WHY MOMMY DRINKS

Gill Sims

WHY MOMMY DRINKS

A Novel

HarperCollins*Publishers*

HarperCollins*Publishers*
1 London Bridge Street
London SE1 9GF

www.harpercollins.co.uk

First published in the UK by HarperCollins*Publishers* 2017
This edition published 2018

19 20 21 22 LSC 10 9 8 7 6 5 4 3 2

A catalogue record of this book is
available from the British Library

ISBN 978-0-00-830016-6

Printed and bound in the United States of America
by LSC Communications

For more information visit: www.harpercollins.co.uk/green

To D

A NOTE TO THE READER

This US edition has been lightly Americanised for your reading pleasure. We have kept certain British words and slang intact but made some changes for clarity. And Mummy insisted on being Mummy throughout the book, although she kindly let us change the title.

CONTENTS

SEPTEMBER	1
OCTOBER	29
NOVEMBER	55
DECEMBER	95
JANUARY	151
FEBRUARY	173
MARCH	197
APRIL	233
MAY	253
JUNE	275
JULY	309
AUGUST	329
ACKNOWLEDGEMENTS	342

SEPTEMBER

Tuesday, 8 September

First day back at school. I am going to 100 per cent nail being a school mummy this year. I can absolutely do this. This year my school runs will go like this:

6 a.m. Wake up, have a shower, put on the stylish and elegant outfit from my minimalist capsule closet that I laid out last night, before applying some light but sophisticated makeup, as suggested by Pinterest, complete with chic, flicky eyeliner. Dry hair, then style into an 'easy' chignon – again according to the diktats of Pinterest – thus creating an overall 'look' that is modern yet classic, with an individual edge. Now looking perfect, I'll tidy up the house so that we have a calm and welcoming environment to return to at the end of the day.

7 a.m. Wake up my precious moppets and offer them a choice of wholesome homemade breakfasts. Happily agree that of course they can help me make the pancakes/waffles/scrambled eggs. Smile with maternal love at the concentration etched on their glowing little faces as they work together to create their delicious concoctions while I pop something yummy into the slow cooker for dinner.

7.45 a.m. Send my adorable children to get washed and dressed, which is of course a quick and simple activity because their uniform was laid out the night before.

While they are getting dressed I can quickly pop the breakfast dishes into the dishwasher, then simply remove the bento boxes from the fridge filled with their nutritious packed lunches, complete with sandwiches fashioned into amusing characters and a wide variety of fresh fruit chopped into quirky shapes.

8 a.m. Brush Jane's hair and style it into French plaits or something similar. Run a comb through Peter's hair and then have ten minutes to read them a lovely story before a final, quick five-minute tidy up and the shoes and coats go on.

8.25 a.m. Leave to walk to school, possibly singing rousing songs, with a detour via the park for the dog to have a run on the way. Watch my darling cherubs tumbling amongst the falling leaves and frolicking with each other and my lovely dog. Feel smug at how the fresh air and exercise before school will have stimulated their youthful brains so that they are now ready to absorb information like sponges.

8.50 a.m. Fondly wave my beautiful children off into the playground with many hugs and kisses, before briskly marching home again with the dog. Then, once the dog is settled in his basket to quietly await the dogsitter coming to let him out at lunchtime, I jump into my freshly valeted car and go to work.

3.15 p.m. Pick up the delightful poppets from school. Chat pleasantly with the other mums in the playground about safe and neutral topics.

3.30 p.m. Give children a nutritious snack, possibly involving homemade granola. While they are eating this, go through each child's schoolbag and carefully read each letter and make a note of all events/trips/requests. Possibly have colour-coded files for each child to keep such letters in, so they can be easily located whenever required. Check homework diaries and draw up a balanced timetable so various homework tasks can be accomplished each night.

3.45 p.m. Send children to get changed for obligatory middle-class extra-curricular activities.

4 p.m. Take children to swimming/music/tennis/dance/jiu jitsu, as appropriate. If only one child is at an activity, spend the time bonding with remaining child and discussing their day/hopes/dreams/ambitions. If both children are doing an activity, catch up on work emails like proper twenty-first-century efficient career woman.

5 p.m. Supervise homework tasks chosen from the carefully planned timetable.

5.30 p.m. Serve up mouthwatering yet effortlessly produced homemade dinner from the slow cooker. Have brief smug moment about what an excellent mother I am and feel sorry for those who lack my razor-sharp organisational skills and unparalleled maternal instincts.

6 p.m. Oversee piano practice and run through spellings/times tables.

6.45 p.m. Permit a half hour of screen time.

7.15 p.m. Bathtime.

7.45 p.m. Bedtime. Read another chapter of the educational book the children have chosen.

8 p.m. Reward myself for my productive day with a nice cup of green tea.

This year we will absolutely have no repeats of last year, where the days all too often went more like this:

5 a.m. Wake up to hear a small child thundering down the stairs. Stumble down after them to discover said small child hunched on sofa and glued to iPad. Snarl at beastly brat monster to get back to bloody bed this instant. Crawl back into bed and seethe with rage. Finally fall back asleep just before alarm goes off.

6 a.m. Hit snooze button.

6.10 a.m. Hit snooze button again.

7.10 a.m. Wake up in panic. Jump in shower. Throw on first clothes that come to hand. Have mild meltdown because arse has expanded to full width so can't get panties past knees. Realise in my haste to get dressed I'd not noticed there was a pair of Jane's panties in my drawer and am trying to haul them on. Sob in relief that while my arse may not be the tiniest or perkiest, I defy any grown woman to manage to shoehorn her arse into an eight-year-old's underwear. Turn head upside down and blast with hairdryer. Survey mad porcupine hair in dismay and tie back with a Hello Kitty hairtie. Try to look as though I *want* to be wearing a Hello Kitty hairtie, as an expression of my unique and quirky individuality. Fail.

7.30 a.m. Go downstairs and shout at precious moppets to disengage themselves from bastarding electronic devices and come and have some breakfast.

7.37 a.m. Snatch bastarding electronic devices from children's hands and howl that they are now confiscated forever and demand once more that they come and have breakfast. Children look up in surprise, having failed to notice my demented banshee-esque presence for the last seven fucking minutes.

7.40 a.m. Hurl Coco Pops at children. Break up fight over the stupid plastic toy in the cereal box. Answer eleventy billion inane questions on subjects such as, 'Who would win in a fight – a vampire squirrel or a weasel cat?' and, 'Can you eat wart-hogs?' Shout: 'I don't know, I don't know, I will google later, stop playing with your food and just eat it, please, come on, hurry up, it's only a bowl of cereal, how long does it take to eat, no, please don't do that, you will spill it, yes, yes, well done, I *told* you that you would spill it if you did that, no, LEAVE IT, I'll clear it up, come on, HURRY UP!'

8 a.m. Send the children to get washed and dressed. Despite laying out their school uniform the night before, now must deal with them insisting they can't find it and claiming it is not there. Stomp upstairs to point out uniform sitting in plain sight on their chairs where it is every sodding morning. At the same time try to make packed lunches and throw something in the slow cooker that the children might actually eat – spaghetti bolognaise. Feed dog. Watch dog inhale food and choke, then vomit. Mop up dog puke.

8.20 a.m. Attempt to untangle the Gordian Knot that is Jane's hair. Explain again that I CAN'T DO FRENCH PLAITS and put in pigtails instead. Listen to Jane telling me that I am a rubbish mummy because everybody else's mummy can do French plaits and actually even Tilly Barker's *daddy* can do French plaits. Endure a lengthy diatribe from Jane over her ruined life and the utter futility of her entire existence due to her French-plait-less hair while chasing Peter around the house attempting to flatten down the strange tufts that have appeared in his hair overnight, while he squeals and dodges like I am attempting to catch him and stick pins in him.

8.35 a.m. Start bellowing at the children to put on their shoes and coats and get their school bags now, *now*, *now*, NOW! Try not to actually foam at the mouth with rage when met with blank stares and complete denial of any knowledge of the existence of shoes, coats or schoolbags. Child informs me of very important permission slip that *must* be returned today. Search futilely through many piles of paper, eventually find the letter, try to dredge up the £5 the letter is also demanding from down the back of the sofa, as I only have a £20 note.

8.47 a.m. Finally leave the house, hustle the children to school while dragging the dog behind me as he attempts to pee on every lamp-post.

8.57 a.m. Push children into playground, smile weakly at dragon headmistress standing at the gate to judge parents under the pretence of greeting them. Stop dog lifting leg on her American tan pantyhose. Scuttle home as fast as possible, mumbling apologies to the poor dog for his lack of a proper walk.

9.07 a.m. Leave a note for the dogsitter asking if she could take dog out for an extra five minutes if she has time, hurtle into car, wonder vaguely what that smell is and drive to work while attempting to put on makeup as I try to convince myself that applying lip gloss when driving is neither dangerous nor illegal. Try not to think about pit of hell bombsite of house left behind.

3.15 p.m. Pick up children. Make half-hearted conversation with other parents while trying to avoid the Coven of Bloody Perfect Mummies, led by the Most Perfect of All, Perfect Lucy Atkinson's Perfect Mummy. Attempt to refrain from making any more social faux pas, such as remarking that a certain much-beloved children's TV presenter looks to me like a sexual deviant.

3.30 p.m. Feed children chips while attempting to tackle the chaos.

3.45 p.m. Send children to get changed for middle-class extra-curricular activities. Argue with them about why they have to go and why swimming/music/tennis/dance/jiu jitsu lessons are not a stupid waste of time. Get told once again that I am a stupid mummy who is ruining their lives. Swear that if I hear the words 'But it's not fair!' one more time I will not be responsible for my actions. Tell Peter that I do not want to come upstairs and smell his fart. Go upstairs and find the clothes they once again claim have vanished. Try to go to the toilet, find large turd staring up at me, shout a lot about the Phantom Shitter while the children wander about in only their underpants. Scream 'We are leaving in FIVE MINUTES!' for at least ten minutes. Get told again that it is not fair. Snap back that *life* is not fair. Wonder how soon I can have wine.

4.05 p.m. Take children to pointless and ridiculous middle-class activities that they don't even want to go to in futile attempt to turn them into well-rounded members of society. If only one child is in activity, allow the other to play on an electronic device despite this morning's hollow and empty threats about eternal confiscation while I stalk people on Facebook on my phone. If both children are in activity, open up work emails, stare at them despondently, then stalk people on Facebook.

5 p.m. Give in to the clamour and permit more electronics time.

5.30 p.m. Realise I didn't turn the bloody, bastarding piece-of-shit slow cooker on this morning. Give children cheesy pasta instead. Force them to eat a piece of fruit afterwards in a feeble attempt at nutrition. Google scurvy and show them photos when they object. Get told they don't even care if they get scurvy.

6 p.m. Ask if they have any homework. Receive staunch denials. Agree children can have just five more minutes on their electronics. Open wine. Attempt to tidy up the bombsite that was once my tastefully decorated, elegant home.

6.30 p.m. Tell children to turn off electronics and do piano practice/spellings/times tables while I vacuum and throw eleventy billion loads of laundry into the washing machine.

6.45 p.m. Realise the children are suspiciously quiet and there is no sound of piano practice or anything else. Discover children have merely swapped one electronic device for another, claiming that I only said they were to put down their iPods, I did not mention any other things.

7 p.m. Tell children it's bathtime. Children announce they have very important homework to do that must be handed in tomorrow. Mutter every single swear word I know under my breath. Do homework with children while trying to refrain from asking them if they are really that stupid as they claim to have forgotten

what number comes after three and are suggesting that C-A-T spells 'dog'.

8.30 p.m. Finally have children bathed and in bed. Slump on sofa and glug the same glass of wine I poured at 6 p.m. and am only now getting to drink. Mutter 'FML!' repeatedly, as my soul dies a little more.

Yes, this year is definitely going to be much better, I will be far more organised. Unfortunately, I have not actually managed to buy the bento boxes or the tasteful capsule closet yet, and I will have to learn to like green tea, as it is foul, and I also have not yet mastered the flicky eyeliner or French plaits, but I am quietly confident that these are mere details in my grand master plan.

Friday, 11 September

FML. I am thirty-nine today. I don't want to be thirty-nine. How did that happen? *When* did that happen? I wasn't meant to get any older than twenty-eight at the most – and even that seemed impossibly ancient – and now I am staring down the barrel at forty and a future that will probably consist of quirkily patterned skirts from catalogue companies and perhaps a 'statement scarf' if I am feeling really daring.

A future where my social life dwindles to people asking me if I want to come to their advanced yoga classes, or their polite book clubs where they only read earnest and improving books and everyone wears their 'statement scarves' tied over turtleneck sweaters and they are all 'tiddly' after a glass of indifferent Pinot Grigio. Then they say things like, 'Oooh, gosh, are you having another glass? Aren't you brave?' while I fight the urge to reply that actually I am not brave, I am not brave at all; a brave person would be able to endure their wittering inanities without the aid of anesthesia, and actually it's not another glass of this cheap wine I need to make them bearable, it's an entire bottle of vodka, and possibly some crack. And, oh, for the love of God, WHY ARE YOU ALL SO BORING?

Perhaps if I refrain from shouting that at the Other Mummies I may have the book club tedium broken up by the occasional invite to jewellery parties, where at least the drink will flow more readily to induce you to buy, buy, buy. But I will then wake up the next day with the sinking realisation that I have spent £150 that I do not have on an array of poorly made tat that I do not need.

I had always assumed that in the unlikely event of me reaching forty I would by then be an elegant and sophisticated woman of the world, fluent in French, pursuing a lucrative, yet humanitarian career, knowledgeable about art and literature and politics – the sort of person that people seek out at highbrow parties to ask their opinion on the situation in the Middle East. Then we would have an informed and illuminating discussion during which it would be obvious that I am much cleverer than them.

Instead, people seek me out at parties because someone told them I had cigarettes, and the reality is that I work part-time in a really boring IT job because it fits in around the children and thus saves on childcare, rendering my lengthy and expensive education redundant. Sometimes, in the more dysfunctional periods of my twenties, I actually wanted to be older and more grown up. Twentysomething me was stupid.

Now, being a grown up sounds like hell. I do not want to go quietly into that good night of women with sensible haircuts who 'live for their children' and stand in the playground trying to trump each other by relating their revolting offspring's many extra-curricular activities and 'achievements', competing about their husbands' high-powered jobs and boasting about their most recent exotic vacations.

I want to drink too much whisky in smoky jazz clubs wearing an inappropriate skirt while an unsuitable man whispers in my ear.

I want an interesting career that makes use of my wit and intelligence (I'm sure I must still have some somewhere …).

I want excitement and romance and danger again.

I want to run away to Paris and fall in love in a garret (though without the poverty and starvation aspect, obviously).

I suspect Simon and the children might find some flaws in my plan, though, quite apart from the fact that I hate jazz.

Saturday, 12 September

In lieu of smoky jazz clubs, Parisian garrets and unsuitable boys, Simon took me out for birthday tapas last night and I got a bit more drunk than I meant to. I did achieve the inappropriate skirt and the whisky, though. Sadly, the whisky was just part of a cocktail in a very wanky hipster bar. I fear hipster bars are probably the new smoky jazz clubs anyway, now that smoking is banned everywhere.

I also have a vague and unfortunate recollection of shouting 'WANKY HIPSTERS!' somewhat louder than intended before Simon managed to hustle me out of there and into a less-pretentious bar, with proper glasses rather than jam jars. The evidence on my phone suggests we had pretty much run out of conversation by that point and so I just took a load of selfies and photos of my cocktails and put them on Facebook with illegible captions, but it was about 11.30 p.m. by then, so Simon had to go home to bed or he would turn into a pumpkin. Remarkably, though, we had managed to dredge up enough to talk about that I didn't resort to posting an annoying Instagram photo of my dinner.

I did actually wake up this morning feeling marvellous, and very clever indeed for sticking to spirits instead of mixing my drinks and turning my teeth black with red wine. No, not me. Not this time. I was elegant ladylike refinement, sipping away on my cocktails.

But then I got out of bed, and felt slightly less clever, and the pain has increased ever since. It quickly became apparent that I wasn't actually clever in the slightest, because I had not dodged the hangover bullet after all. Instead, I had an epic slow burner of a hangover – the sort that tricks you into thinking you are all right, so you start going about your day like normal, but then it suddenly smacks you in the head like an evil gorilla and then you just want to die. I think a badger shat in my mouth.

There were also some terrible hangover flashbacks. After the wanky whisky cocktail I had moved on to gin cocktails and there were unfortunate recollections of sobbing with the gin fear in the taxi on the way home and asking the taxi driver if he thought I looked like I was going to be forty in a year. I think he said no, but that was most likely out of terror rather than honesty.

And then, as I prayed only for the pain to end, Hannah rang in floods of tears to say that Dan was leaving her. There is not really anything you can say when your best friend in the whole wide world rings you up to announce her arsehole husband is leaving her, other than, 'Do you want to come round?' and, 'No, no, just bring the kids, not a problem at all.'

Hannah is devastated, of course, and I am very sad for her, but to be perfectly honest, none of us could ever work out what she saw in Dan, who managed to simultaneously be the most boring man in the world and a nasty little control freak. Obviously, one can't yet say these things in case he changes his mind, or she loses hers and takes him back, but to be honest this is probably going to be a Good Thing for her. I also at no point said, 'Please can you cry slightly less loudly, because I have a very bad headache and I think I might throw up?' I don't know if that makes me a good or a bad friend.

Wednesday, 16 September

Today, as part of my excellent resolution to be a better, kinder, more caring Mummy, instead of panting up to the school gates at 8.59 a.m. while yelling 'Run, RUN! LATE! LATE!', I arrived at school at 8.50 a.m. and walked the children all the way to the playground, chatting delightfully to them about what they thought they might be doing today and the fun things they could look forward to in the new term.

Unfortunately, though, thus it was that as I cheerily waved the little darlings off, Bloody Perfect Lucy Atkinson's Perfect Mummy and her Coven of Bloody Perfect Mummies bore down on me to ask if I had 'had a nice break'. Questions like these are always asked with a sympathetic head tilt and steely glint in the eye. They do not give a rat's arse about whether I had a 'nice break' or not, they just want to make sure I know that they have been to Tuscany or Barbados and to check that I haven't been anywhere better than them so they can humble brag about how they wished they'd had such a 'nice simple vacation' while gloating about their tans.

Obviously I did not have a 'nice break', because a nice break implies lounging around somewhere decadent, reading splendid books by the likes of Jackie Collins and Judith Krantz while a nice man brings you cocktails. Drunkenly shouting at Simon to see what he can make with the supermarket gin and the dodgy bottle of mystery liqueur we got in Malta twelve years ago and have been too scared to open, while scrolling through Netflix to find something, *anything*, that the children haven't watched, other than *The Inbetweeners* (which, it turns out, is actually highly unsuitable for children, as was evidenced by Peter asking his teacher how she got to school and then telling her that she was a Bus Wanker) is not 'a nice break'. Obviously I was not going to admit this to the Bloody Perfect Coven, though.

So we danced the dance whereby they asked if we were 'just at home' and then they sighed about how exhausted they were from dragging their many perfect children around the world all by themselves because The Nanny had insisted on having a week off to visit her own family. Meanwhile, I smiled and gritted my teeth and swore to myself that the next one to make a patronising remark would get smacked soundly round the head with her own duck-egg-blue Céline bag (obviously, I would not do any such thing. I would wallop them with my own cheap designer copy bag and steal the nice Céline bag for myself while she was still stunned from the blow).

FFS, is it any wonder I drink when I have to endure the Coven? It's a wonder I don't drink more. I was going to be very good tonight, but after the Coven, and then an hour of Peter telling me 'jokes' after school (the very best one was: 'What do you get if you cross a goat with the moon? MOONGOAT.COM!' The others were even worse …), I was a bit broken. So when I noticed there was a bottle of Sauvignon Blanc in the fridge with only a glass-worth left in it, it seemed rude to leave the poor wine to be lonely by itself when it could happily join its companions from last night. It turned out to be quite a big glass, actually.

Friday, 18 September

Wine is my friend. Wine is Hannah's friend, too. She made Dan look after his children then she came round and we glugged pink sunshine wine and shouted 'Dan is a wanker' a lot. Simon hid from Hannah, as he copes badly with emotional women at the best of times, let alone if there is an excellent chance that his wife's best friend might cry in front of him and he might be forced to talk about feelings. Simon's idea of a frank and open exchange about one's emotions is to pat one awkwardly on the arm and mumble, 'There, there', while frantically seeking the nearest escape route.

We did manage to corner him at one point as he tried to slink into the kitchen to get another beer when he thought we were preoccupied with singing Gloria Gaynor songs. We insisted that before he left he must admit that Dan was a massive dickhead. Luckily he has never liked Dan either, in fact, he had often complained that he looked like a goblin (he did rather), so there was no boring awkwardness about him 'not taking sides' because obviously there is no question that he is to be on Hannah's side – she is my best friend, and he is my husband, so he is obliged to take the side I tell him to. Obviously I would do the same for him if one of his friends got divorced and would declare the wife to be a shameless harlot. Unless it was one of his wanker friends, of course.

I fear wine will not be our friend tomorrow.

Monday, 21 September

Muchos excitement in the playground this morning. There was A MAN there! Obviously there have been men in the playground before – this is not some completely Stepford Wives' suburb –

but the men in the playground usually take the form of either Super Busy And Important Daddies In Suits who burst in and out, either throwing the children in at the gate or dragging them out at high speed while talking loudly on their cell phones so we are all aware that they are Super Busy And Super Important and only here because The Nanny was so inconsiderate as to get appendicitis; or the House Husband Daddies, who are lovely, but always look in need of a bit of a wash and seem to be a bit lost and teetering on the brink of tears. There are lots of other perfectly nice, normal men who do the school run sometimes, too, but they just sort of blend in, not really standing out or fitting into any of the categories above.

Today, though, today there was A Sexy Man. There had been A Sexy Man once before, it's true, but that 'man' was in fact twenty-three and the French boyfriend of one of the gorgeous nannies, and we all felt like dirty old ladies as we peered at him and mumbled 'YOUNG MAN!' to each other while cackling lasciviously. He never came back, oddly enough.

This new man is age-appropriately sexy. He has got that tousled hair, stubble, leather jacket thing going on, but in a really cool way – not a sad, midlife-crisis way. In fact, he looks exactly the sort of man who would sit beside you in a smoky jazz club and whisper indecent proposals in your ear. And he has a really nice arse.

I am very ashamed of myself, as a respectably married thirty-nine-year-old mother of two children, to be looking at another man's arse in the playground, surrounded by the innocent hearts and minds of impressionable children, but fuck my old boots, it was a *really* nice arse. Anyway, Simon might deny checking out the nannies' arses when he picks up the children, but he's blatantly lying, it is impossible not to notice the nannies' arses. The mummies in the playground spend much time discussing if we ever had arses like those of the nannies. On reflection, we suspect probably not, due to being British and so spending our formative years drinking hard cider and eating fries, unlike the healthy Continental people who eat salad and go cycling.

Anyway, back to this fine arse. Even Perfect Lucy Atkinson's Perfect Mummy was all of a tizz. (She will get thrush if she keeps getting that overexcited in her lululemons.) The jungle drums had already been beating, of course, so she was able to breathlessly reveal that the name of the object of our attention is Sam. (Of course it is. Naturally a splendid, manly arse like that would have a solid, no-nonsense, manly name like Sam. An arse like that could not be called something like Norman.) He is a single dad because his wife left him for another man and callously abandoned the children as well (BLIMEY, what sort of arse must his rival have had?), he also works in IT (really? He doesn't look like it, but oooh, something in common) and he has two children – a boy in Peter's class and a girl in Jane's (more in common!).

Would I be a terrible person if I tried to encourage my children to befriend his children so I could get a better look at that magnificent backside? Yes, obviously I would be, but you could see every other mother with children in those classes thinking exactly the same thing.

My precious moppets offered up very little by way of information about the new children in their classes; Jane managed to recall that the girl is called Sophie and is 'quite nice'. Peter looked blank when asked about a new boy and eventually said, 'Oh, do you mean Elliott who had the Ultra Rare Golden Moshi Monsters?' Elliott left last term. I despair of my children sometimes.

Obviously, I am only going to start brushing my hair and putting on extra makeup for the school run as part of my new resolution to make more of an effort and be less of a lazy slattern.

It is a complete coincidence that Sam and his arse have happened to arrive in the playground. Nothing more.

Wednesday, 23 September

This morning Jane reminded me at 8.30 a.m. that it was her school trip today. This caused panic stations enough as I tried to remember if I had signed the slip and given the school the enormous sum of money it apparently costs to take the children to visit somewhere free (it appears hiring buses is a very expensive business. Maybe I should go for a career change and buy a bus and hire myself out? Mrs Rabbit in *Peppa Pig* seemed to enjoy her job. Was Mrs Rabbit the bus driver? I refuse to google *Peppa Pig* on principle, and see Peppa's irritating face again. Maybe it was Miss Rabbit who did all the random jobs. Oh bugger, I googled it. It was Miss Rabbit. I feel dirty now).

At 8.40 a.m. Jane casually enquired if I was looking forward to coming on the trip too … ARGH! Surely I hadn't ticked the 'I would like to help' box, had I? I had, though why I would have done that was beyond me, unless perhaps I was drunk when I filled in the form? Why would I offer to help on my 'day off' – known to me as my 'Trying To Make The House Less Of A Shit-tip Day' and to bastarding Simon as my 'Having Coffee Day'. Not only had I accidently ticked the box, I had also not bothered to check the children's homework diaries and therefore had missed the nice note from the Lovely Teacher summonsing me to render assistance with supervising the cherubs, which is a task more akin to herding cats.

Ten minutes. That was all I had. Ten short minutes to make myself look presentable and respectable and also just a little bit sexy just in case Sam's Arse was on the trip, too. NO. No. Bad and wrong. I did not need to look sexy, Sam's Arse or no Sam's Arse.

In the end I settled for brushing my teeth, tying back the crazy hair and slapping on a bit of makeup to cover the worst of the horror. When I got to the school I was quite glad of the lack of time to transform myself into a radiantly glowing Sex Goddess because the playground was a moist sea of lip gloss and fluttering eyelashes and *slightly*-too-tight sweaters, with everyone clearly thinking the same impure thoughts about Sam's Arse. However, there was not a sight of the Sacred Butt to be had because his childminder was dropping the kids off (and looking fairly glammed up herself, it had to be said)!

The trip was vile, obviously. I had no idea of the stench that a bus load of children can create. What are their parents feeding them? Thirty children, in a combined space, apparently farting non-stop from the moment we got on the bus until the moment we reached the very large museum containing many priceless artefacts for the children to be educated by, while the adults tried to stop them stealing or smashing anything. My eyes were watering and my lungs were burning by the time we disembarked. I actually thought someone must've soiled themselves, the smell was so bad.

Teachers should be issued with gas masks if they have to spend all day in that fetid fog, though when I remarked on the farting to the Lovely Teacher, she laughed merrily and said, 'Oh, you soon stop noticing it!'

I don't think this is true; Peter came home puffed with pride last year, announcing that he had made his teacher feel sick with a particularly rancid fart he had done. Peter is quite revolting, though. One poor little girl had to be moved away from him as she found Peter farting and then laughing hysterically each time to be quite distracting. You would think that living with Peter, and my foul dog and his cheesy bum, that I would have become immune to the stink, but I haven't. Maybe the Lovely Teacher is on drugs. That would explain a lot.

Anyway, the trip was horrible. The class ran amok; I saw Freddie Dawkins wiping bogeys on one of the glass display cabinets, but at least since everyone is now suspected of being a pedophile I didn't have to take anyone to the toilet.

Apparently they were there to learn about the Egyptians. I suspect they learnt exactly nothing, except how to squander their money on crap in the gift shop. Jane seemed to be under the impression that I was there to provide her with an endless supply of cash to purchase *all* the said crap and became quite huffy when I declined to spend £35 on an umbrella with a ballerina on it. £35! On an umbrella! FML, I didn't even know it was possible to spend £35 on an umbrella, although in fairness I tend to buy very cheap umbrellas and they die or I lose them after three uses, so in the grand scheme of things I have probably spent considerably more than £35 on umbrellas over the years, and maybe what is missing in my life is a statement umbrella. Maybe I *should* have bought Jane the £35 umbrella, and then perhaps she would grow up to be a well-rounded and functioning adult who would not still think 'when I'm a grown up' even in her late thirties? Bollocks, I have failed in my parental duty again.

Being a virtuous and saintly person who helps on school trips and doesn't paint her face like a harpy in order to look alluring to a man with a nice bottom has clearly earned me Wednesday wine, though I have to go to boring work tomorrow because it turns out buses are quite expensive and you have to pass a test to be able to drive one. Since I barely passed my test when driving a very small car – getting the same examiner for so many attempts that he finally said he had only passed me because people were starting to talk about us – there is no chance I could pass a test driving a bloody enormous bus.

Friday, 25 September

Breathing. Breathing. Breathing. Today I had a half day at work, as I had a dentist's appointment and it wasn't worth going back to work for half an hour before I picked up the children, so I took the dog for a walk round the park before school finished. And who should I have met there but the gorgeous Sam and his Arse as I chased my buggering pig dog round the duck pond, bellowing at him to come back and stop trying to do that to the ducks. Sam was walking his rather lovely Stafford, and although my pig dog made a show of me by behaving very badly as usual, he did decide to run up to Sam and jump all over him, while I shouted ineffectually for the wretched beast to stop it. But on the plus side, it gave me an excellent excuse to actually talk to Sam, without looking like a sad desperate slut (because 'Obstreperous Terrier Owner' is a *much* better look, obviously). So we talked about the dogs, which both turned out to be rescues, and then he said he had seen me at the school (gasp) and weren't our children in the same classes?

Sam Noticed Me! Sam. Noticed *me*. Me!

And *then* he said (which was a bit of a let-down, suggesting that perhaps Sophie had pointed me out as Jane's mum, rather than Sam being struck with wonder across the playground by the way that I totally rocked the run in my stockings and frizzy, caught-in-the-rain hair yesterday) that Sophie had said she liked Jane and wanted her to come for a play date after school, and what about this afternoon? And to bring Peter as well, because he could play with his son Toby.

I hesitated for a second, wondering if I could wangle myself an invitation too, just so I could nosy at Sam's house and see if he is as perfect and gorgeous as he seems, and also because then I could casually drop it into conversation with the Bloody Perfect Coven who have been twittering around him like hormonally charged starlings, but who, as far as I know, have not yet received an invitation for either themselves or their children. Then Sam said, 'I know it is a bit weird, your children going to a stranger's house, so please come along too, I quite understand.' Ha! So I got to tag along, having again dodged the desperate saddo bullet, even if the flip side was that he thought that I thought he might be a pedophile/child trafficker/criminal overlord. One can't have everything.

Sam's house was not actually what I was expecting at all. I'd assumed he would live in a super-cool, gadget-filled glass box complete with stylish but uncomfortable-looking twentieth-century furniture – basically the minimalist vision that Simon hankers after, complete with the Mies van der Rohe chairs that he covets and that we cannot afford, not least because the pig dog would chew them and the children would jump on them and break them.

The house was in fact much more like my vision of a home; with squishy sofas and beautiful painted French furniture and tasteful clutter, unlike the clutter-clutter that fills my house. Slightly tactlessly I remarked on this to Sam, but he was very nice about it and said the lack of clutter-clutter was largely due to him just moving in and half the furniture and stuff going to his partner Robyn in the split. Robyn is apparently an interior designer, hence the Very Lovely Things.

I longed desperately to ask more about the errant Robyn, and how and why she would leave a man like Sam, who added to his general perfection by having lots of very good cake, but he changed the subject quite firmly so we ended up talking about the various children's after-school activities in the area – which are good, but not worth the vast sums of money that they cost. It was a dull but safe conversation, and it in no way provided opportunities for me to say anything like, 'Would you mind terribly if I licked you? It's just that you're rather sexy.'

Then Sophie and Jane appeared, screaming, because Toby and Peter had interrupted their game of 'Makeovers' to attack them with Nerf guns, which was perhaps just as well, given how much makeup and glitter the girls were already plastered in, despite apparently only being halfway through the makeovers. Amidst a lot of shouting and scuffling I hastily removed my juvenile stripper look-alike and the tiny Rambo and dragged them home while there was still a semblance of Sam thinking we were a nice, normal family that he and his children would like to befriend.

All this, AND it is Fuck It All Friday. Hurrah and huzzah! So I can give up the unequal battle to save the children from scurvy and abandon the broccoli in favour of frozen pizzas. I can also give up all pretence of limiting their screen time and plug them into the electronic babysitters while I get quietly sozzled on indifferent wine and stalk old boyfriends on Facebook and Simon falls asleep on the sofa in front of *Wheeler* Fucking *Dealers* yet again, and, despite snoring like an angry warthog drowning in a vat of porridge, shouts 'I'm watching that!' if I try to prise the remote out of his clutch. Not that it will do me any good even if I do get custody of the remote, as Simon is such a massive bastarding Gadget Twat that he has rendered using the TV beyond my capabilities with all his various boxes and 'streaming' devices, each with their own remote that needs to be tuned to a different channel. As I can never remember *which* remote is for which box though, I end up jabbing hopelessly at All The Buttons until one of the children takes pity on me and makes it work.

The dog is looking at me most disapprovingly this evening. I fear he has somehow sensed that I am harbouring impure thoughts about Sam and he is judging me as a shameless harlot for using him as a conversation opener.

Saturday, 26 September

Simon spent the afternoon in his shed and I spent the afternoon painting the sideboard in the dining room in an effort to replicate the quirky shabby-chic vibe of Sam's house. While I did this the children attempted to do something creative with what had once been glitter glue, but as the glitter glue had dried out and I had attempted to revive it with some warm water and PVA glue, the substance they were smearing over themselves and the table looked more like unicorn sperm.

Simon was a bit shirty when I revealed the revamped sideboard in its chalk-painted glory, as it had been his grandmother's and is a family heirloom, apparently. Harshly, he insisted it was 'Just shabby, with no chic', which may have been because I got a bit carried away with the 'distressing'.

Due to Simon's lack of vision about my upcycling, the last qualm I had about abandoning him to go out for a drink with Hannah vanished. He actually looked surprised when I appeared in Going Out Clothes, with hair brushed and lipstick *and* mascara on. So much so that he said, 'You look nice. Is that for me?' despite the fact I must have told him at least nine times that he would be looking after the children tonight, including washing the unicorn sperm out of their hair, because I was going out to keep Hannah company so she doesn't have to sit alone in her empty house while Dan has the children for the night.

I may have snapped that at him at bit more brusquely than was necessary, as he actually looked a bit sad and deflated that the effort was not for him, so I said, 'Do I really look nice?' to which he just responded, 'Yeah, you look okay', which is exactly what every woman wants to hear. Twat.

Poor Hannah has fallen back into the pit of despair having found out that Dan has been shagging some twentysomething slapper he met at the gym and being utterly unapologetic about it when she asked if that was why he had left her. Dan is such a dick. At least Simon won't find any nubile twentysomethings in his shed.

I wonder if I should try to set Hannah up with Sam when she is over Dan a bit? That would be both a kind and altruistic thing to do, to help them both find love again, as well atoning slightly for my shameless crush on him. Maybe if he was taken I would fancy him a bit less? Also, it would piss off Dan no end if he saw Hannah with someone as gorgeous as Sam. What price his twentysomething gym bunny against That Arse?

An evening hearing about The Dickishness of Dan over a bottle of Sauvignon Blanc actually made me feel quite kindly disposed towards Simon, and I even planned to tell him that when I got home, except he was out cold on the sofa with bloody motorbike racing blaring out of the TV. How can he sleep through that? He was snoring and wearing his oldest and nastiest fleece and refused to wake up even when I threw a cushion quite hard at his head. So I left him there and went to bed.

When did Simon get so old? We used to stay up all night, talking and listening to music. Not even talking about anything in particular – we couldn't claim to be setting the world alight with our radical views on art and politics. In fact, I don't know what we talked about, but I know we did. When I met him, he was a something between a Goth and a New Romantic, wearing a big black coat from a thrift shop and chain-smoking Marlboro Reds, and I thought he was so cool. Maybe he looks at me and wonders what's happened to me, too? I still remember what I was wearing the night I met him – a very short black skirt, Dr Marten boots, a sort of fisherman's sweater I had stolen off an ex-boyfriend and an over-sized tweed jacket I had stolen from my dad, who phoned me every week demanding its return, except I couldn't return it now because it reeked of cigarette smoke and hash. With hindsight, I must've looked insane, but I was very pleased with myself.

We were at university, in Edinburgh, and I had seen him around in first year but had never spoken to him, as he was older, in the year above me, and part of a cool, arty lot and I, well, I was neither cool nor arty, despite my best attempts to be both. It was towards the end of my second year that he came over to me one night in the Pear Tree pub and asked me for a light, confessing later that it was just an excuse to start talking to me, which was possibly the most absurdly flattering thing that had ever happened to me.

And now here we are, with two children and a mortgage slightly larger than we are comfortable with, and jobs neither of us are terribly happy in, and a ruined sideboard that I have to admit does not look better now the paint has dried, as I had very much hoped it would (actually it looks like it belongs in a dumpster, so there goes my plan of a career change to interior designer). And the other day a radio DJ played 'Disco 2000' on the Golden Oldies slot. 'Disco 2000'! 'Disco 2000' is not an 'oldie', it is the best song in the world ever, and it was only out about a year ago, wasn't it? How the fuck can it be an oldie? FML. My youth is dead.

OCTOBER

Sunday, 4 October

Simon is still going on and on about the wretched sideboard.

'What possessed you, Ellen? What are you going to do about it, Ellen? Do you know how long that has been in my family, Ellen? What's my mother going to say when she sees it?'

Eventually I lost patience with his whinging and bellowed, 'It's just a sideboard! It's just a lump of wood! It's not the end of the world! It's not even worth anything!'

Simon looked hurt and pathetic and sniffed, 'It has immense sentimental value, Ellen, and *you* ruined it, without even consulting me. I think I'm entitled to be a bit upset, don't you?'

'Well, Simon, darling,' I snarled. 'Perhaps if you didn't spend all weekend in your fucking shed, avoiding any interaction with me or your children because apparently you have busy and important things to do in there, then maybe you might have been there to discuss it with me. Hmm?'

To which he retorted, 'I'm very bloody sorry that I think I'm entitled to a bit of time for myself at the weekend, *darling*, but *some* of us have to work full-time. *Some* of us don't get to finish work at lunchtime and have days off in the middle of the week, *darling*, so *some* of us are a bit fucking shattered by the weekend actually.'

'SOME of us don't fucking finish at lunchtime, SOME of us finish just in time to drive like a maniac to the school to pick up SOMEONE'S children, DARLING! SOME of us then spend the rest of the evening taking SOMEONE'S children to their various clubs, making dinner, doing laundry, supervising baths and homework and putting SOMEONE'S children to bed, because of course SOMEONE is too fucking tired after work to do anything except sit in front of the fucking television with a beer. SOME of us spend our so-fucking-called "day off" trying to restore some sort of order to the shit-hole of a house, and SOME of us then spend our weekends also cleaning, doing laundry, ironing and entertaining SOMEONE'S children! Actually. DARLING!' I shrieked.

I felt I had made some very valid points but I was afraid my rage may have reached such proportions that my voice had become so shrill only a dolphin could have heard my excellent argument for why Simon was a selfish bastard.

'Oh for God's sake, Ellen. Why does everything always have to be a competition with you? You've wrecked my grandmother's sideboard, but it's all about how hard done by *you* are.' Simon groaned.

'It's not a competition; I was merely pointing out how *I* spend *my* "free" time. And now, if you will excuse me, I will spend some more of my leisure taking your children on a delightful playdate.'

'We're going to Sophie and Toby's house,' put in Peter.

'Sophie and Toby haven't got a mummy; they live with their daddy, Sam. Lucy Atkinson's Mummy says Sam is lush,' announced Jane helpfully.

'Who is this Sam?' Simon enquired coldly.

'He is a new father at the school. He's a single dad.' I informed him.

'And is he, indeed, lush?'

'I can't say I've noticed, to be honest,' I lied brazenly, hoping I wasn't actually blushing.

It was lovely to be out at Sam's. I do love his house. I caught myself more than once wondering what it would be like to sit having coffee in the morning at his duck-egg-and-cream kitchen table, with Sam all tousled in a bathrobe opposite me. No, not a bathrobe. So unsexy. Maybe some Calvin Klein pyjama bottoms and a nice T-shirt, quite a tight one, and some stubble … STOP IT, ELLEN! STOP IT NOW!

Saturday, 10 October

To the park with the children this afternoon. Somehow the park is never quite the japesome frolic that I feel it should be. To start with, there is the lovely task of scouring the play area on arrival to make sure there are no broken bottles or condoms lying around, abandoned by bored teenagers the night before (though I suppose one should be glad they are at least taking precautions, even after a bottle of cheap vodka, but the conversation about why the children mustn't touch the 'special balloon' they have found is not a particularly enjoyable one to have with a hangover). Then, of course, one has to run the gauntlet of the Coven of Bloody Perfect Mummies dispensing their healthy homemade date and granola cereal bars to their rosy-cheeked offspring while you have not brought any snacks because you were under the impression that now your children were school-aged they could possibly go for a whole hour without shoving food in their gobs every thirty seconds. But as you are the only mummy there without snacks, it seems you were wrong, and they must be fed constantly, like squawking baby birds – only it is quite frowned upon if you let them eat worms, as I discovered when Peter was three.

I was digging through my pockets in search of sustenance, so far having located a fluff-covered object that may once have been a jelly bean, when who appeared but Sam, also apparently unfettered by enough food to sustain his children for a month-long siege, and he actually came over and sat down next to me, despite Perfect Lucy Atkinson's Perfect Mummy and her acolytes cooing greetings to him as he passed and attempting to bribe his children by proffering zucchini traybake ('Don't worry, there's no *sugar* in it, I only use apple juice as a sweetener in my baking.'). It is possible that Sam only chose to sit next to me because by arriving at the park first I had cunningly annexed the only bench with a modicum of shelter from the howling east wind that sweeps through, threatening hypothermia to parents, while the children cast off their expensive warm jackets and run amok, oblivious to the cold.

'I'm confused, Ellen,' said Sam. 'Why are all these children eating? Do they not get fed at home? And *what* are they eating? Toby just told that blonde one that he "doesn't do" green cake, which seems a fair point.'

'Haven't you come across Competitive Mummying before?' I asked. 'Maybe they don't do it to you because they all too busy looking at your … er … fathering skills.' (So nearly said arse!) 'Watch them, the idea is to demonstrate, via the most disgusting snack possible, how well rounded and balanced your children are. Extra points for the longer your offering takes to make – ideally you will have soaked chia seeds in almond milk overnight at the very least – and the more obscure the revolting ingredients, the better. It's quite funny when it backfires, though. Last week Emilia Fortescue threw up on her mummy's Chanel ballet pumps after an attempt at force-feeding her a hemp and spirulina muffin. Once snacktime is over they will start shouting instructions to the children to demonstrate their gymnastic skills on the climbing frame, or their architectural skills in the sandpit. Perfect Lucy Atkinson's Perfect Mummy used to like to shout her instructions in French, but she was totally trumped last week when Tabitha MacKenzie's Mummy issued her instructions in Mandarin. Lucy's Mummy's face was to die for.'

To my astonishment, I realised Sam was actually laughing at this. I hadn't meant to be funny, it was mostly a judgemental and disgruntled rant having spent the last hour freezing my arse off on this bench while staring resolutely at my phone because I lacked the strength to be patronised into the Vortex of Inadequacy that is inevitable in any conversation with the Coven of Bloody Perfect Mummies, looking up only at the more blood-curdling screams to make sure they weren't coming from or had been caused by Peter or Jane.

'Why on earth do they do that?' Sam asked incredulously.

'I dunno,' I shrugged. 'I think it's something to do with them once being terribly important in their careers but giving it all up to have their children brought up by an Eastern European nanny while they go shopping, or, occasionally, if they want to pretend they still "work" they play at being a "designer" of some sort – any sort will do; children's clothes and jewellery are the usual, though, and cashmere baby-gros are currently trending as the Mummy Business *du jour*. Though of course if your husband has a large property portfolio you can call yourself an interior designer if you've bought some cushions. All this is done in between going to yoga and Pilates and checking their very rich husband's phone to see if he is having it off with The Nanny (nannies don't get names), and so they need to validate their continuing importance by competing and showing off to each other about who is the most organic and loving and thus who has the most well-rounded, nurtured and, most importantly, *gifted* children. Oh, and also they lie. See that one? Fiona Montague. She used to knock two months off her baby's age at Mummy and Music and Me so he appeared more advanced than he actually was. She hadn't really thought it through as far as his first birthday, though.'

My God, having started on the judgemental ranting, it seemed I couldn't stop.

'And you don't feel the urge to join in?' asked Sam. 'To break out your bento box full of, I dunno, savoury Vacherin cheese slices seasoned only with the tears of Pyrenean mountain goats?'

Ooooh, Sam is judgy too!

'DAIRY? Are you MAD? They are all lactose and gluten-free, with a whole host of other "intolerances" too. In fact, last year's in-thing was finding the most obscure ingredient to declare your child allergic to and trying to get the school to ban it. I tried to claim mine were allergic to glitter, but it didn't bloody work.'

'Seriously, though, how have you not been sucked into their crazy?'

'Oh, I'm not allowed to be in their gang anyway. They are more bloody cliquey than schoolgirls, and I am deemed not suitable because I am not rich enough and I have to work for The Man, because we are too broke for me not to, due to foolishly deciding to marry my boyfriend from university instead of waiting until I had a suitably important job and snaring a nice rich stockbroker, then setting up my own business "designing" frou-frou fripperies to flog to other bored rich women. Oh, and also I don't entirely manage to hide the fact I find them patronising bitches, which doesn't help. They would quite like you to be in their gang, though; a hot, single daddy to flirt with and make their husbands jealous would be just the job.'

I stopped abruptly, realising I had committed the ultimate British faux pas of oversharing. Sam was looking horrified, so I mumbled something about checking on the children.

'They're fine,' said Sam. 'They're over there with my green-cake-rejecting starving urchins. Oh wait, hang on, I think there's an incident unfolding.'

I had never been so relieved to have to intervene in a Jane-related incident. There is a sort of spinny saucer thing in the park that children sit in while other children spin them round. Jane had persuaded Perfect Lucy Atkinson into this, and then proceeded to spin her as fast as possible while cackling slightly maniacally. The more Lucy Atkinson screamed at Jane to stop it and sobbed that she was going to throw up, the harder Jane spun. I got there just in time to rugby tackle Jane to the ground and stop the spinny thing with my foot. Unfortunately, it was now going at such speed that when I stopped it so abruptly, it made Lucy Atkinson catapult out to land in a pea-green, snotty sodden heap at her mother's impeccably clad feet. By the grace of God she didn't actually puke on her Perfect Mummy's Perfect Shoes, but alas she did smear quite a lot of snot over them. They looked expensive.

I hustled Jane away, trilling, 'SO sorry, just a misunderstanding, Jane thought she was screaming because she was enjoying it and wanted to go faster! Kids, eh? Ha ha ha! PETER! TIME TO GO!' and made a hasty exit. This also had the benefit of meaning I didn't have to talk to Sam again, having just announced to him that he was a hot single dad and all the mummies wanted to shag him.

Simon was in his shed when we got home, ostentatiously trying to sand down the shabby sideboard. It wasn't working. He will see the funny side soon, I'm sure.

Friday, 16 October

Hurray once more for Fuck It All Friday! Simon was apparently 'working from home' today, which roughly translates as 'reading the *Daily Mail* website and eating all my bloody cookies' (in fairness, I do the same when I manage to wangle a day 'working from home'). This also meant that he was actually here to deal with the joy of dinner time while I got ready to go out with Hannah and Sam, as I had decided that the best way to get over my impure thoughts about Sam was to set him up with Hannah. I have, of course, claimed to them both that this is just a fun, casual drink; a chance for Sam to meet other people in the area, blah blah blah, as opposed to admitting to my hidden agenda of both nipping my thumping great crush in the bud AND giving me the opportunity to buy a lovely hat for the Wedding of the Century, where of course I would be able to take all the credit as it was all down to my amazing matchmaking skills. I would probably be asked to make a speech, too. Maybe I could help organise it? I do often think I would like to be a wedding planner – I feel I would be very good at it.

Getting ready wasn't quite the peaceful, relaxing time I had hoped it would be, because in addition to the interruptions from Peter and Jane, Simon was not coping particularly well with the whole dinner/bathtime/bedtime thing and kept trailing hopelessly into the bedroom to wail plaintively 'What's *wrong* with them? Why do they behave like this?' as screams issued from the bathroom and waves of water lapped beneath the door.

'They are behaving like this, Simon, because you let them have Gummy Bears, which turns them into demented, hyperactive hell demons.'

'Well, why did you let me give them Gummy Bears then? Why didn't you warn me?'

'I have told you repeatedly not to give them Gummy Bears, Simon. It's just that you usually leave me to deal with the fallout afterwards while you tit about doing something else.'

'But why do we even have Gummy Bears in the house, then, if they have that effect on the little bastards?'

'I don't know. I don't know how the Gummy Bears get in the fucking house. They're just there, and however many they eat, there's always more. I assumed you bought them, but if it's not you, maybe it's just one of life's mysteries that we will never be destined to find the answer to, like why there are always carrots in puke, even if you haven't eaten carrots. And right now, I DON'T CARE, because I am going OUT.'

Simon did at least tell me that I looked nice as I waltzed out of the house, swishing my hair, and he did so without even being asked, so I then felt rather bad about buggering off and abandoning him again and wondered if I should have asked him along too.

When I got to the pub, though, I decided it was probably just as well that Simon hadn't come, because if we were two couples then it would have been totally obvious that I was trying to set up Hannah and Sam, and one has to be subtle about these things.

Sam seemed quite uncomfortable, and not at all the chilled-out hunk of gorgeousness who haunted my dreams. And, worse, his body language was showing no interest in Hannah (I could tell this because I used to obsessively pore over those 'How To Tell If He Fancies You' articles in my youth, so beloved by female magazines like *Cosmopolitan*). Clearly, I thought, they were going to need a bit of help if I was going to be the guest of honour/wedding planner extraordinaire at the Wedding of the Century.

While Sam was at the bar I talked to Hannah at great lengths about how lovely he was – such a good father, such a nice man. I stopped short of saying 'And just look at his amazing arse! I mean, LOOK AT IT!' because I did not want Hannah to think I viewed her future husband as a mere sex object. Hannah, though, seemed unconvinced and claimed it was too soon after Dan for her to even think about such a thing.

Nothing daunted, I waited for Hannah to go to the toilet and then very casually remarked to Sam,

'Isn't Hannah lovely?'

'Errr, yes, she seems very nice.'

'She's very pretty, don't you think? And she has wonderful hair.'

'Ummm, yes, yes, very nice hair.'

I was wondering whether I should press the point by adding that she also has cracking tits, when Sam said, 'The thing is, Ellen, if you're trying to set me up with her, she's, well, not exactly my type.'

Oh. I was momentarily deflated as the Wedding of the Century and the glorious hat slipped from my grasp (I was thinking a stylish pillbox affair with a flirtatious little veil; it is probably okay to wear a veil to someone else's wedding when you are the guest of honour and have orchestrated the whole thing), but then I perked up again at the thought that perhaps I was Sam's type and that was why he didn't fancy Hannah.

I tried not to be too coquettish as I coyly asked, 'What is your type then?'

Sam looked a bit awkward, then replied, 'Well. Not women.'

Not women? OH! The penny finally dropping, I could only gabble, 'Oh God, so sorry, didn't realise, so rude of me, so sorry!'

'You weren't to know,' said Sam. 'It's just not something I make a big fuss about. No one expects straight people to say "Hi, I'm so and so, and by the way, I'm heterosexual" so why should gay people be expected to introduce themselves by high-kicking to a Judy Garland number complete with jazz hands? Anyway,' he brightened up, 'you see, I shall be quite safe from the Yummy Mummies, since I may be a hot, single dad – thanks for that, by the way – but I am of no use to them.'

I laughed for quite a long time at his optimism.

'Ha! You will be more in demand than ever! They will all be clamouring to have you as their Gay Best Friend and imagining they are in an episode of *Will & Grace*. You will never escape them now. You are DOOOOOOOOOMED!'

'Or,' he suggested, 'I could just keep hanging around with you and you can ward them off for me? Perhaps your unsuitability will rub off on me, and they will leave me alone?'

Poor Sam. It will take more than using me as a human shield to ward off Perfect Lucy Atkinson's Perfect Mummy once she realises his potential to be her essential must-have accessory, but he can try if he wants.

Once it had been established that, alas, my matchmaking skills were not quite as honed as my body language skills (the magazines never said much about matchmaking your friends, I think, because we were all supposed to be in competition for The Boys and were to keep them to ourselves if we got one), we proceeded to get really very drunk. More relaxed now, Sam finally told us, with many shouts of 'BASTARD', how his dastardly ex, Robin (not Robyn) had buggered off and left him.

Apparently Robin had claimed that his passionate interest in restoring antique French Provincial furniture for his business was the reason for his many trips away, but actually it turned out he was shagging a French bloke called 'Jean Claude, or René or somethin' stupid an' French', as Sam informed us after several cocktails. (He introduced us to Manhattans, which are very nice and taste of cherries even though they are just neat booze and get you extraordinarily bedrunkled.) Apparently he then buggered off with the French chap, leaving Sam with the children. Only it didn't work out with Jean Claude/René and so a few months ago he tried to get back together with Sam. 'But I tol' him, I said "Fuck off". I tol' him.' So Sam decided that he and the children needed a fresh start and so here he is, only he has to be civil to Robin ('Bastard') for the children's sake and can't tell him to fuck off as much as he would like to. Sam talks quite a lot when he's drunk.

Hannah then told us that Dan (who also had 'BASTARD' shouted about him a lot) has announced that his floozy (I didn't even realise people still said 'floozy' until Hannah spat the word across the table) will be staying with him this weekend and the children will be meeting her.

'Bastard!' said Sam. 'Even Robin (bastard!) din't introduce wasshisname, Henri Twat, to the kids.'

'More cockingtails,' I slurred.

Astonishingly, Simon was still up when I got home, which was nice. Unfortunately, I was really quite drunk and unable to mumble anything other than 'Toast. Need toast. Toast now. Mmmmm, toast. More toast. I love you, thingy.'

Despite my frankly appalling drunkenness, instead of lecturing me for being a shameful lush Simon laughed and said, 'Looks like you had fun, darling!' and put me to bed. This is one of the many reasons why I love him, even though he gets on my tits sometimes. I think I shall keep him. I think he likes me too.

Saturday, 17 October

Today I have mostly been broken. So very broken. I think maybe Manhattans are not such clever things after all. When I got up there was Marmite all over the kitchen. I would very much like to blame Simon or the children for this, but as I am the only person in the house who eats Marmite, and everyone else retches at the smell alone, it appears I must take responsibility for Marmite-gate, though I have no idea how I managed to get it up the walls. The only consolation was texts from Hannah and Sam enquiring if I happened to know how they got home. I do at least remember getting a taxi home, so I might actually have been slightly less hammered than Hannah and Sam.

Apart from the Marmite, the house was actually remarkably tidy, given it had been Simon's watch last night. He had even taken off his revolting fleece in favour of a rather nice sweater, which, because I am shallow and vain despite my pretensions to be otherwise, and because he was so lovely about me being completely hammered last night, led to me feeling rather kindly towards him, especially in view of the dastardly behaviour of the errant Dan and Robin, so I finally managed to apologise for wrecking his grandmother's sideboard. He was remarkably nice about it in the end, and said not to worry, it was just a sideboard after all (THAT'S WHAT I SAID!).

He did, however, suggest that maybe I might now finally accept that renovating furniture just isn't my thing, reminding me of several other failed attempts at upcycling when we were students and I still believed it was acceptable to bring home things that you had found in a dumpster. I found an Australian in a dumpster once, shortly before Simon and I got together. I didn't bring him home, though he was rather lush. I just gave him directions to the nearest youth hostel. I rather regretted letting him go, but at the back of my mind was the thought that if I took him home and he turned out to be The One, then for the rest of our lives, when people asked how we'd met, I'd have had to say 'I found him in a dumpster'.

Simon being so nice about the sideboard, and laughing together about back when we were young and carefree and even more broke than we are now, led to something of an amorous moment, and he suggested we took advantage of it while the children were catatonic in front of *SpongeBob SquarePants*. In all honesty, my ready agreement was mainly because the thought of lying down in a darkened room was quite attractive in my hideously hungover state, rather than from a mad desire to be ravished senseless. Nonetheless, off we sneaked, only to be interrupted by Peter bellowing in fury outside the (fortunately locked) bedroom door, just as Simon was removing my bra, because Jane had committed the unforgiveable act of changing the channel without asking him. And then there was something about *Ninjago* and unfairness, by which point the mood was spoilt.

The children are good, I'll give them that. They seem to have some sort of built-in radar to detect when we might be on the verge of a shag and work as a seamless tag team to ensure it doesn't happen. I did tell Simon that just putting a lock on the bedroom door wouldn't be enough to thwart them; we would need to build some sort of nuclear, underground, sound-proofed, lead-lined sex bunker if we actually wanted to do it without them barging in, and even then they would probably find some way to breach the defences.

Tuesday, 20 October

Poor Peter is sick. He was absolutely fine when he went to bed last night, but he appeared at 3 a.m. complaining he had a sore throat, which was not solved by drinks of water, or cuddles, or a story, so eventually I dosed him up with Tylenol and he finally fell asleep. He shuffled through this morning with a general air of feeling very sorry for himself and groaning pitifully that his throat was still terribly sore. I had quite a lot to do today, and I was still hopeful that I might be able to get away with pouring another spoonful of Tylenol down him and bundling him off to school anyway. However, when I applied my patented 'Are You Really Sick Test?' by informing him that he would have to stay in bed and read quietly if he was too ill to go to school, he needn't think he could sit and play on his electronics all day, he just nodded feebly and said, 'Bed sounds nice. I'm so cold, Mummy, can I go back to bed now? I just want to go to sleep.'

Given that Peter would generally rather endure torture than voluntarily spend a single minute more in bed than he has to, I decided he must be actually properly ill, instead of faking it in the hope of spending the day achieving the next level on his wretched Pokémon game. I duly took his temperature like a loving and responsible mummy. It was 101.5°F – which I then, of course, had to google because I can never remember what temperature the human body is meant to be at anyway, and at what point a fever becomes 'dangerous' (103°F according to Dr Google), and because I was too tight to buy the special thermometer that flashes lights and sounds alarms when it deems your precious moppet's temperature to be beyond the pale.

I gave Peter another dose of Tylenol – every parent's best friend. (I wish I had bought shares in bloody Tylenol when the children were born, nobody tells you how much of it you will go through, whether it is for genuine illnesses, or placebo doses for those mysterious aches and pains that only arise at bedtime.) Although despite now being six, Peter is strongly resisting going onto the 6+ strength and whimpered pathetically for 'The pink one, Mummy, please, I like the pink one.' I tucked him up on the sofa with a blanket and even agreed he could have a cup of tea, as a special treat, since he was so ill, and he appeared enfeebled enough that even a combination of caffeine and drugs seemed unlikely to rally him to his usual level of hyperactivity, let alone to the demonic Energizer Bunny state that any caffeine usually induces in both my children.

Simon had already left for work this morning, so Sam kindly agreed to drop Jane at school and pick her up for me, which meant I didn't have to take the ailing one out into the cold, harsh world. Jane was most unhappy at being sent to school when her brother was off, so she attempted to cough up a lung to demonstrate why she should also be allowed to stay at home and guzzle the Magic Pink Elixir of Life. However, she spectacularly failed the Test by immediately explaining to me why she should be allowed to watch TV all day, because even though she wasn't *that* sick, there was a good chance she was contagious, and did I even know the incubation period for what Peter had, and what if it was something really serious like Ebola and I was sending her out there to infect the whole school? (Jane has obviously been watching the Discovery Channel behind my back again.) So she was duly waved off, still wailing pitifully about how unfair it all was.

I rang the office and told them I would be working from home, as I had a very sick child (Peter obligingly coughed throughout the phone call, to add some realism to this claim) and then the sofa began to look awfully appealing, given I had been up half the night with Peter.

I cunningly asked, 'Would you like Mummy to come and give you a cuddle, darling?'

To which Peter replied, 'Yes please, Mummy, that would be lovely.'

I duly curled up under the blanket with him and he snuggled in. It was actually rather lovely; there are not many opportunities for cuddles with my children these days, because we are always busy rushing here, dashing there, running around like headless chickens to after-school clubs and doing homework and trying to get some sort of meal on the table and the laundry done. There is never enough time for anything.

Peter was always a cuddly baby, who loved nothing more than nestling into me for hours, but once he started walking he suddenly found that there was a whole new world out there waiting to be discovered, and dismantled, and sitting on his mother's knee interfered terribly with his important plans to stick his fingers into electrical sockets and remove the washing machine filter. As he got older, he found even more things to do, and cuddles became rather passé – not helped, of course, by Jane, who at the grand age of eight has declared cuddles to be 'babyish' and takes great delight in pointing this out to Peter on the rare occasion that he does want a hug. Jane, it must be said, was never a cuddler; even as a baby she hated to be held and screamed to be put down, before becoming the most fiercely independent toddler in the world. 'MY DO IT!' and 'NO!' were mostly all she yelled for the first few years.

So all in all, even if it took my darling son being poleaxed by illness, it was awfully nice having someone to cuddle again, especially since it was a sore throat and not a vomiting bug, so I could relax safe in the knowledge that he was unlikely to puke down my cleavage while he was burrowed in next to me.

Wednesday, 21 October

Peter is still too unwell for school but is clearly on the mend, as today when I snuggled up on the sofa with him he fidgeted wildly, and instead of lying quietly watching the film he argued vociferously at the end of *Up* that it was a very silly film, because the man needed his house, and what was he going to do without his house? Meanwhile I was sobbing that all anyone needed was love, just love, to which Peter insisted that no, you need a house as well. When I wailed, 'Come and give Mummy another hug, darling' he claimed to need a poo and wandered off, still muttering about the need for bricks and mortar, not stupid love. I am glad he is getting better, of course, but I am rather missing my cuddly little boy.

Jane, meanwhile, although apparently in rude health, has been googling obscure and archaic diseases and is still threatening to come down with the plague, because she was even more incensed that Peter got a *second* day off school. Her claims of feeling faint and her self-diagnosis of 'quinsy throat' were somewhat spoiled by her eating an enormous breakfast, and by the fact that her capacity to argue about everything has not been diminished one little bit. I rather regret reading *What Katy Did* to Jane recently, as ever since she has rather fancied herself as a tiny domestic tyrant, lolling in her bed and ruling the house, commanding all below to come and pay homage at her court. This scenario is doubly alarming, as I fear I may be cast as Aunt Izzie, and I'm pretty sure Jane would have no qualms about bumping me off, the better to seize control of the household. She seems to have somewhat overlooked, a) the whole bit where Katy is paralysed for several years, and b) our complete lack of any domestic staff to facilitate this vision once she has done away with Aunt Izzie/me and taken to her bed to rule the roost. God help us all once she's old enough to read the Brontës.

I would obviously feel dreadful if Jane does get ill, especially after accusing her of faking it, so I spent the day anxiously checking my phone to make sure the school hadn't called me to come and collect my poor ailing moppet, but so far she is soldiering on, probably to her great indignation.

Monday, 26 October

It is half term. How is it half term already? They have barely been back at school for two minutes and now they are off for a whole week. Simon has refused once again to take any time off for half term, as he is Far Too Busy And Important and claims the moral high ground by dint of earning more money than me, somehow overlooking the fact that the only reason he earns more money than me is because we, not just me, but *we*, looked at all the childcare costs involved in us both working and decided that it made much more financial sense for me to work part-time to reduce the childcare needed, rather than working full-time just to pay for daycare or a nanny.

Starry-eyed and optimistic, we agreed that we would both spilt the childcare in the school recesses, but somehow Simon always has a very important work trip to go on, or project to complete when they are off school, so it's my bloody annual leave that gets eaten up with vacations, school concerts, open days and Christmas shows because he is so Super Busy. I don't believe he is that super busy, I think he is just cunning. I need to be more cunning.

Sadly, my boring office IT job doesn't allow me jaunts the way being an architect does, what with 'site visits' and conferences, so he has buggered off to Barcelona and I am here with the children, who are very hungry. So very hungry ... Every five minutes they appear, wailing that they are hungry, especially Peter, who consumes an obscene amount of food every day and never puts on weight. I occasionally wonder if he has a tapeworm. If he did have a tapeworm, he could at least share it with me. I would love to eat as much as he does and stay that skinny, to the point that I did once google whether or not you can buy tapeworms on the internet. (You allegedly can, but only from very dubious websites which are not to be recommended, not least for the viruses they will probably fill your computer with, let alone what horrors they are passing off as 'tapeworms'. Assuming they don't just skim your credit card and sit there laughing at the poor, deluded, lazy, fat women.) Occasionally I wonder if I should worm him, but I fear the results and being summonsed to view them. It's disgusting enough when I worm the dog. Peter is entirely foul enough that he would probably want to keep his worms as pets.

Foolishly, I had had high hopes that this week 'off' would allow me some time to sort out the house, clear out the fridge, find the source of the ever-present stench of stale urine in the bathroom and generally turn our home into a clean, tasteful, elegant and Pinterest-worthy living space. Sadly, though, I had forgotten that there is no such thing as an actual week off with the precious moppets. Aside from the constant lurking threat of potential starvation to be staved off, there are fights to be broken up, lost treasures to be found and entertainment to be provided.

When did entertaining children become so expensive? At the risk of sounding all 'in *my* day', my mother would have told me to bugger off if I had spent every day of the vacation whining at her 'What are we going to do today?' and demanding to go to the cinema, or soft play (dear God, let me not become so desperate this vacation that I succumb to the fetid, overpriced charms of soft play. Let me stand strong against the lurid, shit-smeared, Padded Cells of Doom).

The fridge was full yesterday, and now it is almost empty. Peter is only six, how on earth am I going to afford to feed him when he is a teenager? I remember when they were little and I used to suggest to my friend Claire that we went for coffee/to the park, etc. Claire had a teenage son as well as a little girl of Jane's age, and she often used to insist that we went to her house if she had just been to the supermarket because she had to guard the fridge against her son, otherwise he would eat everything if she went out and left him. I thought she was exaggerating, but then I encountered Peter and his tapeworm and now I see the hungry future staring at me.

Wednesday, 28 October

Oh God, I crumbled. We went to soft play. My ears are ringing and my head is thumping and I want to scrub myself and both children from head to toe with disinfectant and a wire brush, and there is not enough wine in the world to ease the pain. Peter got into a fight with a terrifying skinhead child, who had an equally terrifying mother who had 'Juztin Beebor 4ever' tattooed on her neck. I thought we were all going to die, then Jane managed to stand in a puddle of piss in the toilets and get stuck at the very top of the bastarding climbing frame thingy, leaving me with the option of clambering up there to try to rescue her and getting my arse stuck in the foam rollers again, thus having to endure the indignity of the bored teenage staff trying to extract me like Pooh Bear from the rabbit hole, or standing at the bottom shrieking at her in my shrill middle-class voice as I tried to coax her down with cries of 'Please darling, please just crawl through there and come down the slide, darling, and then we can all go home and have a nice pain au chocolat', all the while clutching my handbag to my chest and hoping no one stabbed me. Fuck wine, I'm going straight for gin. Lots of gin. *All* the gin.

Friday, 30 October

Simon is home, hurrah! AND he brought me a present. I like presents. The present, and the fact the demented budgie children are wittering at him instead of me and demanding that he puts them to bed almost, *almost* makes up for him sighing about how exhausted he is by a week in a nice hotel, eating hotel breakfasts and delicious tapas, and then saying in a pathetic voice that he would just like something really simple for dinner, like lasagne. Lasagne takes many pots and pans. It is not simple. But I am making it anyway for him, even though it is Fuck It All Friday, because I am a good wife and I quite missed him and it does give me a legitimate excuse to hide in the kitchen drinking the dubious Spanish gin he also brought home, while the children jump up and down on him and jabber inane questions in his ear – although I had forgotten just how long bastarding lasagne takes, and am muttering darkly to myself over the number of pots used. Also, if Simon tells me one more bloody time about how staying in hotels is not as exciting as you might think, I will not be responsible for my actions.

Saturday, 31 October

Well, that was a fun Halloween. It actually turned out that having to make Peter a last-minute vampire costume out of an old pair of my lace panties because he changed his mind about being a bat approximately fifteen minutes before we left to go Trick or Treating (or, as I like to call it, 'begging door-to-door like starving Victorian urchins' while swearing under my breath at the ridiculous commercialization of an ancient pagan tradition) was the high point of the evening. Jane managed to escape my watchful eye at the Halloween party organised by a kind neighbour for after the begging expedition, and succeeded in stuffing her own body weight in sweets down her throat before I caught her. Trying to contain the screaming rubber ball that used to be my daughter from bouncing off the walls was bad, but I really thought I was home clear once I finally calmed her down and got her into bed, along with Sophie, who had come for a sleepover. However, just as I had sat down with a tiny (enormous) glass of lovely, restorative red wine (I decided I was keeping in the spirit of Halloween by giving myself 'vampire fangs' if I knocked it back in big-enough mouthfuls), there was a plaintive howl from Jane's bedroom.

Jane and I have spoken several times about how, if she is going to throw up, I would really, *really* appreciate it if she could manage not to just lie in her bed and vomit over it. This lesson had evidently sunk in, because instead she had leaned over the side of her bed and puked over Sophie, who was sleeping on a blow-up bed beside her. All. Over. Sophie. Sophie has very long, thick hair.

Simon is quite good with vomit. I am very bad with it. He dealt with the vomit-covered bedding (because despite her attempt to not puke on her bed, Jane had still got quite a lot of it over her duvet) and sleeping bag and carpet, while I shoved a hysterical Jane and a sleepy and confused Sophie under the shower and attempted to get all the puke out of Sophie's hair, while gagging to myself and alternately muttering 'FFS' and 'FML' to myself. So much puke. It was worse than the time Peter spewed off the top of his cabin bed and the resultant splashback made me very much regret the decision to put laminate flooring in his room. I threw away a lot of Lego that night.

I can still smell vomit, and I daren't even drink my wine in case Princess Pukesalot strikes again. Luckily Sophie was very nice about it, though I'm not sure she was actually awake enough to fully take in what was going on, but I am mortified at the thought of having to tell Sam in the morning.

NOVEMBER

Thursday, 5 November

Bonfire Night, hurrah! The smell of woodsmoke and crackling fires. Baked potatoes and sausages. Excited little faces glowing with awe in the light of the fireworks. What's not to love? Well, for a start, one's darling husband decreeing that there was no need to go to an official display because he was going to indulge his inner pyromaniac by setting off our own fireworks in the back yard. What larks, I thought, and promptly invited all the neighbours for a fireworks party so that they too could enjoy the munificence of the woodsmoke/baked potatoes/glowing faces, etc.

Alas, foolishly, Simon entrusted me with the buying of the fireworks and I got a bit distracted because I had filled up the car with gas before I went to the supermarket to buy them and had managed to spill gasoline over my boots and was wondering whether they would even sell fireworks to someone who was reeking of gas or whether they would just call the police to report a deranged fire-starting maniac in their shop. I was so excited that no one mentioned the eau de gasoline aroma drifting from me that I got very carried away and bought many boxes of the biggest fireworks they had (in my defence they were also on sale as three-for-two, and I cannot resist a special offer).

No one noticed (including me), until it was too late, that I had managed to buy several boxes of display fireworks which carried stern warnings that they MUST NOT be set off within 100 metres of any buildings or people. Our house does not in any way have 100-metre clearance around it from any other buildings (aka 'the neighbours' houses'), and it was now too late to return to the shop and buy more fireworks (and anyway, these ones had already cost a bloody fortune, 'special offer' my fat arse).

Nothing daunted, Simon and I decided to press ahead with the party and the fireworks, as Simon airily assured me that the warnings were just a precaution, so you couldn't sue the fireworks manufacturers if you were the sort of idiot who managed to accidently burn your shed down with a sparkler. And *of course* it was perfectly safe, supermarkets didn't actually sell display-size fireworks (do fireworks have a size? Strength? How are fireworks scaled? By 'bang'?) so it would be fine, we would be the wonder of the street.

The neighbours duly assembled, I merrily doled out sausages and baked potatoes and imagined I was some sort of Martha Stewart, domestic goddess, fantasy hostess.

The children all waved sparklers around, at which point I abandoned my serene Martha impression in favour of screaming 'Gloves! Gloves! You must have gloves for sparklers! Don't touch the hot part! Don't set your sister on fire! Please be careful! *Be careful! Be careful!* BE FUCKING CAREFUL WITH THAT, IT IS FIRE!'

And then Simon began the firework display. In an effort to prove he could put on just as good a show at home as one could see being jostled in a muddy park or field with several hundred other people, he had carefully arranged all the fireworks in the back yard in advance and ran around lighting them all at once, so they would go off one straight after another, like a proper display …

So it turns out that supermarkets DO sell display-strength fireworks. It also turns out the stern warnings are *not* just a precaution.

The initial 'Ooooohs' and 'Ahhhhhs' and happy faces bathed in the light of the fireworks very quickly turned to mutterings of 'Is that safe?', 'Fuck, that was really near my house', 'Should someone call the fire brigade?' and 'Holy shit, this maniac is going to burn the street down!' Small children were sobbing, and there was talk of forming a chain of buckets to try to douse the conflagration we had potentially started.

Instead of everyone mingling happily around the bonfire afterwards, sipping mulled wine and exclaiming about the marvellous fun we were all having, the neighbours started to leave hastily to go and check if we had set their house on fire, until there was only Simon and me, and Peter and Jane, huddled at the far end of the back yard, watching us turn our quiet suburban street into an effective re-enactment of 1980s' Beirut. The children were highly impressed. So far there have been no sirens, suggesting that we have not actually burned anyone's ancestral home to the ground, nor have the police appeared to enquire exactly what we thought we were doing with our rocket launchers and grenades.

When the fireworks finally finished, Simon wandered sadly around the blackened wasteland that was once his lovingly tended lawn, muttering darkly to himself about the scorch marks.

Apparently this is all my fault, but I blame the shop – what do they expect will happen if they sell eleventy billion fireworks to people who smell of gasoline?

On the plus side, we are probably off all the neighbours' Christmas card lists now, so that is one less thing to do, and I got to drink all the mulled wine and am quite drunk, due to my misplaced belief that really, mulled wine is hardly even alcoholic.

Saturday, 7 November

I feel almost like an actual person with an actual life! Having two divorcees as friends mean their other halves (BASTARDS) have the children every other weekend so they get to go out and Do Things. Obviously the breakdown of their relationships is very sad for Hannah and Sam, and their children, but it is very good for me, as I get to go to the pub with them.

Tonight, once we had covered the many shortcomings and wrongdoings of the exes, except for Hannah or Sam shouting the occasional random 'BASTARD' as some other iniquity happened to occur to them, Sam finally admitted that I had been right about his pursuit by the Bloody Perfect Coven. Apparently Sophie had told Perfect Lucy Atkinson that she had two daddies and Lucy's Mummy has now asked Sophie round to play no less than five times this week, only Sophie is having none of it, because apparently she hates Lucy Atkinson 'because her face is stupid', which seems as valid a reason as any. The rest of the Coven have also been hovering, suggesting he 'pops in for coffee'; pressing terrifying homemade 'health muffins' on him and, with a staggering lack of tact, even by Fiona Montague's standards (I haven't forgotten the time she told me how 'brave' I was to go out without putting my makeup on especially when I was 'under the weather', despite the fact I was perfectly healthy and wearing a full face of slap), attempting to set him up with her hairdresser 'Because I'm sure you chaps have lots in common.'

'They're like ninjas,' said Sam. 'I feel like I'm in some sort of a computer game on the bloody school run, ducking behind hedges to avoid them hurling their disgusting baking at me and demanding I come to their jewellery parties. I'm fucking gay, I'm not a bloody drag queen, why would I want to spend the evening cooing over their shitty costume jewellery?'

'Do you remember the *artisan* vaginas?' sniggered Hannah. She has never forgiven me for the time I made her come to one of these parties with me, only for us to discover to our horror that the 'designer' mummy hosting the party had, for reasons known only to herself, decided to create an entire range of jewellery based on her own genitalia, to celebrate its fecundity. Given the eye-watering price tags attached to the jewellery (earrings, pendants, rings and bracelets!), her front bottom was extremely fecund indeed. However, all the raised eyebrows at the prices were dismissed with the retort that the jewellery was *artisan* and thus it was perfectly justifiable to charge the GDP of Luxembourg for a necklace with a sterling silver twat hanging from it. It appears that a similar justification is made in the local cafés, should anyone baulk at paying a tenner for a bacon sandwich; apparently this is quite an acceptable price, as the bacon is from a special pig that went to tap dancing lessons and enjoyed skydiving in its spare time or something.

I have never seen anyone look quite as appalled as Sam as Hannah explained about the 'artisan' jewellery. He actually looked even more horrified than Simon (a man who cannot even utter the word 'vagina') had when I told him about it, but I suppose Simon was at least safe in the knowledge that no one is ever going to try to make him go to a jewellery party.

So horrified was Sam that he declared tequila to be a medical necessity to numb the horror of the thought that someone believed that making replicas of their own unmentionable bits to sell to their friends was a good idea.

After a couple of tequilas, I couldn't shake off the feeling that Sam had said something earlier which had given me an awfully good idea, but I couldn't for the life of me remember what the clever idea was, except that it was quite astonishing in its great cleverness. That is the problem with tequila. Well, one of the problems with tequila.

Monday, 9 November

Blimey, we really must have annoyed the neighbours with our grenades and rocket launchers last week. The Jenkins across the road have put their house up for sale.

Of course, the first thing I did when I saw the sign was exactly what the rest of the street was doing at that moment, which was rushing off to look it up on the internet and frantically calculating if the asking price for the Jenkins' house meant the value of our own houses had gone up or down since the last time someone moved. Then, of course, I had to look through all the photos and judge their décor, muttering things like 'OMG, those *curtains*! What was she thinking?' and 'FFS, lazy slatterns, they could have put the lid of the toilet down and hidden the bottles of cleaning stuff before the photo was taken.'

I do love the internet, it is so much easier than in the olden days when you had to ring up the real estate agents and pretend you were actually interested in buying the house before you could stalk your neighbours. You can also nosy over dream houses you will never ever be able to afford – the sort of houses that you used to only be able to look at in the front pages of *Country Life* magazine when you were at the dentist.

I got rather side-tracked this morning, though, and started coveting a wildly romantic Scottish tower house and a grimly brooding, Manderley-esque Cornish manor house. There was even a rather nice little Oxfordshire Queen Anne rectory that I could settle for at a push (actually, that one cost more than the Scottish tower and Cornish manor house combined). Anything other than my dull surburban villa.

All this sighing over dream houses meant that I suddenly realised it was 8.45 a.m. and I hadn't even begun the lengthy process of repeatedly shouting 'SHOES ON, ARE YOU READY?

WE ARE LEAVING NOW! HAVE YOU GOT YOUR SHOES ON? WHAT THE FUCK ARE YOU DOING? JUST PUT YOUR BLOODY SHOES ON! NOW! WE ARE GOING NOW! IF YOU ARE NOT READY, I WILL LEAVE YOU HERE! NO, I DIDN'T MEAN IT; NO, IT'S NOT A JOLLY GOOD IDEA! JUST PUT YOUR SHOES ON, I CAN'T LEAVE YOU HERE, IT'S ILLEGAL!'

All of this seems to be the ritual chant to enable the children to leave the house in the morning, and so without it we were late for school, which resulted in knowing looks amongst the Coven gathered chatting at the school gate in their yoga kits, clutching their little Starbucks cups of soya decaff skinny latte with an extra shot of smugness. Seriously, who has time to stop and get a cup of takeaway coffee on the way to school? Why don't they just drink coffee in their own houses before they leave like normal people? Is it just to show off that they are sooooo super organised they can leave the house with an extra twenty minutes to spare (probably because their nannies got the children ready) and are rich enough to pay £3+ for a tiny cup of coffee?

Of course, I was then late for work, so I had no time to buy a scratchcard on the way to attempt to make my Dream House dream come true (because scratchcards are obviously a far better investment than £3 cups of coffee. I'm so Jerry Springer sometimes, I'll be going to the supermarket in my pyjamas next).

Luckily no one noticed I was late, so I was able to nip out at lunchtime and get a scratchcard then (okay, *five* scratchcards), none of which won. I don't know why I am still so surprised when scratchcards fail to provide the fortune I am eternally hoping for, as I have never, ever won more than £1 on one, which obviously I promptly 'reinvested' by buying another card.

I should know by now that I never win anything, whether it is on scratchcards, raffles or even tombolas. The sum extent of my raffle wins are a furry Kleenex-box cover in the shape of a dog, which I won when I was seven, and, more recently, a turnip. A. Turnip. Who even puts a bloody turnip into a raffle at a school fete anyway? I was very upset about the turnip, as I feared winning it had used up the whole lifetime's worth of luck that I had accumulated by never winning anything, but on reflection, I decided that there could be fewer things more unlucky than winning a turnip, so therefore my luck was intact, ready to all be squandered on one big win, probably on a scratchcard, as I like the instant gratification and can't be arsed with waiting for lottery draws.

Since my scratchcard failings meant my latest property porn dream had been crushed and I wasn't about to move to my dream house, I rang Hannah instead and told her of my new Very Good Idea, which is that rather than trying to buy Dan out of their house, she should just sell up and buy the Jenkins' house and come and live across the road from me. She was a bit dubious about this plan, as she was unconvinced that she would be able to afford it, once Dan had taken his cut and the lawyers had been paid, but I pointed out that after Fireworks-gate it will be easy for us to continue with the anti-social behaviour and thus successfully manage to lower the house prices in the street. I could get Simon to go about in a stained under shirt and chuck some empty beer cans in the back yard. We would have to return to being middle-class once Hannah moved in, of course, so we didn't affect prices too much (i.e. the price of our own house).

I should adore Hannah to live across the street; we could pop in and out of each other's houses for a glass of wine in the evenings instead of meeting up once a month if we are lucky, having carefully synced childcare/children's activities, etc., to let us out of the house, at which point we tend to be so excited to see each other and be out that we generally end up getting hammered.

Instead, we would sit at each other's scrubbed kitchen tables and laugh merrily, while throwing together effortlessly delicious and wholesome suppers that everyone would eat without complaining. I have attempted to pursue this vision with the odd neighbour that I thought might be a kindred spirit, but so far they have all proved sadly disappointing and say things like 'Oh no, no wine for me, it's Tuesday', or 'Sorry, I'm doing Weight Watchers – do you know how many "points" are in wine?' I have rubbish neighbours. I need better ones. Like Hannah.

This afternoon, all the managers were out of the office doing something managerial like team building, so I spent the time browsing further on property websites under the guise of 'research' to demonstrate to Hannah why her buying the Jenkins' house makes perfect financial sense. The good thing about being in IT at an untechnical company is that everyone is afraid of computers, so no one has the slightest idea how long anything should take. This means I actually get to laze about quite a lot, as I can convince people that a job that will take me about two hours will actually take two weeks, but at a push, just for them, I might be able to do it in ten days. Then, if I am feeling magnanimous, I might even deliver it in a week, so everyone thinks I am a genius superstar when actually I spend most of my time shopping online and reading celebrity gossip forums.

Being so very cunning at my job also means they let me work from 9.30 a.m. to 3 p.m., and I have every second Wednesday off. These perks almost make up for all the times at parties when people ask what I do and I say I work in IT and you can see their eyes glazing over before I have even got the 'T' out. However, I do live in fear that one day they might decide I am clearly horribly overworked and get someone else in to help me, which would be fine if it was a like-minded lazy bastard but I would be completely buggered if the worst happened and they employed someone with an actual work ethic.

Thursday, 12 November

AAARRRRRRGHHHHHH. The Christmas emails have begun. IT IS NOT CHRISTMAS UNTIL DECEMBER! Why are my stupid family doing this to me? In fairness, I suppose at least by waiting until November they have heeded my mega meltdown last year when they started sending them in August and I told them all to fuck off and die, they were RUINING THE MAGIC OF CHRISTMAS.

The first email arrived this morning from my smuggety-smug-smug-pants, super-clever, corporate-fat-cat, rich-as-Croesus, practically-perfect-in-every-way sister Jessica:

> Hi Ellen,
>
> Just thinking about what we are going to do for Christmas, with Mum and Geoffrey on their cruise, and Dad and Caroline going to her children. I know it's my turn to have everyone to mine, but I'm just totally snowed under at work and there is no way I have time to host Christmas, sorry.
>
> So what I thought might be nice was if we all went away somewhere together – have a look at Ferraton Hall, it's a gorgeous country house hotel and they're doing an amazing deal over Christmas, two nights for only £500 per person, and they'll do Christmas dinner for £75 a head as well (plus wine), but we'll have to book now, they've only got space because they've had a cancellation.
>
> Also, if we went there, we could just get each other treatments in their spa as Christmas presents, there is a list on the website.
>
> Best wishes,
> Jessica

What the actual fuck?

A) My own mother is buggering off with my stepfather on a cruise over Christmas and hasn't bothered to tell me. When was she going to do that?

B) Okay, fair enough, I knew Dad would be going to stay with his wife's children because it's their turn to have them for Christmas, but I still feel vaguely huffy and like he loves his 'new family' more than us, even though I was twenty-nine when he married Caroline. I sort of want to stamp my feet and shout 'BUT HE'S MYYYYYYYYYY DADDY, NOT YOURS!'

And most of all, C) £500 each to stay, plus £75 a head for Christmas dinner? Just because my darling sister likes to modestly protest that she doesn't *quite* earn seven figures (thus hinting that she is not far off it) she expects us to shell out £2,300 before I've even bought a present, because she is too bloody busy to host Christmas. She knows perfectly well that we just don't have that sort of money to spend on two nights in a hotel, and also Peter and Jane are not quite like her perfect moppets Persephone and Gulliver (so-named because 'we just wanted something classic and yet unusual'), and are likely to run amok, either smashing or stealing the tasteful antiques that such hotels tend to have scattered about. Also, what sort of cold-hearted witch ends their emails to their own sister with 'Best wishes'? It'll be 'Kind regards' next, you mark my words.

I emailed back:

Hi Jess,
Hotel looks fab, but bit on the pricey side for us at the moment, sorry.
    E xxx

Bing! For someone who is too busy to think about ordering a Christmas dinner online from Wholefoods, she is pretty quick off the mark to reply to emails about it.

Hi Ellen,
That's such a shame about the hotel, it looked so nice – I hope you're not still wasting money on scratchcards, ha ha.

Persephone and Gulliver are so looking forward to seeing their cousins at
Christmas, and it is a time for family, after all. Maybe if you don't want to go
to Ferraton Hall we could come to you for Christmas Day? I know it is my turn,
so I wouldn't be expecting you to do all the work. I will bring the Christmas
pudding.

Best wishes,

Jessica

And she's done it again. Somehow, she has guilt-tripped me into
hosting Christmas, and in the space of two sentences turned it
into a fait accompli – 'I will bring the Christmas pudding' –
before I have even agreed to them coming here. Apparently
because it's 'a time for family', when even our own parents can't
be arsed with us! There will be no escaping Jessica's decree that
we are to spend Christmas as a family by pointing out our absen-
tee mental parentals, though, she will just reply that that is all
more the more reason for us to spend it together.

Of course, all the children are a year older now, so surely it
will be more civilised? Last Christmas Peter and Jane had eaten
an entire box of chocolates each for breakfast by the time Jessica
and her almost mute husband Neil arrived (they have been
married for fifteen years and I still don't know whether Neil does
not speak because he hates us or because he is too scared of
Jessica to voice an opinion, or whether he is just rendered dumb
with horror by the chaos of my house and the feralness of my
children. Either way, he tends to sit in gloomy silence, respond-
ing only to direct questions by mumbling, 'No, I'm fine, thanks,
yes thanks, I'm fine', while occasionally twitching).

Persephone and Gulliver had received tasteful, quiet and ethical gifts from their parents, whereas Peter and Jane had mainly
received noisy, annoying computer games from us, which they
were attempting to play at the same time as hurling themselves
around the house like sugar-crazed fiends.

Persephone had written a composition for the piano as her present to everyone and demanded to play it as soon as she arrived, which meant she was crying within ten minutes of setting foot in the door, because apparently our rather rickety upright piano that came courtesy of Gumtree was not of the same standard as the piano that she was used to playing, and also Peter and Jane wouldn't turn off the PlayStation during her recital. Then when Simon forcibly wrestled the controls from their hands, they made up words to Persephone's song which went along the lines of 'Persephone is a poo face, a stupid, stupid poo face' and Jessica's mouth got so like a cat's bum that I thought her whole head was actually going to turn itself inside out, which really beggars the question why she even wants to come to us for Christmas?

I did once ask her why she is so set on us always spending Christmas together, and she looked surprised and said, 'I just want our children to have the same sort of magical Christmases that we had – you know, everyone together, the big family meal, the games and traditions. Not like it was ... afterwards.'

I think Jessica might have got the Christmases of our childhood muddled up with a Coca-Cola advert, as my recollections are of Mum swearing behind closed doors because Granny (Dad's mum) was being a complete bitch to her, while she tried to beat the lumps out of the packet stuffing and neck enough gin to numb her to Granny's comments about her weight. Dad would snatch any toys involving batteries from Jess and me because clearly we couldn't be trusted to put the batteries in by ourselves and so he would have to 'set them up', by which he meant play with them himself, while we whined to have them back. Mum having failed in her wifely duty to provide him with a son and heir, furnishing only two feeble girl children instead, meant that Jess and I got a lot of battery operated presents like train sets and car racing tracks, which were clearly destined for his non-existent sons.

By lunchtime Mum would be on the verge of a nervous breakdown and would burst into tears halfway through eating the Christmas pudding because she had only just remembered about the stuffing she had left in the oven and which was now incinerated. By the time we got to the Queen's Speech, which Granny insisted on watching, no one would be speaking to each other. At about 6 p.m., despite no one ever wanting to see any food ever again, Mum would make a martyred performance of laying out the 'Christmas Tea', consisting of various leftovers fashioned into sandwiches and, for some inexplicable reason, quantities of pickled beetroot. Mum would then shout at us all until we ate a turkey sandwich and a slice of Christmas cake, and only then would we be permitted the high point of the day, which was to watch the comedy Christmas Specials.

To be fair, the 'Afterwards' Christmases do actually make those Christmases look quite rosy – 'Afterwards' being the years after Dad got caught shagging his secretary and Mum kicked him out. 'Afterwards' Christmases were always accompanied by a nagging guilt about whichever parent we weren't with, despite the bright assurances from them that they would be absolutely fine, and not to worry about them.

Poor Jessica. I shouldn't be so mean about her. Even before 'Afterwards' she was always the perfectionist, trying desperately to shape Christmas into the ideal she had in her head – distracting Granny from her spiteful remarks with games of Trivial Pursuit (though part of me still suspects she always picked Trivial Pursuit to show off how clever she was), and valiantly stuffing down Christmas cake in an attempt to stop Mum storming out of the room while shrieking she didn't know why she bloody bothered. I still remember the first 'Afterwards' Christmas, when we went to stay with Dad, and at teatime on

Christmas Day Jess produced the jar of pickled beetroot she had bought especially on her way home from school, in an effort to make Christmas seem more like 'Before'.

However, all this just makes it even more baffling as to why the devil she always seems to wriggle out of hosting Christmas at her house and wangles having it at mine. I would've thought Jess would've been in her element, being the Queen of Christmas, casually shrugging off her immaculately tasteful decorations as 'nothing' while dishing up a Michelin chef-inspired feast, before berating us all to play charades while Persephone entertained us on the Baby Steinway. Oh God. What if Jess always refuses to do Christmas because my children are too awful to have in her perfect house? Maybe she would do Christmas if I offered to drug them or something?

I am not caving in to Jessica that easily anyway, so I replied:

Hi Jess,
I'm not sure what our plans are yet, I'll need to talk to Simon and get back to you.
    E xx

Ha. She will get her own way in the end, she always does, but at least I will get to waste some of her Super Busy and Important time with vague emails. Which will make me feel like I am in some way getting back at her for that jibe about the scratchcards!

FML. The thought of Christmas with Jessica is enough to make anyone turn to drink. Anyway, it's nearly the weekend, so a tiny glass of wine is perfectly acceptable. The dog just gave me one of his looks and shook his head in a most disapproving manner. 'Don't you judge me,' I told him. 'You don't have to deal with Jessica!'

Friday, 13 November

Friday the thirteenth. The unluckiest day of the year. I am not superstitious, but I think there might be something about Friday the thirteenth because this morning I got an email from Simon's sister Louisa. Or rather, 'Amaris', as she recently announced she would now be known, which apparently means 'Child of the Moon'.

Louisa/Amaris and her husband Bardo run an 'alternative spiritual retreat' somewhere in the Highlands of Scotland. They share their retreat with an ever-increasing number of grubby children that Louisa/Amaris seems to pop out on a distressingly regular basis. I think last time I counted they were up to four.

Louisa/Amaris' email went like this:

Namaste, Ellen,

The Goddess has blessed us with another gift, who we have named Boreas. Bardo and I would like Boreas to meet the rest of the family and thought Christmas (or the Winter Solstice Feast, as we prefer to call it) would be the perfect time. We will be closing the retreat for this important occasion and we plan to arrive with you on 22 December. We can sleep in Gunnar (our camper van, it means 'Bold Warrior' – lol) if you don't have room for us in the house, and then we don't need to bother you, apart from for cooking and using the bathroom. We thought we'd head home around the 29th, to give you all lots of time to get to know Boreas. We are doing a digital detox for the next two weeks and so won't be answering emails, so if I don't hear from you by noon today I will assume that is OK!

　　Peace and love,

　　Amaris

Sent at 11.52 a.m. Bitch!

I am not entirely certain exactly what form of 'spirituality' Louisa/Amaris and Bardo (meaning 'Son of the Earth', formally known as Kevin) practice. They seem to have a vague pick'n'mix approach to Druidism, Wicca and Buddhism, all mixed in with a generous dollop of what can only be described as New Age Wank. All I am certain of is that they float through life with a general air of superiority towards Simon and me, enslaved as we are to 'The Man', which at least gives them something in common with Jessica, who also feels superior to Simon and me and our dull suburban life.

At least Jessica and her children are clean. Louisa/Amaris and Bardo/Kevin and their eleventy billion children all look like they need a damn good scrub with a wire brush and a bottle of neat disinfectant. I still have not recovered from their 'wedding', which was a Wiccan hand-fasting ceremony, which I'm not even sure is legal. Despite my misgivings, I gave it my all and I turned up to their big day in an adorable fascinator and my best LK Bennett shoes, doing my utmost to channel my inner Kate Middleton. The ceremony turned out to be in the woods. The woods were muddy and my heels pegged me nicely to the ground, so the happy couple and a wide assortment of grubby people dressed in baggy tie dye and chunky silver jewellery (some of which looked suspiciously similar to the artisan vagina necklaces), got to look on and snigger while Simon hauled me free. Worse, it was raining, so not only was my frou-frou fascinator fucked, but my mascara ran, which meant I soon looked as unwashed as everyone else.

Louisa had recently sprogged and had generously kept and dried her placenta, which she had then ground up and invited us to sprinkle on our food if we wished. Until that point, I genuinely hadn't thought that anything could have made Bardo's 'Lentil Surprise' more unappetising, but after that culinary suggestion I couldn't even bring myself to try a mouthful for fear of what the 'surprise' might be – Bardo's scrotal scrapings perhaps? Simon kicked me repeatedly and told me to behave, after all, it was his sister's wedding.

Louisa used to be perfectly normal; she was a graphic designer at a big advertising agency and earned a decent amount of money. Then she met Bardo, who had once worked in banking but one day he suddenly had an 'epiphany' on a Circle Line train, 'And I just realised, man, what was I doing? I was like that train, just going round and round forever, and I knew something had to change, man.' (Bardo seems to think he is some sort of 1960s' hippy festival movie – 'man'.) So he jacked in his job, sold his flat and went off to travel round India, which was where he found himself as Bardo. 'So I built a fire on the beach, man, and I burnt everything that had belonged to Kevin, and I took this new name, and I left Kevin there.' Basically, he got completely off his tits on drugs and set fire to all his stuff and we are supposed to somehow think this makes him deep and profound, instead of a pretentious tosser.

Having found himself, Bardo decided it was time to come home and spread the message so that others could also find themselves. His decision to come back clearly had nothing to do with him having no clean underpants or money, because he'd burnt it all. Actually, I have a horrible feeling Bardo probably doesn't wear underpants. Ew.

Back in London, he met Louisa, who was always quite suggestible, and convinced her to step off the Circle Line too, and between the remains of the proceeds of Bardo's flat and Louisa cashing in everything she owned as well, they buggered off to Scotland, where they bought 100 acres of scrubland on which they planned to be self-sufficient and run their retreat so that others too could see the unique light cast by Kevin's underwear burning on a beach.

And now they have spawned again. Boreas. What sort of a name is Boreas? I can't even be arsed to google it. I know Louisa will tell me at length what it means when I see her, which seems inevitable as I failed to answer her email in the brief window given before their 'digital detox'. For that matter, what is a digital detox? I'm assuming it's giving up all the horrid modern technologies, despite the fact that the few deluded souls who actually come to the retreat tend to book online. Maybe they've had their electricity cut off again, as using the last of their cash to install solar panels, in a wood, in the North of Scotland, wasn't their most cunning move. It might've been okay if they had consented to cut down the trees around the panels, but apparently they couldn't, because that would anger the Goddess.

No doubt Simon or his parents will have to bail them out again if they've been cut off. I know I shouldn't begrudge Simon giving Louisa money, she *is* his sister after all, but nonetheless I do begrudge it, because really there is absolutely no reason why Louisa and Bardo couldn't go out and get ordinary jobs like everyone else. They are both well-educated and more than qualified for a range of jobs that would pay perfectly well, yet they choose to faff around with their alternative lifestyle, wasting what money they have on things like those stupid solar panels and then expecting the rest of us to finance their ridiculous ideas because they are on a Higher Plane to us and so can't be expected to bother themselves with foolish mundanities like employment or money.

Anyway, Boreas. Is that a boy or a girl? Louisa has now had so many children that I can't remember if I counted the Boreas bump when I thought there were four, or if Boreas is now number five. Either way, that is another present that will have to be bought, for Louisa to sigh pityingly over and explain why they only give presents knitted from organic yak pubic hair.

I still haven't told Simon about Jessica, and now I am going to have to tell him about Louisa too. Although he makes a lot of fuss about how close he and Louisa are, I know that secretly he much prefers it when she stays far away in Scotland with Beardo (Simon's joke, not mine). Also, Jessica v. Louisa could get messy.

FML, why is Christmas so complicated? Why are our families so complicated? Is everyone's family like this? At least Simon's parents have retired to France and show no signs of wanting to visit for Christmas, preferring to have their own wine-soaked Joyeux Noël in their bijou chateau with various amusing neighbours, instead having the hordes of grandchildren to visit in the summer when they can be safely corralled outside in the pool.

I *really* hope Louisa doesn't bring her placenta …

Saturday, 14 November

FML. I forgot to do the online shop, so now we have no food, no toilet paper (where does all the toilet paper go? How can we go through so much bloody toilet paper in a week? Are the children eating it? Do they smuggle it out of the house to sell in some kind of secret toilet paper black market? It is astonishing. Perhaps it is Simon who uses it all, as he is very proud of how much time he spends in the bathroom anyway) and worse, NO WINE!

As Simon claimed he had some work to do this morning, due to him being so Very Busy And Important, I was forced to drag the children to the supermarket with me, which is vile at the best of times but even worse on a Saturday morning when you are likely to encounter the Coven 'just popping in' on their way home from their moppets' new class in Ancient Greek Philosophy Taught In Mandarin, or the like.

These encounters were doubly annoying this morning because for some reason there were many Red Label marked-down bargains to be had. I joyously filled my shopping cart with things like an enormous slab of brisket for £3.42 and filet mignons for £2.54, delighted to think of the bounteous munificence my freezer would henceforth hold, instead of several bags of peas that have been repeatedly defrosted and refrozen due to being used as icepacks on Peter to thwart his ongoing attempts to end up in the ER again and have me reported to Social Services. The Coven judge the Bargain Love, and having spotted Perfect Lucy Atkinson's Perfect Mummy and Fiona Montague lurking, a game of Supermarket Ninja had to be enacted, as we sidled around corners to check the aisles for them, before I charged up the aisle lobbing necessary items into the cart at speed and hissing '*Shut up, shut up, shut up*' at Jane as she asked in her loudest voice, 'BUT WHY DON'T YOU WANT TO TALK TO LUCY'S MUMMY? DON'T YOU LIKE LUCY'S MUMMY? IS THAT WHY YOU SAID LUCY'S MUMMY WAS A TWAT YESTERDAY?'

It was all to no avail, of course, for Lucy Atkinson AND her Perfect Mummy cornered us in the grains and pulses aisle, just as Peter was asking repeatedly what would happen if you kept holding farts in forever – 'Would you explode? Would you? But what if you DID hold them in forever? But JUST SAY, Mummy, would you explode with blood and guts everywhere?' – before he re-enacted what he thought exploding from held-in farts would look like.

Lucy's Mummy looked at us aghast as I hurled bags of quinoa into the cart to cover the lovely Bargain Love within and Peter writhed on the floor, making dramatic vomiting noises.

'Gosh, Ellen, what an *imagination* he has,' said Lucy's Mummy, and then, peering at the lovely, middle-class quinoa, 'Oh, how *fun*. You still eat quinoa. You should give the Carmargue red rice a try, sweetie, you'll find it really helps with that bloating …' And with that she sashayed off, Lucy walking demurely beside her

(Sophie is right, her face is stupid), as I dragged Peter off the floor and replaced the quinoa on the shelf, because there is as much chance of getting Simon and the children to eat it as there is of getting Lucy's Mummy to eat a Chicken Nugget sandwich (Peter's current favourite meal – white bread only, obviously, and don't try to fob him off with any of that half-and-half pretend white bread, he can smell the fibre). Also, I already have a perfectly good packet of quinoa in the cupboard. It may have expired in 2014, but it still counts.

Further humiliation was awaiting at the check-out when the cashier looked at the number of wine bottles in my cart, along with the litre of Export-strength gin, and chirpily asked, 'Ooooh, having a party, are we?' I should have just said yes, but instead all I could do was gesture at Peter and Jane, Peter now attempting to lick the conveyor belt and Jane wittering dementedly in a faux American accent as she doggedly recounted the entire plot of some appalling children's TV show she is addicted to, and say 'No. No, I am not.'

Soul-destroying and hideous though the trip to the shop was, the game of Supermarket Ninja did at least finally remind me what the nagging sensation was that I had had for weeks about that clever notion I had had at the pub, before tequila shots wiped it from my addled brain. It had been Sam talking about dodging the Coven and the other Uber Mummies at the school gate and in the playground, and saying they were like ninjas. In a moment of genius, I mulled that perhaps there should be a computer game or app for mums about doing the school run and all the other parenting scenarios you find yourself in, in which you have to successfully negotiate them. Perhaps you could earn glasses of wine for each hazard you avoid, maybe progressing to gin as you move up through the levels. I could call it 'Why Mummy Drinks'! It might even make a bit of money, and I could have the ruined sideboard professionally restored as a surprise for Simon. I may have finally had a Good Idea (which obviously deserves wine) …

I dashed home from the supermarket to start working on my app straightaway, which so far has consisted of googling how much successful apps can make; gnashing my teeth at articles about twelve-year-olds selling their brilliant apps to corporate giants for billions and squillions of pounds; the discovery that Flappy Birds allegedly made $50,000 a DAY at its height (if you'll pardon the pun); imagining what I would do with all that money (put it to better use than any spotty teenager ever could); choosing which Louboutin shoes I would buy with $50,000; working out how much $50,000 is in pounds; looking at the clock and wishing it was time for wine, and getting up every ten minutes to get someone a snack or shout at them to stop hitting each other. When I am rich beyond the dreams of avarice with my lovely app, I am so getting a nanny. Or at least an au pair.

Wednesday, 18 November

Jane was going to a friend's house after school today, so in a fit of maternal optimism I thought it would be nice for Peter and me to spend some time together, bonding. We would go to a lovely café and he could have hot chocolate and I would have coffee and we would share a cake and chat about our days and it would totally be a special moment. Also, I could probably take a photo of him with his hot chocolate and put it on Facebook and tag it #happymemories so that people think I am a loving and functional parent and might envy my close relationship with my darling son.

Things got off to a slightly sticky start when Peter point-blank refused to consider sharing a cake with me and demanded his own. He also took shameless advantage of my attempt to create a special moment and rejected hot chocolate and insisted on Coke. I knew deep down that I was going to regret that Coke, but in the end I caved, so that I looked like a nice mummy.

Peter then proceeded to witter at me mercilessly about wretched Pokémon …

'What is your favourite Pokémon, Mummy? Not that one. No, that's a rubbish one. No, not Pikachu, everyone says Pikachu. Eevee should be your favourite, Eevee is a good one! Why isn't Eevee your favourite? How haven't you ever heard of Eevee? Just say Eevee is your favourite, okay?'

Finally, worn down by all this I said, 'Darling, do you think we could talk about something that isn't Pokémon?'

Peter looked blank for a moment, because talking about something that wasn't Pokémon clearly did not compute. Eventually, he thought of something to say.

'Who is the best Jedi, Mummy?'

'The best Jedi? Oh that's easy! Luke Skywalker, obviously.'

Peter looked at me in horror. 'NO, MUMMY! YODA is the best Jedi! Everyone knows Yoda is the best Jedi. How do you not even know that, Mummy? Why are you so stupid?'

I remonstrated with Peter that he should not call people stupid, but he stuck to his guns and insisted that anyone who didn't know that Yoda was the best Jedi *was* stupid and there was nothing he could do about it. He also wouldn't let me take his picture, on the grounds that I was so stupid.

Later, when Jane came home, he took great pleasure in telling her all about how I taken him out for cake, which was clearly proof that I loved him more, to which Jane retaliated by telling Peter that he was adopted. Much screaming then ensued from both of them as I attempted to persuade Peter that he was not adopted and Jane that I did not love Peter more than her, until I gave up and bribed them with iPads to go away and be quiet.

Once they were in bed, I indignantly related the Yoda/Luke Skywalker conversation to Simon, and how outraged Peter had been, and how he really shouldn't have called me stupid.

Simon looked at me with the same expression Peter had and said, 'But Ellen, Yoda *is* the best Jedi. Peter's right, everybody knows that Yoda is the best Jedi, and if you don't then you are stupid!'

FFS. Fucking Jedi. Fucking Pokémon. Who knew that despite all my qualifications, I'm stupid, because I don't know about that bollocks. I shall have a tiny glass of wine to numb the looming existential crisis that is threatening to engulf me due to my ignorance of foolish things. The dog needn't give me any of his judgy looks tonight either, he looks like a Wookiee at the moment. See? I do know stuff about *Star Wars*.

Saturday, 21 November

Drinkypoopoos with Hannah and Sam. In a fit of Pollyanna-ish optimism it has occurred to me that if the Jenkins' house has not sold by Christmas, Louisa and Bardo and four or possibly five small children living in a camper van on our driveway for a week should be more than enough to lower the price of their house to something Hannah can afford. The downside of this is that property prices in the street may never recover. I pointed this out to Hannah in an attempt to cheer her up, but she still maintains that she won't be able to afford it, and refuses to even view it. This is selfish of her, because I would love a proper nosy round the Jenkins' house – there is only so much you can glean from the photographs.

Obviously I didn't tell Hannah how selfish she was being, because instead we had the now obligatory 'Bastards, bastards, twatting bastards' rant about Dan and Robin, where Sam revealed that Robin, having cancelled his last two weekends with the children, claiming 'work commitments' ('I didn't realise he'd taken to shagging for *money*,' sniffed Sam) has casually announced he is now expecting to have the children for Christmas, because by his reckoning of when 'his' weekends are, he thinks that he gets Christmas. Sam is spitting feathers and snarling 'Over my dead body!'

Hannah was also in a state because Dan is being a complete dick about money, being late with his share of the mortgage and his payments for the children, and generally being a wanker, pleading poverty and crippling overdrafts, but he has now announced that he won't be able to see the children at all over Christmas, because he is going on vacation. To the Caribbean. With his perky-arsed bit of fluff from the gym.

'We hadn't been on vacation for two years before he left me, because he always claimed we couldn't afford it,' mumbled Hannah indignantly while necking Pinot Grigio and inhaling salt and vinegar chips, which surely is a recipe for heartburn if ever there was one.

'BASTARD!' roared Sam. 'Shall we have a lil' tequila shot?'

'NOOOOOO!' I shouted. 'No tequila, bad and wrong!'

The hideous memory of the last tequila hangover is still lingering with me. I swear to God I could taste tequila for at least three days afterwards. To my astonishment, Hannah, who had also sworn she was never drinking tequila again after the last time, and had *insisted* when she arrived that she was not getting shitfaced this time and would only be having a couple of glasses of wine (though she was now well into her second bottle) said, 'Yes! Tequila! I need tequila, I have something to show you.'

Due to me having the self-control of a child the night before its birthday, I clamoured muchly for Hannah to do her show and tell NOW, but in the event, it took two tequila slammers before she pulled out her phone and found a photograph on it.

'Look!' she wailed, brandishing the phone at us. 'Look at it!'

Sam squinted at the phone somewhat owlishly before pronouncing, 'S'a dick, Hannah. S'definitely a dick.' Although I hadn't seen any penises but Simon's in many years, I couldn't disagree with Sam's pronouncement that it was definitely a dick. It was most definitely a dick.

'Not a ver' big dick, though,' added Sam.

'I KNOW it's a dick!' shouted Hannah. 'I can tell a fucking dick when I see one!'

'Thass good,' said Sam. 'Good that you can tell a dick. But, babe, why you got a dick pic on your phone?'

'A man sent it to me!' said Hannah. 'Why would a man send me a photograph of his bits? Why?'

It transpired that Hannah had decided to dip her toe into the world of online dating. Hannah has led a sheltered life. Even at school, when most of us could think about nothing but getting a boyfriend, Hannah wasn't really that interested. She didn't have a boyfriend until the last year of university, and then when he dumped her after a couple of years, she went into a decline, then she met and married Dan, who was literally the first person she went out with after Eddie, the boy from university. She has only ever seen two dicks in her life. Maybe I am not one to comment on getting married too soon, having married the boy from university, but I made up for it before I met Simon.

Anyway, somehow Hannah was entirely unaware of the joyous phenomenon that is dick pics, hence when a chap made contact through a dating site, Hannah assumed he was The One, had the wedding planned, and was more than slightly perturbed when he sent her a photograph of his penis, before she even knew his last name.

Sam, unhelpfully, fell about laughing at this.

'HOW can you not have known about dick pics?' he cackled, as Hannah sniffed tearfully, 'Why should I know about dick pics? NOT EVERYONE'S OBSESSED WITH DICKS, YOU KNOW!'

'Just because I'm gay, doesn't mean I'm obsessed with dicks!' said Sam indignantly. 'Anyway, mine's much bigger than his.'

At this point we realised the entire bar was listening in to our conversation, with several of them craning their necks to try to get a glimpse of the dick pic and see if it was really that tiny. (It was. Apart from the whole complete inappropriateness of sending strangers photographs of your penis, there must be something quite insulting about being sent a photo of such a very inadequate member, as if 'you must be so desperate, love, that you'll even be impressed by my tiny wiener'.)

I told Simon about Hannah's horror when I got home, and he laughed nearly as hard as Sam. He has known Hannah for almost twenty years and said, 'Oh my God. Poor Hannah, can you imagine her face, the first time she opened it?'

'I know!' I said. 'Hannah wouldn't even read the antiquated copy of *The Joy of Sex* that was inexplicably in our sixth-form common room.'

'You had *The Joy of Sex* in your common room at your all-girls school?' Simon exclaimed, laughing even harder at the (fairly accurate) image in his head of all those sexually frustrated schoolgirls poring over the pictures, as we realised we were not quite the liberated women of the world we thought we were from studying a couple of issues of *Cosmopolitan*.

'Yes.' I said. 'The old seventies' one, with the drawings of the Beardy Man and all the pubic hair. I think one of the teachers may have planted it in there as a form of contraception, in the hope that we'd be so horrified that we would Never Ever Do It With Dirty Boys.'

'Oh Christ, no wonder poor darling Hannah is so repressed! Is that why you have forbidden me to ever grow a beard?' said Simon.

'I don't think school is to blame,' I protested. 'I went to the same school, and I am not repressed!'

'No, my darling, you are not,' purred Simon hopefully. 'Maybe we should go upstairs and see just how unrepressed you are, eh?'

Simon was in luck, as I had managed to hit the Holy Grail of drunkenness where sex seems like a very good idea. This is a tiny drunken window, where even a few mouthfuls more booze can tip you over into just falling into bed mumbling, 'Tired now. You get me shome toast, mmmm toast, ni ni' before passing out with a slice of toast stuck to your face.

Afterwards, loath as I was to spoil Simon's rosy glow, I decided that while he was in a good mood, and I was drunk enough to be brave, it was probably a fortuitous time to tell him that his sister and a camper van of children were descending for a week over Christmas, along with my sister and her family for Christmas Day. Oh, and that I might've invited Sam and Hannah and whatever children they have in tow for Christmas lunch, too. He took it quite well.

By which I mean he said, 'Oh fucking hell', and then, 'Remind me again why I gave up bloody smoking?'

Sunday, 22 November

Simon has informed me that Boreas is in fact Louisa's sixth child. I have somehow missed one out. I don't think I have, because even Simon can only name three of them off the top of his head, but he is adamant that there are six. I also woke up to texts from Hannah and Sam asking me if I am *sure* about them coming for Christmas, because if I am *really sure*, then they would love to come. Obviously I cannot reply, 'No, sorry, I was shitfaced, what on earth was I thinking?', so instead I had to say that *of course* I was *really sure* and we would love to have them. There should be a law that says that any invitations issued while drunk are null and void in the cold light of day.

I love Hannah and Sam, and frankly they will be welcome voices of sanity as Persephone slams the lid on the piano because no one is listening to her, Peter and Jane give Gulliver a wedgy as he holds forth on the novel he is writing in French 'just for fun', various of Louisa's children pee on the rug because she doesn't want to stifle their creativity with potty training, both Louisa and Jessica bollock me for failing to cater for their many dietary requirements, and I hide in the pantry with a bottle of gin. (I love my pantry. We couldn't really afford this house, but we bought it anyway, because having seen the proper, north-facing pantry I declared myself unable to live without it. No one has yet noticed that I have installed a lock on the inside of the door.) But this now means that I will be catering for somewhere between twenty and twenty-two people for Christmas dinner. I don't have twenty-two plates. Or twenty-two chairs. Also, that number of people means that there is no way I can justify buying everything pre-prepared and just bunging it in the oven. I will be hitting Costco for supplies for Christmas dinner, though I will have to lie and tell Jessica it is all from Wholefoods, otherwise she will invent an allergy that prevents her from eating. Maybe I could just get the pickled beetroot from Costco?

Talking of children peeing everywhere, I spent a full hour today trying to get the stench of stale piss out of the bathroom. I scrubbed, I bleached, I sloshed around bicarbonate of soda, as recommended by Google; I even added lemon juice, as I remembered something about it being good for cleaning. I also recoiled somewhat in horror from the frothing explosion I had created by combining lemon juice and bicarb (I should really have paid more attention in Chemistry at school, instead of trying to flick pieces of paper into the teacher's hair when she was telling us for the eleventy billionth time about how esters smell like pear drops, even though it was the nineties not the fifties and so none of us had the slightest clue what pear drops smelt like). AFTER ALL THAT, when I went back into my sparkling shiny, gleaming 100 per cent piss-free bathroom half an hour later, the smell was back, and there was an unflushed turd lurking in the toilet bowl! FML. I am so thrilled I bothered to spend my day doing this. I may have muttered this rather a lot as I stomped around the house ostentatiously flinging countless loads of laundry into the gaping maw of the washing machine and picking up the trail of shoes that seems to endlessly snake through the house. No fucker noticed; not my tidying up, not the fact that they have an endless supply of clean clothes, not the spanking clean bathroom, and definitely not my irate muttering. I am going to run away to a desert island and live alone with my dog and see how they get on without me. I wonder how long it would take them to notice I had gone?

Wednesday, 25 November

It was my day off today, and I was determined I was going to spend it all working on this bloody app, because I really want to get it finished before Christmas. I have not yet told Simon what I am doing, or that it will cost me $100 to register it, because I have decided that, a) it is an investment, and b) the credit cards are now in such a perilous state that I am pursuing the theory that if you owe the bank £1,000 that is *your* problem, but if you owe the bank £1,000,000, that's *their* problem. This is probably not very sound financial planning, but it's currently all I have. $100 probably isn't very much in pounds anyway.

The day was meant to go like this:

8.35 a.m. Leave to walk to school, chatting merrily with darling children, as adorable dog prances beside us.

8.50 a.m. Wave them off happily into the playground, with hugs and kisses as they cry, 'You are the best Mummy in the world, we love you.'

9.45 a.m. Back home after taking the dog for a bracing walk.

10 a.m. Make self a delicious cup of coffee and start work on app.

1 p.m. Pause for a healthy and nutritious lunch, involving much salad and vegetables.

1.15 p.m. Resume work.

3 p.m. Leave to walk back to school to collect darling children, adorable dog walking obediently alongside.

3.15 p.m. Greeted with joy and love by moppets.

4 p.m. Serve up healthy and nutritious snack for children involving fruit.

4.30 p.m. Homework time, as I impart wisdom and knowledge to my offspring and feel a warm glow at the light of understanding that spreads across their innocent and childish faces.

5 p.m. Start cooking delicious dinner for beloved munchkins.

5.30 p.m. Beam fondly as beloved munchkins gobble down delicious food that I cooked with love.

6 p.m. Pop a creative and innovative meal, involving interesting combinations of exotic spices, into the oven for Simon and myself.

6.30 p.m. Supervise bathtime.

7 p.m. Allow the children half an hour of screen time before bed, while I do some more work on my app.

7.30 p.m. Greet loving husband, then tuck the clean and sleepy children into bed, with many hugs and kisses all round.

7.40 p.m. Enjoy a civilised gin and tonic with my loving husband as we discuss each other's days and make supportive remarks to each other.

8 p.m. Sit down to the delicious and creative meal. Husband is stunned by the taste explosion I have presented him with.

8.30 p.m. Do some more work on my app.

10 p.m. Have a glass of wine and watch *Question Time*. (Or is it *Newsnight* that's on at that time? Anyway, some sort of grown-up, political, newsy programme.) Debate it maturely and intelligently with husband.

11 p.m. Go to bed. Possibly shag.

However, this is in fact how the day actually went:

8.49 a.m. Leave house to walk to school; speed-march there, shouting at the children to hurry, hurry, we're going to be late, while the over-excited dog hauls me along.

8.59 a.m. Shove the children unceremoniously through the gate, still shouting at them to run.

9 a.m. Marvel at the entire day stretching before me, a veritable ocean of productivity awaiting.

9.10 a.m. Decide to treat myself to a coffee from Starbucks while I'm walking the dog, because I'm worth it. Balk slightly at the price. Find the dog hoovering up mystery items of rubbish he has found in the street when I come out of the coffee shop.

10 a.m. Bastarding dog has rolled in something unspeakable. Bath him. He still stinks and now the smell is lingering on my hands. Remember tomato sauce is supposed to be good for removing fox poo smells, etc. Cover my hands and dog in tomato sauce. Dog shakes. Entire bathroom, including ceiling, is now splattered with tomato sauce, as am I. It looks like something out of *The Texas Chainsaw Massacre*.

11 a.m. Have cleaned bathroom and changed clothes. The smell is still lingering. Fuck it. App time. Will just have a very quick look on Facebook first. Oooooh, Susannah Ellison from school has got very fat! I will just message Hannah about this, it will make her happy. I might have a chocolate cookie, too.

12 p.m. How have I lost a whole hour messaging Hannah and googling other people from school to see if they are fat? How? Right. App time. Now. I should really have a look at Twitter to see what is happening in the world; I follow lots of journalists to make myself feel important, so really looking at Twitter is the same as reading the news and everyone knows it is important to keep abreast of current affairs. Hmmm, dull, dull, dull … Ah, look, a lady who presents TV programs about moving house is

angry about something! What is she angry about now? Buggeration, Twitter is such a jumbled mess! There we go, having read back through twenty-seven tweets, I have discovered that the source of her rage seems to be that there was a loud man on her train. Fair enough, that is quite annoying.

1 p.m. ARRRGHHHH! Well, no one can work on an empty stomach, I'd better have some lunch. Healthy salad. Except none of the three open bags of salad in the fridge are now edible. Cheese and ham grilled sandwich it is then.

1.30 p.m. Right. App.

2 p.m. Look at that squirrel on the bird feeder. I should video it and put it on Facebook. Maybe it will go viral.

2.30 p.m. No point trying to work now, will have a cup of tea and chocolate Hobnob. And maybe a quick look at Facebook again to see if my squirrel video has gone viral yet. How has it not? Maybe I should put it on Instagram, too?

3.10 p.m. Bollocks, it's time to pick up the children! I will have to drive and be judged.

3.15 p.m. Children shout at me because I mixed up the sandwiches in their lunchboxes and gave Peter cheese and Jane ham. Apparently it was unthinkable that they should be either expected to eat the wrong sandwich or to swap with their sibling. They tell me I am the worst mummy in the world.

4 p.m. Feed children potato chips.

4.30 p.m. Shout at the children to do homework. Demand to know how they can have 'forgotten' to read? Argue with them about how to do long division when they tell me my way is stupid and wrong. Fight the urge to say 'Oh fuck it, what does it matter, I've never done bloody long division since I left school! That's what calculators are for, and that's why I had to google it to help you tonight.'

5 p.m. Make pasta. Wonder if eating too much pasta can cause children health implications. Add broccoli to pasta in a fit of guilt about letting them eat pasta every night, except the nights they eat pizza.

5.30 p.m. Listen to the children having a complete screaming shit fit because there is broccoli in their pasta. Die a little inside.

6 p.m. Lob a chicken in the oven for dinner for Simon and me. Bung some wilted parsley and a lemon up its arse in a vague attempt to make it look like I've made an effort.

6.30 p.m. Start trying to get the children into the bath. Once they are finally in the bath, hide downstairs and look at Facebook on my phone, on the basis that as long as I can hear them screaming, they are not drowning. Decide I hate everyone on Facebook, as they are all having lovely dinners with their shiny children and 'snuggles' before bed. Peter and Jane bite if you try to snuggle with them. Have a gin.

7.15 p.m. Try to get children out of bath. Survey the post-apocalyptic wasteland of sodden towels and pools of water that is now the bathroom. Start mopping up the floodwaters, while shouting 'HAVE YOU GOT YOUR PYJAMAS ON? STOP HITTING EACH OTHER!' over and over again.

7.35 p.m. Bellow 'Why haven't you got your pyjamas on?' at the naked children.

7.40 p.m. Tell Simon when he walks in the door that he will have to put the children to bed because they have asked for Daddy. Omit to mention 'and also because I will strangle them'. Have another large gin.

8 p.m. Dump the slightly cremated chicken in front of Simon. Clench the carving knife very hard when he sighs and says 'God, chicken again? Can't we have something different? I'm so fucking bored with chicken.' Put down carving knife in a calm and serene manner and take a tin of baked beans out of the cupboard. Slam the beans on the table in front of Simon and enquire if that is enough of a change for him. Exercise ALL my self-control and restraint when he says, 'There's no need to be like that!'

8.30 p.m. Look at LK Bennett sale online. Buy shoes. Convince myself they are a bargain and actually investment dressing. Have some wine.

9.30 p.m. Watch soap operas on my laptop while Simon watches *Wheeler Dealers* on the big TV. Look at the internet. Have some more wine. Spend another two hours reading about conspiracy theories.

Midnight – Fuck! I'm hammered and convinced the CIA are watching me and I have to get up and go to work tomorrow. Simon pretends to give me a 'cuddle' under the guise of trying to grope me in the hope of a shag. I threaten to bite him if he doesn't leave me alone. Perhaps that is where Peter and Jane get it from?

DECEMBER

Tuesday, 1 December

IIIIIITTTTTTTTT'SSSSSS CHHHHHHHRRRRIIIIIISSSS-TTTTTMMMMAAAAASSS!

I love the first of December. All the hope of the festive season stretching ahead of you, a whole month of cinnamon- and clove-scented potential for peace on earth and goodwill to all men. The joyous anticipation of a month of advent calendars, carols, cheesy Christmas songs, fairy lights, decking the halls with boughs of holly, mince pies, sleigh bells ringing are you listening, Bing Crosby, old films, pristine snow, all deep and crisp and even, roaring log fires and apple-cheeked moppets tumbling around, giddy with excitement.

This is possibly the best day of the whole of Christmas, because all of that potential is still there and the dream has not yet been crushed by pissing rain and wanting to tear your own ears off if you have to hear 'Last Christmas' again in one more shop or elevator, even though when you hear it today you will be singing along with all your heart. Before you realise that the apple-cheeked moppets are actually just off their tits on sugar as they have been for the whole month, and you have already drunk all the Christmas Baileys Irish Cream by the fifteenth.

But today, today the vision is still intact, as you imagine the whole family carrying the tree home together through snowy darkened streets, before sipping hot cider (what is hot cider? Is it just cider that is hot, or do you need a special sort of cider? I'm imagining just microwaving a bottle of Strongbow would not give the festive vibe I am aiming for?) while you sing carols around the piano.

It is mildly unfortunate that I can no longer hold the threat of Santa not coming over the children's heads, because Olivia Brown's older brother told her that Santa doesn't exist and so she told the whole class this. Then, of course, once Jane had stopped complaining about being lied to for all these years, she felt the need to enlighten Peter, so I can no longer claim that the smoke alarms are Santa cameras and he is watching them (which is mildly pervy when you think about it), in a desperate effort to achieve one month of the year where they behave like normal and civilised children. I may threaten to withhold their advent calendars instead, if they do not toe the line.

But even so, today, we still have everything to play for. Bring on the festive cheer!

Thursday, 3 December

Jane has just handed me the fourteenth version of her Christmas list. I have added up everything she wants and it comes to £2,378.73. Jane, needless to say, will not be getting much from her list. Peter, feeling that writing is too much like hard work, has taken to just standing glassy-eyed in front of the TV, shouting 'I WANT THAT!' when the adverts come on. Yesterday, he was so sucked into the Vortex of Consumerism that he shouted 'I WANT THAT!' at an advert for women's products. I'm still not entirely sure which part he wanted – the roller blades, the pretty blonde girl, the beach or a packet of Tampax – he just looked baffled when I asked him if he knew what the advert was even for and mumbled 'Want it. Want it.'

After three days of advent calendars, I have decided I hate the person who thought it was a good idea to put chocolate in the damn things. Bad enough that the darling children get hit with a sugar rush before they have even had their breakfast, then refuse to eat anything but super-sugary cereal as everything else apparently tastes 'horrible' after their calendar, but then you get smug twats like Simon who 'forget' to eat their calendar for several days and then sit there savouring their chocolate in front of you and refusing to share.

Every year I threaten that I am not going to get bloody Simon an advent calendar, telling him that he is far too old, but then I remember how he threw a massive hissy fit the first Christmas we were married because his mother had not bought him an advent calendar, so he had a tantrum that would have done a toddler credit. He didn't quite lie on the floor, kicking his legs and screaming 'ADVENT CALENDAR! WAAAAAANT ADVENT CALENDAR NOOOOOOOWWWWWWW!' but it was close. His mother informed us that she had assumed his *wife* would be buying his advent calendars for him, now he was married, which came as something of a surprise to me, as I did not remember anything in our wedding vows about 'To Be Your Bloody Mother From This Day Forth …'

I bought him a calendar the next year as a joke, but he didn't seem to realise the joke part, going so far as to tell me that for future reference, he actually preferred a Hotel Chocolat calendar to a Cadbury's one, but he appreciated the thought. And so I continue to buy my forty-year-old husband an advent calendar every year, because apparently I am his mum now, and he is a spoilt child.

Friday, 4 December

Email from Louisa:

> Hi Ellen,
> We are all looking forward to our Christmas break. Can I bring anything?
>   Namaste,
>   Amaris

How do I tactfully reply 'Please, for the love of God, do not bring your dried placenta'?

There was also an email from Jessica:

> Hi Ellen,
> I have been thinking about the Christmas pudding. Do you think I should get a Fortnum & Mason's one or a Harrods' one? Apparently the Wholefoods one is not very good this year, though it's sold out anyway. Mum says you have a good recipe for one, though, would you rather make the pudding?
>   Best wishes,
>   Jessica

'Fuck off, Jessica. Just fuck off. You have dumped the whole of Christmas on me and now you are turning THE ONE THING YOU HAVE TO DO into a massive performance and trying to make me make a Christmas pudding, and anyway, I don't actually have a recipe at all, I just lied to Mum because she was making such a fuss one Christmas about how much stuff I had bought pre-prepared and so I told her I had made the sodding pudding to shut her up, and then she just went on about how I should've got the supermarket pudding *Good Housekeeping* had recommended, because that was by far the best one she'd ever tasted, even though IT WAS THE SAME BASTARDING

PUDDING GOOD SODDING HOUSEKEEPING RECOMMENDED! Ellen x'

I should probably redraft that before I send it. I'm bloody tempted not to, though. But the momentary bliss of telling Jessica to fuck off is probably not really worth her looking martyred all Christmas Day.

The wretched Christmas emails have quite ruined my pleasure in Fuck It All Friday, as I seethe and mumble to myself about puddings and placentas and beetroot. Christmas never looks so complicated on the TV – even the flu remedy adverts make it look idyllic. Why is it so much harder in real life?

Monday, 7 December

More letters from the school. Letters and letters and letters. I am drowning in letters. Letters about nits, which make my head immediately start itching. Letters about book fairs, and Christmas fairs, and Christmas concerts, and the complex ticket lottery for the concerts. And, of course, the festive letter that all parents love – the one detailing the costume required for the school Christmas concert.

This year, the letters tell me, Peter is a space ghost and Jane is a stable mouse. The Christmas concerts have got increasingly strange in recent years since the arrival of a rather progressive drama teacher who writes her own productions. So instead of the old format, where each class got up and sang an out-of-tune rendition of 'Rudolph the Red-Nosed Reindeer' or 'When Santa Got Stuck Up the Chimney' (I always sniggered at the line about him getting soot on his sack. I am a bad person) and then all the nursery tinies came on and did a nativity and sang 'Away in a Manger' and one could have a lovely little Christmas cry at them, instead we have had *Christmas in WW2* (which was as full of festive joy as you would imagine it to be, with moping evacuees bemoaning a lack of bananas) and *Christmas in the Big Brother House*. God knows what this year will involve, with its winning combination of space ghosts and stable mice.

No doubt whatever weird fantasy Miss Elliott the drama teacher has plucked from the drug-crazed dreams of her misspent youth, Peter and Jane will excel at their roles as usual. Back in the happy nativity days, Jane's starring role was as a 'Person of Bethlehem', which involved her standing at the back and glaring murderously at the audience. Peter, though, Peter made my heart almost burst with maternal pride when he was in nursery and was cast in the coveted role of Joseph. I bustled into the hall, pushed my way to the very front, loudly announcing to everyone I passed, 'Sorry, my son is playing Joseph, I MUST be at the front, yes, excuse me, Joseph's Mummy coming through, make way, I AM JOSEPH'S VERY PROUD MUMMY!' On they came, Peter adorable in his dish towel and Simon's old shirt, surrounded by tinsel-decked angels and a rather gloomy Mary, and I almost wept with the sheer loveliness of it all. Once Peter was centre stage, he jammed one finger up his nostril and spent the rest of the Nativity having a thorough root around. Despite my hissed threats and attempts at violent sign language to try to get his attention, he only occasionally removed his finger from his nose to munch on a particularly juicy morsel he had found up there. I was mortified. When I asked him afterwards why he had done that, he just looked at me in surprise and said 'Done what?'

So, to be a space ghost Peter will apparently need silver body paint, a roll of tin foil, old white leggings and a t-shirt 'that you don't need back' and a 'space pack' – whatever that is. Peter helpfully informed me it was 'a pack you wear in space'.

Jane needs 'old brown leggings and t-shirt', to be cut up.

Funnily enough, Peter doesn't possess white leggings, and Jane doesn't have a brown t-shirt, so now I am going to have to go out and buy brand-new ones to be trashed in the name of mouse-haunting space ghosts.

Oh FML, just looked at the letter, it is from last week and they were supposed to take their costumes in today. On the plus side, as it is the Festive Period, weekday wine is perfectly acceptable, isn't it?

Wednesday, 9 December

I have finally finished my 'Why Mummy Drinks' app game (I may have done quite a lot of it while I was at work, but we won't mention that part …). I am really quite pleased with it. From Level 1, where you have to get out the door in the morning while gathering children, lunchboxes, homework and forms for the school, while preventing the children removing them from your bag, to the second levels, where you have to find your way to school in an allocated time, dodging dog poos, stopping children hurling themselves under the wheels of passing SUVs and answering questions on long division and homophones along the way, to the mid-levels, where you have to make your way across the playground without being kicked in the teeth by the scary blonde Ninja Mummies who are lurking behind the play equipment, armed with organic quinoa muffins to floor you with, right up to the final level, where you have to find your way home from the pub while shitfaced, including stopping to buy pizza *and* then not dropping your pizza. It is a poorly animated digital snapshot of my life, but it is the first thing in bloody forever that I have done for myself and which is even vaguely creative. It was also very therapeutic, as I put every arsehole that has ever pissed me off in it. I particularly like the special challenge where you have to dodge a flying cup of soy latte at the school gate. If it doesn't hit you, a Yummy Mummy's yoga pants split up the back and you earn yourself a G&T. I may have sniggered out loud to myself as I did this.

I have paid my $100 to register it and am thinking of adding 'App Developer' to my resumé. In fact, sod it, I shall. It takes a day for it to be approved, while they make sure I am not an evil internet genius planning on bringing down civilisation with my seemingly innocuous platform game, although, if I WAS clever enough to disguise digital Armageddon in a game about baking and homework and wine, I'd like to think that I would manage to outwit the checks by the app people. Obviously I am none of these, I am a bored borderline alcoholic trying pass myself off as a semi-functioning adult.

Oh God, oh God, what if they reject it? What if they think it is pants? I have been checking my phone obsessively ever since I pressed the magic 'submit' button this morning, even though I knew it would take a bit of time, but now I am pacing the floors.

I will cry if they hate 'Why Mummy Drinks'. Even if they don't hate it, I will still cry if nobody buys it. Hannah will buy it. And Sam. But what if no one else does and it was all for nothing? I suppose at least I can take some satisfaction in sitting and playing it myself and laughing hollowly every time Game Me outwits the Game Coven, in between weeping bitterly into my wine and contemplating the general futility of life. Or maybe schools will buy it to discourage teenage pregnancies?

I wonder if I am having an existential crisis?

Friday, 11 December

My Fuck It All Friday was sacrificed on the altar of the work Christmas party tonight, ever the glittering highlight of the social year. Because who doesn't love having to fork out £57.50 to be crammed into a function room in a third-rate hotel, along with twenty-nine other office Christmas parties, all of which seem by law to be forced to include one very drunk middle-aged woman in a rather too-tight polyester party dress and flashing reindeer antlers, who spends the evening cackling raucously at the top of her voice before trying to snog a colleague young enough to be her son, then throwing up, and eventually being put into a taxi while she loudly tells everyone within earshot, including strangers that she has never seen before, how much she loves them? Surprisingly, I do not fulfil this role in our office, it having been bagsied long ago by Sandra from Sales. Throw in a lukewarm Christmas dinner and the 'complimentary wine' which everyone races to neck as much of as possible in a desperate bid to get their money's worth out of the evening and, really, who could fail to be excited by such a night?

What was the best part of the evening this year? Was it Jenny from Marketing calling me a Grinch and trying to forcibly cram the flimsy paper crown from the cheap crackers onto my head, before telling me to 'take a joke' when I snarled that I would cut her if she ever, ever touched me again (my personal space issues are sorely tried by such evenings, due to the venue allocating approximately six square inches per person in an effort to rake in as much dosh as possible).

Or perhaps it was Iain from Accounts spending forty-five minutes giving me a detailed account of his health problems leading up to his gall bladder operation and then a blow-by-blow account of said op? Or was it Pizza-faced Paul from the post room grabbing me on the way back from the toilets and dragging me onto the dance floor, where he pressed his suspiciously bulging crotch up against me while he panted moistly, 'I've always fancied you, Chrissie …' There is no one called Chrissie at work.

Ho ho and buggering ho. And tomorrow, I get to do it all again at Simon's Christmas do, although that tends to be a slightly classier affair, which means better-quality crackers and a 'jus' instead of gravy.

And there has still been no word about whether the 'Why Mummy Drinks' app has been accepted, despite obsessively checking my phone approximately every twenty seconds, along with checking websites that tell you the average wait time to get your app approved, which all say 'a day'. Maybe it is to do with time differences? Maybe it is not work time in America? Or maybe they just hate it.

Saturday, 12 December

Simon's work do was actually very posh, and alas came complete with my nemesis – an open bar. I do love an open bar. I am assuming the day will eventually arrive when I do not treat an open bar as a challenge to drink as much as I can in as short a time as possible, but unfortunately for Simon that day has not yet arrived.

Getting rat-arsed wasn't *entirely* my fault, I found myself at dinner sitting next to Simon's colleague Brian's wife. I think she was called Soozie. Actually, I know she was called Soozie, because Soozie was sufficiently self-obsessed that she felt the need to spell her name for me, so I knew exactly how quirky Soozie is. Soozie has just had a baby. Soozie also has a toddler. Soozie apparently is the first person in the history of the world to ever have had a baby, and therefore Soozie felt the need to tell me all about her amazing children, and how they have changed her life, and how she has decided to bring them up, and the incredibly funny thing Gabriel said the other day even though he's only two, and look, that's Gabriel there, isn't he gorgeous, and that's Gabriel with Celeste, the new baby, yes, we *did* think the names were clever, because they *are* our angels, and there's Gabriel on the swings, and there's Celeste's one-month birthday … and her two-month birthday … and her three-month birthday … And there's Gabriel using the potty for the first time, we were so proud, and that's the contents of the potty, and don't you think breastfeeding is *so important*, what sort of monsters bottle feed and then leave their children in cages to be raised by wolves while they return to work? Oh, you're a working mummy, are you? Gosh, I don't know how you find the time, I just couldn't leave mine like that, they are my life. Oh, I must show you the photo of the amazing drawing Gabriel did, even though he's only two.

What option did I have but to drink through this relentless barrage about the astonishing achievements of little Gabriel and Celeste? And drink. And drink …

And anyway, mistaking the live band afterwards for karaoke and demanding to sing 'Eternal Flame' is an error that anyone can make, and if anything, my very enthusiastic dancing was a compliment to them.

I also wasn't to know that the very nice man I met at the bar and decided was my new best friend was Simon's boss, but in my defence the flaming Sambucas were *his* idea, not mine! As were the second and third rounds. And we totally bonded and therefore this was definitely not a career-limiting event for Simon.

AND I didn't throw up in the taxi on the way home, I just kept demanding a burger. And pizza.

Once in bed, I very much wished the room would stop spinning round. And then I had a sudden thought! The email about Drinky Mummy app might be in my junk folder. Where was my phone? Where was my bag? Where were my shoes? I followed the trail of devastation … there was my dress on the landing, and a shoe on the stairs. Another shoe, and hurray, my bag! And phone! And YES! The app had been accepted! Oh frabjous day! At that point, having a very quick celebratory nap on the stairs seemed like an excellent plan.

Sunday, 13 December

Eurgh. I was woken up on the stairs this morning by Peter and Jane climbing over me to get to the TV. They looked at me with disgust. At least I had somehow managed to put my pyjamas on last night and wasn't sprawled there stark naked. Simon is unimpressed with me and keeps asking what *exactly* I said to his boss, who apparently isn't the very lovely man he seemed to be last night. I would tell Simon what I had said if I could remember, I really would; I do recall being extremely witty and charming, but can't quite put my finger on the nuances of the conversation. I do seem to have some vague memory of showing someone a lot of photos of my dog, but I have feeling that was Boring Soozie, in revenge for having to sit through an endless slideshow of her frankly rather ugly children. I don't know what Simon is worrying about, as I recall his boss and I got on like a house on fire. Or rather a Sambuca on fire. Oh God, I think I'm still drunk!

The dog could not look more disgusted with me if he tried. I looked pitifully at him and whispered 'Please don't judge me!', but he just snorted disapprovingly.

Tuesday, 15 December

ARRRRGGHHHHHHHHH! I realised this morning that it is the middle of December already. How? HOW HAS THIS HAPPENED AGAIN? I have not posted Simon's parents' Christmas presents to France. I have not BOUGHT their presents. In fact, I have not bought *any* presents, and I have not written any cards, and now it is far too late to send cards to people in any Abroad place apart from France.

I did not panic, though, I approached the situation calmly and rationally. Amazon Prime is my friend. Amazon Prime will make everything okay. Everything is twice as expensive from Amazon Prime. Sod it, doesn't matter, needs must. A small fortune later, a ludicrously over-priced cushion with a pug on it, a silk scarf and bottle of perfume are winging their way to Simon's mum, along with more bottles of whisky and aftershave and some cufflinks for his dad. And I am never, ever, ever typing 'Gifts for men' into Google again, as this opened my eyes to a whole new world that, frankly, I was happy without. In no way has my life been enhanced by the knowledge that somewhere out there are vagina-shaped lollipops (not even artisan ones), 'wiener washing soap' (with a selection of holes in a variety of sizes), and something called 'blowjob undies', which I couldn't even bring myself to click on, yet a lingering part of me still wonders what exactly they are … Crotchless underpants? Oh God, I need to stop thinking about this.

Next problems: lack of Christmas cards, lack of posting time, lack of any inclination whatsoever to write Christmas cards, lack of annoyingly smug achievements by family to swank about in a bastarding Round Robin unless I include 'designed an app based on my deep and abiding hatred of humanity, but haven't actually made any money from it', or 'Children only got nits three times this year. #winning'.

I refused to be daunted by the Christmas card problem, though, as I am a very clever app-designing technical person, and so I decided clearly the answer was to film an adorable video of Peter and Jane and the dog in Christmas sweaters, partaking adorably in adorable festive pursuits, which I would edit together with some cheesy Christmas music and conclude with them shouting a cheery 'Merry Christmas, one and all!' I could even put it on Facebook and watch it go viral, and then I would be in the *Daily Mail* as the Most Christmassy Person Ever and would never have to write another sodding Christmas card again! It was a genius plan. What could *possibly* go wrong?

Peter and Jane. Peter and Jane is what could possibly go wrong. And the wretched dog. How do I keep forgetting that my children's primary purpose in life appears to be to thwart every hope and dream I have ever had? By the time I had managed to bribe, threaten and cajole them into their Christmas sweaters, which apparently were 'horrible' and 'itchy', and I had wrestled the dog into *his* Christmas sweater, and I had stopped the bleeding from where he bit me in indignation (which actually makes him more evil than the children because they only threatened to bite), it was dark, and the dog had managed to remove his Christmas sweater and shred it. This meant it was too late for the outdoor frolics I had planned for the video, but that was fine, because there were plenty of lovely indoor things they could do, like pretending to wrap presents, open advent calendars, put up decorations and make gingerbread houses.

Instead of the shining-faced, smiling moppets of my imagination, they slouched around the house scowling. Jane attempted to sellotape Peter to the floor during the simulated present wrapping, they both demanded extra chocolates for the pretend advent calendar opening, Peter managed to smash the snow globe he was supposed to place festively on the mantelpiece, and instead of sprinkling icing sugar over the (bought) gingerbread houses, each with an endearing smudge of flour on their freckled noses, they hurled such a cloud of icing sugar around the kitchen that I couldn't actually see them to film them. Finally, I sat them on the sofa, both looking somewhat ghostly due to the icing sugar, although I had attempted to vacuum the worst of it off them and snarled, 'Just say Merry Christmas, one and all, and say it *nicely*!'

After fifteen attempts, I did not have one single shot where they both looked into the camera and spoke at the same time, let alone with the cheery cry I had envisaged. I had hoped some clever editing might yet save the day, but the result was more like a Salvation Army advert than the envy-inducing festive joy I was aiming for.

I will have to send a text, with a screenshot of a donation to a homeless charity, explaining I have gone for a green and worthy option. Although in my heart I know this is a better thing to do anyway, I also know it will in no way abate the mounting rage at the pile of cards with their accompanying smug letters about how Jocasta has just passed her Grade 7 flute while climbing Kilimanjaro to raise money for orphaned kittens, and how she is really looking forward to starting school next year, and Sebastian is doing so awfully well at Some Obscure Sport, and is now the youngest person to play for the British Obscure Sport Team, and aren't we just simply maaaarvellous?

Fucking fuck my fucking life.

Saturday, 19 December

Another Christmas party tonight. One of the mummies at school invited all the parents in the class, so after some deliberation, Sam and I decided we should risk it. I didn't know the mother very well, she was quite new and tended towards artistic scarves and 'worked in TV', so I must confess there was a part of me that thought there might be famous people there. Sam said this was shallow and shameless of me.

Simon grumbled a great deal about having to go to the party, but as he failed to come up with any better excuse than 'there will be people there' and as I had already booked the babysitter, I insisted he came. People are already starting to think Sam is lying about being gay to cover up the fact that he is having a rip-roaring *affaire* with me, which, given how much I fancied

Sam when I first met him, now seems nothing short of hilarious, but nonetheless I did not want to give the rumour mill any more grist to grind.

So poor Simon was forced out of his favourite fleece and into a respectable shirt and off we went, clutching a bottle of reasonably priced Pinot Grigio and a poinsettia (because Christmas …) from which I had carefully peeled off the red 'reduced' sticker while leaving the original price label intact.

Our hostess, Alicia, greeted us at the door, draped in an unfeasible number of scarves. She had actually managed to achieve the impossible and was wearing even more scarves than Simon's mum. I didn't think anyone could ever wear more scarves than Simon's mum. She looked unimpressed by the poinsettia and vaguely waved us through to the kitchen, murmuring something about 'You'll know lots of people in there.'

It quickly became apparent there was some sort of party apartheid going on, with the school people in the kitchen while the glamorous TV friends were granted the hallowed environs of the sitting room, and sofas. Perhaps Alicia was unsure if we could be trusted with soft furnishings? Even the Coven had been corralled in the kitchen with the rest of the B-list, to the immense indignation of Perfect Lucy Atkinson's Perfect Mummy, who had apparently, so Sam told me, tried to make a break for the sitting room and the Beautiful People, only to be efficiently netted by Alicia's scarves in the hallway and shepherded back to where she belonged.

Rumours abounded that in the sitting room there was champagne and canapés from caterers, as opposed to the kitchen, where there was indifferent white wine and a French stick and some sweaty cheese. I had never seen Lucy Atkinson's Perfect Mummy so close to tears as she knocked back tepid Chardonnay, whimpering, 'I only wanted to see their TV awards!', while Fiona Montague patted her shoulder consolingly and said soothingly, 'We will, sweetie, we'll get there soon. It's obvious we shouldn't be in here.'

As the wine kicked in, a sort of truce began in the kitchen. Still smarting from the unaccustomed rejection, the Coven drew closer to the scorned rubbish mummies, and fragile bridges were built.

Fiona Montague approached me with a slightly glazed expression. 'Y' know, Ellen, I've always envied you,' she informed me. 'I mean, you jus' don' give a fuck, do you? Whatever it is, you jus' don' give a flying fuck! I wish I could be like that. How do you not give a fuck?'

Blimey. Fancy Fiona Montague saying 'fuck'. Fiona Montague doesn't even say 'fart', she coyly refers to farting as 'making smells' if the subject must be discussed at all. Fiona Montague was plastered and it appeared we were drunk bonding. I think. One can never be sure with Fiona, it was entirely possible that she was still just about to deliver her coup de grâce, off her tits on bad wine or not. But no, she had her arm around my shoulder and was saying earnestly, with tears in her eyes, 'I really like you, Ellen. Why aren't we better friends? You're lovely! Lesh have shome more wine.' I was very, *very* afraid.

Lucy Atkinson's Perfect Mummy had her head on Sam's shoulder and was slurring, 'I mean, ish jush so hard, bein' a mum, innit? Well, you's not a mum, ha ha, but y'knowhadd-amean, don' you? Ish hard. I'm sho tired of it. I wanna see the shiny awards. S'not easy, ish it?'

At this point, Simon, who had nipped to the bathroom some time ago and had been gone so long I was starting to fear that he had become fatally entangled in Alicia's scarves or, worse, touched an Oscar and been stoned to death with mini Beef Wellingtons and tiny baked potatoes stuffed with caviar, reappeared, saying, 'There you are, darling, what are you doing lurking in here? There are some people I'd like you to meet' and off we went, walking hand in hand into the Golden Light of the sitting room, leaving behind Fiona Montague and Perfect Lucy Atkinson's Perfect Mummy slack-jawed with envy and booze.

It transpired that Simon had gone to school with Alicia's husband Tristan (what else would he be called?) and they had fortuitously met outside the bathroom and fallen upon each other like the long-lost friends they were – as Simon refuses to use Facebook for the purpose it was intended, which is obviously to stalk your school and university friends in the hope that you are thinner than them, with a better life. Simon claims the only reason he is on Facebook at all is to try to gauge what sort of mood I will be in when he gets home, and to read articles from the *Onion*. Anyway, Simon and Tristan's fond recollection of the time they swapped the lithium and the magnesium in the chemistry lab and almost blew old Dr Everett's face off, and how funny he looked without eyebrows for the rest of term, was deemed sufficient to admit us into the Land of Soft Furnishings, where it turned out there was not actually any champagne and canapés, but there was actually an Oscar, which I was even allowed to hold (surprisingly heavy).

Sam filled me in on the rest of the evening in the kitchen after I abandoned them. Lucy Atkinson's Mummy had a fight with her husband because he suggested she might be better with a glass of water than more wine, to which she shouted, 'STOP TELLING ME WHAT TO DO, YOU'RE ALWAYS TELLING ME WHAT TO DO!' Then he left without her, at which point she had a breakdown and told Sam she thinks her husband might be gay, and Fiona Montague threw up in the flowerbeds outside Alicia's house as her husband tried to get her into a taxi. It seems the Coven do not cope well with rejection. Or alcohol. Somehow I suspect that despite Fiona's insistence on my being her new best friend this evening, normal service will resume on Monday.

As I got into bed, a thought came to me that we should have

a party. Actually, I may have already decided we are having a party and invited everyone at Alicia's tonight. Simon won't mind. And it will be fun!

Sunday, 20 December

Hurrah! Tree Day today. Despite last night's party I was not hungover at all, which suggests that the wine in the sitting room may have been of better quality than the kitchen wine, not least because I had amused texts from Sam with screenshots of awkward messages from Fiona Montague and Perfect Lucy Atkinson's Perfect Mummy proffering vague apologies along the lines of 'having a bit too much wine'. Oh dear. I wonder how much of last night they will admit to next week?

But to the tree … In my festive vision, buying the tree should consist of us tramping through snowy streets as Simon manfully shoulders the tree and carries it home and we all laugh and frolic in his manly wake. In reality it usually involves going to B&Q and having an argument because I pick an enormous tree that won't fit in the car and he picks a tiny tree that a mouse would be ashamed of, so minute and unfestive is it.

This year, though, I had found a Christmas tree farm, where you had a lovely drive into the countryside, then a ride on a tractor, and then you chose and chopped down your own Christmas tree! What could be more divine? Off we went, me merrily carolling 'OHHHHHH CHRISTMAS TREE, ohhhh Christmas treeeeeeeee!' at the top of my voice while Simon muttered about being quiet so he could concentrate on driving and Peter and Jane whined in the back because they weren't allowed to bring their iPods. But so what, we were going to have a Magical Day and create Happy Memories that would stay with them forever.

Peter fell into the mud within five minutes of arrival and

spent the rest of the visit crying that he was so cold he thought he was going to die. Simon turned into Mr Caveman Hunter as soon as he was entrusted with the saw to chop down the tree and did a lot of shouting along the lines of 'STAND BACK! STAND BACK! I am CHOPPING!' Unusually, since now his hunter-gatherer skills were being called into question by having to forage for a tree, he insisted on one so enormous that even I was dubious about whether it would fit in the house, let alone the car.

However, Simon did make it fit into the car, mostly by sheer bloodymindedness, although the children were somewhat crushed beneath it; Jane claimed she almost lost an eye and Peter insisted he had pine needles in his pants.

Once home, we had the obligatory row over getting it into the stand, which involves Simon shouting 'IS IT STRAIGHT? IS IT IN?' and me shouting 'YES, IT BLOODY IS!' before he lets go and it topples over and we repeat it all over again at least six more times until the tree is finally stable and semi-vertical. Then Simon insists on putting the lights on, because apparently lights are a man's job, because his dad always did the lights, and only then can I create the magic of the baubles.

I love decorating the Christmas tree; it is one of my favourite things in the whole world. The first year I was away at university, I was so upset when I came home and found that Mum and Jessica had already done the tree without me that I cried until they took all the decorations off and started again, so I could help decorate it.

In the early days with the children I had lovely ideas about us all doing it together, but then I realised that I am a Tree Nazi and the children do it All Wrong, so mostly I shout at them for the first ten minutes until they lose interest and bugger off and I can rearrange the baubles they have clearly put in stupid places (i.e., move their handcrafted glitter- and snot-caked monstrosities to the back of the tree, out of sight, so my tasteful and expensively smashable glass decorations are front and centre). Thus I can turn the tree into a Glorious Vision of Festive Joy while singing along loudly to carols and trying to stop the dog from pissing on it, because as far as he is concerned, why else would there be a tree in the sitting room?

And so now I sit by the twinkle of the fairy lights, my heart glowing with happiness, though that is possibly due to the fizzy wine I drank while I was decorating, crying 'Look at the tree! Isn't it Christmassy? Doesn't it smell wonderful? Look at it! DON'T TOUCH IT! JUST LOOK. LEAVE THE CHOCOLATE DECORATIONS ALONE! No, they are *not* for eating. I don't care if they are edible, you are *not* bloody eating them. That goes for you too, Simon.' And all is well with the world, and this is possibly the most Christmassy day ever, although, again, that might just be due to the wine, and I think I shall have a little more.

I wish I liked sherry, I am sure such an evening calls for a nice glass of dry sherry.

Tuesday, 22 December

Louisa arrived today, complete with Bardo and the six children (Simon was right). There is not enough wine in the world.

As I have taken time off work while the children are off school over the Christmas holidays, I was here to greet them when they appeared, conveniently, just before lunch. Despite Louisa's breezy announcement that they could all sleep in the camper van, not even I can make six children sleep in a camper van in December, so they are all crammed into our not-very-large house. Louisa and Bardo and the new baby and the toddler are in the guest room, and Peter and Jane are sharing their bedrooms with the rest of the children. Louisa and Bardo were at least considerate enough to have two boys and two girls for their oldest four, so there are no complaints from my children about how it is not fair that one has to share with more than the other.

There have been plenty of complaints about how unfair it is that they have to share at all, though, which they voiced loudly in front of Louisa ('*Please*, Ellen, try to remember to call me Amaris! I left Louisa behind when I dedicated my life to the Goddess'), who took it as a golden opportunity to deliver a lecture on how her children were being brought up to understand that we truly own nothing except our souls, blah blah blah. The way her children's eyes lit up when they spied our iPads suggested they may not agree with Louisa's views on ownership. I'm going to have to frisk those little buggers before they leave.

Lunch was somewhat awkward, due to Louisa having declared the family gluten-free as well as vegan since the last time we saw them, so the pasta bake I had thought would be safe was rejected. But it was okay, she announced, I was not to worry, because Bardo would make us all one of his special soups instead. Cue Bardo rifling through my cupboards, demanding lentils and chickpeas (I am somewhat anxious about our plumbing, with eight of them staying here for a week and stuffing themselves full of so much fibre) and Louisa poking through my fridge, bewailing my lack of organic vegetables, 'These are just full of toxins, you're basically poisoning your family, Ellen! I know organic produce is more expensive, but why don't you just grow your own, like we do? It's so easy, and so satisfying and being in touch with the soil like that is just the most wonderful feeling, it really makes you appreciate every mouthful!'

She then rummaged through the eleventy billion canvas tote bags they had brought instead of suitcases (perhaps suitcases are a symbol of male oppression and the rape of the planet? Who knows? Who cares?) and thrust a bulging sack at me. 'We know there's a lot of us to feed, and we didn't want you to feel we were taking advantage, so we brought a contribution!' She beamed at me proudly, as I peered suspiciously at various wizened, mud-encrusted lumps lurking in the depths. 'It's some of our vegetables, all grown sustainably and organically. Once you taste these, you'll never go back to that horrible, plastic-wrapped supermarket veg! We'll have you up to your elbows in the Goddess' bounty before you know it!'

She emptied the sack on the table, scattering mud everywhere as she did so – 'It's just good clean dirt, don't worry about it!' – and brandished various mystery objects at me. 'Look! Potatoes and onions and beetroot and kale. Delicious. Bardo will put them all in the soup, you'll love it.'

I attempted to hide my outrage at the fact that, a) Louisa clearly doesn't understand the importance of beetroot in my family Christmas and she needn't think that misshapen testicle she waved at me is in any way replacing the sacred jar of pickled beetroot on my Christmas tea table, which is at least something Jessica will back me up on, despite sharing Louisa's views on all non-organic vegetables causing instant tumours if you allow them to pass your lips, and b) I am supposed to feed her and all her filthy children for a week but she expected me to be grateful because she had brought enough vegetables to make one pot of soup.

By the time Bardo's soup was ready Peter and Jane were rolling on the floor, clutching their stomachs and insisting they were about to die of hunger, while Louisa snapped at the older children (Cedric, Nisien, Idelisa and Coventina – not sure which is which) to step away from the iPads, away, they were not poisoning their minds and bodies with those toxic tablets and their killer rays, Boreas, the baby, had emitted a constant stream of noxious smells while squawking indignantly and resisting Louisa's determined attempts to thrust a boob in his face, and Oilell, the toddler, had pooed on the floor twice; 'We're still working on our elimination communication, but she doesn't like the feeling of diapers, and she will tell us when she feels ready to use a toilet. Or she might not, she might prefer to just go outside, as nature intended, like Nisien does.' Bloody hell, one craps on the floor and the other is going to crap in the back yard? Who is going to pick that up? It's bad enough having to pooper scooper after my dog, but I am not picking up after Nisien's desire to express himself through the medium of rejecting the bourgeois horrors of lavatories in favour of SHITTING IN MY FUCKING YARD!

Bardo dumped my best Le Creuset pot on the table, brimming over with some sort of unidentifiable sludge.

'It looks like poo!' announced Peter.

'It *smells* like poo!' Jane added.

'Please don't be rude, children,' I said, although they had a valid point. 'You know, Louisa, I mean Amaris, I'm sure there's not enough for us, it looks *delicious* but I would hate us to eat it all, so we'll just have the pasta. No, no, it's fine, we're used to the toxins.'

If the revolting mess burnt onto my saucepan was not off-putting enough, the black crescents of dirt (good and clean or not) under Bardo's fingernails were enough to turn the strongest stomach.

After lunch, Louisa said, 'Gosh, Ellen, I'm exhausted! It took us three days to drive down and we got up terribly early this morning, so we could get here in time to join you for lunch. Do you think I could possibly have a bath?'

Despite not being entirely convinced that a hot bath quite squared with Louisa's eco credentials, I had little choice but to say through gritted teeth, 'Yes, of course. I'll get you some towels.'

'Oh, you *are* kind,' said Louisa. 'Bardo, do you want to join me? You'll watch the children, won't you, Ellen? Boreas will probably sleep anyway, and Oilell might want to as well, so there's not much for you to do.'

No. Not much for me to do at all other than clean the mud off every surface in my kitchen and wash up every single pot, chopping board and knife I own, all of which were apparently required by Bardo to produce his culinary masterpiece of Sludge à La Mode, while watching EIGHT children, including a baby and a floor-shitting toddler. Not much at all.

As Louisa skipped off out the door, she paused to watch me putting the lunch plates in the dishwasher. 'I do hope you don't use that too much, Ellen,' she cooed. 'It uses so much water and electricity; it's really bad for the environment.'

Two hours later, Louisa and Bardo emerged from their bath, not actually looking any cleaner, but reeking of my best Molton Brown bath oil which I never use, because I am keeping it for something special. The children were all catatonic in front of the TV, as I had encouraged Peter and Jane to put on the most mindless, annoying, screechy programme they could find so they didn't come and irritate me, but despite the gargantuan quantities of lentils Louisa's children had eaten at lunch, at least none of them had felt the need to practise their elimination communication again.

Louisa immediately switched off the TV to snarls of fury from Peter and Jane, and plonked herself down on the sofa and *took her top off*.

'Milk time, children!' she cried. 'Who wants to go first?'

Peter, Jane and I looked on aghast as the biggest one, who I think is Cedric, and must be at least eight, launched himself at Louisa's tit and latched on, closely followed by the rest of the pack.

'Don't be shy, kids!' Louisa shouted cheerily at Peter and Jane, 'you can have a go too, if you want. It's perfectly natural!'

We backed out of the room, ashen-faced and trembling. Even Jane was lost for words for once, though I fear the words may come to her later.

When I went into the bathroom it was in a worse state than the children leave it in, with water all over the floor, wet towels everywhere and my precious Molton Brown bottle drained of every last drop of bath oil. There was also a black ring around the bath that took me twenty minutes to scrub off. I bet they had sex in my bath. I don't think I can ever get in it again, and Molton Brown will now forever smell to me of betrayal and loss and Bardo's hairy bollocks.

Louisa was still on the sofa with various children hanging off both boobs when Simon came home from work.

'Hi Si,' she called. 'Great to see you!'

Simon took one look and walked straight out of the room.

'God, you are so repressed, Si,' shouted Louisa after him. 'It's probably because Mum didn't breastfeed you, you know.'

I followed Simon out of the room and said, 'She's your sister. I have to go out now.'

I went straight round to Sam's, pausing only at the corner shop to buy two bottles of wine and a packet of cigarettes, then I poured out the whole story while he laughed his head off.

'You won't be laughing when her tits are dangling in your Brussels sprouts over Christmas dinner,' I pointed out.

Simon grabbed me when I got home. 'You've been smoking!' he said accusingly.

'Yeah, and, so what?' I mumbled, doing my best sulky school-girl impression.

'Well, bloody well give me one,' he hissed. 'I've been made to watch the video of Boreas' birth in the woods and she freeze-framed on his head crowning. *I have just seen a human head come out of my own sister's twat.* Oh, and Bardo was also naked throughout the birth, and a friend filmed it for them, so his dick also featured heavily. I need a fucking cigarette!'

We sneaked into the back yard.

'Watch where you stand,' I warned him. 'Nisien prefers to poo outside, surrounded by nature.'

'Oh God!' said Simon. 'How are we going to get through this? I know she's my sister, but ...'

'She's a sanctimonious, pretentious, hypocritical, freeloading pain in the arse with dubious personal hygiene and no respect for my fucking bath oil?' I suggested.

'I was going to go for "hard work",' said Simon, 'but your version covers it, too.'

We both drew deeply on our cigarettes.

'What would she say about smoking?' I asked him.

'Same as she says about everything, probably – our smoking is evil and wrong, but Bardo's spliffs are natural and health-giving and therefore she is once again morally superior to us. I don't think I can do this. Let's run away. We could leave the kids with Lou, she'd never notice another two, we could pretend we are just nipping into the garden to pick some organic quinoa and then bugger off and book into a hotel for Christmas. They won't even know we're gone.'

'She would notice,' I said, 'as soon as she realised that she had no one to make patronising remarks to and chide about their carbon footprints. And if we left our children, I would give it about three hours before they cracked due to the lack of electrical waves frying their susceptible childish brains and ran amok with the kitchen knives, brutally slaughtering anyone that came between them and a screen.'

'You're right,' said Simon sadly. 'We're fucked, aren't we?'

'Still,' I said. 'Look on the bright side – at least they haven't blocked the plumbing yet with a lentil-charged turbo shit!'

Right on cue, Louisa shouted, 'Ellen? Ellen, there's something wrong with the toilet; we're just going to use your ensuite, okay?'

FML. Why has no one bought my app yet?

Wednesday, 23 December

The list of things I am going to have to throw away when Louisa leaves grows by the hour. This morning I came downstairs to find her making herself a smoothie in my blender, with what appeared to be the entire contents of my fridge and fruit bowl, including the eye-wateringly expensive melon and raspberries I had bought to attempt an ironically retro starter for Christmas Day. Apparently Louisa can overcome her organic principles if the raspberries cost £3.99 a punnet.

As I stood, aghast once more at the carnage and destruction that Louisa leaves in her wake, seemingly without trying, she picked up a little pot containing some white gel-like substance and popped it into the blender. Remarkably, it appeared to be the only thing that hadn't been plundered from my kitchen, and although I knew I would regret asking what it was, as it would probably turn out to be the organic sap of a Peruvian plant that could only be harvested by the light of a full moon, and really, I should try it, I couldn't help myself.

'It's semen!' said Louisa brightly.

'Ha ha ha,' I said. 'Sorry, Louisa, I thought you said it was semen, what did you actually say?'

'I said it was semen,' said Louisa. 'Bardo gives me some every morning. It's so nutritious – full of B vitamins and protein. It also makes a marvellous face mask. Haven't you noticed how young I look and how my skin glows? Here, do you want to try some smoothie?'

I couldn't actually answer for dry retching in my mouth. Louisa had just put Bardo's hippy jizz *in my KitchenAid blender and was offering me a taste!* What is wrong with her? Why can't she just give him a blow job? Does she 'harvest' it herself, or does he vanish into the bathroom with a dirty magazine? WHY

WOULD ANYONE DO THAT? Why am I even thinking about this? Also, while we are on the subject, since 'finding Amaris' Louisa has looked about ten years older than she actually is, and no one can tell if she is glowing or not because she is usually too grubby, even after availing herself of all my bath oil, which, yes, I am still bitter about, and will be for some time.

By the time I had collected myself to say anything other than 'What the actual fuck?', Peter and Jane had appeared in the kitchen demanding Coco Pops – 'We asked Auntie Louisa for breakfast but she said we could have a disgusting smoothie or some horrible porridge she was making,' they complained.

For once I was grateful for Peter and Jane's staunch aversion to anything they suspect may contain vitamins or nutrients, as at least I can be sure there is no way they will taste anything Louisa or Bardo creates, and therefore I can be sure there will be zero chance of them ingesting any stray bodily fluids.

'Oh, that reminds me, Ellen,' said Louisa. 'I couldn't actually make my chia seed porridge because I couldn't find any chia seeds. Where do you keep them?'

'I don't have any,' I muttered, bracing myself for the inevitable. I am not actually even sure what chia seeds are, except that sometimes I hear Perfect Lucy Atkinson's Perfect Mummy wittering about them to the rest of the Coven.

'Oh, that's no problem,' Louisa chirped. 'I expect you'll be going to the shops today, you can just get some then. Actually, I've got a list of a few things we will need, maybe you could pick them up for me? Or, even better, I'll come with you. Girly shopping trip, won't that be fun?'

Yes, it would be totes fun. In a really awful 'kill me now' sort of a way.

It could've been worse. No, really, it could've. Louisa might have got her way and made us all, eight children included, go in Gunnar the Camper Van, but I at least vetoed that by pointing out the immense illegality of cramming twelve people into a camper van with seatbelts for four people. Louisa huffed and insisted that in Scotland no one bothered about silly things like that, which I am 100 per cent certain is untrue – it's only in Louisa's deluded head that no one bothers about seat belts. I put my foot down, though, while painting dire pictures of Louisa languishing in prison while her moppets wasted away without her life-giving breast milk and she herself became a shrivelled crone without the remarkable rejuvenating properties of Bardo's semen, and probably by the time she got out she would be so wizened he would have taken up with some youthful sprite and the children would have forgotten who she even is. She eventually capitulated, so we went in my car and left most of the children with Bardo and Simon, so at least we didn't all die in a hideous fireball, which is actually about the only way that the shopping trip with Louisa could've been worse, on reflection.

Costco was vetoed first of all, as they didn't have any chia seeds, or suitably obscure organic coffee, though they did have a very useful-looking little generator for an excellent price, which I suggested to Louisa she should buy to save on electricity costs due to the ineffective solar panels, but she recoiled in horror.

'FOSSIL FUELS, ELLEN!' she shrieked. 'No, no, no! I couldn't live with myself, bringing a horrible gasoline-burning monster like that into the Goddess' haven at our retreat!'

However, driving the length and breadth of the country in an antiquated camper van that drinks diesel and belches black smoke from the exhaust is just fine, unlike my beloved SUV, which also earned me a lecture on 'Gas Guzzlers' and a plea to consider an electric car. Sometimes I wonder if Louisa can even hear the words coming out of her mouth.

Wholefoods, although providing the Essential chia seeds and all the organic produce you could want, was poo pooed as 'so corporate, so tediously middle class'.

I *am* tediously middle class, as, for that matter, is Louisa, who was privately educated and went to Durham, and I love Wholefoods, especially the jars of pretentious grains, but after twenty minutes of walking round with Louisa sighing loudly and tutting and shrieking about 'Oh GODDESS, the *food miles* on this are too much' (although food miles don't seem to matter when it comes to coffee), I cracked and gave in to her demands for 'just a little farmers' market, or an artisan healthfood shop, Ellen. I saw one back there, I really think that would be much better'. As she was also threatening to stop and breastfeed Cedric, the eldest, in the middle of the bakery aisle, it seemed best that we left, as people were starting to stare and Louisa was spoiling my happy place.

When we got home, a hollow-eyed Simon met me at the door, holding an indignantly squawking Boreas at arm's length (I had refused to let Louisa bring him, as they didn't have a car seat, and I was unconvinced of her argument that he would be perfectly safe on her lap in his sling).

'Come on,' said Simon, thrusting Boreas (who smelt hideous) into the loving arms of his mother and grabbing me by the hand, 'we are going to the pub.'

Sam, the angel, had popped round to see if Peter and Jane wanted to go for a sleepover at his house. 'They had their bags packed and coats on before I had even agreed,' said Simon.

We recounted the horrors of our afternoon to each other as we numbed our pain with lovely, lovely, life-giving booze.

'She has no idea of irony, refusing to buy her organic coffee in Wholefoods because it is "too middle class" and then in her wretched artisan healthfood shop she filled a cart with hugely expensive bird seed, then when we got to the checkout, announced she had actually forgotten her purse, because she is so unused to using money, as they just "barter with friends" for what they need! So I had to pay for the bloody lot.'

'They followed me into my shed. My *shed*! Even Peter and Jane don't go in my shed.'

'In fairness, darling, that is because your shed is dark and smells funny and you told them there were Venezuelan Vampire Squirrels living in the corners that would attack small children on sight.'

'And then they started *touching things. In my shed*! And then that little one, what's it called? Not the baby, the next one up, the really snotty one?'

'Oilell. These are the fruits of your sister's loins, darling, you should really remember their names.'

'Fuck off, darling, please don't mention my sister's loins after that birth video. Anyway, yes, that one squatted down and tried to do a poo. *In my shed*!'

'Oh, the humanity! It crapped in the kitchen yesterday, I've no sympathy. Is it a girl or a boy, do you reckon?'

'I have no idea, I have tried not to get close enough to find out. Anyway, fucking Beardo was eying up my tools and didn't even notice, but the biggest girl –'

'– Coventina –'

'How do you remember all their names?'

'Years of listening to how Tilly said to Milly, so Milly said to Katie and then Katie told Lucy, so then Lucy said to Sophie and then Sophie said that Tilly and Milly should totally do that, and so then Lucy was crying, which was stupid of Lucy, and Katie said she didn't even care, and then Sophie said to Tilly and so then Milly, etc., etc. And then you have to work out who they all are so you don't accidently ask arch enemies over at the same time, and you invite the right Tillies, Millies, Sophies, Katies and Lucies to birthday parties.'

'Are they all called Tilly and Milly and Katie and Sophie and Lucy?'

'No, darling, don't be silly, some of them are called Olivia.

And there's a couple of Poppies. Anyway, what happened with the floor shitter?'

'Oh, the biggest girl –'

'– Coventina –'

'– Coventina saw the look in my eye and the steam coming out of my nostrils and grabbed it and hauled it outside and it shat on the patio. Which was still better than *in my shed*. And then Beardo asked if I would mind if he borrowed my mitre saw and I said what for and he said to take back to the retreat to do some work. He basically tried to steal MY mitre saw, Ellen.'

'More importantly, what happened to the patio poo?'

'Oh, Coventina got some of the dog's poo bags and picked it up. She seems quite normal, I like her. I caught her stealing sausage rolls out the fridge with Peter and Jane, and when I asked her about being a gluten-free vegan, she sighed and said she didn't want to talk about it and ate another sausage roll.'

'Hurrah for Coventina! She will probably end up changing her name to Susan and becoming a stockbroker to rebel against her parents.'

It was actually rather lovely being out with Simon, as usually if I suggest we go out, unless it is a special occasion, he grumbles he is too tired, or it is too cold or wet, and can't we just stay at home because there will be People if we go out? It says something for the horrors of his sister's family that they have driven Simon out into the world of People. We laughed, and we got mildly (really quite) drunk and when I checked my phone, there was an email to say that ten people had bought my app, which means, I think, if my drunken arithmetic is right, that I have so far made the princely sum of £7! If another ninety people download it, I will even have made back the $100 I paid to register as an app developer. Someone having bought it, I finally thought I should probably tell Simon about it, just in case it does make our fortune. He was slightly confused about what it was and why I had created it, but the key phrase of 'money' pierced the fog of beer and he said it sounded very clever of me.

We even held hands as we walked home together, though he wouldn't let me look in the dumpster outside number 27, which I felt was unreasonable, but as he pointed out, if there had been anything worth having in there, Louisa and Bardo would have had it out hours ago.

Thursday, 24 December – Christmas Eve

Scrap what I said about 1 December being the most hopeful day of the festive season, I was foolish and wrong, for of course that day is Christmas Eve! A day for kissing under the mistletoe and listening to *Carols from King's* on the radio and being pleased that they use the proper old-fashioned King James Bible for the readings and not the nasty modern version they use in the children's carol service at school, because despite being not in the slightest bit religious, if I am going to have a bit of Bible going on, I want it to be the proper one with plenty of 'unto theeings' and 'thou artests'.

It is a day for watching *It's a Wonderful Life* snuggled on the sofa with my apple-cheeked moppets and wrapping presents by the fire in a tastefully kitsch Christmas sweater while drinking mulled wine (still haven't remembered to find out what hot cider is) and eating Christmas cookies, before reading *The Night Before Christmas* to the children and putting out a large Scotch for Santa (Simon did away with the 'glass of milk' idea at Jane's first Christmas) and a carrot for Rudolph. Then it's time to hang the stockings and send the kids off to bed so that I can curl up with my beloved husband and watch *Love Actually* over a delicious glass of good-quality red wine, then yawn our way up the wooden hill to Bedfordshire.

It is *not* a day for waking up to nine texts from Jessica agonising about which Christmas pudding to bring, as she has now bought puddings from every supermarket ('Great news, I managed to get the last one on eBay!'), Selfridges, Harrods and Fortnum & Mason. I think Jessica has spent more on Christmas puddings than I have spent on the whole of the rest of Christmas dinner! There were also five texts from her checking whether I had the pickled beetroot for the Christmas Tea ('OF COURSE I HAVE THE PICKLED BEETROOT, JESSICA, WHAT THE FUCK DO YOU TAKE ME FOR?').

It is not a day for wrangling with a sleep-deprived Peter and Jane while clearing up the mess left in the kitchen by Louisa yet again, or realising that peeling enough potatoes for twenty-two people actually takes far longer than the *Carols from King's* service, and trying to wrestle with a giant bastarding turkey that you are not even sure will fit in your oven while Bardo hovers and demands that the sludge roast that he is creating for his monstrous brood in no way comes into contact with the slaughterhouse horror of my turkey.

It is not a day for spilling a vat of turkey stock over the floor and mopping it up while sobbing 'I just want to watch *It's a Wonderful Life*, IS THAT TOO MUCH TO ASK?'

It is most definitely not a day for discovering that Peter and Jane have been at the Gummy Bears, although thank God for small mercies, they only shared with Coventina ('Do you think you could just call me Tina, please?'), but the three of them were then smacked off their tits on sugar and bouncing round the house.

When I looked out of the kitchen window Nisien was straining in the middle of the lawn, and there is a suspicious smell in the dining room that suggests that Oilell has paid it a visit and left a surprise Christmas present in there.

By 8 p.m. I was a frazzled wreck. No presents were wrapped, for anybody. It was now impossible to tell the Gummy Beared children from the non-Gummy Beared as they had all reached such a fever pitch of excitement that attempting to sit them all down to listen to *The Night Before Christmas* was akin to herding cats, though Tina did attempt to help by screaming 'SHUT THE FUCK UP, YOU LITTLE SHITS' at her siblings, which woke the baby, who started to scream, and I declared I could not do this and took the bottle of Baileys Irish Cream and retreated to my bedroom to start wrapping the presents.

Peace to wrap was not forthcoming, as there were eleventy fucking billion interruptions: from Louisa, wanting to borrow scissors; Simon asking if he should do the whisky for Santa yet; Peter and Jane howling that something or other was unfair; Louisa again, wanting clean towels (MORE towels? What is she doing with them? Is she planning on giving birth again, in some sort of Christmas Miracle?); Cedric peering in beadily, claiming he just wondered what I was doing, but I suspect he was actually casing the joint for things to steal, and finally Bardo wanting, well, I don't know what the fuck Bardo wanted because at that point I flung myself wholeheartedly into what has now become my traditional Christmas Meltdown.

I sobbed that I JUST wanted five minutes' peace, just five minutes' peace, Christmas was magical and they were all RUINING THE MAGIC, and then I shrieked 'FML' several times and grabbed my somewhat startled dog, a blanket (I have done this before and learnt from experience), and the Baileys, and stomped off to the garage, where I watched YouTube clips from *It's a Wonderful Life* on my phone and cried into the dog's fur.

The dog doesn't really like being cried on; he is not a concerned and empathetic creature who feels my pain, like everyone says dogs are. He wriggled a lot and farted at me. I think he's part cat. So then I cried some more because even the dog hates me, and it was bloody freezing in the garage but pride forbade me from going back in, so I had some more Baileys to keep warm.

After about an hour and half, Simon came out to find me. 'Are you okay?' he asked.

'Noooooo,' I snivelled drunkenly. 'Everything is ruined and there's too much to do and I can't do it all!'

'You don't have to,' said Simon. 'Why do you do this to yourself every year, instead of just asking for help? Anyway, the children are all in bed, and I've told them if one of them sets foot out of bed before 7 a.m. tomorrow morning, it will be Rudolph steaks for Christmas dinner. I've finished the wrapping, and Louisa and Bardo are actually clearing up the kitchen. I don't know that they'll make much of a job of it, but at least they are giving it a go. And look, it's snowing! We're going to have a White Christmas! Which will be ...?'

'Magical!' I sobbed. He was right. Fat white flakes were billowing down, covering the hideous trampoline and the discarded Swingball set and transforming our dull little suburban street into Narnia.

'Oh God, I've been such a dick,' I said to Simon.

'You have,' he said. 'But you're *my* dick. Well, you know what I mean, and I love you.'

And then he kissed me, and everything was indeed magical.

Friday, 25 December – Christmas Day!

The magic did not last, as I suddenly remembered that no one had picked up Nisien's poo from the middle of the lawn, so I had to rush out and remove it so that the children did not stand on it when they went out to frolic in the snow in the morning.

Simon had made heroic attempts to wrap, but had not found the many presents I had stashed around the house throughout the year, so there was still a fair amount left to do, and we finally fell into bed at about 2 a.m., which is still earlier than I have managed in other years.

Unfortunately, sleep was delayed by Louisa and Bardo deciding to take the opportunity to indulge in a bout of noisy sex. I can't even go there, except to say they are both extremely vocal and I was not able to look either of them in the eye this morning, after their various exhortations to each other.

The children managed to hold to Simon's decree that they stay in bed until 7 a.m. or Rudolph would die horribly, but once they were up, their excitement was at fever pitch once more. Peter and Jane had received their customary quantities of evil corporate consumerism, while Louisa's children had homemade gifts, carved by Bardo, and clothes from me, for fear of Louisa's shunning anything else. This caused some controversy, as Louisa's older children demanded to know why Santa had brought them such rubbish and given all the good stuff to their cousins, to which Louisa and Bardo cooed that Santa knew each family's values and gifted accordingly, and exhorted their darlings to remember that you only really owned your soul, and possessions were just shackles.

At this point Cedric attempted to stage a revolution and demanded the redistribution of the bourgeois wealth amongst the masses, by announcing it would be much fairer if Peter and Jane gave them some of their nice, shiny, mind-rotting electronics, at which point Jane produced a knife from her pocket and declared that she would cut anyone who touched her stuff, which suggests that she had already got wind of Cedric's plans and armed herself accordingly.

We distracted them by suggesting they all went to play in the lovely snow, so half an hour later, having removed Jane's knife, frisked the rest of them for weapons and wrestled them all into hats and gloves and coats and boots, they went forth to frolic while the grown-ups exchanged gifts.

I had given Louisa expensive soap and toiletries and also a nice scarf, because that is my default panic-buying gift. Bardo got beard oil, a nail brush and posh shower gel. I had carefully made sure everything was organic, ethically sourced and lovingly handmade by artisans; the scarf was even made of hemp, so there was no way that they could sneer at my thoughtful (if pointed) gifts and reject them.

They gave us 'treatments'. I got off quite lightly, with a Reiki session from Louisa, which at least meant she wouldn't touch me. 'I didn't know you were trained in Reiki, Louisa,' I said.

'*Amaris*, please, and I didn't need to be *trained*, Ellen,' she replied scornfully. 'Reiki is all about channelling the universal energy through yourself and letting it flow into the other person. I have such a strong connection with the energy that I am a natural. Sometimes it is all I can do to *stop* the energy overflowing and channel it where it needs to go. Feel this!' She waved her hands in front of me. 'Do you feel it? The heat, and the energy? That is flowing through me all the time, Ellen, *all the time*! It's incredibly powerful. I think I might be one of the most powerful Reiki masters ever. I have a *calling*!'

I didn't actually feel anything, except a wish that Louisa would wash her hands more often.

'Errr, right. Can you actually call yourself a Reiki master if you've not had any training?'

'Power like this can't be taught, Ellen. It just is. I just "am". It's my blessing from the Goddess, and also my curse.'

'Great. Well, thanks!'

Poor Simon had been given a past lives regression session with Bardo.

'Amaris is always saying you're so repressed, man!' enthused Bardo. 'So, we're going to get to the bottom of it and find out why.'

Simon was speechless.

Louisa chipped in, 'Bardo is incredibly good at this. It's one of our most popular sessions at the retreat, it's amazing! People say that it helps them to understand themselves so much better, just knowing who they were in a past life. I mean, just last month, we had a woman who had been Marie Antoinette, Emily Brontë, Queen Victoria and Marie Curie! Imagine the weight of grief and emotion and trauma she was carrying with her. Bardo helped her understand that this had built up over centuries, and she had to learn to *let it go* and forgive herself for her pain. Of course, something like that can't be overcome in a few hours, it took many, many sessions for her to let go of her past selves and live in the present, but Bardo worked wonders.'

Bardo added, 'She had been Cleopatra too, Ams. Don't forget that.'

Simon inquired, 'Didn't Marie Curie, Emily Brontë and Queen Victoria's lives all overlap?'

Curious, I asked, 'How much do you charge for these "sessions" exactly?'

Horrified, Louisa exclaimed, '*Simon*! It won't work if you don't *believe*!', while Bardo mumbled something about it not really being about the money, it was about using his gift to help others, 'Although obviously we do have to cover our costs.'

'And how,' asked Simon, 'do we go about this "regression" exactly?'

'Well,' said Bardo, getting excited. 'Usually we would do it in our yurt, but I reckon we could use your shed. We will light that woodstove you have in there and strip naked and then I burn certain herbs, I can't tell you what, because it is a closely guarded secret that a yogi in Omnatoli told me, and then I chant and put you in a trance, and take you back.'

Simon, who had looked for a moment like he was going to play along with Bardo's 'regression' if only to mess with him and expose him as the snake oil salesman that he really is, now looked aghast at the thought of full-frontal male nudity in his shed.

'And how do you put me in the trance?' he asked.

Bardo looked confused. 'Um, I just tell them they're in a trance and they go into one …?'

'Yes, well, we have a busy few days before you leave, so it's very thoughtful of you, but I'm not sure we'll have time.' Simon said briskly, clearly suspecting Bardo of planning to drug him and steal his precious mitre saw from under his very nose.

Luckily, at that moment the children decided they had had enough of the snow, having spent a full twenty minutes playing in it (and trampling my winter wonderland into a churned-up post-apocalyptic wasteland in the process) and decided a much better game was to come inside and trail snow and mud all through the house. I abandoned Simon at that point in favour of retiring to the kitchen with my hangover and a bottle of gin to check on the turkey and the other mountains of food, and fret there would not be enough to go around.

Jessica and Neil arrived about 12.30. 'I thought we'd get here early and give you a hand, and of course Persephone and Gulliver were simply longing to see their cousins, weren't you, darlings?'

Persephone and Gulliver were hiding behind Jessica, looking appalled at the scenes of carnage strewn around my house. Frankly, I couldn't blame them. Louisa and Bardo were shouting encouragement to Oilell, who was squatting on the patio, as I had put my foot down about the floor-shitting, while Nisien stood looking outraged at having his thunder stolen.

Peter, Jane and Coventina, who had abandoned all pretence of being on her family's side, were sprawled in front of the TV, playing something mindless on a games consul and screaming a lot while shoving the contents of chocolate boxes in their mouths.

Cedric was marching up and down and singing 'The Red Flag', while occasionally launching an assault on the children in possession of the technology to try to take a controller for the people.

Idelisa, the middle girl, who everyone seemed to pretty much ignore, lacking as she did her brothers' psychopathic tendencies or Coventina's spirit, was attempting to change Baby Boreas' diaper. Boreas was objecting strenuously.

'Gosh, what a busy little house you've got here, haven't you?' said Jessica.

Neil mumbled something.

Persephone and Gulliver tugged at Jessica's hand and whispered in her ear.

'Oh, that's sweet! Persephone and Gulliver want to know when they can give everyone their presents. Persephone has been so busy with taking her Grade 8 piano and viola that she hasn't had time to write her own composition this year, so she's just going to play the first movement of the symphony she learnt for the school concert, and Gulliver has written a series of sonnets, in Latin – they are a sort of loose homage to Catullus. Isn't that nice?'

'Marvellous,' I said weakly, while thinking didn't Catullus write some fairly saucy poems?

'And I just brought all the Christmas puddings so you can choose which one to use,' (so if it's rubbish it will all be my fault) 'and you didn't tell me where you had got the beetroot from, so I just picked up a jar in Fortnum's while I was there. Now, what can I do to help?'

Mainly out of malice, to see her wriggle out of it, I said, 'Well, you could make a start on peeling those carrots, if you didn't mind?'

Jessica sighed.

'Oh Ellen, would you mind if I didn't? I had my nails done yesterday for a party we are going to tomorrow – the Cholmondeley-Featherstonhaugh's, do you know them? – and I don't want to wreck my manicure. Anything else, though, just say the word!'

'Well, maybe you could keep everyone's drinks topped up,' I said, handing her a couple of bottles (the booze was disappearing at an alarming rate, between Simon and me self-medicating and Louisa and Bardo miraculously finding that their ethical, organic scruples didn't extend to guzzling drink at someone else's expense).

'Perfect, of course! And fizz, what fun!' said Jessica, squinting at the label and barking 'Drinks!' at Neil as he scuttled off.

'Darling, I can't help but notice that the fizz – what is it actually? Prosecco? Oh, CAVA, lovely! But it isn't organic. I do hope you don't mind but I only actually drink organic wine these days because otherwise the sulphides give me the most awful migraine,' (obviously Jessica can't just have a hangover like the rest of us) 'so I've brought a few bottles of some lovely organic wine we get from this *amazing* little vineyard we stayed at in the South of France …'

Ha ha ha, I thought. Good luck getting to drink much of that once Louisa and Bardo get wind that there is actual organic wine in the house!

With her usual impeccable timing, Louisa appeared at that very minute and embraced Jessica at length. Jessica has even more issues with personal space and uninvited physical contact than I do so she twitched noticeably, and although I could see her mentally reaching for her hand sanitiser, good manners forced her to settle for discreetly wiping her hands on her skirt.

'JESSICA!' cried Louisa. 'Long time no see! How are you? Did I hear you saying you had brought organic wine? That's just amazing of you, you are so right about the sulphides. I keep telling Ellen, but she won't listen – you know her, quantity over quality! That's why she married my brother.'

Louisa then indulged in some sort of hideous 'nudge nudge wink wink' routine before Neil reappeared with my bottles of cut-price Cava and, for the first time in days, Louisa put her hand over her glass at the sight of a bottle.

'No, thank you. Neil, Jessica was just telling me about some amazing organic wine she says I have to try, so I'll have some of that, please. Bardo! Bardo! Come and try Jessica's organic wine.'

'Oh thanks, man!' said Bardo, putting down the possibly leaking baby and sloping over.

Jessica and Neil both had fixed rictus grins as they realised that the bulk of their precious Châteauneuf du Unicorndust was probably going to be poured down Louisa and Bardo's gullets before we had even sat down to eat.

'Oh, you don't mind, do you, Jessica?' asked Louisa innocently.

'No, no, of course not, help yourselves!' Jessica ground out through gritted teeth.

'Just say when …' she added as Neil began to pour.

'Ha ha ha, WHEN!' Louisa shrieked as her glass threatened to brim over. 'Ooooh, Neil, are you trying to get me drunk, you naughty boy? You better give Bardo the same, or he'll think you fancy me!'

The apoplectic bulging of Neil's eyes – Neil, who is married to Jessica, the scrubbed and shining Ice Maiden – at the thought that he might be trying to get into Louisa's doubtlessly crusty underwear, was the best thing I had seen all day.

Sam and Hannah arrived about 2 p.m. Sam had got his way and had Sophie and Toby for Christmas, not so much due to Robin seeing the light and deciding to do the right thing, as Robin getting a last-minute offer to spend Christmas on a friend's yacht in the Caribbean. Sam was chuntering a little about the latest 'friend', but mostly he was just delighted to have his children with him for Christmas. Hannah also had her two children, Emily and Lucas, who despite owing half their genes to Dastardly Dan are generally polite, pleasant and clean.

Persephone had been crying for the last hour over wanting to perform her 'present', and Gulliver had been muttering increasingly menacing Latin phrases to himself that I wasn't at all sure were his sonnets and not some foul curse upon us all (when I said this to Simon, he said Gulliver would be hard-pressed to come up with a curse fouler than Louisa's oozing children), so once everyone had arrived, I suggested we did the rest of the presents.

There was only one awkward moment when Cedric decided he was going to provide a percussion accompaniment to Persephone's recital, which caused further tears and also a somewhat tactless (if true) wail from Persephone that 'The DIIIIIRTY boy is spoiling it all, Mummy', but other than that, it was a perfectly pleasant exchange of bland middle-class gifts purchased at the holy altar of discreet beige department stores.

Louisa continued to offer treatments as gifts, and Jessica choked on a Brazil nut and turned purple when Louisa announced that she would like to give Jessica a reflexology session there and then. Jessica pays a 'marvellous little woman' in Harley Street a sum roughly equivalent to my mortgage for weekly reflexology sessions and there was no way on God's earth she was going to remove her Jimmy Choos and let Louisa's grubby paws get anywhere near her.

I finally got the dinner on the table about 4 p.m., after spending a good hour debriefing Sam and Hannah in the kitchen over a bottle of Jessica's (admittedly delicious) wine that I had managed to liberate from Louisa's grasp.

The children were corralled in the kitchen around a medley of play tables drafted in to supplement my kitchen table and fed off plastic plates. I hurled food at them and then closed the door on the howls of how unfair it was, to leave them to go feral while the grown-ups ate in the dining room. Louisa waited until everyone was assembled around the table before remarking loudly, 'I do think it is *wonderful* of you to let the children express their creativity by painting the furniture, Ellen, but what a *shame* you had to let them do it on darling Granny's beautiful sideboard.'

'Don't worry, Louisa!' snapped Jessica. 'We don't possess anything except our souls, remember; the sideboard is just an *object*!'

I wasn't sure if Jessica was actually defending me out of loyalty or whether she was just smarting over Louisa glugging all her special wine, but either way, I was grateful.

By 8 p.m., everyone but Neil (who was driving) was hammered. Several of the children were also swaying in such a way as to suggest they had been taking liberal nips of something while they were shut in the kitchen. The Christmas Tea was upon the table, admittedly only about an hour after we had finished the Christmas Dinner, and Jessica and I insisted everyone conducted a blind tasting of our respective beetroots. Everyone looked a little frightened as Jessica and I sang the special 'Song of the Hallowed Beetroot' that we had made up twenty years before, and then snarled 'Go on, which is better?' The consensus was that both were 'delicious' before Jessica and I also embarked on the tasting and then cackled uncontrollably as we concluded both were disgusting because pickled beetroot is vile.

By 10 p.m., Jessica and I were even bonding.

'We'sh shishters,' slurred Jessica. 'N'I fucking luff you. Pershephone, pleashe jus' fuck off an' watch TV with the othersh, 'kay? Mummy talkin' to Auntie Ellen. I's so glad you do Chrishtmash, Ellen, cos it like we a proper family. All the people …' she gestured vaguely at the comatose forms of Louisa and Bardo on the floor (Simon and Louisa had provided the obligatory family Christmas row by having a shouting match about who was their parents' favourite, because they had

FaceTimed Simon's iPad to wish us all a Merry Christmas and hadn't called Louisa separately. She stamped her feet and Simon told her he wished she had been given away for adoption and then they slammed some doors and generally behaved like petulant children), Sam, Hannah, Neil and Simon attempting to play Trivial Pursuit and various children skulking in corners, plugged into a variety of electronic devices. 'It'sh lovely. S'what Chrishtmash's about. Wish I was more like you. Wish I could jus' not give a fuck like you do.'

Why do people keep saying that to me? Does no one realise the amount of time I spend worrying and fretting about getting things right, or what people think about me? Or if everyone thinks I don't give a fuck, maybe that suggests they spend even more time worrying about that stuff? Maybe everyone is anxious and thinking they are just muddling through while projecting a different image to the outside world. Maybe no one is as perfect as I think they are, not even Perfect Lucy Atkinson's Perfect Mummy? Too much wine had been had to think about this. It's Christmas. It's magical (ish). More wine.

Saturday, 26 December – Boxing Day

Eurgh. Headache. Hangover. General inability to cope with reality while mourning the passing of the magic. The snow has turned to slush. The turkey is a sad heap of bones that should really be made into soup, but in the fridge are vats of pigs-in-blankets and stuffing and there are still five more Christmas puddings to eat that Jessica left behind. Today, everyone can fend for themselves. Today, I am going to loll in my pyjamas and eat chocolates and read the books that Hannah and Sam gave me for Christmas and stuff Turkish Delight in my mouth until I feel sick and remember I don't actually like Turkish Delight, and generally not give any of the fucks that everyone seems to think I don't give anyway. I will just tidy up a bit first, obviously, so I can loll properly. And put some clean pyjamas on – I am not an animal.

Monday, 28 December

I hate this yawning chasm of time between Christmas and New Year. After the hype and excitement and build-up to Christmas, it is all suddenly over in a flash of smoke, like the bang from a cracker, and all that remains is piles of tat, bad jokes and some tiny screwdrivers that will be very useful at some point in the future if only you could remember where you put them when the time comes.

The Christmas Food – the Important Cheese, the snacks, sausage rolls and canapés and other morsels of deliciousness that had to be guarded so carefully against the marauding hordes intent on plundering my fridge before Christmas Day are now declared 'boring' and declined by all, as I desperately attempt to press the vol-au-vents and turkey sandwiches on anyone who pauses for long enough on their way around the house.

Tonight we are having turkey and ham pie for dinner (well, Simon, the children and I are, obviously Louisa's vagabond tribe cannot be expected to poison themselves with such muck and will be feasting on another Bardo Special – I have had to unclog the toilet three times now and have informed Simon in no uncertain terms that next time, it is his turn). Simon sighed when I told him of tonight's culinary delights and said, 'Oh God, Ellen, I'm just a bit over all that rich food, I'd really like just a nice salad or something!'

In truth, I would also like a salad, but THAT IS NOT HOW CHRISTMAS WORKS, and on a point of principle, we are not having anything else until all the Christmas food has been eaten. Simon claimed that there was no need for me to shout that at him while menacingly banging a knife against the worktop. Rude.

Tuesday, 29 December

The end finally arrived. Louisa and Bardo have departed, the rickety camper van crammed to the gunnels with children, backfiring black smoke as it lurched up the road. Truly I thought this day would never come. Louisa, obviously enjoying my hot water and central heating, offered to stay for a 'few more days', but Simon, who was growing increasingly twitchy about Bardo's forays into his shed and garage (I found him last night looking anxiously at his special jars of screws, weighing them in his hand and wondering aloud if Bardo had been pilfering them. Quite probably, I would say) briskly intervened, barking, 'That would be lovely, sis, but you'd better get back to the retreat, eh? The children must be missing their own beds, and after all there's no place like home, is there? It's been wonderful to see you, we must do it again soon. Not that soon. Safe home!' and practically shoved her out the door.

Bardo, however, made one last-ditch attempt to get his hands on the precious mitre saw, mumbling, 'Oh Si, remember you said I could borrow the saw, man? I'll just go get it …'

Simon was having none of it and said firmly, 'SO sorry, Bardo, old chap!' (old chap? WTF? Has Simon turned into some sort of spiffing 1930s caricature in rebellion against Louisa's hippy-dippy, New Age witterings?) 'I'm awfully afraid the mitre saw's broken. Yep, completely buggered, absolutely kaput! What a shame.'

Bardo, credit where credit is due, was not so easily deflected and cheerfully offered to take it anyway, as he is 'good with fixing things' and apparently if it was beyond repair he could 'just use it for parts'.

The testosterone in the room was palpable, as Man faced down Man over the holy grail of Power Tools. Simon's love for his power tools is not a force to be underestimated, though.

'I'm afraid I've taken it to the shop already,' he said coldly. 'A special shop, a long way away. I took it this morning, early. What. A. Shame. Goodbye, Bardo.'

There was one final scene, when Peter and Jane hurled themselves upon Cedric, not as I initially thought in an eleventh-hour demonstration of cousinly love, but because he had secreted their iPods and various portable games consuls about his person and was attempting to make off with them.

Louisa, seemingly more concerned by her offspring's desire to fry his budding brain cells with 'awful microwaves' (not really sure iPods emit microwaves, but who are we to argue with Louisa's cod science) rather than the fact that he is a thieving hooligan, announced that Simon was probably right, and it *was* time for them all to return to the 'purity' of life at the retreat. She didn't actually denounce our house as a den of iniquity, but it was on the tip of her tongue.

I have never felt such relief as when waving them off. I will quite miss Coventina, but I fear she and Jane in combination would have turned into a pair of juvenile criminal overlords, selling black-market Gummy Bears and X-rated, under-the-counter comic books while using poor Peter as their minion.

And, oh, what bliss to have the house to ourselves again! I feel like I have done nothing but cook and clean for months.

Wednesday, 30 December

Ha ha ha, the tree is gone. Gone. GONE! I could bear it no more, the poor tree, borne into the house with such joy, such festive pomp and circumstance, but now reduced to a sad desiccated shrub instead of the glowing beacon of festive love that it once represented. I think I will be vacuuming up pine needles until about March, but fuck it, the sitting room now looks so big – in fact, the whole house looks much bigger now all the cards and tat and holly and ivy are no longer decking the halls. Even though the house isn't actually particularly clean, because I got bored with cleaning after spending an entire hour doing nothing but vacuuming up pine needles and then another half hour unblocking the vacuum cleaner which had clogged with all the bastarding pine needles, it *looks* much cleaner. Maybe Simon has a point with his endless whining for minimalism? Perhaps a stark white box wouldn't be SO bad?

The dog is also delighted that the tree has gone, because he was finally able to pee on it when it was lying outside the back door – something he has been longing to do since the day it arrived.

Thursday, 31 December – New Year's Eve

Why, oh why, oh why did I decide, in a haze of wine and unexpected bonhomie at TV Alicia's party that it would be a good idea to have a party myself? And WHY did I decide to have it on New Year's Eve, probably the worst night in the world EVER to have a party, with the hours leading up to midnight being filled with forced fun and hilarity, because it is New Year's Eve and you have to have a wild and crazy time, IT IS THE LAW!

And then after midnight, after all the counting down and getting pawed by sweaty men under the guise of wishing you 'Happy New Year', there is just nothing, except a sense of disillusionment and despair, as the last glowing sparkles of December are brutally extinguished and all you have looming ahead of you is the dark void of January and another year in which you will probably fail to become a proper grown-up.

Why didn't I see sense and reason (that is a rhetorical question, obviously, because the answer, as it so often is, is 'booze') and realise that spending NYE watching fake parties on TV wasn't so bad actually, as you get to see random celebrities trying to pretend they are not actually being filmed in August, all corralled in a studio together, where they too are forced to have the 'best time ever'. Why did I think this was a good idea?

I am frantically cleaning and cooking and assembling canapés in between looking at Facebook, where everybody I know ever is posting statuses like 'Looking forward to a fabulous NYE party at Ellen's!'; 'Can't wait to see New Year in with Ellen and the gang!'; 'Cheeky bubbles before Ellen's party!'; 'Getting glammed up for Ellen's party, Happy New Year in advance everyone!'

I HATE THEM ALL! I am not having 'cheeky bubbles' or getting 'glammed up' because I am panic vacuuming and frenziedly assembling Caesar fucking salads on sticks and trying not to burn the profiteroles and this is all my horrible friends' fault for accepting my stupid invitation in the first place and Simon's fault for letting me have a party, and if he offers one more time to do something stupid and selfish like pour me a glass of wine or run me a bath (the bath is still dead to me anyway, after the thought of what horrors might have happened in it over Christmas), I will beat him to death with a honey-and-mustard-glazed mini sausage.

Breathe. Breathe. I can do this. These people are my friends, except for the ones I hate that I only invited to show off what a calm, capable and welcoming hostess I am. And the ones I invited because we went to their party and so we 'owe' them. And the ones I just invited because I was sloshed and they seemed less annoying than usual. It'll be fine. MOST of these people are my friends.

At least the children are sleeping over at Sam's house with his babysitter, so they will not appear halfway through my elegant and sophisticated cocktail party demanding that the guests guess who farted – Peter or the dog? – and making kind offers such as 'I'll give you a clue, mine are more cabbagey and his are more meaty!'

Cocktails! Bugger. Has Simon started making the cocktails yet? Simon's cocktails are my secret weapon. He is very good at making extremely strong cocktails that somehow just taste like fruit juice, so I will get everyone hammered as soon as they arrive and it will all be fine, they will not care about anything else and will probably wake up tomorrow morning with little recol-lection of the evening, so I will easily be able to convince every-one that I am the party hostess of the century. Hurrah! It will be fine. Still hate those smug bastards tagging me on Facebook, though.

Arrrghhhh! People are arriving already!

JANUARY

Friday, 1 January – New Year's Day

Oh God, my head. Oh Jesus, what happened? Oh fuck. Sam was there, Sam and Hannah came early to help me finish getting everything ready. We had a couple of cocktails …

Everyone else arrived and I was utterly charming – enthusiastic and witty and welcoming. I introduced people to each other and encouraged them to circulate. Did I actually shout 'FOR FUCK'S SAKE, CIRCULATE, YOU MISERABLE BASTARDS!' at everyone? I might've. Well, they probably thought I was being ironic and amusing.

Food. I did feed people, didn't I? I seem to have woken up clutching a cocktail sausage roll in one hand. Yes, I fed people. I have a vague recollection of ranting to a husband of one of the school mummies who had turned out to be a GP about why everyone is gluten-free now, while ramming mini filo parcels in my mouth and trying to force-feed them to him.

Music? Yes, we had music. And dancing! At least I had dancing. I insisted the floor was cleared while I performed Kate Bush's dance from 'Wuthering Heights'. I sang along, too. I do remember being surprised by the shocked silence at the end instead of the rapturous applause I had expected for my virtuoso performance. Shit.

Actually, double shit, where am I? Why am I in the guest room? Oh God, was I so awful that Simon is now divorcing me?

Maybe I did my routine to the 'Patricia the Stripper' song again. Actually, that rings a bell. I *did* do Patricia the Stripper, but I wasn't alone. Who else did it with me? Fucking hell, it was Fiona Montague! I feel a bit better now, if Fiona Montague was wasted enough to be doing Patricia the Stripper, I wasn't the only one there being a 'bit much'! And 'Patricia the Stripper' and 'Wuthering Heights' are pretty much par for the course as my party pieces. Just as long as I didn't try to do anything really awful, like pinch TV Alicia's scarves for the Dance of the Seven Veils or anything.

I wonder if I text Simon he would bring me a cup of tea? I had to eat the sausage roll, to keep my strength up. I would literally give almost anything in the world for a bacon sandwich right now.

Saturday, 2 January

Oh dear. It appears I was a 'bit much'. I forced Fiona Montague to take part in the Patricia the Stripper dance, although Simon says she seemed to rather enjoy it once she got going, and has, I quote, 'quite a hip action'. After that, apparently I decided profiterole juggling was going to be a new Olympic sport and attempted to give a demonstration. When Simon remonstrated with me, I took a huff and went to bed in a strop, in the guest room, to spite him. No one appeared to notice my absence, though, as everyone thought I was just in another room.

More excitingly, Alison Evans brought her rather hot brother Mark along, and he went home with the phone number of none other than young Sam, and he has already called and they are going on a *date*.

It is fairly obvious that it has been some time since Sam has been on a date, as he has suddenly lost all his urban cool and turned into a wittering, love-struck teenage girl. He has already sent Hannah and me photos of at least ten different shirts, demanding our opinions, and with accompanying worries about each one: 'The blue one really brings out my eyes, but the green one shows off my pecs, but I don't want to show them off too much, I don't want him to think I'm some 'roid raging meat head, but then I don't want to look easy either, and I like the tartan one, but is it too pretentious, because I don't want to look like a hipster wanker, so I think I'll go for the blue. I'm going to wear the blue. Unless you think I should wear the green? Maybe I should buy a new shirt? Do you think it will be really obvious it's a new shirt? I don't want to seem desperate. I could say I got it for Christmas. Who gave me it? Not my mum, obviously! Okay, one of you gave me a shirt for Christmas, if you see him, remember that. Remember to tell Mark you gave me a nice shirt, then I will look like I have tasteful friends who like me enough to buy me expensive presents. Yes! Nailed it.'

What does he mean it will 'look like' he has tasteful friends? He *does* have tasteful friends; we are very tasteful – apart from the sideboard, which could happen to anyone.

Besides trying to soothe Sam's obsessive shirt worries (ooh, I wonder if he's had a dick pic yet and that's why he's in such a flap? No, I digress), now my hangover has subsided, I have come up with a list of excellent and improving New Year's resolutions, which I am definitely going to stick to this year. I shall be forty in a few short months and I need to learn to be a grown-up. Forty-year-olds do not climb atop their rickety pianos and perform lewd dance routines to 'Patricia the Stripper' (even though it is actually quite challenging to dance on an upright piano). Forty-year-olds are Proper People. With that in mind, this year I shall:

Learn French. Proper French, with a French accent, enabling me to converse eloquently, beyond my current limits of '*Je voudrais aller le discotheque'*. I am thirty-nine; that is too old to tell people that I like to go to the discotheque in any language.

I will also read interesting novels in the original French, perhaps while reclining upon a *chaise longue*. *Madame Bovary* was a good French book, and also very saucy. Actually, have I read *Madame Bovary*, or did I just watch the rude TV series where people kept shagging in a forest? I will read *Madame Bovary*, in French. Or at least in English.

I will also force the children to learn French with me, and once a week we will have French Night, like in the Chalet School books, where we only speak to each other in French, saying things like '*Voulez vous passez le petit pois, s'il vous plait?*' On these nights, I will be sure to invite the children of the Coven for tea, so they go home and report how cosmopolitan and intelligent we are, and the Coven mummies will feel a bit inadequate, despite their perfect Pinterest boards and their #soblessed Instagram feeds. Ha!

Get a different job. I do get to mess about a lot at work, but the actual job part of it is very dull. Simon says all jobs are dull and I'm lucky to have a job I can fit around the children, but I would like to do something exciting and fun that challenges me creatively.

Simon says, 'Wouldn't we all, my love, please stop being such a pretentious twat,' but it's all right for him, titting about being an architect, leaving his genius behind him for posterity, or at least a few years, though he seems unconvinced by his great legacy of office conversions and blocks of city centre apartments.

Along with being a clever and creative app developer, I am thinking of becoming a social media entrepreneur. I have no idea what this means, but I keep reading about people who claim it as their job description. Perhaps the first part of the resolution should actually be 'find out what a social media entrepreneur is'?

I am also going to properly pursue promoting my app and making some money out of it. I was pleased to see this morning that 100 people have now bought it, which means I have pretty much broken even. Pure profit from here on in! Between that and the social media entrepreneurship, I shall be a millionaire soon.

Drink less wine. Instead of buying a cart full of anything on special offer, I shall visit quirky independent wine merchants and buy one or two bottles of high-quality wine, which I shall sip on reflectively, savouring each delicious mouthful.

It will probably be French wine, to reflect my newfound sophistication and elegance. Anyway, I will be too busy with learning French and becoming an app mogul/social media entrepreneur to get shit-faced on supermarket Pinot Grigio anymore. I simply will not have the time to spend my evenings watching soaps; dicking about on Facebook and necking cheap wine in a vain attempt to dull the ringing in my ears from the incessant witterings of the children and also to silence the nagging fear that everybody else seems to have a much better life than me. Anyway, the children will not be wittering anymore, they shall be uttering cultured observations on life, in French.

Be nicer to Simon. We shall schedule time for each other and go on Date Nights, where we shall discuss art and politics and not whether it was him or one of the children who left a big poo in the lavatory and did not flush it.

We shall walk hand in hand by moonlit rivers and remember that we are soulmates. I will not call him an annoying twat or a fuckwit (to his face anyway) and I will make more of an effort and wear matching underwear often enough that he no longer assumes that because for once I am wearing a bra and panties in vaguely the same colour, he must be 'in there'. I shall appreciate all the many nice, kind and generous things he does for the children and me, and not just focus on the annoying things. I will not sulk when we have a row and make him be the first one to apologise, even when I'm in the wrong. Anyway, with my new mature and responsible approach to our relationship, we probably won't even have rows anymore. Perhaps we shall have 'family meetings' instead, where we take it in turns to air our small dissatisfactions in an adult way without apportioning blame and work together to find resolutions, rather than hurling the cookie tin at his head because he asked me once again if there 'was a reason' why the oven was on, when any blithering idiot could see that the oven was on to COOK HIS BLOODY DINNER!

Politics. I shall learn all about this. Not only British politics, but world politics.

I will understand the American political system; I will know the difference between the French Prime Minister and President; I will find out who is in charge of Spain (do they still have a king? Or is that Portugal?).

I will also look up where is Spain and where is Portugal, so I know where people are going on vacation. There will be no repeat of the unfortunate time that I thought Cologne was in France (which is, frankly, an easy mistake to make. Why would you have 'eau de cologne' if Cologne is in Germany? Why wouldn't it be called something German?).

Not only will I learn who is in the Cabinet, I will also know who is in the Shadow Cabinet. I will stop reading the *Mail Online*, especially the Sidebar of Shame, and I will read improving newspapers like the *Guardian* and the *New Statesman*. I will become a caring, compassionate and informed person.

TV. BBC2 and BBC4 only. Also, Sky Arts.

There will be no more binge-watching soap operas. *Game of Thrones* is probably okay because I saw somewhere that there are a lot of political analogies, so I could still watch that as part of my politics resolution – but only for the analogies and not for the dragons and the shagging and my weird fixation with Jaqen H'ghar.

I will also strictly limit the children's screentime. By which I mean actually limit it and not pretend not to know they are still watching Netflix in their rooms after I've made them turn the TV off. It will be CBBC only for them, especially *Newsround*.

Children. I will do interesting and educational activities with them, and I will not shout at them or tell them they are stupid, EVEN when they glue their hands to the table during the interesting and educational activities.

I will also read up on better ways to resolve conflict between them when they try to kill each other, instead of just howling 'For the love of God, will you stop fucking fighting! I don't CARE who started it, just bloody stop it NOW!'

I will listen to their thoughts and feelings and emotions that led up to them trying to twat each other around the head with an iPad and I will quietly explain to them why that is not acceptable behaviour, while helping them to explore different ways to express their frustrations. Possibly through the medium of interpretive dance.

Money. I will be sensible about money. I will not bury my head in the sand and pretend that credit cards are free money. I will log on each week to our accounts and keep a note of how much we are spending, and I will attempt to reduce our debts. I will do this quite soon, because I screwed up the courage earlier to look at the credit card account and then had to immediately shut it down in horror, and then had to open it up to look again, because I was hoping it must've been a mistake, we couldn't have spent that much over Christmas? But it appeared we had. I will also tell Simon about this very, very soon and we will deal with it like responsible and mature adults.

What else? Oh yes, get thin, obviously. That's on pretty much every woman's resolution list, isn't it? Get thin, and get fit. Ideally,

I will get thin enough that people will talk about me behind my back and say things like, 'I think she's actually a bit *too* thin now', but I would settle for just thinner generally.

I have just read over all my resolutions. They are very good resolutions but they are possibly going to turn me into the smuggest, most annoying twat of all time. Anyway, it is too late to start today, and there still some wine left. It is best I finish up the bargain wine before I start on the grown-up wine resolution, because the children keep waving posters from school in my face about reducing wastage, which is what I will be doing by drinking the wine.

I will finish up the cheap Chardonnay and just have a little stalk on Facebook, but only of the more worthy people who share all the *Guardian* articles, to introduce me to my new world of informed political stances.

I wonder what 'Fuck My Life' is in French?

Wednesday, 13 January

Simon has seen the credit card bill. It was inevitable really, in this day and age, it's not like Mum used to be able to hide the bills from Dad by shoving them under the mattress, though he would always find them, too, and then there would be a row much along the lines of the one Simon and I just had.

It was fairly standard actually. The size of the bill and amount of money spent were entirely my fault, because I was the one who had bought most of the stuff. Simon conveniently ignored the fact that this was because I had done all the food shopping and bought all the presents, most of them for his wretched family and his sexually incontinent sister's ever-increasing tribe of unwashed brats. Describing Louisa and her family like that was possibly a mistake, as Simon is allowed to criticise his sister, but I am not, unless he has opened the proceedings.

Finally Simon roared, 'For fuck's sake, Ellen, how are we ever going to get ourselves on a sound financial footing if you keep spending money like this? I am working flat out to provide for you and you just fritter money away.'

There were so many things I could've said to this. Like how *I* wasn't the one who'd had five years of student loans to pay off after university. Like how when we first graduated, and indeed for some time after we got married, I had actually earned considerably more than him. Like how the *only* reason I work part-time now is to look after his children and if I am frittering money away, what the fuck is he doing with all his sodding gadgets and power tools that he never actually uses?

I didn't, though. I tried to be positive. I said, 'It's not that bad, Simon. We just need to economise for a bit, that's all. And maybe my app will –'

'Jesus, Ellen, shut up about your fucking app, all right? How many have you sold? A hundred? Or have you gone global and reached the heady heights of two hundred yet? Your precious app is not going to get us out of this financial hole, okay? At least I am trying to save money. I have ordered some smart light bulbs that will use much less electricity and energy meters to monitor how much electricity we are using.'

'Oh right! Right. Fucking marvellous, Simon, just fucking marvellous. You always have to be the smug, sanctimonious arsehole, don't you? It's all MY fault we've no money, you tell me, while informing me of how YOU are economising by SPENDING MORE MONEY!'

'I wasn't the one who spent a fortune on Christmas, Ellen. That's all I'm saying. If you could just plan ahead a bit better, and shop around for better value, I'm sure we wouldn't have needed to spend nearly so much. If you would just organise your life, things would be much easier. And yes, my light bulbs will save us money in the long run, actually, so they're an investment, unlike you spending £180 in some health food shop. On what? What do you even buy in a shop like that? Lentils? Only you could be so fucking profligate to spend that much on lentils when we don't even eat lentils!'

'It was your bastarding sister that spent that! Because she's such a special snowflake that she can't be expected to eat my toxin-loaded supermarket food. And the other reason why the bills were so high over Christmas is because we had EIGHT EXTRA PEOPLE TO FEED FOR A WEEK! Which is not cheap, because I'M NOT THE MESSIAH, SIMON, I CAN'T ACTUALLY FEED THE FIVE FUCKING THOUSAND ON FIVE LOAVES AND TWO FISHES, and even if I could, your sodding sister would turn up her nose at it because it wasn't organic, gluten-free or FUCKING VEGAN! Ditto, unfortunately I can't turn water into wine to satiate her endless thirst nor my own need to anesthetise myself against all her bullshit. And when exactly am I supposed to trail around six different supermarkets so I can get 5p off a bag of carrots and then go to another shop for the potatoes because they are 10p cheaper? Tell me that? I work; I look after your fucking children; I clean this house; I cook, and what do you do? You work one day more than me and apparently that means that you get to spend all weekend sitting on your arse while I still run around after the children and cook and clean and do the laundry, while you do exactly fuck all squared to help me –'

'Oh, well, I'm very sorry that I'm too tired after working a sixty-hour week to do the dusting, darling!' spat Simon. 'I'm very fucking sorry that I had the nerve to ask for a bit of time for myself, and while you're blaming MY family for the expense of Christmas, can I remind you that YOUR family came too?'

I wanted to kill him. I actually had visions dancing through my head of how immensely satisfying it would be to hit him over the head with Peter's cricket bat and then bury him in a shallow grave in the woods. Or maybe I could use a frozen leg of lamb like in that *Tales of the Unexpected* story? I didn't have any lamb in the freezer, though. There was a big piece of brisket, I wondered if that would do? Probably not, you probably need something like a leg of lamb to get a good swing on it – with brisket you'd probably need to get them on the ground first and it would be more like trying to bash their head in with a rock. Instead of murdering him, I took a deep breath and said, 'Simon, do you remember the pigeon?'

'What the fuck are you on about now?' said Simon. 'I'm trying to talk about saving money and sorting our lives out and you are wittering on about pigeons?'

'It doesn't matter. Forget it. Just fuck off and leave me alone, since everything's all my fault, like usual. I'll just start shopping in frozen-food shops, will that make you happy? Frozen lamb? Hmm?'

He's right about one thing, though. What's the point in constantly checking for emails to see if another ten apps have sold? It's never going to happen, despite me sending it off to various websites that review and recommend apps. It was a stupid idea.

We are not speaking now, after the row. Well, *I* am not speaking to him and I am mainly relying on flouncing round the house and slamming doors and passively aggressively crashing round the kitchen to prove my point. I have a horrible feeling that despite the door slamming and passive aggression he is quite enjoying the peace and quiet. Maybe I should start speaking to him again, just to spite him. Ha! It is very difficult to keep up anyway, when every fibre of my body is screaming 'AND ANOTHER THING …'

Saturday, 16 January

In an effort to avoid Simon, because I am Still Not Speaking To Him, I decided to take Peter and Jane on an outing to a free art gallery and museum. This trip had two advantages: firstly, not having to look at fucking Simon and hear him tutting if he discovered a tub of houmous with a smear left at the bottom that went out of date yesterday, and thus having to endure another of his lectures on 'wastage', and secondly, being free, it was an excellent way of demonstrating my great frugality and fiscal prudence.

In a further attempt at economy, I also decided we would not drive my gas-guzzling SUV into town and then pay a king's ransom to park; we would get the bus, which would be both cheap and fun.

Using public transport regularly instead of driving would also mean that we were not straying into the Perfect Atkinsons' territory, as Lucy's Perfect Mummy once told me that they have a 'Public Transport Day' each year, when they leave the Range Rover Overfinch at home and pick a destination and then have to work out how to get there and back by only using public transport. This is, Lucy's Mummy informed me, 'tremendous fun'.

Unfortunately, it turned out the bus cost a bloody fortune and it would probably have been cheaper driving. The free museum and art gallery is crammed to the rafters with treasures and artefacts from the four corners of the earth but Peter and Jane only wanted to look at the dinosaur poo, and pay the obligatory visit to the Egyptian Room, as it is the law that at any given time when you have primary school age children at least one of them will be doing a project on the Egyptians.

Afterwards I dragged them to look at the Art. They were underwhelmed, until they found a nude, at which point they sniggered and pointed and then, unable to contain themselves any longer, burst out with 'BUTT! BOOBIES!' and cackled loudly.

'Stop being so childish!' I hissed, to which they replied in confusion, 'But Mummy, we *are* children? How do we stop being childish?'

My attempt to refresh my mind and soul by standing in silent contemplation of the Impressionists was rather spoiled by Peter standing behind me chanting 'Butts butts butts, I want to see more butts', and the always worrying realisation that Jane was silent. A small part of me hoped that she was dumbstruck by the beauty around her, but in my heart I know her better than that, and in fact she had sidled into the next room and found a cabinet of rare and priceless jewellery and was trying to work out how to pick the lock.

In fairness, I wasn't too devastated by the children's distractions as I have spent a lot of time in my life standing in art galleries, trying to 'feel', to absorb and drink in and understand art, but mostly I only feel self-conscious and awkward, but having stopped, I have to stand for a suitable amount of time before walking on, in case people judge me and think me a philistine for not showing suitable appreciation – a bit like when you realise you are walking in the wrong direction and you can't just turn around and walk the other way, because then People Will Know, so instead you have to pretend to go into a shop and then come back out and go the right way.

I caved after that and took them to the gift shop like they had been asking me to ever since we arrived. I still refused to shell out £35.99 for a ballerina umbrella for Jane, even though it was now in the sale reduced to a mere £22.99.

The bus on the way home was a double decker and I made the mistake of sitting upstairs on the basis it would be 'fun'. I have not been upstairs on a bus since they stopped you smoking on buses.

It was not 'fun', it was very loud with screaming teenagers excitedly Snapchatting each other and then discussing the messages they'd just sent across the bus at the tops of their voices with much squealing and shrieking. On the plus side, they drowned out the noise of Peter and Jane squabbling about how the other was cheating at I Spy.

I had forgotten what a wonderful view the top deck of a bus affords into other people's homes and lives, though. It was dark by then, and the houses were lit up as people came home, and I watched all the scenes passing – the couple standing in the kitchen, chopping things for dinner, a woman in her sitting room with a glass of wine and a magazine, an empty room, full of books and paintings, with a fire lit, the occupants obviously about to come in and fling themselves down on one of those big squashy sofas.

It always astounds me, passing all these houses, all these windows, that behind every one of those front doors is a story; a family that think and feel and shout and argue and eat pasta and watch TV, just like we do. Do people think the same when they pass my house? Do they look in my windows and see a nice house, a woman who has everything she could want, two beautiful children and a husband who loves her?

That's what I see, through all those windows – the good stories. The couple are cooking in companionable quiet, not silent and tense-jawed, chopping aggressively after a massive row as she wonders whether to dice the onion or plunge the knife through his heart. The woman with the wine is enjoying a well-earned bit of me-time after a busy day in her glamorous job, not drinking herself to oblivion to try to forget the fact that her married lover has decided to go back to his wife. That empty room is waiting to welcome a loving family for a convivial evening, it's not empty because someone has gone into the hall to answer a phone call bringing them terrible news.

When people pass my house, they don't see a woman who wonders if she has made the right choices in life, who is sure she is a terrible parent, who doesn't know if her husband loves her anymore – because he certainly doesn't seem to like her very much right now and they barely talk or have anything in common these days – and who doesn't know how long she can keep plastering on the bright smile that says to the outside world that everything is fine, it's *fine*, it's all marvellous, before she cries drunkenly into the dog's ears because nobody understands her.

Or maybe it's all much more ordinary than that. Maybe the couple just have nothing more to say to each other as he wishes he had bought a sports car and toured the South of France instead of spending all their money on a ludicrous wedding and a mortgage they can't afford, and she thinks about the boy who once kissed her on a beach on the Mull of Kintyre. I wish I could remember that boy's name, as that kiss was possibly the second most intensely romantic moment of my life.

Simon was responsible for the most romantic gesture anyone has ever made for me, and also the most ridiculous. We were in Edinburgh, we hadn't been going out for very long and we were walking through a park when we saw these pretty pink pigeons pottering around on the path in front of us. I was quite delighted by the notion of pink pigeons (at a distance), so when Simon said 'We've got some of those at home,' I exclaimed, 'How lovely! Bring me one next time you go home, I want a pink pigeon.'

We carried on our way and I forgot all about the pink pigeons. A few weeks later, Simon went home for some family celebration. We weren't at that stage where I was invited as well, so I stayed in Edinburgh and probably went out and got drunk.

On Sunday night, Simon appeared at my flat, clutching a cardboard box and insisting I come outside. He hustled me into the gardens of the square opposite and handed me the box. He was grinning like a little boy on Christmas morning, he was so very pleased and proud of himself.

I opened the box, screamed at the top of my lungs, dropped it and fled.

Simon had gone and caught a pink pigeon from the dovecote at his grandmother's house, brought it on the train with him all the way from Hampshire (getting very odd looks when he opened the box to give it food and water) and finally lugged the sodding thing halfway across Edinburgh to give to me, because I had once expressed a whim for a pink pigeon.

Poor Simon was not to know then that I am utterly phobic of birds and moths and bats and anything else that flaps or flutters, and short of Gwyneth Paltrow's head, literally the worst thing I could possibly open a box to find was an irate pigeon. I screamed so much people thought he was trying to mug me and a homeless person kindly tried to perform a Citizen's Arrest.

It was the single most lovely thing anyone has ever done for me, and once everything had calmed down, I had stopped screaming and Simon had been released from the headlock, the pigeon had flown off (and Simon had assured me that it was definitely a homing pigeon and it would be fine, so that I would stop crying about the poor, lonely, country pigeon all by itself in the big city, because just because I am shit scared of pigeons didn't mean I wasn't worried about the horrible, flappy, terrifying bastard), then, with dusk falling in an Edinburgh garden, Simon put his arms round me and told me he loved me for the first time. (What he actually said was 'I love you, even though you are crazy', but we will leave that last bit out for the sake of the story.)

Now he moans if I ask him to bring the washing in. I don't think he'd bring me a pigeon again.

FML, these January blues are a killer. No wonder people say public transport is depressing.

Sunday, 17 January

I was looking through old photos today, pretending I was sorting them out, but actually I was just rifling through them and marvelling at how young we all were. There was a terrible one of Hannah and me at a Vicars and Tarts party, dressed up as slutty vicars in dog collars with fishnet stockings and suspenders and far too much burgundy nineties' lipstick.

I think that was the night I broke my wrist while being spun enthusiastically round the dance floor and I refused to go to hospital dressed as a tarty vicar for fear of what they would think, so instead I self-medicated heavily with cheap gin and woke up with an agonising wrist and a very bad hangover. It might have been a different night, though – there were an awful lot of Vicars and Tarts parties back then.

What happened to Vicars and Tarts? Was it just a flash-in-the-pan nineties' thing, or are they still going on amongst younger, cooler people than us sad old farts? For a moment I thought I should have a Vicars and Tarts party, maybe for my fortieth, but then I realised that it was not the easiest look to pull off when one was nineteen and lithe and slender let alone now, after two children and too many chips. The flab oozing through the fishnets would not be a good look. Most of us would have to go as portly bishops now. Even back then it was galling how the boys would borrow my slutty dresses and hot pants and (from the back anyway) look so much better in them than me – even then I struggled somewhat with my 'curves' and was only as slim as I was due to mainly living on cheap white wine, vodka and Diet Coke, an endless supply of Marlboro Lights (God, I wish I could afford to smoke that much now) and the occasional pizza on my way home from clubbing.

Then I started looking through photos of Simon and me,

from the obligatory photo-booth strips to parties with me striking silly poses and Simon being Mr Cool behind me, but always with his arms around me. And then I got onto our wedding photos and I started crying, partly because we were so young and full of hope and looked so happy and partly because my dress was so awful.

Seriously, *what* was I thinking? Mile upon mile of stiff, shiny, white taffeta, puffed sleeves (*très* Anne of Green Gables), the odd ruffle and flounce. Given the eighties had been over for some time when we got married, I still wouldn't have looked out of place in *Dynasty*. The only consolation was Hannah's equally awful bridesmaid dress.

Simon, the bastard, got to be all timeless classic elegance in a suit, which frankly is just unfair, like how boys get to buy one dinner suit that lasts their whole lives provided they don't get too fat (which in fairness, Simon hasn't), whereas women are supposed to have a different dress for every 'do' they go to, and heaven forbid if someone else should turn up in the same dress as you, even though the men are all dressed identically.

I was still sniffling a bit and muttering to myself about double standards while trying to find Hannah's and my first ball photos, because if my wedding dress was bad, my first ball gown back in the early nineties was truly the stuff of nightmares – emerald-green, be-ruffled and be-bowed taffeta with a bolero jacket (what has happened to taffeta, while we are on the subject – has it gone the same way as the Vicars and Tarts parties?) when Simon came into the bedroom and saw I had been crying.

They say women marry their fathers, and certainly my dad and Simon's most striking characteristic in common is their inability to cope with emotional women. My father used to deal with this by offering us money to stop crying, which Jessica and I soon worked out was an excellent source of revenue in our teenage years – a wobbling lip was worth at least £5, but if you

could squeeze out some actual tears, you were in for £10, sometimes even twenty if you could manage a few sobs. We didn't
even need to come up with a reason why we were crying, we
could just wail we were sooooo saaaaaad about the divorce and
the resulting emotional blackmail would open his wallet even
wider. Jessica used to put half her windfalls in her savings
account and use half to buy Savings Bonds, whereas I used to
spend mine on vodka, cigarettes and clubbing. This difference in
our fiscal prudence is possibly why Jessica now has a big house,
lots of money and a proper pension and I cannot afford the
Botox I need for all the lines round my mouth caused by years
of smoking.

Simon's approach to crying women is sadly less generous, he
tends to just hide in his shed until such a time as he thinks the
storm has passed, so I was surprised when he carried on into the
room and sat down on the bed. I assumed he had come in to
pack, as he is leaving tomorrow on a work trip for a week, and I
was braced for him to start moaning about the mess of photos
over the floor.

Instead he picked up a photo of us together, the background
too dark to make out if we were in a pub or at a party. I am
laughing up at him and he is looking down at me in a way that
he hasn't looked at me in a long time.

'God, we were so young!' he said.

'Too young,' I said coldly, because I was still pissed off about
the fight the other night.

'Do you think? I do remember the pigeon by the way. I don't
think it's possible to transport a pigeon 500 miles in a cardboard
box, including across London on the Underground, and forget
the experience.'

This did make me laugh, despite myself.

'I'm sorry,' he said. 'I don't want to go away with things like
this between us.'

I was still very, very angry with him, but it was hard to stay that way when there were all the photos spread over the floor of us looking so happy (and thin), and anyway, he had apologised first, so technically, I had won the argument. I didn't say that, obviously, tempting though it was. But I knew that he knew that I knew I had won.

It was probably a bad start to the resolution about having a mature relationship and discussing things like adults, but I still maintain he was in the wrong and so I was totally justified in not apologising first this time. Even so, I do love him really. Apart from when I am fantasising about shallow graves in the woods, obviously.

FEBRUARY

Monday, 1 February

Sam is in luuuuuuurrrrrrrve. If Sam was any more of a besotted teenage girl he would be writing into a problem page and asking how he could tell if a boy liked him or not. His current dilemma, which he spent twenty minutes debating after school this afternoon and then continued via group texts to Hannah and me, is whether or not he should celebrate the one-month anniversary of his first date with Mark in a couple of days, or whether he should hang on and go all out for Valentine's Day. He literally shoe-horns Mark's name into every conversation, it's so sweet. I wouldn't be the slightest bit surprised if he has been practising signing his name 'Sam Evans' and doing that sum where you add up all the letters in your names to work out your 'compatibility'.

Hannah, meanwhile, has decided that if Sam can find love again after the cheating pig rat Robin, then maybe she too should dabble in the dating pond again (her analogy, not mine, personally all I could think of was pond scum when she described it thus).

Anyway, she has discovered a nice, middle-class website where your friends describe what a fabulous person you are and why people should want to date you, and has decided that it is a much better bet, because the men on there don't look the dick-pic sort. Sam snorted at this and said all men are the dick-pic sort given half a chance, and Hannah took umbrage.

Poor Hannah, I really hope she knows what she's doing. She definitely deserves somebody lovely, unlike dastardly bastardly Dan the Dick, but I'm not sure meeting men online is right for her. She has at least asked me to write her 'blurb' for the website, though I am not entirely certain what I should put: 'I've known Hannah since we were eleven. Be nice to her and don't send her photos of your penis, or I will find you and chop it off.' Too much?

'I've known Hannah for many years. She likes cheese and wine and films and having a laugh with friends. She enjoys reading and travelling and spending time with her family. She is a lovely person with a positive personality.' Too bloody bland. That could be anybody. Oh God, this is much harder than it looks.

'Hannah is great fun.' Nope. I'll be describing her as 'zany' or 'madcap' next. Maybe I shouldn't try so hard to 'sell' her?

'Hannah is kind, loyal and loving.' Hannah apparently is a Golden Retriever now. Who knew writing a short paragraph about why someone should shag your best friend would be so hard? Maybe I should just go up to some bloke at the bar next time we're out and tap him on the shoulder and say 'My mate's really into you, do you want to snog her?' like we did when we were about fourteen.

I wonder if fourteen-year-olds still snog, or by that stage have they moved on to making hardcore pornos? I have all this joy to come with Peter and Jane. Mind you, I'm not sure Jane will ever find someone brave enough to shag her, and I pity any boy brave enough to try to sext her, as she will probably stab them through the heart or at the very least shove their phone where the sun doesn't shine. She is still traumatised from the 'how babies are made' talk and DVD at school and has frequently announced that she is Never Ever Doing 'That', so hopefully she will stick to her guns once those teenage hormones hit.

When it comes to Peter, though, I can see visits from angry fathers objecting to him besmirching the honour of their maiden daughters. Peter has been a shameless man whore since he was a baby; Simon is still traumatised by the time when a toddler Peter leaned out of the shopping cart in the supermarket and pinched a lady's bottom, and the lady, understandably, thought Simon had done it and threatened to call the police. Simon still cites this incident as the reason why he can't be expected to take the children with him if he has to go to the shops, even though these days Peter is more likely to just fart and then cackle as the whole aisle gags. Anyway, back to Hannah's sales pitch.

'Hannah is lovely. She is warm and funny; a great mum and a good friend. She deserves to meet a man as wonderful as she is. Who won't show her his dick before he has even met her.' Maybe not the last line. Oh God, it will do. I have been reading other people's descriptions for inspiration and they all say pretty much the same thing. Everyone is interested in travel and reading, even if the closest they've come to either is perusing a Chinese takeout menu.

Apparently they are all wonderful people who only drink socially (obviously, who is going to put 'functioning alcoholic' or 'I enjoy sitting alone, wearing only my stained underpants and guzzling cheap vodka until I pass out'?) and are looking for someone 'special'.

I do think Hannah is incredibly brave to be doing this. Simon might get on my tits sometimes but I don't think I could face trawling through thousands of men trying to work out from one tiny photo if they look like my soulmate, and wondering if they describe themselves as 'cuddly' if that actually means they are really fat, or if they describe themselves as 'athletic' does that mean they are just showing off or would they actually be expecting me to do sporty things, too?

Simon, God love him, has never expected me to be sporty. I did join a gym once, when the children were very small, which was more to take advantage of the crèche they offered than a burning desire to get my figure back. For a while, though, I actually went to some classes and got quite fit. I rather loved a kick-boxing class, which was very good for taking out any pent-up rage and frustration on a punchbag, though apparently you weren't meant to announce you were picturing your husband's face as you battered seven bells out of it.

The thin end of wedge for the gym was when I went to an awful class where you had to try to balance on a wobbly board and do various exercises. The class was taken by a very over-muscled man in an unfeasibly small undershirt who kept caressing his own biceps in a most disturbing way.

Apparently, though, I was the only one not gripped by lust for his oiled pecs, as all the other women in the class were in full makeup and frantically batting their false eyelashes at him and trying to get his attention. I was in my trusty old baggy t-shirt and leggings, and was so appallingly bad at the class that he spent most of it trying to show me what to do, to the outrage of the Lycra-clad gym bunnies.

The final nail in the coffin of my fitness, though, was when I went to a 'core' class, where they made us kneel on those giant bouncy balls. I insisted I could not possibly do this, the instructor insisted everyone could, it was easy.

It was not easy. I managed to wobble on top of the ball for a microsecond before I fell off, but somehow I didn't just collapse to the ground, instead I flew across the room at high speed, before I collided with a pillar and slid to the floor, somewhat dazed.

Everyone saw. Many people rushed to assist as I woozily scrambled to my feet, insisting, 'Fine, I'm fine, ha ha ha, no, absolutely fine!' and limped out of the room to grab the children from the crèche and flee, never to return again.

I kept paying the membership for another six months, though, so they wouldn't guess I was too embarrassed to return, until Simon objected to the waste of money and made me cancel it. Now the sportiest thing I do is run around looking for the bastard dog when he does a bunk after rabbits.

Of course, the lack of sportiness is another reason why I don't think I could put myself out there like that. I just couldn't take my clothes off in front of someone else, not after having two children and gaining rather more pounds than I care to think about.

Simon saw the stretch marks as they appeared, and the changes (ravages) of pregnancy and child birth and eleventy billion chocolate cookies on my body, and he was partially responsible for them (maybe not the cookie bits, in fairness), but how could I just whip my clothes off in front of anyone else and go 'Ta daaaaa!', after almost twenty years of no one but Simon and medical professionals seeing any of my bits in all their glory?

I should really stick better to my resolution to be nicer to Simon. He has never once grumbled that I am no longer a lithe and youthful sexpot; he laughs and tells me he thinks I am gorgeous when I grumble about how fat I am or obsess over the horrible stretch marks, and if he doesn't bring me flowers very often, he does bring me a lot of cups of tea, which, to be honest, are probably more welcome. And if he spends too much time in that bloody shed, or filling my house with pointless gadgets that he claims save time and effort but actually waste time and effort, with the trouble of finding the right remote or app that controls them, well, that's got to be better than him being out shagging other people and breaking my heart, like Sam and Hannah's horrible exes.

Tuesday, 9 February – Pancake Day

There are pancakes on the ceiling. There are pancakes on the floor. There are pancakes on the dog. I watched YouTube tutorials on tossing pancakes for an hour last night. A whole sodding hour. For this.

Admittedly, declaring I would have a pancake party and inviting Sam's children round after school as well was perhaps overstretching myself somewhat, but how can a few pancakes go so far? My cunning plan was I could call the pancakes crepes and it would be one step closer to my 'learning French and becoming a cultured and sophisticated international style person' plan (apparently 'fuck my life' in French is '*baise ma vie*'. I think I prefer 'FML' as 'BMV' sounds like something catching).

Unfortunately, my crepes were another reminder of why I don't cook with the children, as Sophie and Jane carefully sifted flour all over the floor and then Peter and Toby managed to break five eggs and not get a single one in the bowl. So, after innumerable attempts at making the batter, there were no more eggs or milk and I snatched the bowl off the children and threw it all in the KitchenAid and hoped for the best.

The best was still rather lumpy, but I ladled it into the frying pan nonetheless, where obviously the first three pancakes stuck, probably due to me casually disregarding the stern instructions from 'celebrity chefs' that one absolutely *must* buy a special frying pan for one's pancakes, available from their selected supermarket of choice for a very reasonably enormous sum of money.

Eventually I scraped something semi-edible out of the pan, and once the children had finished fighting like a pack of rabid dogs over it, they pointed out that I was not *tossing* the pancakes, merely turning them with a spatula and obviously this was completely wrong, and I must try to toss them.

As the tossing had been the subject of all those YouTube videos last night, I decided to give it a go, but it was my poor tossing technique that was responsible for the pancakes stuck to the ceiling. Meanwhile, the children insisted they could do better, and thus their tossing attempts resulted in the pancakes splattered all over the floor and my poor dog, who was somewhat nonplussed.

Sam, as ever, tried to be a good sport when he arrived to pick up his cherubs and found them so liberally coated in flour, eggs and batter that you could be forgiven for thinking I had planned to deep-fry them, like some sort of high-calorie version of the Hansel and Gretel witch.

Sunday, 14 February – Valentine's Day

Ah, and they say romance is dead! It is dead here anyway. Simon has always refused to participate in Valentine's Day as it is also his birthday. Apparently his mother was quite keen to call him Valentine but luckily his father talked her out of it. I am not sure I could have married a man called Valentine. Does that make me shallow? No, probably not: a boy named Valentine would probably of necessity grow up into a very different person to one with a sensible name like Simon.

I am not desperately keen on Valentine's Day myself, as for me it still carries with it the tang of desperation of going to an all-girls school and having to slouch in on the morning of Valentine's Day pretending you had left before the post had come, while all the swishy-haired, blonde popular girls (who would inevitably grow up to be School Playground Bloody Perfect Coven sorts) waltzed about fluttering their sheaves of cards and, if they were in possession of a boyfriend, a nasty, cellophane-wrapped single rose.

Somehow I never ever managed to have a boyfriend for Valentine's Day, or even a secret admirer. Some of the girls got Valentines from their fathers, and I was never sure if this was better or worse than not getting any at all – my father certainly had no truck with such notions.

My first year at university, though, I got no less than four Valentines! I was delighted. I swished my hair and I waltzed with glee. I was a popular person. I would find true love. The next year I got some, too, but by the next Valentine's Day I was going out with Simon, and since then the only Valentine's card I have received was made by Jane at playgroup. It was very sweet, they posted them out to all the mummies and Simon was quite outraged at the thought of me having an admirer, until I explained where it had come from. I wasn't sure whether I was flattered that he was jealous or insulted that he was so surprised someone might have sent me a card.

This year, though, I have the joys of dealing with Peter and Jane's respective takes on Valentine's Day, as well as various melt-downs from Sam. Peter has declared his undying love for Poppy Hodgkins, an overly perky little girl who reeks of synthetic strawberries ('She smells lovely!' says Peter staunchly), who I suspect will grow up to be a complete ho-bag, but Peter none-theless has given her a Valentine's card and asked her to be his girlfriend. Poppy is 'thinking about it' (tart).

Jane, meanwhile, was appalled and incensed that Freddie Dawkins had the temerity to give her a card (none of them seem to have really grasped the concept of Valentine's cards being anonymous), because Freddie is, in Jane's words, 'a stinky, ginger, speccy four eyes'.

I have tried to tell Jane that she shouldn't judge people on their appearances and Freddie is probably a lovely boy, but the truth is that he *is* a most unfortunate-looking child, with more than a whiff of stale cabbage about him and a very odd manner that makes me suspect his true path in life will involve burying people in shallow graves in the woods.

It's likely that Jane has not helped Freddie's social awkwardness and possibly will be the catalyst that leads him to embark on a lifetime of dysfunctional relationships at the very least, as apparently her reaction to his card was to tear it into tiny pieces and stomp on it (and his heart) in front of everyone. Unlike Poppy Hodgkins' parents, I definitely don't think we need to worry about teenage pregnancy being an issue with Jane.

Sam, meanwhile, is trying to cook a romantic meal for Mark, and it is all going wrong. Finally, after the seventeenth anguished text because his Coquilles St Jacques had gone awry, I told him to just call UberEATS and get dinner delivered and hide the evidence. It's what I did for Simon's birthday dinner, as he refuses point-blank to venture into the world on Valentine's Day, but it gives me a night off from cooking while he thinks I have lovingly prepared a gourmet meal for him.

Simon has spent the day oblivious to his children's emotional anguish because he was busy playing happily with his birthday presents. Simon and I agreed long ago that I would stop buying him presents because Simon is a bloody picky bastard, and if something is not exactly the thing he wants, it is dead to him. Which would be absolutely fine, if he would only return the offending gift to the shop and get a refund, or the thing he *did* want, but he refuses, instead putting whatever it is aside and insisting that no, it is *fine*, yes he likes it, no, no need to exchange it, while it lies, unloved and never touched again.

So when offered the choice of having the expensive watches, shirts, scarves and gadgets I have bought him over the years shoved up his arse or buying his own present and giving it to me to wrap up for him, he chose the latter.

I still buy him the odd bottle of posh gin or cashmere scarf to make it feel like I've made an effort, which I then steal back for myself, so it's win-win for everybody. This year he has gone for a variety of little black boxes to plug into the TV so we have even more remote controls to lose, thus making turning on the TV a NASA-esque challenge, and a jig saw, to keep the holy mitre saw company and make Simon feel manly and Bardo even more envious next time he visits.

The lengthy argument with my precious moppets over why they really did have to go to bed and were not staying up to join us for our romantic meal unfortunately led me to have a bit too much of Simon's birthday gin while I was lovingly reheating his thoughtfully pre-ordered dinner, and so it was that I gazed into his eyes over the tiramisu and said, 'Do you remember the first time I cooked you dinner, darling?'

'Of course,' said Simon. 'How could I forget?'

I glowed. 'It took me ages. And it made such a mess, I don't know what on earth possessed me to think that making spinach and ricotta "pancake cannelloni" was a good idea.'

Simon said. 'That isn't what you made, the first time you cooked me dinner.'

I grew slightly shrill with indignation that he did not, in fact, remember the first time I cooked for him.

'I DID! They were incredibly fiddly, but I made them especially, because you were a vegetarian then.'

'I don't know who you made that for, it sounds disgusting. Not me anyway, because I've never been a vegetarian. And the first time you made me dinner was unforgettable because you had tried to brown meat on the stove in a Pyrex dish which exploded, and when I arrived, your kitchen was full of firemen and broken glass and you were having hysterics.'

Ooooh, awkward. Who on earth did I make those pancakes for then? (Simon's right, they were pretty grim – very soggy as I recall.)

'Oh. Yes. That does ring a bell.'

'And then the next time you tried to make me dinner, you managed not to involve the fire brigade, but you'd tried to roast the wrong cut of lamb and it was inedible. At the time I think you were the only person I knew who could cock up any recipe. And then you got a copy of *The River Café Cook Book* and life became much less dangerous as you only made pasta for about a year. That's when I decided you might be safe to marry.'

'Safe to marry? What the fuck does "safe to marry" mean? That's not very romantic. You married me because I was "safe"?'

'No, my darling,' sniggered Simon. 'No one could call you a safe option. And I knew I wanted to spend the rest of my life with you after that first night. It was just, with your unusual culinary skills, I wasn't sure how long that life would be!'

I was slightly mollified by this, as I demanded, 'But you like my cooking now, don't you? It's improved, hasn't it?'

'Yes, sweetheart,' he said. 'You've got incredibly skilled at hiding the take-out boxes. You're a wonder in the kitchen.'

Rude. But I was really quite drunk and sentimental and determined to fish for as many compliments as I possibly could because it was Valentine's Day.

'Did you really know you wanted to spend the rest of your life with me that night?' I wheedled.

'Of course. I'm not going to ask if you felt the same way, because given you've already mixed me up with one old boyfriend tonight, I'm not sure I could trust your answer. I'd fancied you for ages, I just never got a chance to talk to you before then, because either I was too drunk, or you were too drunk, or there was some other dickhead bloke hanging around you. I didn't think you even knew I existed. And eventually, there you were, one night, on your own for some reason, and there I was and so I thought, fuck it, what have I got to lose? I'm going to go for it; at least for once I won't have an audience if she knocks me back. And the rest is history.'

'Yes, even though I put out on the first night, despite all the lectures about boys won't respect you if you do that. Go on then, what made you fancy me so much?'

(I was shameless. He has told me this before, but sometimes it's nice to hear it again. Actually, it's always nice to hear again. I wondered if I could surreptitiously turn on my phone and record him to listen to it next time he's fannying about in his shed or snoring in front of *Wheeler Dealers*.)

'You had cracking tits!' I tried to hit him. 'Okay, Okay. You *still* have cracking tits. And you always looked so happy, like you were just having the best time of anyone in the room. I wish you looked like that more these days, actually. Right then, your turn. It's *my* birthday, you should be the one telling me how irresistible and gorgeous I am and how much you want my body.'

So I told him how dark and mysterious I had always thought he was, and how the way his hair fell into his eyes made me think very impure thoughts about him, and how I had assumed he didn't know I existed either, thinking he would be more interested in fellow dark and moody arty girls, rather than someone as ordinary, as boring as me. And then we went to bed, Simon having rather annoyingly proved himself better at being romantic than me, on account of that stupid vegetarian boy and his sodding spinach pancakes.

Wednesday, 17 February

Sometimes I wonder what the actual fuck is wrong with me. Like a fool, I agreed to a conference call this afternoon, at home, after I had picked up the children from school. What sort of idiot tries to make important phone calls with children in the house?

Despite settling them down with various iPads and all the fries and snack foods they could possibly desire, making sure they had both been to the toilet so there could be no unfortunate 'wiping' incidents like the last time I tried to make a work call at home, even though Peter never actually bothers to wipe any other time, and then tiptoeing away more silently than a mouse, as soon as the call connected, their antennae pricked up and they appeared at the door to shriek and wail and bellow and whine. Thus I discovered, to my chagrin, that trying to emotionally blackmail them into being quiet and leaving me alone because I have very important work to do is basically like a red rag to a bull and they are immediately seized with the desire to make as much noise as they can while plaguing the everlasting fuck out of me.

Attempts to tune them out were unsuccessful, and I actually have no idea what I agreed to do on the call because I couldn't hear what anyone was saying – hopefully it is nothing too taxing … I thought I had got away with it all by claiming that the howling noise in the background was clearly a bad connection and then brightly suggesting they put everything in a follow-up email so I could still get some gist of what was actually going on. Then I opened the door to demand why my precious moppets had seen fit to spend the duration of the call banging on the door and screaming, despite my hissed threats of what would happen if they didn't bugger off.

Peter was scarlet and sobbing, but looking slightly sheepish, standing behind an indignant Jane, who was the one who had been attempting to batter down the door.

'MUMMY, WHY DIDN'T YOU OPEN THE DOOR?' demanded Jane in outrage. 'Peter has got a pea stuck up his nose!'

WTAF? Ten minutes. That was all they had to entertain themselves for, but in that time Peter had managed to get a pea stuck up his nose.

'Why?' I said. 'Why did you put a pea up your nose? And where did you get a pea? We haven't had peas in weeks.'

Peter shrugged. 'I found it in a corner of the kitchen. I dunno why I put it up my nose.'

Marvellous. Just marvellous. As if being a neglectful mother wasn't bad enough, now I could add 'slovenly housekeeper' to my ever-growing list of crimes for the children to hold against me.

'FML,' I muttered.

After much strenuous blowing by Peter, and enthusiastic excavations, the pea appeared to be more firmly lodged than ever and there was nothing else for it but to take yet another trip to the Minor Injuries Unit, while frantically hoping that I hadn't exceeded the quota of visits you are allowed before they call Social Services. Simon, needless to say, was off somewhere exotic being Busy And Important, so I had to take both children with me.

Even on a minor injuries scale a small boy with an antiquated pea stuck up his nose is not high on the list of priorities, so we had quite a wait to be seen at the hospital. Ignoring my best attempts to entertain them, the children were adamant that grubbing about on the floor was far more interesting, despite me hissing 'Get up! Get up! You will catch something unspeakable. OMG, your middle-class immune system will never be able to cope.'

Finally we were called through to a cubicle to await the poor overworked nurse with her special pea-extracting tool, who must wonder why she spent all that time and money training to save lives only to be faced with the likes of Peter and his pea. Jane had been unusually quiet for the last ten minutes, but once we were in the cubicle, she mumbled something at me.

'Darling, I can't hear you, you'll have to speak up. And open your mouth and talk properly, don't mumble like that.'

Jane opened her mouth and announced, 'I *said*, I might have got a paper clip a bit stuck between my teeth.'

Once again, WTAF?

Stunned by this revelation, all I could do was say, 'How? Why? Where did you even get a paper clip?'

Jane looked defensive and said, 'I found it on the floor in the waiting room.'

Oh dear God. What is wrong with my children? What would possess someone to put a random item they found on a hospital floor *in their mouth*?

'I just wanted to see if it would fit between my teeth,' Jane added. 'But now it's stuck.'

'What the FUCK did you do that for?' I exploded.

'Mummy, you shouldn't swear at me, it's not kind. Nice mummies don't say things like that to their children,' said Jane primly. Or as primly as one can say anything with a paper clip stuck between one's teeth.

'Nice unsweary mummies,' I thought grimly, 'do not have children who do things like this.'

The paper clip turned out to be well and truly stuck and could not be dislodged. Thus it was that when the nice nurse came in with her pea extractor, and once she had deftly flicked the pea out of Peter's nose, I had the shame of then having to ask her if she could possibly perform some similar magic to remove the paper clip from Jane's teeth. I have never seen such pity in anyone's eyes as I explained the situation, before she found a pair of pliers and removed the paper clip. I am going to have to find another hospital, I cannot endure the shame of returning there after today.

Fucking fuck my fucking life. And people wonder why I drink? I am beyond the aid of mere wine tonight and have had to resort to gin, while muttering darkly to myself. 'Enjoy every moment', they say. 'They grow up so fast', they say. 'Children are such a blessing', they say. I defy anyone to have enjoyed every second of today with the blessings that are my precious moppets.

I nearly smashed my phone when Simon sent a text asking how my day had been and complaining that he is so tired of restaurant food and can't wait to come home and have something simple to eat. He means lasagne; he always means lasagne when he suggests something simple. One day he is going to find a lasagne inserted somewhere unexpected. If he has really annoyed me, it might even be a frozen lasagne.

Saturday, 20 February

Simon finally returned last night and drooped most pathetically at my cruel and unreasonable refusal to make him a nice, simple, bastarding lasagne, so I decreed we could each spend the day bonding one-to-one with our precious moppets. I decreed this mainly because I realised this morning that Jane looks like some sort of reject from a Victorian orphanage, as she has had a growth spurt and all her clothes are far too small, not to mention somewhat ragged and worn. Since she has recently started to object to what I choose for her to wear, wanting to assert her own style, even though I was still smarting slightly after the whole paper clip/teeth interface, I decided we should have a lovely girly shopping day, bonding and chattering, without Peter tagging along behind us insisting that he is starving and trying to touch anything that looks remotely breakable or expensive. We would have such fun that when Jane grows up she would say things like 'Oh, my mum was more like a big sister to me!' Though given that Jane seems to feel that that being a big sister means constantly tormenting Peter and repeatedly attempting to murder him, perhaps that wouldn't be such a compliment. Maybe she will tell people I am her best friend instead?

Sometimes people say that about their mothers. That might be better.

Jane rejected every adorable outfit in every bloody shop; all the pretty t-shirts with sparkly bows and kittens on them, the flouncy skirts, the retro pinafores. They were all YUCK, apparently. Yuck, yuck, yuck.

Eventually, as Jane sneered at yet another frock I was waving at her, I sobbed in desperation, 'Well, what DO you want to wear then?'

'I want a t-shirt with dinosaurs on it.'

'A t-shirt with dinosaurs on it? Darling, I don't think we've seen any t-shirts with dinosaurs on them.'

'Yes, we have. In the first shop.'

'The first shop. Why didn't you say so, then?'

Jane shrugged. 'You didn't ask.'

We toiled our way back to the very first fucking shop, where I could see no sign of the fabled t-shirt with dinosaurs on.

'Darling, are you sure this is the right shop?' I asked in despair.

'Yes,' said Jane. 'It's over there,' and she pointed at the boys' department.

'But darling, that's a boys' t-shirt,' I said.

'I don't care,' said Jane. 'I like it. And I like these jeans, not like those stupid ones with glitter on over there.'

In the end, Jane was kitted out exclusively from the boys' department, but by that point I was beyond caring, I just wanted the soul-sucking hell of Jane announcing everything I suggested was stupid to be over. On the way to the café, I made a very quick detour to the shoe section, because I had spotted a 'reduced' sign and I thought perhaps there might be some bargains to be had. I was in luck. One pair of sparkly silver stilettoes later (very good value, reduced from £79 to £23, it would actually have been rude not to buy them) and we made our way to the café.

'We're good friends, aren't we, darling?' I said brightly, over coffee for me and hot chocolate for Jane, having looked longingly at the tiny bottles of wine and regretfully put them back because I had the car.

Jane looked even more appalled than she had when I suggested she might like a pink, sequinned Hello Kitty t-shirt.

'No,' she said. 'Of course we aren't friends. You're my mummy, not my friend. Sophie is my friend, and Tilly and Milly and Lucy-That-Isn't-Lucy-Atkinson. Not you. People aren't friends with their *mummies*!'

'Some people are friends with their mummies,' I said indignantly.

'Hurrumph,' said Jane. 'Then those people are *weird*!'

When we got home, the first thing Jane said was, 'Daddy, Mummy bought more shoes. I told her not to, I said she had enough pairs of shoes, but she bought them anyway.'

The house looked like a bomb had hit it. There were dirty dishes strewn all over the kitchen and the sitting room, and four, yes, FOUR half-finished glasses of orange juice on the coffee table, along with several empty bottles of beer. A pair of Peter's pants were tossed on the back of the sofa and there were crumbs and smears of butter and bits of cheese all over the kitchen worktops. An empty chip packet had been casually chucked on the floor beside the bin, which was overflowing.

'Simon,' I said. 'What the fuck has happened here? What have you done all day?'

Simon looked hurt. 'I have been busy looking after *your* son!' he said. 'We didn't all get to go shoe shopping and gallivanting round the town today, you know.'

'Yes, but what have you actually done? You could've taken out the trash, or put the plates you used in the dishwasher –'

'I *told* you, I was looking after Peter. I made him lunch. *And* I'm jet-lagged, you know. When was I supposed to find time to do the other stuff, while you were out shoe shopping? And actually, I don't know why you complain the children drive you mad, Peter and I have had a great time.'

Yes, yes, I'm sure they have, because Simon had ONE child to look after, which meant no fighting and stopping them trying to kill each other because apparently one of them looked at the other one, and he has done nothing else except 'look after' Peter, who I will bet has not actually been unplugged from one electronic device or another since I left the house this morning. Simon has not been trying to scrub shit off toilet bowls or wrangle five loads of laundry into the washing machine or vacuuming up Lego, all while breaking up fights and fielding constant demands for food and for apps to be downloaded, and answering inane questions about who would win in a fight, a robot or a monkey. No wonder they've had a great time and everyone now thinks Simon is Dad of the Fucking Year! And, of course, shopping with his beloved daughter was such complete and utter fun; indeed, I was living the dream, wasn't I, as she crushed all my hopes and refused to pose for the #girlyday #soblessed Instagram photos, instead lecturing me on how it was violating her human rights to put photos of her on the internet without her consent.

FML. At least I have sparkly shoes. Although the dog looked most unimpressed with them.

Monday, 29 February

Since Sam's children and my children have now all decided they are best friends, Sophie and Toby came to tea today. As is always the case at my house, they managed to get astonishingly filthy, this time somehow managing to smear themselves with what looked like an entire bottle of tomato sauce each.

In an attempt to mollify Sam about the foul state of his
children when he came to pick them up, I offered him a glass of
wine, which obviously turned into us finishing the bottle while
he told me of the latest astounding pronouncements from Mark.
It is all very well going on like that when your new boyfriend is
called Mark, but I never got to do the dreamy-eyed name-
dropping into every conversation because every time I began
'Simon says ...' my friends would immediately shout something
like 'Put your hands on your head!' My friends were rubbish.
Sam, however, is still completely loved up and making jokes
about which one of them gets to propose in a leap year.

After Sam had gone, feeling slightly blurry on half a bottle of
wine and no dinner, I decided once again to be brave and look
at my bank account to enjoy the feeling of actually being vaguely
in the black and see what pittance would be left to me after various direct debits came off the next day.

I was somewhat perplexed, however, to find that there was
about £10,000 more in there than I was expecting. This never
happens. £10,000 *less*, quite possibly, but not £10,000 more. After
squinting somewhat at the screen and going back through my
transactions, there it was: £10,003 credit. From the app people.

Still mildly tipsy, but nonetheless a bit hopeful, I looked at my
emails, at all those messages I hadn't bothered opening for the
last couple of months, unable to bear the depressing news that
another ten people had downloaded my app and earned me
another £7.

It turned out no less that 14,290 people had bought it! There
was also an email from one of the app review websites I had sent
it to saying they were going to feature it in one of their articles,
which is probably how so many people came to buy it.

I was astonished, and overjoyed. Simon was working late, so
he wasn't there to discuss what we should do with this splendid
windfall. Go on the vacation of a lifetime? Buy twenty pairs of

Louboutins? Ten pairs of Louboutins and a weekend in Paris, just the two of us, walking hand in hand by the Seine, and a week at Euro Disney *en famille*?

I opened another bottle to celebrate while I mulled it over. We could use the money to buy a nice car that didn't smell vaguely of rotting apples. Although there's not much point while the children insist on viewing cars as mobile dumpsters.

Finally, reluctantly – and almost unbelievably for me – remembering how stressed and worried about money Simon has been recently, and even more so than usual after the credit card got racked up so much over Christmas, I decided that I would just put the money into paying off the credit card. Actually, that would pretty much wipe the card debt.

I decided I would not say anything to Simon, I would just leave it as a lovely surprise, so when he checked to see what the minimum payment needed this month was, he would just find the balance gone and when he asked what had happened I could just casually say, 'Oh, well, darling, you know that app I created that you said wouldn't make any money and was just a stupid pipe dream of mine? Well, it's only gone and paid off the credit card, hasn't it? Also, look how frugal and prudent I was to use my money for that, instead of squandering it all on Louboutins LIKE I WANTED TO! What price stupid Ellen who can't manage money now, eh?' and then I could be all smug and he would be delighted that there was one less drain on our eternally over-stretched finances.

Buoyed up by a surfeit of red wine, I transferred the money before I came up with a better idea and convinced myself to do something more exciting with the cash.

When Simon came home he looked shattered, and it was all I could do just to smirk at him and not blurt out what I had done, even when he grumbled about me being so drunk on a Tuesday night.

It also occurred to me that if my app had made that much money in a couple of months, then it might make a bit more! My sensible and prudent decision may yet be rewarded with a fabulous vacation and stunning shoes that I can't walk in. I think it is fair to say that I am very, very pleased with myself tonight, though I may be slightly less pleased when I am hungover tomorrow and thinking of all the exciting things I could've done with ten grand.

MARCH

Friday, 4 March

Not a dicky bird. Not a sausage. Diddly buggering squat. That is what Simon has had to say this week about the astonishing news that our credit card has been paid off, as if by magic. Why hasn't he said anything? Has he not noticed? Has he noticed but assumed it is some sort of error or glitch which will turn into something else he has to sort out because his feckless wife is so useless with money? Does he fear what I will answer if he asks me how I paid it off, announcing that I have taken to selling my body or defrauding little old ladies out of their life savings? It is rude to say nothing.

Something out of the ordinary did happen today, though. My car was in the garage (oh, the bliss of not wondering if my card will be declined when I go in to pay) and the children were going straight to Sam's after school for a sleepover, so Simon dropped me off at work. I was going to get the bus home afterwards, now that it is March and I will not sit on the top deck of the bus crying pitifully to myself about all the sob stories I have made up about the people behind the windows I pass and comparing their lives to my own.

Since I didn't have to pick up the children, I stayed on for an extra couple of hours at work, to miss the screaming schoolkids on the bus, but when I got to the bus stop it was starting to rain and there was fifteen minutes before my bus was due so I nipped into the pretty little art gallery across the road, which sells lots of beautiful things that I can't afford, and also nice cards, which I can.

I thought I might as well have a mooch around before stocking up on cards, as I had time to kill, and as I was standing admiring a very sweet little bronze of a sleeping dormouse and thinking that even if I had a spare £450 I wouldn't spend it on something quite so small, the only other person in the gallery, a very large man, came over and stood beside me.

I don't like people in my personal space. I don't even like Simon to lie too close to me in bed, unless there is a good reason. For actual sleeping, I have my side and he has his side, although he stoutly maintains that I am the one who does not adhere to my side and tries to take over his as well. I think this is perfectly reasonable of me. But given I do not even like the father of my children to invade my space, I have definite actual issues when strangers do it.

This man had the whole place to wander round, why was he muscling in on me and my overpriced dormouse? Was he trying to steal my bag? He looked very respectable, but I remembered the time I was on the Underground with Simon and there was a very disreputable ruffianly sort in the carriage as well, and I clutched my bag to me and hissed to Simon to keep hold of his wallet, because I Did Not Like The Look of the disreputable man, who we soon discovered was an undercover policeman, when he pinned a most dapper chap in a suit to the floor and slapped a set of handcuffs on him for nicking a nice lady's phone.

I was taking no chances with this man. I started to move away, but not before I had turned to him and given him a hard stare that Paddington Bear would have been proud of.

Instead of looking abashed and moving on, like he was supposed to, like a proper British person would, he stopped and beamed at me. Oh God, I thought, I am going to have to be polite to some tourist and then I'll probably miss my bus trying to give them directions somewhere because I am too British not to, and it's Friday night and I'm child-free and all I really want to do is go home and have a bath, with an enormous gin, to blot out the thought of what my sister-in-law may have done in my bath, and then put on my pyjamas and eat chips in front of the television. Bloody hell, it's a child-free Friday night and that is the height of my ambition? I am turning into Simon. Bugger, the man was saying something.

'Ellen Green! I thought it was you, and I would know that "please fuck off and leave me alone" glare anywhere.'

'Charlie?' I said. 'Oh my God! Charlie! What are you *doing* here?'

Charlie Carhill. I have not thought about Charlie Carhill in almost twenty years. Correction, I have refused to think about Charlie Carhill in almost twenty years. I treated Charlie appallingly and I have been ashamed of how I behaved ever since, so I put the thoughts of Charlie in a little box in my head and just didn't think about him, because when I did, I felt hot and cold and uncomfortable about myself. And now here he is, standing in front of me, and actually looking rather attractive and, somewhat unbelievably, given the history between us, astonishingly pleased to see me.

Next thing I knew he had enveloped me in a bear hug, before releasing me and saying, 'I can't believe it! It's so good to see you.' And just like that, I remembered how nice Charlie was, and how genuine and how he never, ever held a grudge, and so I said, 'It's wonderful to see you too, but what are you doing here?'

'I work at the hospital up the road. St Catherine's?'

'Of course, you're a doctor now, and at St Catherine's, how lovely!' I said, slightly faintly, thinking, *of course* he is a doctor now, you fool, did you think he had somehow spent the last twenty years still being a shy, clumsy medical student just because that was the boy he was when I locked the box in my head and decided I simply wasn't going to think about Charlie Carhill anymore?

'Yes, not been there long, but, *Ellen Green*! I still can't believe it's you,' he beamed, to which I replied, already a little too sharp, 'It's Ellen Russell now, actually, and it's definitely me, I can assure you.'

'Are you busy?' he asked, undeterred. 'Are you rushing off somewhere, or have you got time for a drink?'

And because it *was* so nice to see him, and I was cross with myself for already being snappy at him within about thirty seconds of seeing him again, and also because it was, after all, Fuck It All Friday, I said, 'Yes, a drink would be lovely' and I went and had a drink with him, and then another drink, and so eventually I got home a little the worse for wear and considerably later than I had originally intended.

Simon was in the kitchen reading a magazine and drinking wine when I got in. I had already texted him to tell him I was going for a drink after work, but I hadn't said more than that.

'Did you have a nice time?' he asked.

I opened my mouth to say 'Oh dear GOD, Simon, you won't believe who I met and who I had a drink with!' but for some reason I just said, 'Yeah, it was okay. You know,' and shrugged, implying it was just a standard Friday night drink with some colleagues.

I had meant to tell Simon I had run into Charlie; I had thought all the way home about what I would say, about how it was such a bizarre coincidence, and how wonderful it was to see him, but at the last minute, I just didn't.

Maybe it was because Simon never really knew Charlie, and the thought of trying to explain who he was, where he had fitted in, would also have reminded me of how I had behaved to Charlie, and I didn't want to be reminded of that – not tonight when Charlie had so clearly forgiven me for being such an awful bitch.

'Hey!' said Simon. 'It's Fuck It All Friday and we don't have any children in the house. Do you want to go out for a drink? Or have you eaten, we could go for dinner?'

How unlike Simon to willingly venture into the world of people. It would've been rude to say no, even though I very badly wanted to take my bra off, so we went out and ate pasta and drank more wine, and we even held hands, and somehow, the right moment to mention that I had met Charlie never quite seemed to come up.

Saturday, 5 March

Sam was supposed to be introducing Mark to Hannah and me properly tonight. I tried to persuade Simon that we should get the older Baxter girl up the street to come and babysit so he could come too, but apparently two nights out in a row was far too much for someone of Simon's advanced age to contemplate and he claimed that he was in urgent need of lying on the sofa and watching *Wheeler Dealers* in his oldest fleece.

'You must remember I am ancient and decrepit now, darling,' he said, 'whereas you are still a woman in her prime.'

'Fuck off, darling,' I said. 'You're only a year older than me. And what is this "woman in her prime" nonsense? You make me sound like Miss Jean Brodie.'

'Mmmm,' said Simon, attempting to grab me, and getting That Look in his eye. 'Wasn't she a bit of a goer?'

'Put me down!' I said. 'If you're not coming, I'm going to be late!'

Alas, the beloved Mark had not been able to come out and meet us, as he was suffering from an attack of norovirus.

'I did offer to look after him,' Sam said nobly. 'But luckily he said no, because I am not very good with puke. He looked ghastly, poor thing.'

'Maybe it was just the thought of meeting us, making him turn green?' suggested Hannah.

'Yes!' I cackled gleefully. 'Our reputation precedes us.' (I'm pretty sure it hasn't actually, I'm almost certain I have never done anything untoward in the presence of Mark's sister, Alison, unless her children have carried home lurid tales of my own darling cherubs. But then again, her oldest boy Oscar is Peter's hero as apparently he once did such an enormous poo that he blocked the entire school plumbing system.)

'I hope he feels better soon, though,' I added dutifully, before proceeding with the proper gossip of the night and excitedly demanding that Hannah guess who I had run into yesterday.

'No, not him. Not her, why would I pleased to see her? Go on, guess, you'll never guess!'

'Well, if I'll never guess, why are you making me guess?'

'Oh, you are rubbish at this! All right, I'll tell you. Charlie! Charlie Carhill! Isn't that bizarre?'

Hannah looked very odd. 'What do you think you are doing, meeting Charlie Carhill?'

'I didn't meet him. I was in that gallery on the High Street, and so was he and he recognised me and said hello, and so we went for a drink.'

'A drink. Just you and Charlie? For Christ's sake, Ellen, what were you thinking? Can't you leave him alone? What happens now, are you going to start playing games with him again? Don't you think you did enough damage there?' Hannah hissed this last sentence across the table with such venom that I actually recoiled.

'Hannah, I haven't seen Charlie for almost twenty years. I can go for a drink with him if I want to, and it's none of your business if I do, I just thought that maybe you'd be interested to know

I'd run into him, and you might want to hear what he has been doing since we left university. *Actually*!'

Sam's eyes had grown increasingly saucer-like throughout this exchange, and now he could no longer contain himself, he was practically bouncing up and down in his seat as he squeaked, 'WhoisCharlieCarhillandwhatisgoingonandwhat didEllen DOOOOOO?'

'She broke his heart!' huffed Hannah.

'I did not!' I protested indignantly. 'I did nothing of the sort, I couldn't help how Charlie felt about me, and I couldn't help that I didn't feel the same way.'

'Oh, no, no, of course you couldn't, could you? None of that was your fault *at all*, was it? Not leading him on for two years, letting him think he might, just might, have a chance with you, and then finally going to bed with him, which I never understood why you did, and then the very next night, there was poor Charlie thinking he had finally got somewhere with you, only you stood him up and went off with Simon. He saw you, you know, leaving the Pear Tree with Simon that night. And then, as if that wasn't enough, you kept him dangling for another fucking year, ringing him up every time you had a row with Simon, pouring your heart out to good old Charlie, so he was always hoping that maybe you and Simon were about to finish and he'd finally get his chance with you. You were horrible to him, Ellen. And you left me to pick up the pieces.'

'Ooooh, Ellen, you *slut*,' put in Sam. 'Two men in two nights! And keeping this chap on the side when you were seeing Simon, *naughty, naughty, naughty*!'

'Shut up, Sam,' said Hannah and I together.

Sam tutted to himself. 'I'm only trying to *help*!' he muttered.

'What are you talking about anyway, you had to "pick up the pieces"? You barely knew Charlie,' I said, incredulous at this unexpected fury from Hannah.

'I did know Charlie. I was there the first night you met Charlie, in Freshers' Week. I was there at dinner with you every night in first year, and Charlie too, and when you didn't bother to turn up because you'd got a better offer, Charlie and I would eat together. When you decided to ruin Charlie's life on a whim, I was the one he talked to about it. I probably knew Charlie far better than you because you never talked to him about himself, all you ever talked about was yourself when you were with him. You treated Charlie like some sort of dog! Actually, I've seen you with your dog, you're nicer to dogs than you were to Charlie.'

This stung somewhat, because there had been a certain dog-like quality to Charlie's unswerving devotion which I had rather enjoyed, even if sometimes it was all I could do to stop myself scratching him behind the ears and asking him if he was a good boy, or rubbing his belly. I was not proud of this, though.

'I did not ruin Charlie's life on a whim!' I retorted angrily, the niggling shame of how I had behaved causing me to react badly to Hannah's accusations, 'and it was eighteen years ago! Why now, all of a sudden, are you so enraged by the thought of Charlie and me having a drink? You never said any of this at the time, and I don't see what bloody business it is of yours now.'

'I didn't see you much then, Ellen,' said Hannah sulkily. 'When you started seeing Simon you were so wrapped up with him you didn't have time for anyone else, unless you wanted something from them. Like you wanted Charlie to make you feel adored and worshipped when you fell out with Simon.'

'But all the rest of it. What good friends you and Charlie were. How awful you thought I was. You never told me any of that then. And I didn't lead him on, I really didn't: I *liked* Charlie. Just not like he liked me.'

'Why did you sleep with him then, when you had no intention of it going any further? If you weren't leading him on. And it wasn't just a shag, was it? You were Charlie's first. You must've known what that meant to him, and then you *joked* to me about it afterwards. You *joked* about poor virgin Charlie and his sweaty palms, fumbling with your bra. "Charlie don't shag" I think was what you said.'

'Ooooh, ELLEN, you *deflowered* him, you heartless wench!' breathed Sam.

'Shut up, Sam!' we said in unison again.

'I don't know why I slept with him, when I knew it was never going to go further,' I said. 'I slept with a lot of boys who were never going to be my one true love. And I had no idea he had never done it before until we were in bed. What was I supposed to say, "Oh, sorry, mate, pop back for another go when you've lost your V plates"? Would that have been better? Told him I wasn't going to shag him because he'd be crap? FUCK, I was DRUNK! I thought I was doing a nice thing. I dunno, I thought maybe if I slept with him, he'd actually just get it out of his system. Move on, find a nice girl. And you were the only one I told about that, because I was under the mistaken impression that we told each other everything. I didn't realise you were so offended by my poor taste, because you had a jolly good laugh when I told you about other disastrous shags, like that engineer who kept his condoms in his calculator case. Didn't know Charlie was a special case and our union was SO BLOODY SACRED! So I'm very fucking sorry that I'm such a whore and not more like you.'

'Not like me, Hannah the Frigid Cow?' Hannah said, her voice trembling horribly. 'Not like me, poor old Hannah who couldn't get a ride on a rocking horse?'

'No,' I sighed. 'Not like you, as in me being a fucking slut. Not like you as in me being the sort of person who just slept with someone because they felt it would be rude not to. Not like you as in me being a horrible person without an ounce of your self-respect and confidence.'

'*Confidence*?' spat Hannah. 'CONFIDENCE? YOU were the one with the confidence, Ellen, you still are! You were the one everyone wanted to talk to, be friends with, date. I was just your sidekick. I WISH I had an ounce of your confidence. You were the one Simon bloody Russell fell in love with, when half of Edinburgh was panting after him. You were the one who had Charlie worshipping the ground you walked on. YOU! I didn't not have a boyfriend because I was so full of self-respect and confidence, it was because I was so bloody shy and nervous. If I hadn't been friends with you, I probably would be some mad old spinster now, living alone in a basement with seventeen cats and no friends. I was just washed along in the wake of you; people only liked me because I was your friend.'

'I wasn't confident!' I howled. 'I was fucking terrified. I hated myself. I hated every single moment when I had to walk into a roomful of people, and you always made me go first, start talking to people first. Do you know how I did it? I pretended I was Jessica. Not me, my fabulous, clever, confident, big sister Jessica. I wished I could be like you, quiet and self-contained, and having the courage to be myself, instead of being a fake, loud, OTT copy of my fucking sister.'

Hannah and I looked at each other. Sam opened his mouth, then thought better of it and closed it again.

Hannah sighed. 'We seem to see ourselves very differently to how other people see us.'

'Yes,' I agreed. 'And I was horrid to Charlie, you're right, but I don't understand why you're so upset about it now, when you weren't at the time.'

'I just don't want you to hurt him again,' said Hannah. 'You almost destroyed him before.'

'But why do you care so much about bloody Charlie Carhill? Why were you so pissed off about me having a drink with him? We haven't had a row in years, Hannah, and we just had one over *him*! Oh my GOD …' a realisation just hit me … 'Did you have a thing with him too? Is that why you're so cross with me for catching up with him?'

Hannah, always a terrible blusher, was scarlet. You could practically see the colour pulsating as the veins throbbed on her forehead.

'NO! There was nothing going on with me and Charlie!'

'Then why are you puce?' I asked, as understanding started to dawn. 'OH! You liked him. You wanted Charlie to be *your* darling. Why didn't you say anything? Christ, I know I was awful, but I'd never have gone to bed with him, never have had anything more to do with him if I knew you liked him.'

'It was a bit more than liking,' said Hannah sadly. 'And Charlie was crazy about you. I didn't want him as your cast-off, knowing he was only with me because he couldn't have you and I was the next best thing. I wanted him for myself. I kept hoping if I could be a friend to him, he'd finally start to prefer me to you. And then you slept with him. And you arranged to meet him for a drink the next night, and for once in your useless life you were early, and started talking to Simon and so as he came in one door, you went out the other door with Simon, with Simon's arm round you. And he was shattered, but once you and Simon were so obviously serious, I thought he would get over you. Only *you* couldn't leave him alone. A quiet drink here, a trip to the cinema there, a walk round Holyrood Park – every time you needed an ego boost, you dragooned in good old Charlie. How was he supposed to move on? So I told him he deserved better, he needed a clean break. And the next time he met you, he told you that, do you remember?'

I did remember. Remembered very well. Charlie, sitting across from me, holding my hand and saying, 'I just can't stand this anymore. I love you so much and I can't bear to be with you and know you're with someone else. I don't think I can see you again, I can't just be your friend.' And then he'd stood up, and kissed me, very gently on the mouth, and said, 'Bye, Ellen'. Then he turned around and walked away, without a backwards glance.

Sam sniffed dramatically and wiped his eyes.

'So, I thought then, when he'd made a clean break with you, he'd finally see me as more than a friend,' Hannah went on. 'Only he didn't. He saw me as he always had, as an extension of you, and he didn't want to see me either, because it just reminded him of you. So I had to accept that Charlie and I were never going to happen, so I started seeing Eddie, and he started seeing that awful law student who had been chasing him for the last three years –'

'Repulsive Rachel!' I interrupted. 'He married that ugly bitch. They're divorced now.' I added hastily, as Hannah's mouth twisted worryingly. 'I imagine she was a complete cow, but we could've told him that. But I can't believe you never told me any of this then.'

'I can't believe you never told me you pretended to be Jessica to be able to go over and talk to people!' said Hannah.

'I thought you knew.'

'No, I always thought that was just how you were. *I* pretend to be you sometimes, if I have to talk to a load of people I don't know. Emily's first day at school, all those mums in the playground to be faced, I thought "what would Ellen do?" and just brazened it out and talked to them like you would.'

'Ha ha ha,' sniggered Sam. 'That's where you're wrong! Ellen doesn't talk to most of them, she doesn't like them.'

'SHUT UP, SAM!'

'Anyway,' said Hannah. 'I'm sorry, you're right, I overreacted. I was just taken aback to hear you'd seen him, that's all.'

'I'm sorry, too, and *you're* right, I was awful to Charlie. I've always felt guilty. I had no idea he'd seen Simon and me that night, though, he never said.'

'Oh well, it's all water under the bridge, I suppose, now.' Hannah began to calm down, as curiosity got the better of her. 'How is he anyway? I can't believe he married Repulsive Rachel. Did she nag him into it?'

'CAN I TALK NOW?' grumbled Sam. 'Or will you just tell me to shut up again? I could've mediated between you two, you know, if you had let me. We could have been like a mini middle-class *Jerry Springer Show*, though obviously I'm much better looking and we all have our own teeth. We could do it again, properly, and I'll tell you each when you can talk.'

'Shaddup, Sam,' we said once more, although much more good naturedly this time.

'Oh, for God's sake! If you won't let me play at Jerry Springer, I'm so over this sharing business,' complained Sam. 'To summarise, Ellen was a bit of a slapper; Charlie Whatsit was some sort of saint who was shit in bed and Hannah needs some dick. Get yourself on Facebook, honey, and send this Charlie a friend request, see where it takes you. It's been eighteen years, he'll be over Ellen by now, and it doesn't sound like his wife was anything to write home about and he's had plenty of time to practise undoing bras with his clammy paws. Just do it, Hannah. Literally, fnah fnah ... Now, you know what we need? TEQUILA!'

Several tequilas later, Hannah slurred, 'Whaddabout Jeshca?'
'Eh?'

'Whaddabout Jeshca? Who you think she pretendsh to be?'

'Jeshca don' need to pretend to be anyone, she'sh shcary Jeshca!'

'Nooo ...' insisted Hannah. 'I pretend to be you, you pretend to be Jeshca, who she pretend to be? Bet she pretend to be shomeone.'

I thought about it. 'Jeshca pretend to be the Queen!' I finally pronounced.

Sam laughed until he fell off his seat. 'I pretend to be the Queen too!' he hiccupped. 'Not tonight, obviousshly, though. Queen wouldn't fall off her sheat. Or her throne,' he added.

I would have no problem if Hannah got together with Charlie. They are both very nice people who deserve to be happy. I only forgot to mention he had given me his number because I was very drunk. I will in fact be virtuous and put right the mistakes of the past by texting Hannah's number to Charlie and nonchalantly suggest he gives her a call to catch up. I will definitely do that. Later. I'm just a bit busy right now, being very drunk.

Sunday, 6 March – Mother's Day

Mother's Day with a hangover is not a thing to be recommended. The children woke me early to give me their cards and gifts. The cards were caked in glitter. The gifts were unidentifiable lumps, covered in glitter. My bed is now full of glitter.

'Mine is a poo!' announced Peter.

'That's lovely, darling,' I beamed weakly, unsure whether he had made a clay poo at school, which would be bad enough, or had in fact simply dried one of his own turds and sprinkled glitter on it. You can never tell with Peter.

'And yours is lovely, too!' I said to Jane. 'It's a, er, it's a, is it a …?'

'It's a thing with glitter on,' shrugged Jane. 'We all had to make them. Will we make your breakfast now?'

'Ooooh, yum, yes please, darlings! Will I come and help?'

'NO! It is Mother's Day, we are bringing you breakfast in bed.'

'How wonderful, darlings, what a treat.'

As the children thumped downstairs, I kicked Simon, 'Go and supervise.'

'What? Why?'

'Because this is Peter and Jane, darling. Do you not know your children at all? They have just been turned loose in a room containing sharp knives and flammable objects. I'm just a tiny bit hungover, sweetie –'

'Self-inflicted, no pity!'

'– And I really don't want to spend the rest of the day having to explain to the ER and Social Services how exactly it was that my darling children came to stab each other and/or set each other on fire. So please, for me, go and supervise.'

'But they'll be aaaaages,' moaned Simon. 'I thought we could take advantage of them being preoccupied …?'

'NO! NO. No sex. How can I concentrate on sex when all I can think about is the fruit of my loins murdering each other horribly in a fight over who gets to break the eggs over the stove under the guise of making scrambled eggs? PLEASE, go and keep an eye on them. I'll make it up to you later, I promise … a little bit of sexy time …?' I wheedled.

'For the love of God, Ellen, please never, ever refer to it as "sexy time" again. It's remarkably offputting,' huffed Simon, as he finally got out of bed. 'Have you seen my slippers?'

I sat up in horror. '*SLIPPERS*? Oh my God, since when do you wear slippers? And you say *I'm* offputting, talking about "sexy time"? Sexy time isn't nearly such a passion-killer as slippers. You'll be wearing a cardigan with leather patches on the elbow and prowling around, doling out fudge to unsuspecting children next. SLIPPERS!'

'My feet get cold,' he said sulkily.

I lay back down. Bastarding slippers.

Breakfast would have been a challenge at the best of times, but managing to eat half-cooked scrambled eggs, seasoned liberally with chunks of shell, served on burnt toast with a tepid cup of tea-coloured milk on the side, all with a tequila hangover, is testimony if ever there was one to the strength of a mother's love.

The rest of the day was uneventful; having trashed the kitchen, Peter and Jane lost interest in the whole concept of Mother's Day, so I dutifully rang my mother to listen to her complain about why she had not received a card from my children as well as me and bit my tongue to prevent me from shouting 'Because you're not their fucking mother', then sat through twenty minutes of the Wonders Of Jessica And Her Children and spent the rest of the day nagging Simon to phone his mother.

I didn't quite get round to texting Charlie about Hannah, but I totally will. He did send me a Facebook friend request, though, which it would have been rude not to accept.

Saturday, 12 March

Every single bloody weekend I decide things are going to change; things are going to be different, we are going to be a happy, wholesome loving family and we are going to have a wonderful time, worthy of being documented on Instagram with suitably cloying hashtags. Every week I think the weekend is going to go something like this:

Saturday

8 a.m. Wake up, spring out of bed rested, refreshed and raring to go. I awake my darling children, who yawn and stretch and tumble out of bed looking adorable in their organic cotton pyjamas.

8.30 a.m. We all sit around the table, chatting merrily of the plans for the day. Simon is tousled and stubbly and rather sexy, but that's okay, because we have already had sex once this morning before we got up. We feast upon croissants and orange juice and coffee while we read the papers and discuss current affairs with the children, who are interested and involved.

10 a.m. I emerge from a relaxing bath to find Simon shaved and dressed in tasteful knitwear. The children are also dressed and we look like something from a pretentious middle-class clothing catalogue.

12 p.m. The children help me to make a delicious lunch of healthy soup and homemade bread. They eat it with delight and exclaim how tasty it is.

2 p.m. We all go for a lovely walk in the woods and finish up at a rustic pub, where the children charm the slightly cross tavern keeper, whose cold heart is touched by their simple childish joy and he learns to love again. The dog lies quietly at our feet.

5 p.m. Simon suggests he makes dinner, and I sip a glass of wine while reading a gripping, yet still highbrow and improving, novel.

8 p.m. We all watch a classic film together. The children make engaged and pertinent comments about it, before going to bed.

10 p.m. Simon and I enjoy a final glass of wine together and discuss art and politics, before we go to bed and have more sex.

Sunday – pretty much the same, except the children go to bed earlier because they want to be well rested for school.

In reality, though, it goes like this:

Saturday

9 a.m. Stumble out of bed a bit hungover and in need of more sleep, but get up to avoid Simon's increasingly determined advances. Find Peter in the sitting room playing some unsuitable-looking video game, wearing only his underpants for some reason I don't even want to know. Find Jane has got up, retrieved the iPad and gone back to bed, where she is now watching YouTube videos about cats. Pray she did not put 'cute pussies' into Google.

10 a.m. Shout at everyone to just stop arguing and eat some fucking breakfast. Simon scratches his balls at the breakfast table. Peter copies him. Jane screams they are disgusting and throws her spoon at Peter. Peter hurls his entire bowl of cereal at Jane, misses, and covers the dog with soggy cornflakes. Banish both children to their rooms as they loudly complain that is not fair because they are still hungry. Clean up carnage. Bath dog.

12 p.m. Go to make delicious healthy lunch and find Peter in the kitchen cramming mini sausage rolls into his mouth as fast as he can. Shout at him to stop it, and as he jumps in fright he manages to choke. Perform the Heimlich Manoeuvre while Jane repeatedly demands if she can have his room if he dies.

2 p.m. Bully, shout and scream at everyone until they agree to come out for a walk. Insist Simon drives to a suitable location for a delightful country walk, because I will not drive him anywhere because he is a bastarding pig of a back-seat driver and the last time I drove him I did an emergency stop and threw him out of the car in the middle of the street because I had had enough of his 'helpful' comments and his foot jabbing for an imaginary brake pedal. The children continue to fight all the way there, as Jane taunts Peter about what she will do with all his stuff if he dies.

The children continue to squabble, the dog runs off, Simon is wearing his oldest, scabbiest fleece to spite me. Jane pushes Peter into the river, on her quest for his death. We find a pub to have a warming hot chocolate for the children. The barman says, 'No dogs', so we have to sit outside. Peter says he is dying of hypothermia. Jane looks hopeful. Simon complains the whole time because I'm having a glass of wine and he is driving.

5 p.m. Refuse to cook dinner and go on strike. Announce we are getting takeout. Referee World War 3 over what sort of takeout. Refuse to order pizzas, curry AND Chinese and declare everyone will have curry. Have more wine.

8 p.m. Everyone is slumped, staring slack-jawed and glassy-eyed at various devices. Suggest a film. Get told my films are stupid and boring. Give up. Drink wine.

10 p.m. Remember the children are still up. Shout at them to go to bed. Finally snatch all electronics off them and tell them they are never getting them back ever, ever, EVER! Simon snores loudly on the sofa throughout. Get the children to bed and try to change the channel on the TV to something that isn't *Wheeler* Sodding *Dealers*. Simon, who has been snoring determinedly for the last two hours, immediately wakes up and says, 'I was watching that!'

1 a.m. Finally stagger to bed, a bit more drunk than intended. Tell Simon to fuck off when he goes in for another grope.

Sunday – much like Saturday but without the outing as no one could face round two, so instead Simon hides in his shed and I do eleventy fucking billion loads of laundry while shouting at the children. The bedtime row comes slightly earlier because they have school in the morning, while they scream at me that it is so unfair that they have to go to bed at 8 p.m. because EVERYONE ELSE at school gets to stay up until midnight, playing *Grand Theft Auto*.

Thursday, 17 March

Simon has finally got around to mentioning the tiny fact that I have been very clever and paid off the sodding credit card. He was less pleased than I had thought he would be. Actually, as I suspected, his first reaction was that I had done something dreadful to get the money, which was not very flattering. Then he accused me of having a rich great aunt I had omitted to tell him about who had left me the money. When I revealed I had made it all by my own self, because I am very clever indeed, he was strangely quiet.

It took me a while to notice this, though, because I was happily babbling on about how clever I was, and showing him how many more apps had been sold since that first payment, which it turned out was just the money up until the end of January, and another 40,000 had sold in February, and the same again this month, which meant that actually there was at least another sixty grand coming our way, possibly more, and what were we going to do with it? We could go on an amazing vacation, we could buy a car, or cars, or we could do both and wasn't it fucking fabulous?

Simon just muttered to himself and then said, 'What about tax, Ellen? You are going to have to declare it and you'll end up paying 40 per cent on it.'

'Is that seriously all you have to say about it? "What about the tax?" Even I do pay 40 per cent, that's still well over £30,000 for us! Fuck the taxman, not literally, I think that is frowned upon, though I suppose somebody must have to, but that is still enough money to change our lives.'

'I mean, if you'd just set yourself up as a limited company, you wouldn't be liable for so much –'

'– FUCK OFF with your fucking limited company. Don't you see what I've done? For US? Despite you telling me it was a stupid idea, and would come to nothing.'

'What do you want me to say? "Well done, you've done brilliantly"?'

'Yes, that is exactly what I wanted you to say, instead of being so negative and talking about tax and limited companies and just bloody implying once again that I'm just some stupid little girl who can't cope with finances, and is going to rush out and spend it all on shoes.'

'Of course I'm happy, and of course it's amazing, and you're anything but stupid, though you are shit with money, you know you are. You openly admit you regard credit cards as free money and you do buy a lot of shoes –'

'Simon, I thought you were being nice!'

'I am! It's just … well …' He went quiet for a minute and looked down, avoiding my eye. 'Well, you won't need me anymore, will you?'

'Need you? Need you for what? What are you talking about?' I asked, bewildered.

'For anything. You've never really needed me, and I've always been so scared you would leave me. You could have had anyone, and you picked me, but I've always thought you would wake up one day and think "what am I doing with this guy?" and that would be it for me.'

'You are a twat,' I told him. 'You are a massive self-centred twat. This isn't about you! What the fuck is wrong with you? Hannah only said the other night about how half the girls in Edinburgh were in love with you.'

Simon perked up a bit. 'Ooooh, were they? Like who? What about that blonde one, with the big tits, what was her name? Sadie? I always thought she was giving me the eye. Was she into me?'

'Shut UP, Simon. Why do you think I will leave you? Why are you not happy about ALL THIS LOVELY MONEY I HAVE MADE FOR US? Because if you don't want any of it, I will bloody well spend it on shoes, just see if I don't!'

'I am happy. And I'm proud of you. It's just when money has been tight the last few years, I did sometimes think "well, at least Ellen can't afford to leave me now, we're too broke". Stupid, I know.' He avoided my eye again, waiting for me to respond. Probably hoping I'd soften and reassure him that he wasn't being a massive twat.

Instead I replied, 'Yes, very stupid. Very, very fucking stupid,' before asking him incredulously, 'What have I ever done that made you think I might leave you?'

'I dunno. I suppose I always just thought you'd get a better offer. Like that medic that was always hanging around you when we first started going out, the one who constantly panted after you with a gormless expression, like a Labrador who'd spotted a plate of sausages.'

'"Like a Labrador who'd spotted a plate of sausages". Thank you, Simon, it's nice to know I have such a lovely effect on men. Has it ever occurred to you for one bloody minute that if I had wanted to marry Charlie the Labrador, I would've married him instead of you?'

'You remember his name, though.'

'You remember Sadie with the big tits.'

'S'not the same. And you're friends with him on Facebook. I'm not friends with Sadie's tits on Facebook,' mumbled Simon sulkily.

'I'm friends with lots of people on Facebook, and you're not friends with Sadie and her hooters because you only have about six friends because you primarily use Facebook to stalk me and, according to you, gauge what sort of mood I will be in when you get home. I also once had a tweet retweeted by a radio DJ, it doesn't mean I am going to run off with one.'

'Yes, but –'

'Simon, you're not the only one who's paranoid. Do you think I don't worry that you'll get some sexy new secretary and fall for her filing skills, or be enchanted by a sloe-eyed señorita on one of your trips abroad? But despite everything, the credit cards and the hell-fiend children we have created, and the rough patches, so far you haven't, and we're both still here, and still together, so I don't know why you think this money is going to change our lives for the worse, not the better. And you are really fucking me off right now by being so fucking negative. But I'm not going to leave you, because actually, when I don't want to stab you for being an obstreperous, up-your-own-arse dickhead, and you're not wearing your terrible fleece or your granddad slippers, I do quite love you. And also, you'll have to sort out the tax thing for me because I still don't understand taxation. So you see, I *do* need you. So will you cheer the fuck up now and come and talk about all the really lovely things we could do with all the FUCKING MONEY, because I LOVE YOU, and you're not getting rid of me that easily?'

Simon immediately began to talk of savings plans and mortgage payments and pensions.

'Bollocks to that!' I said. 'I'm having at least one pair of Louboutins and a bloody good vacation. You can be sensible with what's left.'

This is possibly another example of why Simon is in charge of our financial decisions.

I should really have taken the opportunity when Charlie came up in conversation to mention to Simon that I'd bumped into him, shouldn't I? And maybe dropped in the fact that I'm actually having a teeny tiny drink with him after work tomorrow, not for anything untoward, but because we'd been messaging a bit, catching up on all the other stuff of the last few years, and then he said it would be nice to finish catching up properly and would I like to go for a drink – Simon too, he added. So it is clearly not anything improper, but Simon is hard enough to get out the house at the best of times, let alone to meet someone he barely knew a lifetime ago, so I didn't *quite* get around to suggesting it to him.

Anyway, my motives are pure, because it occurred to me that it would be much easier to talk Hannah up to Charlie in person; just casually mention her and how fabulous she is now, and also slightly single, blah blah, rather than doing it in a message which might make her sound a bit desperate. I *am* a good person! The Wedding of the Century could be back on before you know it. And now I am going to spend the rest of the evening googling impractical shoes and luxury villas in hot places while Simon feverishly compares savings plans.

Friday, 25 March – Good Friday

Simon's parents, Michael and Sylvia, are here from their bijou retirement chateau in France for Easter. They gave us their customary three days' notice that they were coming, as they found 'cheap last-minute ferries' and arrived this morning. Peter and Jane are very excited about 'French Granny and Grandpa', or 'Mamie and Papi' as Sylvia insists on them being called. 'Mamie' is very confusing, because either it just sounds like they are shouting 'Mummy' at which point I turn around and screech 'WHAT NOW!' at them, or if they try to affect a French accent, as Sylvia encourages them to do, it sounds like they are doing a very unfortunate Al Jolson impression, which is not something that is really approved of in public.

Sylvia and Michael have at least brought a bootload of cheap French vino with them, rather than drinking us out of house and home like their charming daughter, which will somewhat ease the pain of their visit. Sylvia has always been quite tricky and hard to read. She likes scarves, that I do know – with the possible exception of TV Alicia I have never seen anyone wear so many scarves as Sylvia. Sometimes I wonder if she actually wears any clothes at all, or just layers and layers of scarves. I mentioned this to Simon once and he turned pale and said 'Don't put thoughts like that in my head! Jesus, she might get hammered and decide to do the Dance of the Seven Veils! Oh God, I'm shuddering at the very thought!'

Apart from scarves, and her pug 'Napoleon Bonapug', I'm not quite sure what else Sylvia likes. Cushions. She likes cushions. I like cushions, too. However, cushions may be the only thing we have in common, as I'm not that keen on scarves and I think Napoleon Bonapug is an evil little fucker. I see the way he looks at me. My dog agrees, and he is an excellent judge of character. He would quite like to eat Napoleon Bonapug (full name to be used at all times), but Sylvia never puts him down for long enough. There is only so much conversation that can be eked out of a shared interest in cushions, though, and so I end up babbling wildly in Sylvia's presence about any random crap that enters my head – perhaps my finest moment being a lengthy soliloquy on otters and how they have opposable thumbs (see? That very expensive trip to the aquarium when Jane tried to drown Peter in the 'petting tank' wasn't completed wasted), while Sylvia looks bored and demands to know what art galleries and exhibitions I have been to recently and I try not to shout that I haven't been to any actually, because I don't really have time to go to art galleries by myself and when I try to take her grandchildren to instill a love of learning and culture in them they run amok like wild beasts and then demand to know where the gift shop is.

Sylvia fancies herself as something of an artiste, as many moons ago, before she married Michael, she had a brief stint as a temp at the BBC, and therefore she likes to shoe-horn 'when I worked in TV' into every conversation she possibly can. She also belonged to an art club when she lived in Surrey, and therefore takes full credit for Simon and Louisa's artistic skills while shaking her head sadly that poor Simon has ended up married to such a philistine.

Simon's father, however, is a splendidly jolly chap. He is charming and adorable, very easy-going and likes red wine, golf, tweed and his grandchildren, possibly in that very order. He tends towards the stoutly tweeded school of dressing, and his main mission in life appears to be to get everyone sloshed, which in my opinion is an excellent intention to have. He is a most enthusiastic topper-upper of glasses and it is in fact distressingly easy to get disastrously drunk in Michael's presence and have no idea whatsoever how that happened, as I discovered the first time Simon took me home to meet them.

Michael and Sylvia lived in a rather posh house in Surrey at the time. Although both my parents were far from badly off, on paper at least, they did not live in particularly big houses, preferring instead to waste their money on bitter divorces and recriminations, and, as they still like to remind us more than twenty years after leaving school, the dreadful expense that was our school fees (though technically that could also be classed as 'recriminations', I suppose).

Sylvia made it quite clear as soon as I arrived that she did not find me in any way good enough for her son and heir, not least due to the fact that she felt having divorced parents and numerous step-parents rendered me deeply morally suspect. I have later come to the conclusion that, a) Sylvia looks down her nose at pretty much everyone unless you have a title or have been on the TV (did she ever mention that she used to work in TV?), and b) no one actually would have been good enough for her precious boy, ever, except possibly a bona fide princess, and even then she would have had to have been from the British Royal Family, foreign royals also being distinctly dubious in Sylvia's eyes. Though that only really left the Princesses Beatrice and Eugenie for him, and Sylvia does not approve of them either, because she feels their mother is very common, as is red hair according to her. Sylvia has a long list of arbitrary things that are considered common, including, but not limited to, buying patterned underpants, dahlias, cable TV, hoop earrings ('Darling, must you look quite so like a gypsy?'), Greece and Finland (no idea), computers, all takeout food, shop-bought jam, tumble driers, magazines and political parties (don't even ask).

At the time of that first visit, though, so grand was Michael and Sylvia's house, so glacially terrifying was Sylvia and so generous was Michael's hospitality, that after he had topped up my glass for the umpteenth time, I found myself leaning over to him and congratulating him on his lovely home, where, I had been most impressed to notice, the whole family could go pee at the same time, and still have two bathrooms left for visitors.

'Errr, well, yes,' said Michael, ever the perfect gentleman. 'I suppose we could. Can't say we've ever really thought of it like that. Perhaps we should give a try sometime, eh? More wine?'

Michael made what he describes as 'an absolute bomb' on the stockmarket in the eighties, and he has a large stock of hysterical anecdotes about that time, most of which tend to end in, 'And then you'll never guess where the stripper produced *that* from', or 'It was only to be expected really, after he'd had that much Colombian marching powder!', while Sylvia tries desperately to hush him, as she does not feel such stories really match her image as the Gracious Lady of the Manor. Unfortunately, these days I also have to try to hush him, as he has a tendency to hold forth with such tales in the presence of the children, which can involve some interesting explanations to questions like 'But why was the lady playing table tennis with no clothes on?'

Michael is an unashamed capitalist (he refers to his son-in-law Bardo as 'that useless grubby hippy' and once incurred the wrath of Louisa for teaching Coventina to play poker, and telling her there was no point playing unless you were in it for the cash), so he was delighted to hear about the success of my app.

I suspect part of his enthusiasm was also relief, as I have noticed Sylvia and Michael making discreet cutbacks in their lifestyle over the last few years, suggesting that the 'bomb' has dwindled somewhat after several recessions, Sylvia's extravagances and the depredations of Louisa and her constant need for bailing out, or 'investment in the retreat', as she puts it.

The cases of champagne and Saint-Émilion they would once have turned up with have been replaced by crates of 'this rather fun, little local wine we've discovered', Sylvia's scarves are still silk, but from French markets rather than Hermès, and Michael no longer buys cars on a whim, only to sell them again a few months later because he's got bored, instead insisting that his trusty Saab is 'a classic' and that there is no need for anything more modern. For all his bonhomie and generosity, Michael is a prudent man, and I don't doubt that they have more than enough money to see out their days comfortably, but our own somewhat precarious finances must have been a worry to him, especially if he was no longer in a position to be able to help us out to the same extent that he had helped Louisa. So he was most thrilled to hear that there was now a good whack of cash coming in, even if he did tease me about it, asking with a completely deadpan face, 'What are you going to do with it then, Ellen? Live your dream by putting in a couple more bathrooms, so you can all go at the same time?'

Sunday, 27 March – Easter Sunday

'Let's have a jolly Easter Egg Hunt,' I said. 'Won't it be fun?' I said. 'Hannah, Sam, bring your children, too!' I said.

Simon also suggested we invite his school friend Tristan, who he discovered at Christmas, and his wife TV Alicia and their children.

As if that wasn't enough, I then decided to ask the nice new family who moved into the Jenkins' house last week, the tales of Louisa's camper van and vagabond tribe sadly not having reached their ears. Alas, despite our best attempts to lower the tone of the neighbourhood to make the house affordable enough for Hannah, it was not to be.

I met the mummy a few days after they moved in, and she seemed very nice, even if I didn't quite manage to work the conversation round to how much they had paid for their house, which was obviously the only reason I had brightly accosted her in the street and then demanded she come in for a cup of coffee under the guise of being 'neighbourly' and also because for once my house was in a relatively clean and tidy state. As I wasn't sure when that might next be achieved, I thought I should take my chance while I could.

Her name is Katie and her husband is called Tim. They have two tiny girls called Lily and Ruby. They are the nicest people I have ever met, and possibly the blandest. They both giggled nervously at everything we said and looked terrified by Michael, who was circulating with an ever-present bottle in each hand and shouting, 'Come on, come on, drink up! No need to endure our families sober, you know. Get it down you. Did I ever tell you about the time old Eddie Harrington-Hughes – what, Sylvia? I'm just telling these nice people about the time we switched Eddie Harrington-Hughes' marching powder for sneezing powder before he went to his in-laws for Easter lunch, and when he popped off for a little toot to make the roast lamb with the battleaxe more bearable he ended up sneezing a mouthful of mushroom soup over his mother-in-law and thought his brain had exploded! WHAT, Sylvia? Not suitable? What on earth do you mean? Oh, the children. Right, sorry, sorry. No, Jane darling, Mamie says I'm not to tell the story about the champion table tennis player I met in Bangkok any more. I know, it *is* a funny story, isn't it? What, Sylvia?'

Sylvia wafted up to me in a cloud of scarves and waved a hand at the gathering, enquiring, '*Chérie*, who *are* all these people? Why have you invited them?'

'They are our friends and neighbours, Sylvia,' I said mildly.

'That one is an accountant!' she said indignantly, pointing at poor Tim. 'Poor Simon. Ellen, you are forcing him to live in a cultural desert. Why can't you cultivate some more interesting people than all these corporate suits?'

'Errr ...'

'And who is that woman in all the scarves! What does she look like? What is she thinking?'

She was pointing at TV Alicia now, who she appeared to have had some sort of Scarf Off with, as I swear she had popped upstairs and added some more, just so she couldn't be out-scarved by Alicia.

'That's Alicia – she works in TV and is married to Tristan, who used to be at school with Simon.'

'Tristan! Oh, do you mean Tristan Barnaby-Soames? Oh, he was a charming boy! His father owned quite a lot of Sussex. Delightful man. And Alicia works in TV, you say? Yes, I could tell she was artistic. I must go and say hello, I expect we know lots of the same people from when I worked in TV. And I must tell Tristan to give my love to his father from me, we got on awfully well. Lovely man. Owned most of Sussex.'

With that Sylvia floated off, giggling coquettishly, so I could turn my attention to the task of getting ten mildly inebriated adults and ten overexcited children into the back yard for the Easter Egg Hunt without anyone breaking their necks by tripping over our dog, who didn't know what was going on but was determined to join in.

The Easter Egg Hunt was not as bad as it could have been. Only half the children cried because they felt their haul of eggs was unfair, a mere two managed to stand in a dog turd I had failed to pick up, and the dog was considerate enough to only steal a load of white chocolate, which resulted in some spectacular projectile vomiting from him, but which at least saved me the expense of an emergency trip to the vets.

In fact, it was all going splendidly until blood-curdling screams sent us all hurtling into the house. Katie and Tim's little girl Lily had brought her beloved toy rabbit 'Rabby' (not entirely imaginative naming, but who I am to talk when Jane has a cupboard full of bears named 'Cuddles', 'Fluffy', 'Fluffy Cuddles', 'Cuddly Fluff', etc., the ever-increasing loot from attending a series of Build-A-Bear birthday parties). In her excitement at the Easter Egg Hunt, Lily had callously cast Rabby aside to go in search of sugar and E-numbers. Sylvia, in a rare oversight, had actually put down Napoleon Bonapug for a moment while she earnestly quizzed TV Alicia about whether she knew Binky Warrington-Jones or Emerald Tuftson-Smith or anyone else who had worked at the BBC over forty years ago, while Alicia tried to explain that actually she worked for an independent production company and Sylvia scoffed and loftily informed her that *everyone* in TV knows each other.

Napoleon Bonapug, relishing this rare moment of freedom, had waddled his way over to where Rabby lay on the floor, abandoned and unloved, and had promptly mounted Rabby with great enthusiasm. Lily had discovered Napoleon Bonapug humping away, wheezing in ecstasy, and set up howls of protest at 'Dat doggy killin' Rabby!'

Sylvia, instead of attempting to disengage Napoleon Bonapug, was instead cooing, 'Oh, isn't Mummy's boy clever? Has 'ooo found a friend, Napoleon Bonapug?' oblivious to Lily's wails and everyone else's horror. I tried to end Napoleon Bonapug's moment of passion with a swift boot, but deep in the throes of bliss now, he paid no heed and the only result was to add Sylvia's screams to Lily's as she shrieked, 'Don't you kick my dog, you bully!'

At this point, my own dog, having rallied after his vomit fest, decided to come and see what the fuss was about, and either deciding to appoint himself the defender of Rabby's virtue or taking umbrage that Napoleon Bonapug was getting some and he wasn't, or finally just seeing his opportunity to kill his arch enemy, launched himself at Napoleon Bonapug's throat.

The screaming now redoubled, as Sylvia and I screeched at the dogs and Lily bellowed hysterically, as Rabby was still lost in the melee, and everyone else got in on the act and danced around, shouting unhelpful suggestions. A sexually incontinent pug is no match for a furious terrier, though, and while I was no fan of Napoleon Bonapug, I was concerned that our dog murdering him in cold blood in front of Sylvia might make future family gatherings a little awkward, while also thinking it was bad enough that most of the street already regarded us as dangerous pyromaniacs after the bonfire party, and I didn't really want, 'You know, the ones with the killer dog!' added to that.

I was attempting to prise our dog's jaws open, at some risk to my own fingers, when Sam had the presence of mind to empty a large jug of fruit punch and ice over the dogs, and they finally parted. Sylvia swooped in and retrieved Napoleon Bonapug with many dramatic sobs, Rabby was restored to Lily – minus quite a lot of stuffing and with a shocked and wide-eyed expression that

I swear wasn't there before – and I realised quite a lot of the very cold punch had gone over me and rendered my t-shirt completely see-through, as well as the unfortunate effect caused by the chill of the ice. I gathered our dog to my bosom, with as much dignity as I could muster, mostly to protect my own modesty, and, gallantly ignoring the fresh mint and strawberries nestling in my cleavage, brightly cried, 'Who would like some lovely Easter cake?'

Everyone left shortly after that. It is doubtful now that Tim and Katie will reveal themselves to be kindred spirits, which is a shame, as it would have been most convenient. Instead, I have a feeling they might take to avoiding us.

APRIL

Friday, 1 April

Michael and Sylvia are leaving tomorrow, which is a relief, as apart from anything else, Sylvia frowns on the concept of the hallowed Fuck It All Friday. It has been a long week, with helpful contributions from Sylvia such as the evening when I was trying to persuade Peter that, yes, he really did need a bath and he could show me all the YouTube clips he wanted about how your skin and hair begin to 'self-clean' if you go long enough without washing, and if he wanted to be a filthy urchin child he could go and live in the woods with his Aunt Louisa, where there are no electronics, when Sylvia, a perfectly able-bodied woman, shouted plaintively up the stairs, 'Ellen! I was just wondering if we are actually going to get a drink at all this evening?'

'Help yourself!' I bellowed down through gritted teeth.

'Oh no, I wouldn't want to be so presumptious. I suppose I will just have to wait until Simon comes in with his father to get a drink, since you are so very busy, because I can't leave Napoleon Bonapug.'

We have also, obviously, had daily updates on Napoleon Bonapug's post-traumatic stress disorder, after his 'near-death experience', as Sylvia refers to it. Apparently he is so traumatised that all he can keep down is roast chicken, hand fed to him by Sylvia. Oddly enough, he also seems to manage to keep down all my dog's biscuits that he steals from his bowl whenever he manages to give Sylvia the slip.

Then there have been her constant references to girls that Simon went out with before me: 'Do you ever hear anything from Catherine MacKenzie, darling? She was a nice girl, wasn't she? I did like her. What about Toggy Wilkes-Cholmondeley? Didn't her parents have a lovely castle? Sweet girl, she was.'

No matter that Simon points out he hasn't seen Catherine MacKenzie since Sylvia forced him to escort her to her school dance when he was sixteen, or that the last he had heard of Toggy Wilkes-Cholmondeley was that she was very happy with her wife Elizabeth, Sylvia steamed on with all the tact and diplomacy of a Panzer tank.

Simon's advice is usually to 'just ignore her', but even he admits sometimes that he doesn't know how his father doesn't throttle her. A couple of weeks of Sylvia is usually mitigated by a cheap vacation when we go to stay with them, in the spring and in the summer, but we haven't usually just had a week of Sylvia drifting around our house first. I was so dreading the prospect of another round of Sylvia in a couple of weeks' time that I had lunch with Charlie and had a thorough moan about her.

Charlie didn't tell me to 'just ignore her'; Charlie sat and listened to me holding forth on the many iniquities of Sylvia, including the first time she held an infant Jane and said, 'Oh dear, I assume she must look like your side of the family, Ellen, because she certainly doesn't take after *our* side!' Charlie provided much sympathy and insisted I should definitely have the chocolate fudge cake with ice cream, as a balm to my frazzled soul.

Charlie didn't sigh and roll his eyes and say, 'She IS my mother, darling. Can't you just try to get along with her?' when I banged my spoon on the table and mumbled, 'She's a witch!'

through a mouthful of chocolate. Charlie did, however, hold me just a little bit too tight and too long when he hugged me good-bye. I must give him Hannah's number.

Tonight, over dinner, Sylvia raised the subject of the vaca-tions. 'When are you flying out, darling?' she asked Simon. 'SO silly that they don't have proper Easter vacations any more, and this ridiculous "Spring Break" thingymabob instead, but at least it will be getting nice and warm by the time you are there.'

'Ah,' said Simon. 'I'd been meaning to talk to you about that. We thought we might go somewhere different this year.'

Did we?

'Oh, how lovely!' said Sylvia. 'Where are we going?'

'Well, *we're* going to Greece. Corfu, to be exact.'

I gasped in surprise.

'Corfu! Marvellous! I adore Corfu, whereabouts are we stay-ing, you clever duck?' cooed Sylvia.

My heart sank at the thought of Sylvia coming too.

'Actually, Mum,' Simon took a deep breath. 'I thought you'd probably want to get home and have a break from us, so I've just booked a tiny villa for Ellen and me and the kids.'

My heart lifted again!

The silence around the table was not so much frosty as Siberian, until Sylvia gave a little laugh, which contained about as much mirth as an icicle smashing into someone's heart (actu-ally, that is something I have always worried about when I see sharp rows of icicles – what if they fall down and stab you? I also worry that if you fart outside on very cold days there might be puffs of condensation from your bottom, like when you can see your breath and so everyone will know you have just let one off. I've never been keen on the idea of skiing trips for these two reasons).

'Very funny, Simon,' she snapped. 'Hilarious! I wasn't born yesterday, though. You are going to have to get up earlier in the morning than that to put one over on me! I *am* aware it is April Fools' Day, you know. Now, when are you coming?'

'Mum,' said Simon. 'We never actually discussed us coming. You just assumed we would be.'

'In much the same way as you just assume you *can* come, you mean! You never discuss with your father and me whether it suits us for you to come and stay, you just inform me when you will be arriving. It may have escaped your notice, but we are *not* running a hotel for your convenience, young man!' (This is actually a fair point. I have quite often said to Simon we should check whether his parents are happy for us to come before he books flights, but he just shrugs and says, 'It's fine, they like us just turning up.')

Sylvia now had something that looked dangerously like a tear in her eye, which came as a bit of a surprise to me, as I hadn't realised that she was capable of emotions that might damage her makeup.

She turned to me, 'I suppose this is all your doing!' she barked. 'You and that stupid game of yours. As if it isn't enough that when my friends ask if my daughter-in-law works, I have to say yes, and admit you work with *computers*, instead of having a nice job like Sukey Poste's daughter-in-law who is an interior designer, now I have to tell them that actually you've also invented some common game about drunken mothers like you!'

'Steady on now, old girl,' said Michael. 'There's nothing wrong with Ellen's job, and let's not say anything we'll regret now? Corfu will be nice at this time of year, though the sea will be cold. Hope you've got a villa with a pool, eh son?'

'Ellen didn't know anything about this, Mum,' said Simon.

'I did, though,' chipped in Michael. 'He told me a couple of days ago, asked me to keep quiet, because he wanted to surprise Ellen with it. I was going to tell you at some point, Sylvs.'

I felt a wave of enormous gratitude towards darling Michael for being so, well, jolly sporting, to use one of his phrases, about the whole thing, and not least for deflecting the wrath of Sylvia from Simon and me onto himself, so Simon's surprise wasn't completely wrecked by Sylvia having a massive tantrum at me.

Sylvia tottered to her feet and clutched Napoleon Bonapug to her so hard that he started choking on the piece of chicken she had just fed him.

'I see,' quavered Sylvia, her lip trembling bravely. 'Well, I assume you will all excuse me, but as I appear to be superfluous to this family and no one feels the need to tell me anything, I think I will have to go to bed. I seem to have one of my migraines coming on. Perhaps I shall see if Louisa and her children would like to come instead.'

Sylvia's migraines are the stuff of family legend, seeming to strike only when she doesn't get her own way, thus leaving her a suitably dramatic exit clause with the additional bonus of emotional blackmail.

Despite talking constantly of the many things that can trigger her migraines (coffee, chocolate and cheese, to name but a few) she happily guzzles all of these things with no ill effects, claiming if anyone remarks on it that it is 'other sorts' of the forbidden foods which affect her. She is also the only person I've ever met who apparently suffers from claustrophobia and agoraphobia. Just sayin' …

After Sylvia had departed stage left, in a whoosh of scarves as she swept out the door, Michael, who had visibly paled at the suggestion of Louisa and the hordes descending on them, stood up and murmured that he might just go and watch a spot of TV with the kiddos, and tactfully ambled off to the sitting room, where Peter and Jane were slumped in front of the cartoons. I turned to Simon.

'Corfu? Really?'

'Ellen, do you have any idea how much money you've made this month?'

'Not really,' was the shameful answer. After Simon's lectures about tax and limited companies I had basically abdicated all responsibility for the app money to him, so he had set up a limited company to put it through and I had just arranged for the money to be paid into a business account instead of into my personal account.

I periodically looked at the emails about how many apps had been sold and tried to work out how much actual money that meant, but Simon's sermons about taxation and everything else had left me with no idea how much remained after the wretched taxmen had taken their many cuts. I had nonetheless popped into town and paid a trip to a shiny store and bought myself a pair of Louboutins. They were stunningly, utterly beautiful, but so very high that when I tried to walk in them I gave a passable impression of Bambi on ice.

'There was the £60,000 from your February sales, which you got today, and then you've sold over 140,000 this month. That's about another hundred grand to come. Before tax,' he added prudently. 'You've done it, darling. You've sorted our finances, and I was the dickhead who doubted you and then acted like a prize twat because I wanted to be the hunter-gatherer caveman who brought home the golden woolly mammoth. So I think you deserve a vacation that doesn't involve my parents, don't you? Especially after you have heroically managed to refrain from strangling my mother with one of her own silk scarves this week.'

'Wow,' I said. 'Really? That much? But why Corfu?'

Simon looked worried. 'Don't you want to go to Corfu? Did I book the wrong thing? Did you want to go to Barbados or something?'

'No, no, Corfu is perfect! I just wondered why you'd picked it?'

'Well, I found a really, really nice villa. It's actually huge, but if my bloody mother thinks there is room for her she will whine at me until I crack and invite her along, so let's just stick with the bijou and compact story. You said that *My Family and Other Animals* is one of your favourite books ever and you always wanted to go to Corfu, so I thought you might like it?'

I did say that. I haven't said that for a very long time, because I can't remember the last time that Simon and I talked about something like books, or travelling; conversations these days are more along the lines of who would be passing the supermarket and thus could pick up some yoghurts for the children's lunch-boxes and why I am the only person who can change a lavatory roll and who had used Simon's good screwdrivers to open pots of paint? But he remembered. And we are going to Corfu.

With extraordinary tact and restraint, I didn't spoil the moment by demanding to know what colour the villa was and then huffing because he hadn't read the book and didn't know what I was talking about. Because he remembered, and we are going to Corfu, and I am extraordinarily happy.

Thursday, 14 April

We are in Corfu. It is unspeakably blissful. Getting here, though, was less blissful, as Simon did his favourite trick of morphing into a complete and utter arsehole before we set off.

This excellent, fun game began as usual a couple of days before we left, as he wandered around the house getting in everyone's way, plaintively asking me if I had seen his sunhat (no, though I have a vague recollection I may have thrown it away in a fit of pique while tidying up because it is so hideous), or if I had bought him his special sunscreen because he can't wear the ordinary stuff because it brings him out in a rash (yes, as I couldn't face him doing his 'scratching' pantomime in a foreign pharmacy again, because he looks like he is doing an overly dramatic impression of a flea-ridden monkey).

By the time we got to the airport I was, as is now customary when going on vacation, extremely stressed and wondering why the fuck I married this annoying twat. Simon was also very stressed because now he had the Important Job of Checking Us In. No one except Simon can ever do Checking In, because Simon Is Man. I am Mere Woman and therefore my job was to try to restrain Peter and Jane from flying around the terminal on their little wheely ride-on children's suitcases that seemed such a good idea when we bought them, and only revealed themselves to be lethal weapons once it was too late.

If we make it through check-in with only a dozen or so other passengers left limping in our wake after Peter and Jane have collided with their ankles, that is generally considered a success. While Simon was checking in, I also had to hold onto his carry-on luggage, because he was holding the passports and would shortly be in charge of the boarding passes as well, so he could not possibly be expected to hang on to his own nasty nylon backpack that he insists on taking on vacation.

I, meanwhile, also had my own carry-on luggage, which weighed slightly more than my actual hold luggage, as part of my Operation Take All The Shoes On Vacation Without Being Charged For Excess Baggage.

After check-in came security, which is always another personal challenge to Simon, as he frantically changes queues approximately every thirty seconds in an attempt to beat the system. I did suggest to him that now we are a bit more flush we should just pay the extra for the Priority Security Lane, but he recoiled in horror, as apparently it is about the 'principle' of beating security and to simply pay for a fast-track lane would not be sporting.

Having changed lanes at security seven times, as Simon repeatedly insisted we had to move to other queues which he thought were moving faster, we finally got through security about fifteen minutes after the people who had been behind us in the first queue and had stayed there. Now Simon embarked on the next stage of his Epic Quest, which was to Find The Gate. No matter that there were two and a half hours before our flight because he always insists on us arriving at the airport stupidly early, in case security is busy and his system-beating antics fail, he had to Find The Gate *now*! No matter that the gate had not been sodding well announced, He Is Man and so can guess where the gate is.

Off he strode, encumbered only by his backpack, the precious passports and boarding passes tucked away in one of the Special Pockets of his Special Travelling Trousers, as we trailed behind, me lugging my bag full of All The Shoes, Peter and Jane's cases slung around my necks as I had confiscated them after a nasty scene when they attempted a hit and run with an elderly lady, the children grasped in each hand lest they make a break for it and topple the giant towers of Toblerone in Duty Free (where obviously we were not allowed to stop, because Simon was Finding The Gate).

Periodically he paused and looked behind him, tutting as we scurried to catch up, Peter and Jane being bodily dragged along by me now, as they usually try to make a break for freedom at some point in the airport.

'Come on,' he said bossily. 'What's keeping you?'

When I hissed that I would stab him as he sleeps he looked at me in bafflement, for was he not Finding The Gate for me?

Heaven forbid that I should have delayed the sacred search by, for example, stopping at a shop to buy water for the children, who had apparently developed a searing thirst and could not go another step without a drink, for that was a major impediment to his plan.

When he finally arrived at The Gate, at least an hour before they had even thought about boarding, Simon had an air of achievement that suggested he had just trekked alone to the North Pole. He sat down as close to the door as he could, so that when they announced they would be boarding by seat numbers he could get in as many people's way as possible, once we had had the traditional debate about whether or not we could make one of the children pass for under five and thus claim priority boarding.

When I arrived several minutes after him, scarlet, sweating, breathless and furious, barely visible under the encumbrances of bags and children, he looked surprised to see me.

'There you are!' he said. 'I thought you were right behind me, what happened to you?'

By the time we got onto the airplane (including the fun of a bus to the airplane, my face pressed in a stranger's armpit, as the children attempted to fall over and break their noses, while Simon stood at the other end of the bus and pretended not to know us), and we were finally in our seats, all I could snarl at Simon was, 'I want a fucking divorce!'

'What's wrong with you?' he asked in surprise as I spat, 'I hate you, you are a massive knobhead, I hate you.'

I then demanded many tiny gin and tonics from the lady with the drinks cart to soothe my shattered nerves and finally started to calm down about ten minutes before landing, when more drama ensued as Simon tried to be the first off the airplane and then shouted a lot and turned the baggage claim into a piece of performance art, before having a fit at the queue for the car hire.

Every single time I travel with Simon it is the same – I don't know why I am even surprised any more. In an added twist this year, he didn't realise the handbrake wasn't on in the hire car, so when he put it in gear it started rolling backwards and almost killed me as I was trying to strap Peter in, which led to recriminations and accusations of attempted murder. I also missed a page of the very complicated instructions to the villa, which meant going round and round Corfu Town in circles until I found it while Simon shouted at me and I muttered at him under my breath to fuck off and die.

When we finally arrived at the villa, it was perfection. High in the hills, looking out over the bay, sitting alone with nothing around it but olive groves. There were hammocks in the olive groves and a sparkling blue swimming pool.

As we lugged the bags out of the car, including the several cases of wine we had stopped to buy on the way from the airport (which was another row, as I madly dashed round the Greek supermarket), Peter and Jane saw the pool and immediately began clamouring to swim.

I opened my mouth to say 'NO! Later,' and then thought, 'We're on vacation. There's not actually any reason for them not to swim right now if they want to,' so instead I asked Simon to go and keep an eye on them, as just because we are on vacation doesn't mean they might not try to drown each other or somehow 'forget' how to swim, despite the small fortune squandered on many years of lessons for them.

Monday, 18 April

I love it here. Freed of the constraints of home – where everyone seems to be constantly rushing from one place to the next without ever having quite enough time to do any of the eleventy billion things that need to be done, and we're always running just late enough to be fraught and shouting – we are all much nicer people.

The children swim all day and barely bicker at all, though whether that is due to the sunshine, the physical exertion or the fact that I am not bellowing at them, I'm not sure. Simon looks ten years younger and for the first time in years I feel like my shoulders are not somewhere up around my ears.

We get up in the morning and make coffee, and the children have even consented to eat fruit and yoghurt for breakfast, so surely that will ward off the scurvy for a few more months, and then we swim and throw stuff on the barbecue for lunch. Peter, having initially point-blank refused to try sardines finally had a mouthful, declared he loved them and ate ten of them, which was galling because I had planned to eat ten of them myself.

The rest of the time we just potter about, and read. Well, I read, Simon listens to his iPod, Peter rearranges the essential Pokémon cards which he couldn't possibly go on vacation without, and Jane looks for dead stuff, having been most delighted on our first day here to discover that there was a dead praying mantis lying on the terrace, being dismembered by ants.

We keep making plans to go and do a bit of sight-seeing, but it is so relaxing here that the most we have managed to do is to totter to the little taverna down the road for drinks and ice creams. Periodically, all the wine somehow vanishes and I have to send Simon out into the world for more supplies, because I don't do foreign driving.

Simon has even managed not to slope off with his laptop on the basis that he 'just needs to do some work' or 'answer a few emails', which confirms my suspicions that when we vacation at Michael and Sylvia's his claims of 'work' are just an excuse to get five minutes' peace from his mother or his children, who tend to spend the vacation hyperactively trying to kill each other because Sylvia has stuffed them full of sweets, while insisting that French sweets are different and the excess of sugar can't possibly be to blame for the children's behaviour. It's possible

Simon also sneaks off to get some peace from listening to his wife complaining about his mother.

Although there is Wi-Fi in the villa, I have even (temporarily) given up my Facebook addiction, apart from a few swanky photos to show off to everyone when we first arrived, which I rather regretted as it prompted Charlie to keep messaging me, once he knew I was contactable. It's not that Charlie sends me anything inappropriate – it's just jokey messages, silly photos and memes, but there are rather a lot of them. An awful lot of them. Anyway, I am not going to think about that. Charlie is a problem for real life, and I will deal with all of that when we get home. *If* we go home …

I am formulating plans whereby we simply stay here and become the next Durrells. In truth, I have not completely given up the internet because I have been secretly looking at Greek property websites and glorious tumbledown villas, where I would drift around the stone-flagged floor, barefoot, quaffing simple local wine from a terracotta cup (I am not entirely certain how pleasant a terracotta cup would be to drink out of, but the idea of it fits pleasingly into my Vision), tossing the odd olive to the children, who would be sunburnt, bohemian urchins by now, before wandering out into the groves with my easel to paint another masterpiece.

In my vision, that school report which declared, 'Although I appreciate Art is a difficult subject for Ellen, as she has no ability whatsoever, it would be nice if occasionally she could concentrate and at least pretend to be working' is no impediment to my watercolour masterpieces. I do recall throwing paint about quite a lot and being generally quite badly behaved in Art. But no matter, for once I was installed in my beautiful Corfiot villa my latent artistic skills would clearly awaken.

Thursday, 21 April

In the evenings, after the children go to bed, Simon and I sit out on the terrace and drink more wine and watch the lights across the mountainside and in the bay below. We can hear the dogs barking to each other in the village further down the hill and the cicadas singing in the garden and olive groves – and nothing else, apart from the very occasional motorbike gasping its way up the mountain.

It is gloriously peaceful and romantic, until at a certain point each night hordes of bastarding crickets decide to investigate the light and start plopping down onto the terrace in huge numbers and blundering about, and trying to jump into our wine, and I run inside screaming while Simon shouts 'They won't hurt you, FFS!' Gerald Durrell never had this problem.

Tonight, though, before the nightly plague of locusts descended upon us, I told Simon of my splendid vision and plan for us to stay in Corfu. He was dubious, as I waxed lyrical about the new life we would have.

'No one ever wants to go home from a vacation, Ellen,' he said.

'But wouldn't it be wonderful? An old stone villa, nestling in the olive groves, with vines growing over the terraces so we could make our own wine. There would be an ancient retainer wandering the groves, called …' I pause to think, '… Nico. He would have a donkey, and has mourned his lost love forever, and he never talks about what he did in the war, until one day he learns to trust us and tells of his exploits in the Greek Resistance, where Maria, the only woman he ever loved, was shot by the Nazis and died in his arms, and since then, his only friend was his donkey, until the lovably eccentric gringo family –'

'– Pretty sure "gringo" is Mexican, darling.'

'– SHADDUP! I'm telling you about my dream vision for our new life! Don't put obstacles in my way. Where was I? Yes, Alexis –'

'Who's Alexis? Wasn't she in *Dynasty*?'

'The ancient retainer!'

'I thought he was called Nico?'

'WHATEVER! Nico, the mysterious, ancient retainer, wandering the groves with only his donkey for company, is taught to feel love and emotion again, through the simple companionship of the British children, and their hapless parents, who will have amusing scrapes and hilarious misunderstandings with the locals but Nico will help them become part of the community and then they will have a marvellous party in the olive groves, with lots of homemade wine and everyone will live happily ever after!'

'Jesus, darling, how many of those chick-lit books with pink covers and cartoons of glasses of wine on the front have you read this week?'

'Some,' I said sulkily. There was an endless supply of such books in the house, left behind by previous vacationers. Surely part of the point of a vacation is to take many worthy, improving tomes with you, which you've been meaning to read for ages but not got around to, and then as soon as you arrive, abandon them for any jolly bonkbuster you can find?

'What would we live on?'

'Why, we would hardly need any money. We would make our own wine, *like I keep telling you*, if you were *listening*. We would need only some simple bread and cheese, we could probably make the cheese from the donkey milk –'

'– can you milk donkeys?'

'– how should I know? I expect so.'

'I have never heard of donkey cheese.'

'Well, we'll get a fucking goat then, okay? Don't bring me

problems, bring me solutions! Anyway, some simple bread and GOAT'S cheese, some wild honey from the hives in the olive groves, our own olive oil, there will be fruit trees around the villa, delicious peaches and persimmons –'

'– What *are* persimmons?'

'I'm not sure. Will you please stop interrupting? The point is we would hardly need any money.'

'I've just googled persimmons, they are a bit like plums. We would need money, darling, how would we pay for electricity and telephones and water and heating? Where would the children go to school?'

'The lovely little local school, like the one in the village here.'

'But they don't speak Greek! WE don't speak Greek.'

'I did Latin at school!'

'Darling, Latin and modern Greek are not even slightly the same thing. Latin and Ancient Greek are not even slightly the same thing. You have still failed to learn any French, after however many summers with my parents, how on earth are you going to learn Greek? We would be like those awful people on the daytime TV programmes who decide they are going to move abroad and then come home two weeks later because they can't find the right brand of orange juice in the supermarkets. The Greek economy is buggered; you'd have to be mad to put your money into Greece right now.'

'Ahhhh,' I said cunningly. 'But surely the state of the Greek economy means that we would get much more for our money?'

'No, darling,' said Simon and droned on about inflation and economics for a while, as I tuned out and thought of my olive groves and watercolours and the attractive shady hat I would wear to paint.

When I tuned back in, he was still crushing my dream, demanding once more to know how I planned to pay for the utilities. I opened my mouth to suggest we would live by oil lamps and draw our water from an ancient stone well, but then I realised that I was veering dangerously into Louisa territory, and also in reality there was no way I would actually be able to live like that.

Fortunately, at that point the locusts decided to swarm, which meant I could make a dignified retreat from Simon's stupid questions about the practicalities of my vision. Or as dignified a retreat as one can make while running indoors shrieking, 'ARRRGH! Are they in my hair? I don't want them in my hair!'

I refused to accept defeat, though, and spent the rest of the evening looking for the perfect house. I have a week to make my dream come true. I can totally do this!

MAY

Sunday, 1 May

I failed to make the dream come true. Simon continued to crush my dream with his insistence on focusing on reality and practicality and the necessities of keeping our children shod and fed, and also the alarming vagaries of the Greek economy. He also staunchly refused to believe my pronouncements on things like it being optional to pay tax in Greece, which I am pretty sure it is, and my sweeping statements about how we would just live off the land and everything would just fall into place once we had found the right house. And so, alas, we have returned to suburbia.

Perhaps this is how Louisa found herself at the 'retreat'? Perhaps she too just had a vision of a simpler life, and freed of the constraints of a dream-crushing husband like Simon she made the dream reality? But then again, I have been to Louisa's reality, and it is distinctly muddy and damp and smells a bit. Also, Louisa's vision is in a soggy wood in Scotland, not on a sun-drenched Greek mountainside, so it is more likely that Louisa is just crazy. I prefer this option, as I try to shy away from anything that suggests Louisa and I may have something in common.

The washing machine has not been off since we came home. I don't understand how this is possible, as I thought I had done all the laundry while we were on vacation, yet somehow there is still an unfeasible amount to do, even though all anyone wore was shorts and t-shirts. I failed to wear any of the shoes I lugged all the way to Corfu and back, as it turned out flip flops were all I needed, but I think I put my back out trying to heave my carry-on luggage and pretending it didn't weigh a thing.

The children are feral again, and have been ever since we landed, when, overtired and scratchy, they fought their way home from the airport. The sky is too low, the bluebells are fading, there is too much traffic and I don't want to go back to work tomorrow. Simon says I just have a massive dose of the post-vacation blues, but I want to be sitting on my *terracio* (that might be Italian, actually. Or possibly just made up entirely) drinking quirky little local wines and watching my lovely children frolicking in the pool, and then later on watching the lights twinkle on, one by one, in the valley. In short, reality sucks and I hate my life and it is all very unfair and I am going to scream and scream until I threw up. Or, just, you know, mutter under my breath a bit.

On the plus side, it is quite nice to return to British plumbing and actually being able to flush the toilet paper down the toilet. I was not so keen on the little trash cans full of shitty paper, I have to say. It is also nice to be able to brush my teeth without Simon bellowing, 'Use the bottled water! Don't use the tap water!' And, of course, it is very nice to see my dog again. I did miss the dog dreadfully, and may have messaged the kennels a bit too often to make sure he was okay. And sent him a postcard.

Wednesday, 4 May

Well, I'll be buggered. I was early for school pick-up today and so I made a rare foray into the playground. Of late I have been avoiding it, by arriving bang on the bell and then walking slowly down the road so I can meet the children as they come out of the gate without actually having to set foot in the playground and talk to the Coven and the other mummies. I know this is very bad and anti-social of me, but I somehow just do not have the strength these days to play the game and dance their dances. My only consolation is that Sam has admitted to doing the same on the days he picks up Sophie and Toby, so at least it is not just me who is an anti-social bitch.

Today, though, I decided to be brave. If Perfect Lucy Atkinson's Perfect Mummy and the rest of her cronies wished to sashay up to me and enquire if I'd 'had a good break', with their sympathetic little head tilt, I could at last turn around and say, 'Yes, thanks, we just popped over to Corfu for a couple of weeks. Yes, it was magical actually. I *know*, it does make such a difference if you can get away' instead of trying to pretend that we'd had a simply fabulous time at Michael and Sylvia's while the Coven grew wide-eyed at the notion and almost cricked their necks trying to tip their heads far enough over to express the faux sympathy needed for being so poor as to have to go on vacation to one's in-laws.

The usual mummies were standing around in their usual cliques when I got there, but they were all tapping away at their phones and muttering urgently to each other. 'Oh fuck,' I thought. What had I forgotten? Or had some momentous world event happened and I was completely oblivious? They all looked quite chirpy, though, so maybe it was a cheerful momentous event? I wondered if maybe I could just get away with smiling and nodding if someone said 'Wasn't it *marvellous*?' about whatever had happened.

Right on cue, Perfect Lucy Atkinson's Perfect Mummy made a beeline for me, followed by the rest of the Coven.

'Ellen, is it TRUE?' she shrieked.

Is *what* true, I thought. What does she know? What? That yes, I am a married woman and I flirted more than I should with Charlie Carhill because I was flattered by the attention? Yes, yes, I am a scarlet woman, but nothing actually happened, we just had drinks and lunch a few times and yes, he is still messaging me several times a day and no, I can't keep pretending I haven't seen them, but I am going to sort this whole thing out really, really soon.

Then I thought, of course she doesn't know about that, how could she? What then? Oh God, I bet someone saw the dog do a poo in the wood behind the park and I didn't pick it up because I had run out of poo bags and I really meant to go back for it, but I completely forgot! Round here, leaving a dog poo unpicked is pretty much punishable by stoning. I hoped if I kept my startled bunny-in-the-headlights look, perhaps I could brazen it out and deny all knowledge. I grinned inanely and opened my eyes slightly wider.

'Oh my God, it IS true!' cried Lucy Atkinson's Mummy. 'Look at her face. I TOLD you, Fiona, but you didn't believe me! Thingy the Nanny (I just can't pronounce her name, you know, I have tried) showed me an article about it, and I knew it must be you!'

'An article?' Oh shit! I am in the local paper for the dog poo. Named and shamed, no doubt.

'Oh, in some dreary computer magazine. Apparently she has a degree in something computery from some Ukranian university, so she likes that sort of thing. Anyway, it was about the latest hit "apps" and their developers, and there it was – "Why Mummy Drinks", developed by Ellen Russell Games Ltd. I knew it had to be you! Fiona said you weren't clever enough, but I said you were.'

Wow, thanks, Fiona! So much for bonding over our 'Patricia the Stripper' routine. I won't be dragging you up on top of the piano with me again – Lucy Atkinson's Mummy can join me instead.

'Um, yes,' I muttered. 'That was me. Have you tried it then?'

'*Tried* it? Ellen, we *love* it! We're all completely *addicted* to it!'

I realised a small crowd had gathered by now, all making weirdly appreciative noises about 'Why Mummy Drinks'. Lucy Atkinson's Mummy was, as usual, the official spokesperson for the playground, though.

'It's just so funny, Ellen! And it's so true. It's exactly what life is like, but you've made it into this brilliant game.'

It's not what *your* life is like, I thought, confused. It's what ordinary mums like Hannah and my lives are like. Not you, with your perfect, swishy, shiny hair and your 'Thingy the Nanny' and your angelic bloody children. But she was still in full flow …

'Even the bit where you have to avoid the uber mummies at the school gate, it's just fabulous!'

YOU ARE THE UBEREST UBER MUMMY EVER, WHAT ARE YOU TALKING ABOUT, YOU DELUSIONAL FOOL?

'I've always felt I had to sort of scurry by the working mums who are looking down their noses at me for not working or having my own financial independence, and I envy you, too, you know, going off to work, getting to have something for yourselves, outside your families. And I do worry about what sort of example I am to Lucy …'

'But I've always felt that I've had to scurry past you stay-at-home mums,' put in TV Alicia. 'I thought you were judging me for leaving my children, for having a career, for not making my entire world revolve around them. *I* worry about what sort of an example I am setting for my children by always being busy with work and not baking with them enough or doing crafts.'

'I fucking *hate* baking!' announced Fiona Montague to no one in particular. 'My life would be perfectly complete if I never saw another bastarding cupcake again. Sodding things!'

Truly, the playground had never felt such a nice and friendly place as it did today, as all the mummies actually joked about how they never felt quite good enough and they all were worried that whether they worked or stayed at home they were doing the wrong thing by their children, and how, however much you might love your children, sometimes being a parent was just mind-numbingly boring and hard graft.

Who knew that everyone felt like that? That even Perfect Lucy Atkinson's Perfect Mummy has on occasion been tempted to tell St Lucy herself to just fuck off and stop wittering, and that sometimes Fiona Montague locks herself in the bathroom and cries because she can't face another episode of *Peppa Pig*, or that super-high-powered TV Alicia found herself singing the *Phineas and Ferb* theme tune out loud in a very important meeting the other day?

I was stunned. The app had begun life as a sort of venting mechanism for me, so I threw everything that annoyed me on a day-to-day basis into it as daily challenges to be negotiated. Although I have been loving all the lovely money it has been making, I was baffled as to why it was so popular, as I honestly thought the rubbish mummies, the muddling-through mummies, the just-barely-good-enough-on-a-good-day-if-they-are-lucky mummies, were in the minority. But it turns out we're not. Most of us are those mummies, even if we give the illusion that we are coping, that we are Super Mum, that our lives are perfect.

Perfect Lucy Atkinson's Perfect Mummy gave me a hug as we left the playground. It was terrifying.

Tuesday, 10 May

Today, I got a phone call from the school asking me to please come in as soon as possible, as there had been an 'incident' involving Jane. Petra, the school secretary, who is usually friendly and jolly, sounded very sombre and restrained and called me Mrs Russell instead of Ellen. She refused to go into any details, saying only that I needed to come in urgently to see the headmistress, and that Jane was unhurt.

Obviously, the main reaction to any such phone call is major panic. I rang Simon, whose phone went straight to voicemail, of course, so I then rang his office, only to be told he was out at a site meeting and to try his cell phone, which was helpful when his first-born child was in untold peril. I may or may not have sobbed that down the phone to his secretary.

I drove to the school in a flap, trying to envisage what on earth had happened to Jane that would necessitate me being summoned to the school in the middle of the day, yet didn't require her to be hospitalised. I abandoned the car in the strictly-forbidden-to-parents staff-only car park, as this was clearly an emergency, and ran into the school.

Jane was sitting in the office with Petra, looking very pale. She had the set, defiant jaw I knew meant she was on the verge of tears, and that she would rather die than shed them in public. Petra managed to give me a sympathetic smile and an eye roll before Mrs Johnson the headmistress came bustling out of her office.

Mrs Johnson is a self-important old bitch. She is clearly one of those people who went into teaching because it was an easy route to having power over people more vulnerable than herself, rather than because, like most teachers, she wanted a vocation to fill young minds with knowledge and instil a love of learning and wonder at the world around them. Unfortunately, she reminds me all too much of my own headmistress, which means that every time I see her I have to fight the urge to slouch and mumble that I'm NOT CHEWING before running round the back of the bike sheds and lighting a cigarette and French kissing with an unsuitable boy.

Mrs Johnson gave me her reptilian smile that never reaches her eyes and said, 'Mrs Russell, come through, please' at the same time as Jane said, 'Mummy, I need to talk to you!'

I stopped and asked, 'What's happened? Is Jane hurt? No one has told me why I am here.'

Mrs Johnson said, 'If you *would* just come through, Mrs Russell, I will explain what Jane has done and why you are here.'

Jane said, 'Mummy, *please!*' There was a desperate tremor in her voice that broke my heart, as clearly those tears weren't going to be held back much longer and Jane hates crying in front of anyone, even me, let alone Petra and Poo-face Johnson.

I took a deep breath and channelled Jessica. In my most frigid voice I said, 'I think, Mrs Johnson, it would be more appropriate if I spoke to my daughter first, before I hear *your* explanation of whatever has happened.'

Mrs Johnson's chilly smile vanished to be replaced by a mouth like a cat's bum.

'I don't think that is appropriate, actually, Mrs Russell. *If* you would please come through.'

Jane shot me a desperate look.

'I don't think so, Mrs Johnson,' I said, totally being Jessica the time a delivery man brought her out-of-date smoked salmon and she had to call and complain about it. 'I really think I should speak to *my daughter* before I speak to you, don't you? Now?'

Mrs Johnson huffed and puffed, but the Angry-Jessica-With-Substandard-Smoked-Salmon Voice will brook no argument.

'Well, I suppose you can both come through to my office with me,' was her last stand, only to have Jessica-Who-Has-Been-Offered-A-Non-Organic-Apple snap back, 'I *don't* think so, I will speak to Jane first, and *then* I would be only too delighted to hear your version of events. Thank you *so* much for offering to let us use your office, though, that's terribly kind of you. Come along, Jane!' and I swept through before Mrs Johnson could say another word – Jane trailing after me, Poo-face mouthing furiously and Petra grinning and giving me a discreet thumbs up ('Sweeping Furiously Through Doorways 101' was courtesy of

Jessica's one and only trip to an all-you-can-eat buffet restaurant when she discovered she was expected to go up to the counter and get her own food).

Once in the office and out of sight of Mrs Johnson and Petra, Jane broke down completely and sobbed her heart out. This was not my brave warrior girl, who ever since she was born has marched to the beat of her own drum and shunned tears as being for the weak and foolish. She sobbed in my arms for a while, and the only words I could make out were the occasional 'UNFAIR' and 'I HATE THEM!' and something about Oscar and Tilly. Eventually, I managed to calm her down and was relieved to see that she seemed to be crying as much with rage as with misery and she finally choked out what had happened.

It seems that Oscar Fitzpatrick has been remorselessly bullying Jane's friend Tilly, hitting her and pinching her when there are no staff around, taking her lunch, calling her horrible names and generally being a vicious little bastard. The school have been less than useless – despite many children standing as witness to his behaviour, the most severe 'punishment' meted out to the little sod has been that he was made to stay in one lunchtime and choose an activity in the classroom, instead of going out to play. Apparently he chose the Lego corner, so obviously he was deeply chastised by this penance.

Today Tilly brought her new doll to school, which she had been given for her birthday last weekend. She was showing it to her friends, including Jane, when Oscar appeared, snatched the doll from Tilly, wrenched its head off and threw the body over the fence into the road and chucked the head into the trash, all while Tilly and the girls were screaming and trying to get it off him.

Jane then decided to take matters into her own hands and, putting all those Jiu Jitsu classes I sent her to into practice, she managed to throw Oscar Fitzpatrick to the ground (which is quite impressive because he is one of those giant mutant children that towers above the rest of the class). Then when she had him down, she booted him in the balls, because, as Jane insisted, 'He deserved it, Mummy, and we are only supposed to use Jiu Jitsu in defence, but I WAS! I was defending Tilly!'

Unfortunately, one of the teachers, despite never being around to see Oscar tormenting Tilly, happened to see Jane launch herself on Oscar and batter him, thus Jane was summarily marched off to Mrs Johnson to give an account of herself. Jane, showing wisdom I wish she could apply to things like finding her school shoes, then refused to say anything until I was present, because, 'I have the right to remain silent, Mummy.'

Once Jane had calmed down and I had assured her that of course she had done the right thing and I would be sorting this out for her pronto, I sent her back to Petra and then Jessica-ed up again and called Mrs Johnson into her office while we discussed the matter.

Mrs Johnson appeared to have swelled to twice her normal size with righteous indignation while I was talking to Jane, like an outraged puffer fish, and she bustled into her office with a sharp 'WELL, Mrs Russell, I assume you see the severity of the situation now!'

'Absolutely,' I replied. 'I completely agree this is extremely serious. I understand your concern; I do see that it reflects very badly on the school that you have been so negligent in preventing bullying that other pupils have to take matters into their own hands to protect their classmates, as they can't rely on staff to deal with situations when they arise.'

Ha! I actually managed to nonplus the bitch, as she mouthed furiously for a moment before spluttering, 'I am referring to Jane's completely unprovoked attack on another child!'

'A child who has been systematically bullying one of her friends,' I retorted.

'Mrs Russell, I cannot comment on other ongoing situations with you, we are only here to discuss Jane's violent attack on Oscar. I'm afraid that in this scenario we have no choice but to see Jane as the aggressor and therefore the bully, and deal with it accordingly.'

'And how, exactly, do you propose to do that?'

'Jane will have to publicly apologise to Oscar, and she will miss her Funday Friday time.'

'And what will she do instead of Funday Friday?'

'She will sit in my office and think about her actions.'

The Mother Tiger in me, who had been growling quietly ever since I saw Jane sitting in the office, roared fully into life. I no longer needed to pretend I was my high-achieving sister in order to savage this bitch who was trying to unfairly punish my baby. In fact, she would be lucky if I left without burning her stupid school to the ground, with her battered carcass within it, if she did not back down and leave my little girl alone. It. Was. On. The tigress' claws were unsheathed.

'But when Oscar was allegedly punished for the time he took Tilly's lunch and threw it in the mud and stamped on it, he just missed lunchtime playtime, and got to choose an activity, he has never been made to apologise or miss Funday Friday,' I pointed out.

'Yes, Mrs Russell, but this incident involving Jane was violent, AND was witnessed by a *staff member*!' said Mrs Johnson.

'And every other incident, including today's and several times when Oscar was violent towards Tilly were also witnessed by several other children who will all corroborate Jane and Tilly's version of events, but you feel that because your *staff member* saw the end of an altercation that their solitary version is more reliable than that of multiple children?'

'Mrs Russell, I really –'

'Do you think Jane is stupid?' I interrupted.

'What?'

'Do you think my daughter is stupid? Do you think she would actually get into a physical fight with a boy who is twice her size for no reason? Jane is many things but she is not stupid. She was defending her friend and she should be commended for that. She will not be apologising, and she will not be missing her Funday Friday. Because –' I bashed furiously at my phone, thankful that I had not used all my data faffing around on Facebook, 'Firstly, and I quote, the Department of Education defines bullying as a "repeated pattern of behaviour", so one single, isolated incident on Jane's part could hardly be described as bullying. And secondly, the school district's bullying policy states that they follow a system of promoting positive behaviour, which you are not doing by punishing Jane like this, and that children must be taught to take responsibility for their actions. How are you teaching the children to do this, when you dismiss the repeated word of many different children as being of less importance than the word of ONE staff member who didn't even witness the full incident? Jane was defending her friend, and you have failed in your duty of care to Tilly and to Jane and to Oscar by failing to provide a suitably supervised safe environment.'

'– Mrs Russell, I'd like to say –'

'– I AM STILL TALKING!' roared the Mother Tiger. 'And *I* would like to say that I suggest you drop all these ludicrous threats and allegations against my daughter *right now*, or I will be only too happy to place the entire affair in the hands of the school board and let them investigate how you have failed ALL the children involved in this disgraceful episode. Do I make myself clear?'

'Mrs Russell, I really don't think there's any need to take this to the next level, do you?' babbled Mrs Johnson nervously. 'I think perhaps this could be resolved quite easily. I possibly was a little heavy-handed with Jane –'

'– And would like to apologise?' I suggested.

'Of course, if I have inadvertently caused Jane any distress, I am very sorry that she felt that way.'

It was a cop-out of an apology, but in all honesty I was astonished that I had even got that much out of her, but while I had her on the ropes, I thought I might as well make the most of it. 'And of course you will not be expecting her to apologise or miss Funday Friday?'

'No, no, I suppose not!' panted Johnson, who was an unpleasant shade of puce. I hoped she wasn't about to have a heart attack, after I had so roundly trounced her. I decided to quit while I was ahead, so I stood up and said as graciously as I could, 'Well, I'm *so* glad we've sorted out this silly misunderstanding, Mrs Johnson. It was very nice to see you, do feel free to give me a call if there's anything else at all that you would like to discuss. Obviously, I'll be taking Jane home for the rest of the day, as she is quite shaken by the whole thing. Goodbye!' And I hurriedly did the outraged Jessica sweep out of the office before she could keel over, lest I be blamed.

I marched out to the car park, Jane trailing in my furious wake.

'Mama?' said Jane. Jane hasn't called me Mama since she was about three. 'Are you angry with me, Mama?' she said in a small voice.

'Of course I'm not angry with you, darling!' I said. 'I'm angry with Mrs Johnson and Oscar and the school, but I'm not angry with *you*. You did a good thing, standing up to him like that, especially when he's so much bigger than you. I'm really proud of you; you defended your friend, even though you might have got hurt too, but you weren't scared, you just did it anyway. You should be proud of yourself too, because that was a really brave thing to do.'

'Oh good,' said Jane. 'Do you think we could go and get ice cream on the way home then?'

I gave a sigh of relief. Jane's pragmatic determination to now milk the situation to her own advantage seemed to suggest that for her, normal service had been resumed.

'And maybe a comic?' she added.

Later, Tilly's mummy rang me to say that Tilly had told her the whole saga of what was now being billed as an epic David and Goliath-style battle between Jane and Oscar, and she asked me to thank Jane for intervening like she did, and I nearly cried with pride, even though Jane had shamelessly managed to milk me of £15-worth of treats when we stopped for ice cream on the way home.

As is always the case with any sort of confrontation, I spent the rest of the evening stomping round the house mumbling, 'AND ANOTHER THING!' to myself, as more and more cutting, scathing remarks occurred to me which would have crushed Mrs Johnson like a flea.

Friday, 20 May

It's Fuck It All Friday again! I wish could say 'already' but the gaping chasm between Monday and Friday seems to widen each week. I hurled the frozen pizza down the precious moppets and went to get ready for a bijou pop to the pub with Hannah and Sam.

I was feeling quite pleased with myself for managing to squeeze into a pair of white jeans that I felt were very summery, and was attempting to put on my mascara when Jane wandered into the bedroom.

'Are you wearing *that*, Mummy?' she said in a horrified voice.

'Well, yes!' I said. 'What's wrong with what I'm wearing?'

'I just didn't realise how big your bottom is, that's all,' said Jane.

Have a baby, they said. It will be fulfilling and life-affirming, they said. I was trying not to cry at Jane's pronouncement on the size of my arse, and wondering if I should change or if I should just say 'Fuck it!' when Peter came in and announced he wanted to give me a hug before I went out. Peter's hug mainly consisted of wiping his chocolatey hands and face over my white jeans, which at least solved my dilemma about whether to change or not, as once he had finished with me, I looked like I had soiled myself. Oh yes, having children is just bloody marvellous! Who doesn't like having their soul crushed or being used as a human napkin by a small, sticky creature?

Once I finally got the pub, slightly late due to the entire outfit change while shrieking for Simon to come and bond with his precious moppets, please, it turned out that Sam is out of love. He has decided Mark is not for him; that he was just a bit of a roll in the hay to help him get back on the horse, so to speak. Also, he said, apparently Mark seems to think I am a homophobe.

'I mean, why would he say a thing like that?' said Sam indignantly.

'Ah, I think I might know …' I said, going somewhat scarlet. 'It was all a very unfortunate misunderstanding between his sister and me, but I thought we had cleared it all up.'

'Ellen,' Sam looked at me with his eyebrows raised. 'What on earth did you say or do to make Mark's sister think you were a massive homophobe?'

'Weeeeeeell,' I mumbled. 'I was at a party, and it was quite noisy and I'd had a couple of glasses of wine and I didn't really know Alison that well, and we were having that polite conversation where you ask inane questions about each other, and I asked if she had brothers or sisters and she said she had one brother and I asked if he was married, and I THOUGHT she said, "No, he's dead" because it was *very noisy*! And she was very matter-of-fact about it, but I thought I should be sympathetic, and so I did the whole, "Oh, I'm so sorry about that!" and she just sort of looked at me, and so I said, "Was it sudden?" and she said no, she'd always sort of known, so I assumed he had had some sort of long-term illness. So then I said, "Oh well, that doesn't make it any easier though, does it?" and she just looked at me again. And then, because I thought maybe I wasn't being sympathetic *enough*, I said, "And how did your parents cope, because I suppose you never really get over something like that happening to your child, do you?" Then she got very huffy at me and said she was surprised at me, and she had thought I was more broad-minded than that, and the way I was carrying on anyone would think her brother was *dead*, not gay! But I thought she had said he was bloody well dead, and she was just some cold-hearted weirdo being all blasé about her sodding dead brother. I did explain about the mistake and how I only said all that because I did think she had said he was dead, and I really thought we had cleared it all up, but obviously not. Why would she say that? She came to my party with her undead gay brother and now she's going round telling everyone I'm some sort of bigot.'

Sam was in tears of laughter. 'You utter fuckwit!' he cackled. 'I can't believe you said "How did your parents cope?" You tit! I wouldn't worry too much. I expect Alison told him that story and he got the wrong end of the stick, he isn't very smart. Pretty, though. You have cheered me up about dumping him, at least.'

Hannah, meanwhile, was gloomy because the 'Please Shag My Friend' website she had signed up for had not yet resulted in a single date, let alone bringing about a meeting with her kindred spirit to share the rest of her life with, and so clearly she was going to be alone forever.

Sam tried to cheer her up by pointing out that at least she hadn't had any more dick pics, but she just sank further into despair, groaning, 'I am too much of a withered hag for anyone to even want to send me photos of their penises. I am a crone. The children will grow up and leave me and move to Australia to get away from me. Even the cats shall abandon me and I will have no one to talk to but a wilting pot plant. It will probably be wilting because it is trying to die, just so it doesn't have to listen to me either. I WILL BE ALL ALONE!'

'You will still have us,' I suggested, in the hope of cheering her up.

'Nooooo,' Hannah wailed. 'No, you will be going on Nile cruises with Simon, and Sam will be off getting loads of dick and I will be ABANDONED!'

'Or you could just lay off the gin, babe?' offered Sam. 'I think you've just got the Fears.'

Nile cruises? What sort of a bloody geriatric does she think I am going to be?

Thursday, 26 May

Sports Day. I hate Sports Day. Peter and Jane have both inherited my sporting prowess, which is to say they have the grace and co-ordination of Bambi on ice, combined with the speed and elegance of a baby hippopotamus. They are also resolutely lacking in team spirit and sportsmanship, managing to sulk both if they don't win and if they get a 'Well Done On Taking Part, Even Though You're A Bit Shit' sticker. Jane especially resents the 'Everyone's A Winner Awards', muttering darkly under her breath as we stand for hours while every child in the school goes up to get their medals. Last year she threatened to stage a boycott and had to be bribed with many packets of Gummy Bears not to make a scene.

Apart from the ineptitude of Peter and Jane, I always feel mildly cheated by Sports Day. Sports Days should take place in glorious sunshine, the mummies should be clad in tea dresses of eau de nil silk, with hats wreathed in flowers, while the daddies should wander about in cream linen suits and panama hats. There should be strawberries and cream in the Quad, though I am not entirely certain what a Quad is, and lashings and lashings of fruit cup, and maybe even champagne. Winners should be acknowledged with a polite round of applause, and perhaps the odd 'Hurrah' or two. Picnic hampers involving chicken sandwiches and salmon mousses may feature. Male teachers ought to be in cricket whites, with nice cable-knit sweaters, and female staff in some sort of fetching tennis attire.

It is possible that I have confused Sports Day with some sort of Merchant Ivory mash-up.

Instead, we have a bleak sports pitch, with hordes of children in violently hued nylon vests that I am sure must be a fire hazard if they run fast enough, though obviously that is not something I need to worry about with my children. These luminous bibs denote what team they are in, for all the sports are done by team, so no one is a loser.

Despite this helpful piece of political correctness by the school, all the children persist in jeering 'LOSER! LOSER!' at the child who comes in last, as what the school and political correctness have failed to grasp is that children are inherently cruel and have a pack mentality towards the weakest. Fortunately, due to a combination of low cunning and downright cheating, Peter and Jane generally manage to avoid coming completely last, which probably makes me prouder than I would be if they were actually good at sport.

The teachers trudge around shoe-horned into 'sporty' outfits that range from skin-tight Lycra for the pert young probationer teachers, which cause several of the daddies' eyes to bulge in a way unbecoming in a man of middle age, to a sturdy tracksuit for Miss Briggs the Religious and Moral Education teacher, which only comes out once a year if the vague whiff of mothballs is anything to go by.

The most terrifying sight, though, is Mrs Johnson the headmistress, who, despite being a stout lady of a certain age, likes to cram her most ample bosom and backside into similar garments to the skimpy skin-tight ensembles donned by the young trainees. The advantage of this is that any lustful thoughts that might have been kindled in the daddies' minds by the acres of firm, prancing, youthful flesh on display from the young teachers are immediately doused with horror as Mrs Johnson waddles into view, her megaphone clutched in one pudgy trotter and her air-horn in the other.

Usually, despite my best attempts to avoid her, Mrs Johnson manages to corner me and makes me feel like a naughty schoolgirl, but after the incident with Jane a couple of weeks ago she contented herself with just glaring at me from across the sports pitch, which, frankly, was an unexpected bonus.

The other mummies are divided into the working mummies who are looking hot and a bit flustered in their work clothes because they have come straight from the office, and the Coven mummies and their ilk, who are also poured into sportswear because they are going to ace the Mummies' Race. There was a terrible scene last year when Perfect Lucy Atkinson's Mummy was disqualified for wearing running spikes, which were ruled to give her an unfair advantage, and so her unbroken record of winning every Mummies' Race since Lucy started school was spoilt.

The daddies are mainly wandering about trying to prove who is the busiest and most important, by seeing who can shout the loudest on the phone to the office about busy and important things, and also by competing to see who has the biggest camera to capture their precious moppets' glorious moments of triumph.

This year, I decided to rebel, and wore a suitably floaty frock to Sports Day. I tried very hard to persuade Simon into a panama hat, but he loftily informed me that he was not dressing up like some dickhead from *A Room with a View*. So then I tried to persuade Sam that *he* could be all dapper and dashing in a panama, but got a similar response. Rude!

I also added to the revolution by stashing a large bottle of premixed gin and tonic in my bag. Initially this was intended just for Sam, Simon and me, but word spread and soon mummies from a variety of years were sidling up to me and hissing, 'I hear you have booze!' I felt rather like a drug dealer, dispensing my contraband to the favoured few. Even Lucy Atkinson's Perfect Mummy limped up after the Mummies' Race, her winning streak well and truly over after a well-timed shove from Fiona Montague saw her come in in second place. Denied a Stewards' Enquiry into the result, she settled for consoling herself with a warm G&T.

The ginny gin gin made the interminable hell of Sports Day pass much faster, even when we had to endure an Olympics-style 'Closing Ceremony' which involved various unco-ordinated children flapping pieces of ribbon about while some pan pipes played in the background. Instead of muttering 'Kill me now', I felt all warm and fuzzy about the little darlings giving their all to the ribbon waving. I wish I had thought of taking filthy booze along years ago!

JUNE

Wednesday, 1 June

I have been a little despondent recently because the lovely emails telling me how many people have bought the 'Why Mummy Drinks' app have not been coming quite so regularly, nor have the numbers contained within been so fabulously startling. I suspect it has run its course and this is the beginning of the end. I know it has made more money than I ever dreamed of and I shouldn't grumble, but I do love the happy feeling of those emails plopping into my inbox. Quite a lot of shoes have also happened as a result of those emails, and several pairs of boots, and one or two rather nice purses, and I don't want my supply cut off. It has been divine going into nice shops and just saying 'I will have that' instead of stroking and coveting and hoping for a really good sale.

Simon and the children have been less impressed with my generosity towards them. I thought I was being such a kind and loving wife buying them glorious designer dresses and shirts and jackets, but Jane declared the outfits I had bought her to be 'stupid' and refused to be parted from her beloved dinosaur t-shirts and Simon first announced that he wasn't wearing that because it made him look like a pimp and then recoiled in horror at the price tag. Peter at least did agree to wear the clothes I had bought him, because he is a small boy and doesn't really notice what he wears, but he managed to spill juice on a brand new t-shirt the first time he wore it, and it wouldn't come out, which I suppose serves me right for spending £75 on a t-shirt for a filthy urchin child. There was a suggestion that if I wanted to buy expensive gifts for my family then the latest and dearest electronic devices would be more acceptable than overpriced clothes, but I declined, as the children do not need anything to feed their screen addictions any further and Simon certainly does not need any more bastarding gadgets to make my life more difficult under the guise of making it easier.

Tonight, Simon spent the evening faffing about on his laptop while I for once had control of the big TV and after pressing eleventy billion buttons on eleventy billion remotes for the eleventy fucking billion gadgets he has already connected to the TV because he is a massive bastarding Gadget Twat, I actually managed to get the TV to work and, even more impressively, got the iPlayer thingy to connect to it through one of the wretched gadgets so I could catch up on my soaps, which was about as much excitement as one can really hope for on a Wednesday night.

So I was a bit annoyed when Simon decided to come in and start wittering at me about money, because it was an especially dramatic episode and I wasn't really in the mood for another lecture about savings or pension plans. However, Simon was determined that what he had to say was more important than 'a stupid soap opera', and he insisted I turn off the TV before announcing that he had been going over all the figures for 'Why Mummy Drinks' and even after all the tax owing (the man is obsessed with tax, I swear to God he has missed his calling as a tax man), it had made enough money to pay off the mortgage!

'Mortgage-free, darling! It's the middle-class dream come true.'

'No,' I corrected him. 'The true middle-class dream is being mortgage-free in a house with a handmade artisan kitchen and a massive duck-egg-blue Aga. But that is still pretty bloody marvellous! Oh my God, can we give up work?'

'No,' said Simon. 'Sadly not. It has made a LOT of money but not quite that much. And you said yourself that sales are dropping off now. But you've still done an incredible thing, Ellen. And even after the mortgage is paid off, there'll be a good whack left.'

'Enough for the other middle-class dream?' I asked hopefully.

'Which would be …?'

'A lovely little vacation cottage somewhere by the sea. Maybe Norfolk. Norfolk's nice, isn't it? OR a lovely tumbledown villa in Corfu. Even if there was only enough for a deposit, then it would still be an investment, Simon, because we could rent it out to other people. And it would be so much nicer an investment than a savings plan …'

Simon droned on for a while about the tax advantages of savings accounts versus an adorable seaside cottage/tumbledown villa while I mutinously thought, 'Yes, but I can't bloody well swank in the playground about how I'm just popping off to my stupid savings plan for a few days, can I? I can't create beautiful Pinterest boards of a share portfolio, can I?'

I tired of Simon wittering about boringly sensible financial decisions and said, 'We should celebrate. Properly!'

'Of course! You're quite right, I've put some champagne in to chill, I'll just go and get it.'

Simon returned and handed me a chilled flute of champagne, those lovely little bubbles popping delightfully. I smugly took an enormous gulp of my delicious, celebratory champagne and choked on what appeared to be sparkling battery acid.

'Simon, what the actual FUCK am I drinking?'

'Champagne, darling. I found it in the wine rack.'

'We haven't got any champagne in the wine rack – if we did, I would have drunk it long ago.'

'Yes, we do,' Simon replied indignantly. 'It was a bit dusty, so I thought it must be something you were keeping for good.'

A terrible thought occurred to me. 'Show me the bottle,' I demanded.

Simon returned brandishing The Bottle. The Unspeakable Bottle of some sort of dubious German sparkling wine that has been doing the rounds of every school, Girl Scouts', Boy Scouts' and sports clubs' raffles and tombolas since approximately 1973. You do not actually 'win' The Bottle, you simply become its temporary custodian until the next fundraiser when you are able to return it to circulation with a sigh of relief. Simon has broken the system. Society may collapse without The Bottle as the backbone of the school fete. Also, what a cheap bastard! The least he could have done was actually buy a bottle of decent champagne instead of trying to fob me off with something he found at the back of wine rack. I grumbled all of this to him at some length until he went to the shops and bought me a bottle of proper champagne.

By the time Simon returned with a bottle of lovely Bollinger, I had obviously come up with many more ways of celebrating our new, grown-up, mortgage-free status.

'Let's go away this weekend,' I suggested.

Simon made his usual noises about 'thinking about it' and 'looking into it', but I was having none of it.

'Fuck that shit, Simon!' I announced. 'We fucking *deserve* this! *I* fucking deserve this, and I am going to go away this weekend whether you like it or not. If you don't want to come, that's fine, I will take Hannah and you can stay here with the children by yourself. But I am going to go away for a glitzy and glamorous weekend. I am going to go to London and stay at … ooooh …

The Savoy, and I am going to drink ludicrously overpriced cocktails while wearing impractical shoes and I shall go to Harrods and a cool retrospective of something at the Victoria & Albert museum and generally I shall have a very fucking lovely time.'

Faced with the prospect of being left alone with Peter and Jane while I swanned around London off my tits on pink drinks with unfettered access to expensive shops, Simon suddenly decided that maybe we could just go away at the drop of a hat, without his weeks of earnest and intense research first. Unfortunately, this plan meant that there was no one available to take the children at such short notice, so they are going to come with us and have a lovely time, too. We will be like a shiny family in an advert. I shall take them to the Tower of London, like my dad used to take me, and it will be a marvellous bonding experience. They are far more civilised than they used to be anyway, and the hotel has a babysitting service so I can still drink my shockingly expensive cocktails in peace. What's the worst that can happen?

Friday, 3 June

'What's the worst that can happen?' What's the fucking worst that can happen, I said. Were there ever words more likely to tempt fate?

After my insistence that we go away *this* weekend to celebrate me being so very, very clever and nouveau riche, Simon and I hastily booked time off work, lied to the school about why Peter and Jane would not be in today and booked first-class train tickets to London, and a suite, no less, at The Savoy, Simon twitching visibly at both the outrageous price and the trauma of being forced to book a hotel without first having spent at least six weeks reading TripAdvisor reviews about it.

Merrily we set off, though I did rather wish that I had a matching set of Louis Vuitton luggage instead of my rather battered, black nylon wheely suitcase and the children's gaudy, vile and dangerous wheely suitcases that they insisted they could not travel without. Simon attempted to bring his extremely nasty ancient backpack as his luggage, but I vetoed that by dint of a lot of foot stamping and shouting 'It's the *Savoy*! They will think you are an aspirational bum trying to come in and use the toilets if you take that scabby old thing with you.'

Simon's counter argument that they would merely think him another in a long line of visiting English eccentrics did not mollify me at all, as I insisted that a visiting English eccentric would undoubtedly have a battered vintage leather suitcase, with many exotic stickers from far-flung locations and also probably a panama hat, and Simon had already made his views on panama hats clear on Sports Day. He finally consented to bring the little suitcase he uses for work trips instead, while I thought covetous thoughts about vanity cases, but couldn't get one delivered in time.

The train was very nice, but ultimately I always find trains a little disappointing. I want to sashay through billowing steam like Marilyn Monroe at the beginning of *Some Like It Hot*, then have an intense and meaningful romance à la *Brief Encounter*. I long for compartments, and silk stockings, and adorable hats, and ticket collectors with smart caps, and possibly a brutal yet curiously bloodless murder or two to solve en route (*Murder on the Orient Express*). The lighting on trains, even in first class, is always extremely Soviet and unflattering. Would it be too much to ask for a little ambience? A little atmosphere? Instead of strip lighting and those weirdly furry nylon seats in distressingly busy patterns, a spot of wood panelling wouldn't go amiss.

Apart from my internal laments about the soullessness of the train, the journey passed without much incident, due to Simon insisting we would all have a much nicer time if I just let Peter and Jane log into the train's Wi-Fi and sit glazed in front of their iPods for the duration instead of chivvying them to hold conversations with us and play I Spy and The Minister's Cat (actually, we can no longer play The Minister's Cat since Jane had the very good idea of playing Rude Words Minister's Cat. Admittedly, it was quite funny, but a visiting child was scarred for life by Jane's winning contribution that the Minister's Cat was a crappy, bastarding, arsehole cat. After that, no one really knew what to say).

The suite was utter bliss. The hotel sent a little man to pick us up from the station. Why does my life not contain more chauffeur-driven cars? I feel this is something definitely lacking in my world. Obviously, because I am pretentiously middle class and pretend to read the liberal newspapers, it was important to me that the little man driving the car knew that I was not elitist or over-privileged, but was in fact 'down' with the 'people'. Thus I insisted on attempting to engage him in conversation, until Simon kicked me on the ankle and made 'shut up' faces at me as I politely asked the man how long he had been a chauffeur. Apparently I was being patronising and sounded like I was trying to be the Queen, which is unfair, as I was only trying to be polite.

After we had checked in and I had made sure we had consumed every 'complimentary' snack and beverage that came with the suite, we set off for the Tower of London. Simon baulked even more at the entry fee than he had at the cost of the hotel, and it was only under extreme duress that he could be induced to pay extra for us all to have an audio guide each.

Once inside the Tower, Peter, obviously, was bored and felt the need to remind us every thirty seconds that he was bored, or that he needed a wee, or a poo, or another wee, or that he was bored, or that this was a boring place and he was bored.

Jane, however, was entranced. She was particularly taken with the torture exhibition and the execution site, becoming more animated than I have possibly ever seen her, as her eyes glowed with zeal at the thought of having anyone who annoyed her either tortured or executed. I attempted to explain to Jane that torture and execution were the tools of bloodthirsty despots and had no place in modern democracy, but she was deep in plans of whose head she would have off first.

While Jane was plotting bloody revolution followed by world domination, Peter managed to dismantle his audio guide and proudly presented Simon with the pieces, leading to more mutterings from Simon about wasted money.

By now I had blocked out Simon's grumblings about money, and when we got back to the hotel I raided the mini-bar – the Sacred Mini Bar! I had never ever been allowed to touch a mini bar before, as my father shared Simon's parsimonious views on Not Spending Money On Vacation. In a fit of generosity, I even let Peter and Jane have the tiny tubes of Pringles and the bar of Toblerone. Then I looked at the actual prices and decided Simon was right and it was extortionate and declared the mini bar off-limits again. Not before I had opened a bottle of wine, though …

The plan for the evening was that we would take the children downstairs for an early dinner in the hotel, and then someone was coming from the hotel's babysitting service to look after them while Simon and I went out and had a grown-up dinner and cocktails.

As we waited for the elevator, it is possible that I was a tiny bit be-drunkled after the mini-bar wine, which I had insisted on finishing due to the ruinous price, and therefore my attention may have wandered slightly. I was squinting in the mirror outside the elevators, demanding of Simon if I should make my hair blonder, when the elevator pinged and we realised that Peter and Jane had vanished. The Savoy is a very quiet hotel, with thick carpets and twisting corridors, and my darling children had sidled off somewhere. After hunting for them for about twenty minutes without any success, we were forced to go downstairs and admit to the reception desk that we had managed to lose our children and request that the staff keep an eye out for them.

Unfortunately, it turned out that hotels take missing children somewhat more seriously than Simon and I did, and they immediately put the entire building on lockdown until they were found. Many angry American tourists were milling in the lobby, demanding to be released to go and have their dinners as I attempted to explain to the manager that I was sure the children were fine and would turn up shortly, and the lockdown probably wasn't actually necessary, and no, please, don't call the police just yet, let's look a bit more, all while trying to talk out of the side of my mouth so he wouldn't notice the drink fumes.

The manager did not share my blasé attitude towards my errant moppets and I think judged me quite a lot when he insisted the lockdown was absolutely necessary, if only so that Peter and Jane couldn't get out and drown in the Thames, and I cheerfully replied that at least if they fell in the river I would finally be getting my money's worth for all the swimming lessons I have forked out for over the years, just in case of such an eventuality. He also seemed dubious about my insistence that no one in their right minds would actually try to kidnap Peter and Jane, because Peter's rancid farting would quickly put them off, in the unlikely event that Jane didn't just murder them.

There was a tiny part of me that was concerned that perhaps Jane had lured Peter back to the Tower of London and tricked him into the torture room and was even now experimenting on him, but just as I started to wonder if maybe someone should see if a Beefeater could pop down and check a small boy wasn't being stretched on the rack by his loving sister, the children were found.

Apparently they had bolted down the fire escape stairs, and from there they had made their way into the bowels of the hotel and discovered a marvellous store room, filled with all the tiny bottles of shampoo and shower gel and other goodies that Simon complains about me stealing from hotels. They had gathered as much loot as they could carry and were attempting to stagger back to the suite with their booty when they were spotted by a chambermaid and turned in. To their immense disappointment, their swag was taken from them by a now-apoplectic manager and we slunk back to the suite in disgrace.

After the shame of the evening, and the fact that pretty much every guest in the hotel now hated us, and the fear that if we ventured out someone might take a photograph of us and sell it to the *Daily Mail*, who would caption it 'Broken Britain', we cancelled the babysitter and spent the first night of our fabulous weekend hiding in the suite, eating fries from room service and hoping the staff hadn't done anything worse than spit on them.

Saturday, 4 June

Ha ha ha ha. How cunning I am. I informed the children that there is a swimming pool in the hotel, so of course they immediately desperately wanted to go swimming. But alas! Such tragedy! Mummy had forgotten her swimming costume. But it's okay, because DADDY has his swimming costume (which I had carefully packed for him) so he could take them swimming while Mummy just went for a little looky round the shops.

Somehow my little meander round the shops took me not in the direction of TJ Maxx or Forever 21 as usual, but towards New Bond Street. So many lovely shops, selling so many lovely things. How convenient that I had happened to transfer all the dividends for 'Why Mummy Drinks' into my current account before I left. But of course, I was only going to look, to press my nose against the windows of the beautiful shiny things.

But as I was pressing my nose, I saw Them. The Most Beautiful Earrings In The World. They spoke to me. 'How shiny we are!' they cooed. 'How pretty you would be if we dangled from your ears! There is literally no part of your life that could not be improved for having us in it. You know you want to. You deserve a treat. A shiny, shiny treat. And we are two treats for the price of one. A bargain really.'

I only meant to look closer, and perhaps enquire of the price, when I went into the shop. My Preciouses were even shinier and more beautiful close up, though, and even though the price was beyond outrageous and entering the realms of the obscene, somehow I found myself handing over my card and then skipping out of the shop with a stiff and expensive little shopping bag clutched in my hand.

I meant to stop there, I really did, but a little further along was the most beautiful luggage shop in the world, and there in the window was a vanity case. A glorious vanity case, one that said steam trains and silk stockings. A vanity case that said swanning into grand hotels in the South of France, with a bell boy running behind trying to carry all your matching luggage while louche men appeared to light the cigarette in the elegant holder that dangled from your bejewelled fingers. A vanity case that whispered 'Take me on the *Orient Express* and I will help you solve the murders. Come inside. Stroke me. You know it's meant to be.'

I didn't want the vanity case to be lonely, so I had to buy a matching suitcase. I shall feel like the Queen on the way home. I may demand my own train, just for me and my lovely luggage. The children will have to be dressed in some form of biohazard suits before they are allowed within six feet of my new bags, lest they touch them with their sticky paws. Simon, too, probably.

This evening, Peter and Jane duly fed from room service

again, to avoid any risk of another bunk, and a former Estonian police officer supplied by the babysitting agency to keep them in order, Simon and I are going out for the lovely dinner and expensive cocktails we were denied last night. My new earrings are sufficiently bling that even Simon noticed them and remarked on them.

'Oh these?' I said casually. 'TJ Maxx.'

He may realise I have fibbed somewhat when I spend the whole night obsessively clutching my ears to make sure I haven't lost one of my beautiful babies, and he is going to do his nut when he finds out how much I have spent today, but fuck it. It will be totally worth it. Maybe I'll mollify him by buying him another pimp jacket for him not to wear.

Friday, 10 June

Right, I decided today that I am a grown-up, and I am going to deal with this Charlie situation. I haven't actually seen him in over two months, since the day we had lunch before Sylvia and Michael went home, but his messages continue apace.

The trouble is I manage to be aloof and ignore him through the week, and then at the weekends I drink too much wine and play on my phone while Simon tries not to fall asleep in front of *Wheeler Dealers* and so then I end up on Messenger chatting with Charlie, because, to be fair, he does make me laugh and also he claims never to have heard of *Wheeler Dealers* (is this really possible? A man who does not watch *Wheeler Dealers*?) and so then the next week the cycle all repeats itself and I am clearly a Very Bad Person.

I need to nip things in the bud, but I am not sure how because it has all got a bit tricky now as Charlie is refusing to be British about things and just skirt vaguely round difficult subjects without ever addressing them head-on and has instead sent me a message getting right to the point, which frankly is just rude. Why can't he just be emotionally repressed and awkward, like British people are meant to be?

I blame it on this new habit that everyone has of hugging and kissing people you barely know. Why do we have to do that now? I don't want to kiss people at parties who I have never met, or have only met twice. My days of kissing strangers at parties involved someone's tongue down your throat and then waking up the next day with a slight nagging sense of shame, not this pecking on the cheek business. And is it one, or is it two? Then there will always be some clever bugger who goes for three, and then I have *ishoos* with the people who actually kiss your cheek with their lips instead of just vaguely brushing cheeks with each other, because now there is a very good chance that I have saliva belonging to someone I barely know on my face, and how long can you leave it before discreetly wiping your cheek? But by then it might have dried, and it is all just too much! What is wrong with a brisk handshake?

I digress. That is how much I don't want to deal with emotions or any sort of direct confrontation. There is no need for it, a quiet mutter under one's breath followed by pretending nothing has happened at all should be sufficient. Anyway, this is what Charlie had to say for himself:

Hi Ellen,

I can't help but feel you're avoiding me? Have I done something to upset you? If so, maybe we could meet for a drink and talk about it?

Charlie xx

Arrrrrrgh! OBVIOUSLY I cannot reply 'Well, Charlie, the thing is, when I bumped into you I was a bit fed up because my husband was being a bit of an arse, and I generally felt underappreciated and so it was awfully nice popping out for drinks with you, and generally being flattered by your attention and feeling as though I had recaptured a bit of my lost youth, and I did think you might still fancy me a bit, which was also quite an ego boost, but actually, I'm getting on much better with Simon now, and I've made potloads of cash and I'm going to buy a seaside cottage in Norfolk or possibly a savings plan but more likely the cottage, maybe in Wells-next-the-Sea, have you been?, apparently it's lovely, so anyway, I'm awfully sorry I led you on again, and that I keep getting slightly drunk and messaging you, which is a very bad and irresponsible thing for me to do, but I'm not actually going to shag you, on account of the whole husband thing, so soz again for being a shameless Jezebel … lol!'

Instead I send this, because one of us has to be British about things, if Charlie insists on being rude enough to address issues head-on:

Ha ha ha, no, of course you've not upset me and I'm not avoiding you. I'm just a bit busy at the moment! Ellen x

But Charlie is not to be thwarted. Why not? What is wrong with him?

Good, I'm glad I've not done anything to upset you. So let's have that drink anyway, if you're not avoiding me. What are you doing next Friday night?

WASHING MY HAIR!

Oh, that's such a shame, I'm actually doing something next Friday. Some other time?

Saturday then?

Ellen? Did you get my message about Saturday? For someone who is not avoiding me, you seem to be doing a good job of avoiding me, lol!

Oh fuck. I'm going to have to go for a drink with him now or he will think I am avoiding him, even though I am *totally* avoiding him, but he mustn't know I am avoiding him or that would defeat the purpose of avoiding him. I wish I was French; if I was French I could just shrug and say 'Boff! Oui, I am avoiding you' and blow a sardonic stream of Gauloises smoke in the air and laugh a wry laugh while sipping my pastis and that would be an end to it. Sometimes being British is rubbish. I put on my big girl pants and message him back:

Yes, Saturday night would be great, if you fancied a quick drink?

Argh, why did I use the word 'fancied'? Will he read something into that? Too late, it is sent. I can stare at the screen and jab at my phone all I like in a twenty-first-century version of getting my hand stuck in the mailbox while trying to retrieve a letter sent in error, but there is nothing I can do about it now.

There is also the small matter of me somehow still forgetting to mention to Simon about meeting up with Charlie, who he thinks is just a Facebook friend and not living round the corner and having cocktails with his wife on Saturday night. Actually, note to self: do not drink cocktails on Saturday night, because that will result in me getting shitfaced and possibly even talking about my feelings. A single glass of dry white wine will suffice. Maybe a large one, though.

Tuesday, 14 June

So I came home from picking up the children from school today to find Simon's car in the driveway along with a battered wreck that looked suspiciously like Louisa and Bardo's camper van.

Why were they here? Why wasn't Simon at work? And why hadn't he said anything about them coming?

When I walked in, I wasn't even sure at first that anyone was there, as the house was surely too quiet to be containing Louisa and the hordes, but when I stuck my head into the sitting room I was greeted by a sea of small, grubby faces, although curiously they were staring transfixed at the TV and appeared, from the debris scattered around them, to have been eating ham sandwiches.

Were these really Louisa's children? Weren't they gluten-free vegans who were forbidden from short-circuiting their precious neuro-networks by rotting their brains with TV? I must confess that there were so many of Louisa's offspring I had never really looked at them properly, and probably wouldn't actually be able to pick any of them out of a line-up of similarly grubby children, so for a moment I feared we had been broken into, only instead of taking the TV, we had been left a load of kids, which was bizarre to say the least, but probably the sort of thing the *Daily Mail* would blame on immigrants. Then the cleanest one waved and said, 'Hello Auntie Ellen, we've come to stay for a few days'. I recognised Coventina, who still appears to be the only one with a semblance of manners or normal behaviour.

Peter and Jane bridled somewhat at this invasion, having neither forgotten nor forgiven the attempts made to steal their beloved iPods by Cedric, but the hypnotic glow of the TV was too strong for them to resist after a whole day of education and they slid in to assume the same slack-jawed, catatonic poses as the other children, while I went in search of Simon and the ruffians' parents and some answers about what they were all doing here.

A clue was offered outside the kitchen door, as there were very soggy sounds coming from the other side, so clearly some-one was in there. I did hesitate for a moment before I went in, because I couldn't help but worry, given the moist nature of the noises, which were interspersed with the odd yelp and whimper, that there was an excellent chance that Louisa and Bardo, with their customary disregard for boundaries and hygiene were having sex on the kitchen table, while Simon cowered in the garage, protecting his power tools from Bardo's thieving habits, but I decided that surely not even Louisa and Bardo would just turn up unannounced and start shagging. I hoped not anyway.

There was no sign of Bardo in the kitchen, just a heaving, gasping Louisa, sobbing pitifully in Simon's arms. Judging by the number of Kleenex scattered over the table, the state of Simon's shirt – the front of which was drenched (I presumed with Louisa's tears and not that he had been taking part in some sort of wet t-shirt competition when she arrived) – and the fact that Louisa's face seemed to have disintegrated into a bellowing, beetroot blob, smeared with snot and tears while her eyes (always rather small) were now so swollen with sobbing that they were almost invisible, she appeared to have been crying for some time.

Simon, given his fear of weeping women, was attempting to console her as best he could, by patting her shoulder clumsily and muttering, 'There, there! Maybe you could cry a bit less now, and have a cup of tea? Hmmm? Nice cup of tea? There, there.' The dog was hiding in his bed, as he shares Simon's horror of emotional females.

Simon looked deeply relieved to see me and ceased his shoulder patting to say, 'Look, sis! Ellen is home. SHE'LL know what to do. Why don't you tell her all about it, and I'll … errrr … I'll make some more tea? Yes, more tea. Or what about a nice drink? Yes! A drinky. Excellent plan. Do you want a G and T, Lou? Ellen?'

Louisa just sobbed, which suggested that plying her with gin was possibly not one of Simon's brighter ideas. 'I think just some tea for now, darling,' I said firmly, as I gingerly attempted to find a seat that was not strewn with Louisa's snot rags.

Gradually, amidst much hiccupping and wailing from Louisa and awkward mumblings from Simon, I managed to piece together what had happened.

It seems that Bardo, as part of the full package for the 'past-life regressions' he performs on gullible, insecure women, has been providing his own 'special therapy' in the yurt as well. Some 'extras', if you will. Louisa, meanwhile, had been blissfully unaware that he was merrily dipping his unwashed wick wherever he could, until things got rather out of hand with his latest 'client', a rich and clearly bonkers American who had come to Scotland to have her theory proved that she was the reincarnation of a Celtic warrior queen, which Bardo obligingly did, and then promptly obliged her in several other ways as well.

The loopy American then decided that Bardo was her soul-mate; the one that she had been searching for across the centuries (she may have watched too much *Highlander*) and that they were meant to be together.

Bardo was not averse to this idea, probably because as part of her quest to find her one true love she had been divorced three times, amassing larger and larger settlements each time, and was prepared to give him access to all her cash.

Therefore, he and Sgathaich (formerly Carol) had gone to Louisa and suggested that they should all live together, with Louisa and the moneyed bonkers woman being 'sister-wives' to Bardo. One must, at least, give Bardo some credit for his sheer unrepentant effrontery, as a lesser cad would simply have buggered off with the rich divorcee.

Louisa, in a fit of fairly justifiable outrage, had responded to this suggestion by loading the six children into the dilapidated camper van, along with whatever possessions she could fit around them, walking out on Bardo and Sgathaich/Carol and the retreat and high-tailing it to fling herself on the mercy of her big brother, who she was now entreating to go and fight for her honour while Simon made excuses of distance and the fact that Bardo is quite a big fellow.

So now it appears that Louisa and the children are to be installed here for the foreseeable future. Quite where they are to be installed I am not entirely sure. It is one thing having them here for a few days over Christmas but Louisa has declared that she is never returning to Bardo or the retreat.

I suggested a hotel, but Simon feels it would be very unkind to dump her and the children on their own when Louisa is so fragile. I am less convinced, but on the other hand, as it turns out Louisa also has no money and we would be footing the bill, perhaps it is for the best that she is here, draining my wine rack rather than draining the mini bar while the fiends rampage round ordering room service and stealing anything that isn't nailed down.

Eventually Louisa rallied a little and mumbled she thought she might be able to manage a tiny glass of wine. I took advantage of the hiatus in the howling to nip up to the bathroom and hide my newly purchased bottle of bath oil. As I was doing so, I found Peter and Jane doing the same with all their electronics and looking gloomy at the prospect of a lengthy visit from their cousins.

It could be worse. Louisa has at least declared that she will be known as Louisa again and not Amaris, as she wants no reminders of that 'bastarding twat Kevin' (although I am not sure how she is going to manage that, given she has six larger-than-life reminders of him sitting in front of my TV) and, hurrah, for she has finally ordered the floor shitters to use the toilet instead.

Friday, 17 June

My house is mayhem. There are children everywhere. I feel like I am living in some sort of hideous commune. Or possibly an orphanage, as Louisa's urchin children are lurking in every corner. Louisa has obviously had a dreadful shock, not least because the prospect of life as a single mother to six children must be rather daunting and I am trying to be understanding, really I am, but I can't help but feel that it wouldn't bloody kill her to shove the vacuum cleaner round while I am at work, or even just pick up some of the trail of destruction that her children leave behind.

Yesterday the baby ate my Crabtree & Evelyn soap from the downstairs bathroom that I only put out when we have posh visitors that I want to impress, and then he vomited foam all down the stairs. Louisa just looked at it, sniffed bravely and said, 'Oh, the poor fatherless mite.'

It has not escaped my attention either that, despite her wallowing in the slough of despair, she still has sufficient wits about to her to have started making covetous noises about the items of furniture we inherited from Simon's grandmother.

As well as the still-ruined sideboard, there are some other rather nice bits that she has been eyeing up, while muttering that she doesn't know how she would even start to manage to furnish a home of her own, and she had always so *loved* Granny's ottoman, a few good pieces of furniture make all the difference you know … And this from the woman who, until recently, had been fond of announcing that all we owned was our souls, and in fact when offered some of Granny's furniture after the old dear popped her clogs, declared she had no interest in possessions and instructed Michael to sell what he didn't want and give her a share of the money instead. I have several tins of chalk paint left and I am not afraid to use them if it stops Louisa getting her grubby paws on our furniture.

I am also not sure that it is entirely necessary for her to hurl herself on Simon with quite such drama when he walks in the door at night and start again on her sobbing, 'Woe is me' routine, given that until she hears his key in the lock, she is quite happy to lie dry-eyed on the sofa, heckling the TV and ignoring her children's requests for food, instructing them to go and ask Auntie Ellen, because Mummy has a headache.

FML is more my mantra than ever, as I crash around loudly, tidying up and stage-muttering (is stage-muttering a thing? If it's not, it should be) that no, NO, don't worry about clearing up the children's lunch, Louisa, I've only been at work ALL DAY. No, of course I don't expect you to wipe down the counter tops or put the cheese back in the fridge or the bread in the bread bin, and don't worry AT ALL that your children have eaten ALL THE YOGHURTS for the packed lunches, I'll just GO AND BUY SOME MORE, will I, THAT'S FINE! Louisa pays no attention at all to any of this and just droops tragically into another room.

Saturday, 18 June

I nearly cancelled my drink with Charlie, as I wasn't sure I could stand any more drama, or talking about feelings, with Louisa flopping hopelessly around the house and wailing, but after a full day of her weeping loudly for Simon's benefit, the thought of actually getting away from it for a couple of hours was very appealing.

When I went into the kitchen to say goodbye, Louisa was in her now customary nightly position of sobbing face down on the table, lifting her head periodically to take another enormous slug of wine (a rather nice Barolo that I had bought for a special occasion, I couldn't help but notice), while Simon cowered on the other side of the table, his major contribution to getting Louisa to man the fuck up being to manage to stop her actually crying *on* him.

There is a niggling part of me that can't help but feel Louisa is rather enjoying her role as distraught, abandoned woman and milking it to the max. She knows there is no point in crying at me, because the first time she tried it, I got out my iPad and cheerfully suggested we made a lawyer's appointment for her, so she could get some legal advice and find out where she stands, whereas she knows perfectly well that Simon will be so paralysed with horror at the sight of her hysteria that he will let it run, for fear that saying anything of practical help will make matters worse.

I gestured at the calendar and mouthed 'I'm going out. It's on the calendar!', because everyone knows you cannot argue with something that has been written on the calendar, it may as well have been written on tablets of stone.

Simon frowned at me and said, 'Are those MORE new shoes, Ellen? Jesus, how many shoes do you have now?'

I staunchly denied that my brand-new shoes were in any way new at all, while Simon looked disbelieving. He is possibly disbelieving because my shoe collection has now reached critical mass and can no longer be contained under the bed. This is another reason why I would quite like to get rid of Louisa because then I could keep my shoes in the guest room. Of course, if Simon would only listen to reason and let me buy my adorable beachfront cottage in Wells-next-the-Sea, I could keep some of my shoes there. Simon insists that my plan to buy a house just to keep my shoes in is in some way unreasonable, but clearly he is wrong.

Louisa heaved her head off the table and looked at me through brimming, bloodshot eyes. 'It must be nice to just go out for the night, Ellen, not a care in the world,' she quavered pathetically. I almost felt sorry for her until she added a pointed, 'And in new shoes, too! I can't remember the last time I bought new shoes, you know.' FFS, she is shameless! Louisa has been hinting a lot about how our feet are practically the same size, but they are not, hers are a good size bigger than mine and she is not getting her (still distressingly grubby) paws on any of my preciouses.

'Maybe you'd like to go, too, Lou?' suggested Simon desperately. 'I could babysit. It wouldn't take you long to get ready. Splash of water on your face, quick hair brush, job done. Ellen could lend you something to wear and some shoes. Might do you good.'

Bloody hell, Simon must be desperate to get a few hours free of his demented sister if he is volunteering to babysit EIGHT children on his own! But I was the one who had cunningly arranged to escape and I was not being thwarted that easily, only to have to sit in public with Louisa ranting about how the bourgeois capitalists have ruined her life and stolen her youth.

Also, it would take more than a quick brush to get through Louisa's mop, which I think last saw scissors or a comb sometime around when there was a Bush in the White House. 'You will have to do better than that, Simon,' I thought grimly, as I caringly patted Louisa on the shoulder (pushed her back into her chair) and said, 'Don't be silly, Simon, of course Louisa's not ready to go out yet. She's in the middle of a very distressing time, the last thing she wants to do is go to some noisy pub full of strangers. I'd stay in if I could and be with you, Louisa, but I just can't get out of this, sorry!'

And with that I skipped out the door, as Simon slumped dejectedly back in his chair, all hopes of bribing the children upstairs with chocolate and iPads while he sprawled on the sofa in front of *Wheeler Dealers* slipping from his fingers and being replaced by the prospect of listening to his sister sob about how ALL MEN ARE BASTARDS for the fourth night in a row. (Louisa's repertoire is rather limited; she starts with how she would like to kill Bardo and Sgathaich, and then moves on to how the Goddess has abandoned her and what will become of her, and ends by shouting furiously about being oppressed by the patriarchy as she nears the bottom of the bottle.) On the plus side, he was too defeated to even ask who I was meeting, which was probably a good thing, as I hadn't quite made up my mind what I should say about Charlie.

In the event, the evening didn't go at all as I had expected. We met at a rather posh new wine bar (is it just me, or are wine bars becoming a 'thing' again? They vanished for a long time after the eighties, but all of a sudden they are popping up all over the place). We did the polite chit-chat thing, the 'how are yous', and the 'what have you been up tos', and I was thinking 'ha ha ha, it is all going to be all right, we are not going to have to talk about feelings, we will just have a quiet drink like two civilised people and go on our way', which was absolutely fine by me, because Louisa has provided enough emotion to last a lifetime, when there a was a pause in the meaningless conversation and Charlie said, 'Why have you been avoiding me?'

Buggeration. I thought we had established that I hadn't been avoiding him by me saying I hadn't been avoiding him. You are supposed to accept that at face value, even if it is a blatant lie. I am starting to wonder if Charlie is British at all. Didn't he do a gap year in America? That was probably where it all started, this desire to communicate instead of living a perfectly happy life of awkward silences and speaking only in clichés.

Obviously I said the only thing one can say under those circumstances, which was to laugh shrilly and squawk, 'Of *course* I haven't been avoiding you! Ha ha ha! So sorry, just busy busy busy.'

I stared at the table as I babbled this, frantically dodging eye contact, as there was no need to make this even more embarrassing. Charlie, however, leaned across the table and put his hand under my chin, lifted up my head, then gently brushed my hair out of my eyes. Fuck. I knew I should have put a bobby pin in, like that super-sensible TV historian, Lucy Worsley, and then he wouldn't have any excuse to do things like that. I wished I was as sensible as Lucy Worsley – she would never get herself into a position like this. Or if she did, she would deal with it in a brisk and no-nonsense, jolly hockey sticks manner, like a school games captain telling the younger classes off for having a crush on her. I bet Lucy Worsley was a games captain at school. Or, actually, she was probably head girl. I wondered if I could google Lucy Worsley under the table to distract me from the inevitable unfortunate scene about to unfold.

My googling plans were thwarted when Charlie reached across the table and took my hand. Oh God. MORE physical contact. Not a good sign. Maybe, I thought desperately, I could just knock my wine over, send it flying over us both, and the moment would be over while we mopped our ruined clothes and then I could just grab my purse and say, 'GOSH! Is that the time? Must go, lovely to see you, byeeeeee!' then run away and move to Outer Mongolia and change my name. And google whether Lucy Worsley was a games captain or head girl.

Only he was holding the hand closest to the wine, so in order to knock it over I would actually have to lean across the table with my other hand and give it a good shove. I could totally do that. Or, I could suddenly shout that I had explosive diarrhoea and had to go to the bathroom RIGHT NOW! I defy anyone to have a 'moment' in the face of the uncontrollable squits. Oh bollocks, he was talking again.

'Ellen, are you listening to me?'

'Yes, of course. Do you think Lucy Worsley was a head girl or games captain when she was at school?'

'What? Who is Lucy Worsley? What does she have to do with any of this?'

'You know, the blonde historian lady off the TV. Very sensible. She always wears a bobby pin in her hair, and comfortable-looking shoes.'

'I have no idea what you are talking about.'

'LUCY WORSLEY! BOBBY PIN! Lots of programmes about Henry VIII! She wears a fucking bobby pin, how many TV historians wear bobby pins, for fuck's sake? You *must* know who she is.'

'Ellen, I don't even know what a bobby pin is, let alone why you are suddenly so obsessed by them. Can we just talk about –'

'It's a sort of hair clip. To keep your hair out your eyes, or your bun in place. But I just think she's very no-nonsense and she was obviously a games captain or head girl at school, but I wondered which? I'm thinking more head girl actually. Our head girl was awfully clever and sensible. I wasn't even allowed to be a prefect, because they said I was a rebel leader to the junior school, because I wore my school socks rolled down round my ankles. It's not exactly *Star Wars*, is it? Shall I google Lucy Worsley, so you know who she is? And maybe Wikipedia will tell us whether she was a head girl or not. I bet you £5 that she was! Actually, I've probably got a bobby pin in my purse too, so I can show you what it is …'

Charlie was looking baffled by this, and I took advantage of his temporary confusion to try to snatch my hand away under the guise of googling Lucy Worsley's school career and giving a masterclass in bobby pins, but he pre-empted me and hung onto it.

'Ellen, I don't really care what some woman off the TV did at school, and as you may have noticed, I don't really have enough hair to have any interest in your bloody bobby pins. I want to talk to *you*!'

'We ARE talking, Charlie! We're discussing a wide range of topics, such as history and television and fashion.'

I succeeded in wresting my hand away from him and dived into my bag, emerging triumphant with a rather grotty bobby pin and my phone.

'LOOK! See, this is a bobby pin. *Now* do you know who I was talking about? Look, I'll just quickly google –'

Charlie removed both the bobby pin and my phone from me, and put them on the table, but not before he looked slightly horrified at the dusty glob of matter clinging to the bobby pin (I think it was probably a bit of a forgotten jelly bean).

'Enough!' he said. (He was quite masterful actually. If I hadn't been so in dread of having to talk about how I felt, I would almost have had a frisson.)

'I don't give a shit about this woman. My life has been in no way enhanced by learning what a fucking bobby pin is! We need to talk. Can we just be honest with each other, please?'

NO! Let's not, please?

'Why are you here, Ellen?'

'Ha ha ha, for a drink! Lovely, lovely drinky poos. Can I have my bobby pin back, please? They're very useful, you can pick locks with them. I've never actually picked a lock with one, but apparently you can. There's probably a YouTube tutorial on it. I could google it! Maybe Lucy Worsley's sensible head girl image is all a front and she is actually a cat burglar in her spare time and that is why she always wears a bobby pin, so she can break in and steal all the diamonds.'

'ELLEN! SHUT UP! If you mention *fucking* bobby pins, or Lucy Fucking Worsley one more bastarding time, I WILL NOT BE RESPONSIBLE FOR MY ACTIONS. WE NEED TO TALK.'

'We *are* talking! We are talking about –'

'We are *not* talking, you are wittering crap at me. Now we are going to talk. Answer me – you could go for a drink with anyone. Why are you here with me?'

Oh FML, he really doesn't give up.

'Because we're friends, of course. Ha ha ha!'

'Please would you stop laughing like that. It's really quite disconcerting.'

'Ha ha ha! Sorry.' Ha! I decided to put him off with my dreadful nervous laugh instead. A shrill cackle is surely as good a passion-killer as threatening to soil yourself at the table or offering a blow-by-blow account of the history of the bobby pin.

'Ellen, please. I do hope we're friends. But I think maybe you have been avoiding me because you're worried that I want us to be more than friends?'

'Oh no! Nono*no*no! Of *course* not, what an IDEA. Ha ha ha!' I wondered whether to stab my eye out with the bobby pin as a distraction technique.

'Please will you shut up now? You're actually being quite irritating, and if we are going to be friends, I think we need to clear some things up.'

'Oh?'

'Firstly, yes, I find you attractive. You were my first love. My first ...'

'Shag?' I supplied helpfully.

'Well, yes, I was going to go for something a little more grown-up, like –'

'First jiggy jiggy? First bonk? First beast with two backs –'

'Lover. You were my first lover as well.'

In fairness, that does sound much better than my suggestions.

'And when I bumped into you again, it did cross my mind that something might happen. Actually, I quite hoped something might happen. And if you were single, maybe it would have. But you're not, are you?'

'Well, obviously not. I never pretended to be. You knew I was married.'

'For fuck's sake, will you stop interrupting me?'

'You asked me a question!'

'A rhetorical question! Anyway, the point is, you're not single, and you're not that sort of girl either, are you?'

I opened my mouth to ask what sort of girl exactly, but Charlie gave me a look, and I closed it again. I did like being referred to as a girl, though.

'The sort of girl who has an affair. Because I do still know you quite well, Ellen, even though I didn't see you for years. I know you can be spoilt, and frequently shallow, and often selfish, and you can be infuriating.'

Really, I thought, if he is trying to convince me to have it off with him, his compliments need a great deal of work.

'And there will never be anyone else for you but Simon. I think I knew that, the first night I saw you both together. Also, I don't think that you would be able to bring yourself to break up your children's home; do the same thing to them that your parents did to you, have them shuttled between different houses every week, and have step-parents and step-siblings to get used to. So I realised pretty quickly that there was no point even thinking about you and me.'

'I could *so* have an affair!' I burst out indignantly, feeling not entirely thrilled with the image of the boring, repressed, spoilt, suburban mummy that Charlie was painting. I could be that woman, in the smoky jazz club, with the inappropriate man and the sweet nothings. I *could*!

'Do you know why my marriage ended?' Charlie asked.

'No,' I muttered sulkily, thinking, oh my God, did I forget to *ask*? Is that another sign of my spoilt, shallow, selfishness? No, of course I asked. Nosiness would have compelled me, if nothing else. I'm pretty sure he just said something vague about drifting apart and wanting different things.

'I had an affair,' he said calmly.

'YOU?' I spluttered. 'YOU had an affair?'

'Is it such a ludicrous idea? That more than one woman should find me attractive enough to sleep with?'

'No! But you are meant to be one of the nice guys. The good ones. The sort who don't have affairs. You're Lovely Charlie. That's what we used to call you, Lovely Charlie. Because you were so straight and decent.'

'Lovely Charlie? I wasn't lovely enough for you, though, was I? Being the good guy didn't do me any favours there. And anyway, I'm not. I'm shallow and selfish as well, and I was bored and unhappy with my marriage and I was flattered and excited when someone else seemed to offer me all the things Rachel didn't. So I had an affair, and Rachel found out, and that was the end for us, and ultimately the affair itself wasn't that exciting or glamorous, it was rather sordid. A lot of motel rooms with beige carpets, and a constant nagging sense of guilt, once the initial excitement had worn off. But I did it anyway. So I'm not this chivalrous, shining noble knight you think I am, I'm a bit of a dick. But I think when we first met each other again, you felt a bit like I did at the start of things with Sarah. You were fed up, and Simon was getting on your tits and you wanted something more. Only I don't think you would go through with an actual affair, because you love Simon too much, whereas I never really loved Rachel – and yes, that probably is something to do with you because I should never have got together with her on the rebound from you, and then somehow we were just on some wedding juggernaut that I couldn't stop, and I'm not proud of myself. But then you felt awkward about seeing me, because you thought you'd been leading me on again, and so you started avoiding me because of your ridiculous fear of actually talking about things and so here we are. Am I right?'

I stared hard at the table again and wondered about changing the subject.

'Ellen?' said Charlie. 'Please say something. And don't change the subject. Were you avoiding me because you thought I wanted more from you? Talk to me.'

'Yeeeeees, I was. But why did we have to talk about it? If you don't want to shag me, why wouldn't you just let me avoid you? Why did you push it?'

'I never said I don't want to shag you. I just don't think it would be a good idea, even in the unlikely event that I got you drunk enough to actually do it. But look, I've recently moved here, I don't know a lot of people outside work. The job at St Catherine's seemed like a good chance to make a fresh start, but I hadn't appreciated how lonely it would be, especially because I lost quite a lot of friends in the divorce – understandably most of them took Rachel's side, although in my opinion she rather overplayed the martyred victim. But whatever … I did cheat on her, so I suppose I deserved it. But I would really like us to be friends, because right now I need friends more than I need another messy, complicated relationship, which is what an affair with a married woman would be. I need proper friends, and nothing more, without worrying about there being some sort of subtext, or either of us getting the wrong idea. But we can't be friends if you are being all weird and thinking I'm still poor old love-struck Charlie. And also,' he grinned wickedly, 'it was bloody funny watching you squirm when you were actually forced to discuss something emotional instead of just brushing it under the carpet and running away.'

'Rude!'

'Also,' he continued, looking more serious. 'I do still care about you. I used to hear bits and pieces from other people, and I would think "Well, I'm glad Ellen and Simon are still together – I may have had my heart broken, but at least it wasn't for some stupid thing that fizzled out after a couple of years". I used to tell myself that clearly you two were meant to be. And I suppose I just wanted to remind you of that. You seem much happier now, in a much better place with him than when I first saw you, which is maybe why nothing happened with us, but if you do find yourself in another rough patch, and are tempted by someone else, it mightn't be someone who has your best interests at heart, and it might end up causing an awful lot of trouble.'

'So be a good girl, Ellen?' I muttered crossly.

'No. Just remember that very few people are lucky enough to have what you have with Simon. So don't throw it away for a bit of excitement when things get tough or boring, because life *is* tough and boring, as is marriage. That's all. Here endeth the lecture. Shall we get another bottle?'

'Maybe,' I said. 'You said you still want to shag me, though, so how can we be friends?'

'Oh, *that*!' said Charlie airily. 'You have a nice arse, and I'm a single man who hasn't had sex in a while. Hence, yes, the thought crossed my mind. In fairness, there's quite a few shaggable women in here, you're not the only one.'

'Again, RUDE! But if that's all it is, then yes, let's get another bottle. And you're buying for making me talk about *feelings*.'

The rest of the evening was much more relaxed, and even enjoyable. We talked about Hannah, and I gave Charlie her number and suggested he give her a call – just as friends, I said. I do hope they will be more than friends, but I feared saying, 'Do please phone Hannah, because she is afraid she is going to spend a number of years as a crazy cat lady, before even they abandon her and she lives out her last days in a dingy basement, weeping alone for her lost youth, and like you she is also desperate for a shag' might not be an entirely tempting prospect.

On the way home I googled Lucy Worsley. Annoyingly, the internet gave no details of whether she was ever a head girl or games captain. I can now pick a lock with a bobby pin, though, should the occasion ever arise.

JULY

Wednesday, 6 July

Louisa is still here. All the children are still here. She has largely stopped crying, at least, but shows no other signs of attempting to get a job, or starting to put her life back together, or finding a home for her children. In lieu of the crying, she has taken to going off on solitary evening walks, leaving Simon and me to deal with the eight children (eight children. Did I mention there are *eight fucking children* living in my house? DID I?).

I get the impression that Louisa is rather resentful that we are unable to provide suitably dramatic windswept moors for her to passionately stride about, bewailing her lot to the heather and the rocks. Instead she marches round and round the park muttering to herself (Sam saw her when he was out with his dog), doing more of an impression of Mr Rochester's first wife than of Cathy Earnshaw searching for Heathcliff.

This morning it was my day off, and I had firmly suggested to Louisa (actually I had just ordered her, I have turned into something between Mary Poppins and Nurse Ratched when dealing with Louisa, brooking no arguments and speaking only in a bright and cheerful voice like the one you use in public to a recalcitrant toddler because you can't scream 'just fucking do as you're told, you little shit' when there are witnesses) that she took her children to the shops and bought some bread and milk as we were rather low. We are permanently low on bread and milk. We have seven extra people in the house to feed.

Unable to face the mess in the house (*eight fucking children!*) I had decided to try to weed the front yard to make the house look less like it was an abandoned junkyard, what with Louisa's camper van (named, we are not allowed to forget, 'Gunnar') parked on the road outside, gently listing to starboard as the tyres deflated, a pool of oil underneath growing larger each day.

Repeated suggestions to Louisa that she needs to do something with her battered heap, like sell it for scrap, or at least take it to a garage and get an estimate for how much it would cost to make it roadworthy, are met with either another storm of grief that we want to 'kill' her beloved Gunnar, who 'saved' her from Bardo/Kevin and Sgathaich/Carol (who she has now declared clearly must be an evil witch who enchanted Bardo and would have enslaved Louisa's poor innocent children, had brave Gunnar not carried them to freedom. I think Louisa has been watching too many old Disney films) or a shuddering sigh of horror that she is being asked to contemplate anything so *sordid* as financial considerations when she is so clearly in the grip of higher emotions.

In the meantime, it can't be long before one of the neighbours makes a complaint to the council about the rust bucket ruining the street by lowering the tone of the neighbourhood and, more importantly, house prices.

As I jabbed away at the parched earth with my trowel, trying to decide whether the wilting specimen in front of me was a weed or something that was meant to be there, there was a nervous cough behind me. There stood dullsville Katie from across the road, who lives in what I must stop thinking of as the Jenkins' house, as now it belongs to Katie and her husband, Thingy. (I have really tried to remember his name, but it keeps slipping my mind.)

'Ummm, Ellen, I hope you don't mind me saying so, but errr, is that your sister-in-law's?'

I sighed. 'Yes. I'm very sorry about it, and yes, I know parking is an issue in the street, and no, I don't know how long she is staying or what she is planning on doing with it.' (This was not the first time I had had this conversation with a neighbour since Louisa arrived.)

'Oh no!' said Katie, going a pretty shade of pink (she is boring as sin, but she does blush prettily in a mousy sort of way. I go a fetching puce). 'I just meant, I wondered if Louisa was in? Since her van is here?'

Has Katie not noticed this bastarding heap of junk hasn't moved in almost a month, since Louisa arrived?

'No,' I said shortly. 'She's gone to the shops.'

'Oh,' said Katie sadly. 'That's a shame, I was going to ask her over for a cup of tea. I've bought the special, organic, herbal tea she likes.'

Katie was going to ask *Louisa* over for a cup of tea? *Louisa*? In all the months they've been here, Katie and Thingy have not so much as asked us over for a glass of water, despite (or perhaps because of) our extremely generous hospitality on Easter Sunday. And now, not only does *Louisa* get asked over for tea, she gets special tea bags bought for the occasion!

This was not right. This was rude. This is not how people in this street conduct themselves. We are respectable people, following a strict code of conduct about invitations to Christmas parties and barbecues and admittedly somewhat dangerous fire-work parties and even *cups of tea*!

You cannot accept someone's invitation and, firstly, fail to return it, then think you can just bypass them and invite their unwashed flake of a sister-in-law round for *a cup of tea made with special tea bags*. THAT IS NOT HOW IT WORKS!

This may have shown somewhat on my face as I narrowed my eyes and scowled at Katie, because she then nervously added, 'And you, of course! Would you like a cup of tea?'

No, Katie, I wouldn't. It was too little, too late, Katie, because clearly to know about the special tea bags you have been merrily teaing away with bloody Louisa while I have been WORKING to put food on the table for the *eight children currently living in my house*, but Katie was not getting away with it that easily, and also I wanted to see what her and Thingy had done with the house since they moved in, so I put down my trowel and said, 'That would be lovely!'

Katie's house is very … cataloguey. It looks exactly like someone has ripped a series of illustrations out of the catalogue for a mid-price furniture shop and made it come to life. It was quite extraordinarily soulless, which made me glad, as I would have been most galled to discover bland, boring, TRAITOROUS little Katie was actually hiding a talent for exquisite interior design.

Katie, it turned out, is harbouring quite the girl crush on Louisa. I found this baffling at first. Katie is so *clean*! She looks like she scrubs herself down with disinfectant and a wire brush every morning. Louisa looks like she *needs* to be scrubbed down with disinfectant and a wire brush. And then possibly fumigated. And just to be on the safe side, steam-cleaned for luck.

Katie, though, thinks Louisa is marvellous. A 'true free spirit' was how she described her. It seems Louisa has seen fit to confide in Katie that her current life plan is to travel around Europe with her children in Gunnar, educating them in life. After Europe, who knows? She might drive across Africa with them, or she might go to Asia. Apparently, it all depends on karma and seren-dipity and where the winds of fate blow her.

Louisa seems to have failed to realise that even phase one of her grand plan, just getting herself to France, will require a working vehicle and money for gas and ferry fares, none of which she currently possesses, before we even touch upon such tedious realities such as how she plans to feed herself and six children as she bums around the world 'educating them in life'. (Also, I think Coventina might raise strenuous objections; she is a sensible child with a remarkable work ethic, who informed me the other day that when she grows up, she is going to make lots of money and spend it all on stuff! For a child of Louisa's, there is no greater rebellion.)

Katie, though, was starry-eyed as she waxed lyrical about Louisa's bravery and strength in undertaking such an endeavour. I wondered whether to disillusion her about the practicalities which mean that Louisa will be doing no such thing, at least until she gets Bardo to start paying her some child support for the tribe. But Katie was in full flow about the wonders of Louisa and there was no stopping her.

'It must just be so amazing, to be so free from a humdrum life!' sighed Katie.

I had had enough. I didn't know what bollocks Louisa had been prattling to her but I was sick of hearing of the wonders of St Louisa of the Great Unwashed.

'It must be amazing, Katie, yes,' I snapped. 'We'd all bloody love not to have to think about filling the dishwasher and going to the supermarket and seeing if there is enough bastarding milk in the fridge for breakfast and getting the car fixed and cleaning the gutters and scrubbing the bath and all the other really fucking boring bullshit that keeps life ticking over, but the unfortunate fact is, Katie, someone has to do those things.'

Katie looked like I'd just slapped her. Her lip actually trembled as she quavered, 'But that's not true. Louisa doesn't have to worry about anything like that. She is just free, to go where she wants and do what she likes!'

I felt a bit bad about Katie's brimming eyes, which had been glowing with zeal until I pissed on her chips, but I was on a roll.

'Louisa doesn't have to do any of those things because Louisa is an irresponsible child-woman who has decided to abdicate all accountability for her own life to other people while she witters a load of New Age bollocks about being true to ourselves and letting The Universe provide what you need. Louisa has got away with this for as long as she has because her bloody father and Simon have been bailing her out and bankrolling her for years, but the fact remains that she is a thirty-eight-year-old mother of six children and it is about time she put on her big girl panties and started taking responsibility for herself and for them. She will not be going off travelling round Europe with her children, or Asia, or Africa, because that rusting tin can of a camper van no longer goes and she doesn't have any money to buy another one or indeed to even feed her children because she is a feckless waste of space, and tomorrow she can stop wafting about being all airy fairy and refusing to confront reality and start looking for a job and somewhere to live because Simon and I are *not* financing another one of Louisa's hare-brained schemes! Why should she get to follow her dreams at our expense? WHY, KATIE? WHY?'

I realised that I had got a bit carried away and had been banging my fist on Katie's lightly distressed kitchen table so hard that one of her wooden letters spelling E-A-T had fallen off the wall. Katie was also openly sobbing. Shit. They already thought we were crazy and now I had confirmed it by taking a massive hissy fit in Katie's colour-co-ordinated kitchen.

'Oh God, Katie, I'm sorry. I'm really sorry, I didn't mean to get so carried away. It's just it can be incredibly frustrating, living with Louisa, and trying to get her to stop being such a –' I was about to say 'complete and utter twat', but I had already shocked Katie enough with my potty mouth. Katie looks the sort of person who not only says 'Oh sugar' but actually thinks it, too, so instead I carried on '– an ostrich and burying her head to ignore anything that doesn't fit in with her life. I shouldn't have shouted, I'm sorry. Katie, please stop crying!'

Katie sobbed harder and mumbled something incoherent.

'Sorry, Katie, I couldn't quite make that out. Do you want me to just go?'

Katie shook her head violently and howled, 'Such a lovely DREAM! Louisa's ideas, just packing up and going where the fancy took you, something new and different every day. Leaving all THIS behind.' She gestured violently at her immaculate kitchen.

'It's always the SAME, Ellen,' she wailed. 'EVERY FUCKING DAY!' Blimey, she does swear. 'I get up. I feed the girls, we go to some wanky baby class where every other mother there is smiling and shiny and perfect and they all love their lives and everyone tells me how lucky I am, and I am, I know I am, I do love the girls, and Tim' (TIM! Of course – that is Thingy's name.) 'But it's so repetitive and tedious and I used to be someone, Ellen! I used to be head of marketing for a really big company, and people respected my opinions and listened to what I had to say at dinner parties and I KNOW I'm so incredibly lucky to be able to stay at home with the girls, but I am so sick of being known as Ruby and Lily's Mummy, instead of as a person in my own right, and then Tim comes home and tells me how tired he is, from being Busy and Important, while implying I've basically been playing with dollies all day and I scream at him that at least he gets to go for a fucking piss in peace, which is more than I do, and I'm so LONELY, Ellen, and I feel so awful for feeling like this, because all the other mummies are so much better at all this, and I'm just a shit person and it was such a lovely idea of Louisa's, just to leave everything behind. To go off and have an adventure. I want an aaaaaddddveeennnntuuuuuuuure!'

I was stunned. I felt bad for judging Katie's house for being bland and soulless when clearly she is just having a bit of a bad time, adjusting to being a stay-at-home mummy. Charlie was right, I am shallow. There was further evidence of my shallowness, because although I did feel for Katie, there was part of me that was thinking, 'Why is my life filled with crying women all the time?' Maybe this is how Simon feels every month.

I patted Katie gingerly on the shoulder (again, I appear to be turning into Simon, but I was wearing a new t-shirt and I didn't want to get her mascara all over it, and also, those personal space issues).

'Katie,' I said. 'It's okay. Pretty much everyone feels like that.'

'NOOOOO!' bellowed Katie, who having decided to unburden was really going for it. 'It's only me, I know it is. Everyone else is so perfect and I try to be, I really do, and it's no goooooood! I just feel like everything I do is wrong.' Then she subsided into gulping and sniffing dolefully.

'Seriously,' I said, feeling like the wise, elder stateswoman of the tribe, though Katie must be about the same age as me. 'We all feel the same. We all sat in those classes and shook our maracas and drank the dreadful coffee at the Mother and Toddlers group and looked at everyone else and wondered how they all had their shit together and why we were so inadequate. It's just nobody talks about it. It's not until later that you are having a glass of wine with someone one night and they suddenly admit that they seriously thought about repeatedly smashing their head on the floor if they had to sing "Baa Baa Black Sheep" one more time, and then you realise you're not alone, and we were all struggling and it would probably have been so much better for all of us if we had just admitted it. I bet if you go to Mummy and Me Music tomorrow and announce you are finding it really difficult and you feel a bit lost, 99 per cent of the other mums there will say "ME TOO!"'

'Won't they judge me?' whimpered Katie.

'They will probably think you are a fucking heroine for having the nerve to stand up and admit it!' I cried. 'I felt like I was the worst toddler mum, because I didn't make homemade salt dough Christmas decorations with them. I felt like I was the worst school mum for working, I felt like all the stay-at-home mums were judging me, and then I made that stupid app, more as therapy for me than anything else, and thousands of people have bought it and it turns out that all the school mummies felt the same as me and we just need to talk about it, instead of pretending we are all fine and everything is perfect and we are coping splendidly without a care in the world. Running away like Louisa isn't the answer, we need to TALK TO EACH OTHER!'

I was banging on the table again. Another letter fell off the wall.

'I never knew,' said Katie. 'I would never have thought you felt like that. You and Simon look like you have such a perfect life, you are so glamorous and exciting. I was terrified of you after that Easter party, because I thought you were so clever and cool. Even your sideboard is cool!'

'Ah ha ha ha!' I cackled. 'The sideboard has been a bone of contention since I painted it. And we are not perfect or glamorous or exciting. The dog threw up in my shoes last night, and I frequently want to stab Simon for being a patronising twat, and NOBODY'S life is as perfect as it might look. NOBODY'S!'

The last letter fell off the wall.

'I hate those fucking letters,' shouted Katie. 'Let's BURN THEM! And open some wine. FUCK, YEAH!'

Thursday, 21 July

Drama abounds. The big guns have arrived in the form of Michael and Sylvia. After the day with Katie I obviously revealed Louisa's travelling plans to Simon. Simon was furious and pointed out all the many flaws in Louisa's plan, and Louisa screamed a lot that he wasn't her father and he couldn't tell her what to do (nor would she ever rule The Universe with him).

Louisa also took an almighty strop with Katie and me for 'betraying' her by telling Simon what she was up to. Apparently, we not only betrayed her, we also betrayed the Sisterhood and the Goddess. She has told me this several times. For someone who announces at least three times a day that she isn't talking to me, she talks to me an awful lot. I rather wish she would make good on her promise to never utter another word to me.

Another contradiction Louisa seems to have no issue with is her declaration that she can hardly bear to be in the same room as me, yet she is perfectly happy to live under my roof, at my expense. Simon, meanwhile, although not her father, as she often points out, is apparently bringing the full weight of the patriarchy down on poor beleaguered Louisa, for no other reason than to oppress her. For fun, probably.

Eventually, in despair, as Louisa refused to listen to any reason and kept insisting that she would be going travelling and that Gunnar was perfectly roadworthy (although for one so keen to travel, she showed no signs of actually getting in that bloody camper van and leaving, assuming it would even start) and therefore she would not be looking for a job, or a home, and with the summer rapidly approaching and the house feeling more cramped and claustrophobic by the day, Simon rang his parents and asked them to intervene with their wayward daughter.

Michael and Sylvia arrived today, and while I must admit I had had some reservations about how much use they would actually be in making Louisa see sense, when it came down to it they were rather marvellous.

Louisa, predictably, threw a massive tantrum as soon as they arrived and started shouting at Simon about running to Mummy and Daddy to tell on her, and Michael, who I had always assumed was a splendidly jolly but somewhat buffoonish character, who took nothing very seriously except his golf scores, *bellowed* at her in a terrifying voice.

'LOUISA CATHERINE RUSSELL, SIT DOWN AND BEHAVE YOURSELF! Ellen and your brother have been more than hospitable, putting you and your children up for over a month. Not many people would do that. Apologise to them this minute.'

'I'll apologise to Simon, but I'm not speaking to Ellen,' muttered Louisa sullenly.

'YOU WILL APOLOGISE TO THEM BOTH. NOW!' boomed Michael. 'AND THANK THEM FOR EVERYTHING THEY HAVE DONE FOR YOU!'

'Sorry, Simon, sorry, Ellen. Thank you both, you've been very kind,' mumbled Louisa, to my astonishment.

'Right. Are you aware, young lady, that Ellen and Simon's attempts to thwart your plans are not, as you have been shrieking, to ruin your life, but rather to keep you out of prison? If you attempt to turn up at a border crossing and a policeman gets one sniff of that deathtrap rustbucket –'

'– Gunnar!' protested Louisa. 'His name is Gunnar!'

'What? Who is Gunnar? I thought that dickhead you married was called Twatto or something? Oh dear God, tell me you haven't taken up with some other hippy fool already. You're not pregnant again, are you? Simon, why didn't you tell me about this Gunnar?'

'Gunnar is my camper van!' sniffed Louisa. 'That's his name!'

'Oh for fuck's sake,' snapped Michael. 'Louisa, you are thirty-eight years old. I am sixty-eight years old. I am not referring to a fucking camper van by name. Kindly grow up. As I was saying, if you come within a country mile of a policeman in that thing, especially with all those bloody children bouncing around inside, you will be arrested sharpish and your children taken into care. Is that what you want?'

Louisa muttered something.

'I SAID, IS THAT WHAT YOU WANT?' shouted Michael.

'No, Daddy,' said Louisa in a small voice.

'RIGHT!' said Michael. 'Now we're getting somewhere. So tell me how you got yourself into this pickle and let's see if we can come up with a plan for what you're going to do now.'

As Louisa started to explain how she was now virtually penniless, due to Bardo having the retreat and everything in it listed as a limited company, therefore entitling her to no share in it, and how she had no paperwork showing the money she had put into it at the start from the sale of her flat, or any of the considerable bailouts Michael had given her, Sylvia nodded at the door and indicated we should leave.

In the kitchen, Sylvia sank down at the table and sighed. She suddenly looked very old and fragile.

'Do you think I could have a drink?' she asked. 'Assuming, of course, that my freeloading daughter has left you anything in the house. Oh God, that wretched girl! What a stupid mess she is in. It's my fault really, I spoiled her. Michael was always the only one who could handle her, and I used to end up just giving into her if he wasn't there, because it was easier than putting up with her tantrums. And, of course, he was always working in those days, so she got her own way an awful lot, which is probably why she's now such a horror. I should've stood up to her, instead of letting her grow up thinking all she had to do was stamp her feet and she'd get what she wanted. Thank you so much for taking her in, Ellen, you've no idea how grateful I am. I can imagine how awful she's been.'

I was gobsmacked: Sylvia was being human. Sylvia was acknowledging that she might have been wrong. And Sylvia was admitting that one of her children was less than perfect. All this as well on a day when someone had actually succeeded in shutting Louisa up and wringing some semblance of manners from her. I was rather scared of what might happen next on a day of such unnatural behaviour from Sylvia and Louisa.

Next door Michael started shouting again, and Simon shot through.

'Best just to leave them to it, I think!' he gasped, as Michael's roars drowned out Louisa's wails of protestation.

'Apparently, she has been hanging around here, refusing to get off her backside because despite all her protestations about how much she hates Bardo, she was hoping he would come after her and declare his undying love, renounce Whatsit, and they would all live happily ever after. Dad's just disabusing her of this notion now. Actually, darling,' he put down the wine bottle. 'Do we have anything stronger?'

Of course we had something stronger. Now I was rich beyond the dreams of app-arice (Simon just looked at me when I told him that quite brilliant pun), I had taken to buying quantities of artisan gin instead of supermarket own-brand. I got out several bottles and suggested we could take our mind off things with a little gin tasting.

Gin may not have been the best choice under the circumstances. Simon was summonsed back to the sitting room by another bellow from Michael, so Sylvia and I were left alone with the bottles. An hour later, we were both rather emotional, as Sylvia gulped, 'I gave up everything up for my children. Everything. There were days when I didn't even know who I was any more. I still have days like that. And what was it all for? Louisa throwing her life away on that bloody unwashed hippy! S'all my fault, I was a bad example, making her think you need a man. Don't need a man. Stupid mans. Fish'n'bicycles, you know! I should've been like you, Ellen. You do horrible 'pooters, but you got your independence. You could leave Simon tomorrow, an' you'll be all right. You won' though, will you? Promish me you won' leave Simon? You're a good example to Jane. Independence! Own money. Wish I'd had my own money. An' career.'

I hiccupped. 'Don' you think I'm a bad mother, bein' away from them too much? Other people bringin' 'em up? Is bad of me. Feel very bad. Guilty 'bout it. Always too busy.'

'Nah,' slurred Sylvia. 'I was always there for my children, an' look how that turned out! An' I's guilty too. Too worried 'bout what people thought. Too busy making sure cushions and curtains and flowers matched. 'Pearances not everthing! Should've been more, whaddaya call it, more "chilled". Never let them in the drawing room, 'cos they would make a mess. Shoulda let 'em in drawing room. Maybe Louisa would be a nice person if I'd let her in the drawing room? Maybe all this hippy bollocks is a, a, I dunno, a rebellion 'gainst me, an' my silk curtains? Though …' Sylvia squinted at me, 'Simon'sh not sho bad. He got you. You're alright. Part from the 'pooters. I don' like 'pooters. Internet. Bad. Scary. S'there any more gin?'

'Oooh, I know!' I chirped as I slopped more gin into Sylvia's glass. Bafflingly, there didn't seem to be much room for tonic. 'I could show you how to use the internet. You can buy stuff! An' you can go on eBay an' win stuff, and learn how to do anything on YouTube. 'Cept flicky eyeliner. Thass tricky. You could do lots of stuff! I love winning things on eBay. Last week, I winned three chandeliers an' a giant crystal pineapple on eBay! Chandeliers was all the same, I din't realise I had bid on them all, I's going to put them in my seaside cottage in Wells-next-the-Sea with the shoes. Less you want one?' I added generously.

By the time Michael, Simon and Louisa came through, Sylvia and I were singing along to Kate Bush and practising the dance moves to 'Wuthering Heights' courtesy of YouTube.

'Michael, LOOK!' shouted Sylvia. 'I CAN DO 'POOTERS NOW! Ellen showed me how, an' I'm gonna win stuff on eBay too! 'Pooters is FABLUS! Ellen, can I win a 'pooter for my own self on eBay?'

'Oh dear God! What the fuck has happened in here?' said Michael in horror as Sylvia attempted a high kick but over-balanced and lurched into his arms.

Friday, 29 July

The crisis talks on How Do We Solve A Problem Like Louisa continue. In fairness, now the summer recess has started she has actually been reasonably useful this week and looked after Peter and Jane while I was at work. Michael must have had a word with her as well, because she even attempts to tidy up and vacuum while I am out. She is useless at it, of course, and I have to redo it when I come home, but I suppose at least she is trying.

I am trying to be nice about all this and focus on the childcare fees Louisa is saving me, and not on how much money she has cost me over the past few months, including having to buy a new blender due to the sperm smoothies. Although having found out just how generous Bardo had been with his special ingredient, I am very glad I did, because there is not enough disinfectant in the world to sterilise that away.

Tonight I met Hannah and Sam for a 'first week of the summer' debrief drinky. I asked Katie along too because I think she just needs to spend a bit more time with grown-ups and a bit less crying in front of *Paw Patrol* and trying not to claw her own eyes out with boredom.

Katie has actually turned out to be rather a kindred spirit, and I wish I had found this out months ago. I have taken refuge over the road from the rows between Louisa and Simon and their parents more than once recently, and had a lovely time putting the world to rights with Katie over a bottle.

Simon was drooping round the bedroom as I was trying to get ready, gloomy at the prospect of another night with his sister and parents, while Louisa alternately wept and raged at Michael and Sylvia's refusal to pay for Gunnar's repairs and allow her to set off on her travels. Michael has, however, got his lawyers onto Bardo to try to wring some cash out of him, which will come as a nasty shock to his hippy arse.

Hannah texted me while I was putting on my makeup to make the mysterious announcement that she was bringing 'someone' for us to meet, so I took pity on Simon and said, 'Why don't you come too? Louisa can make herself useful and babysit.'

He perked up straightaway and said, 'Really? You wouldn't mind? That would be lovely!'

Poor Simon. It is a dark day when he actually feels going into the company of People is preferable to the sanctity of his sofa.

I wasn't terribly surprised when the 'someone' Hannah was bringing for us to meet turned out to be Charlie. I'd had a coffee with him a couple of weeks after That Drink, and then suddenly his messages and suggestions to meet up had tailed off, and Hannah had become elusive as well. I had hoped he had taken my advice and called her, and it seems that he had, because they were like a pair of loved-up teenagers.

Simon was a little stand-offish with Charlie at first, but Charlie, being a good soul and sensing Simon's hostility, made no mention of our meetings, saying only that he had bumped into me by coincidence a few months ago and, learning he was now living in the area and was single, I had given him Hannah's number.

Simon thawed somewhat after that, joking that I always did love a chance to matchmake, and even going so far as to remark that Charlie was lucky I hadn't found out he was single before Louisa arrived, or in my desperation to get rid of her I might have tried to set them up instead, 'Though God knows what you'd have done to Ellen to deserve that!'

I was rather jealous of Hannah and Charlie, not because of Charlie, but just of how besotted with each other they were and unable to keep their hands off each other.

'Awwwww,' said Sam. 'Isn't it sweet! Our little Hannah has found love, and without a single dick pic. You *didn't* send a dick pic, I assume?' he asked a rather startled Charlie, who then had to have Hannah's abortive foray into online dating explained to him.

'What about you, Sam?' asked Hannah. 'Now you've split up with Mark, are you looking for *someone else*?'

'Oh God!' said Sam. 'Not really. Mark was okay, but it was an awful lot of effort. I mean, the sex was great, but I'm not sure it was really worth having to be interested in his opinions on something called *Real Housewives*. I honestly don't know if I can be bothered. I've got the kids and the dog, and my friends, and I'm probably good with that. I know I'm an awful let-down to the gay clichés, I should be running around gagging for dick, but to be honest, I'm pretty happy as I am. I mean, never say never. If I meet The One, then great, but if I don't, it's not the end of the world. I can just snuggle up on my own with my cashmere bedsocks on and watch *Outlander*.'

'Mmmm, *Outlander*. Ooooh, Jamie Fraser! And his magic falling-off kilt ...' sighed Katie, Hannah, Sam and I together, while Charlie and Simon exchanged resigned looks.

AUGUST

Thursday, 4 August

A summit meeting was called this evening. A solution has apparently been found for Louisa and the children which has been agreed as satisfactory for everyone.

A house is for sale adjoining Michael and Sylvia's property in France. It's not huge, and it needs some work, but it's just big enough for Louisa and the children. Michael and Sylvia will be on hand to support Louisa and look after the children, and Michael and Simon have called in every favour they have ever been owed to get Louisa some freelance graphic design work, which will enable her to be at home with the children and earn something of a living as well – the hope being that once she's done a few jobs, word will get round and more will come in. Although Michael and Sylvia's house doesn't have enough space for Louisa to live with them long term (to quote Sylvia, 'it's only a *tiny* chateau'), she can stay with them while the property sale goes through and her house is renovated. This all sounded marvellous, but I had an uneasy sense of foreboding, as everyone looked at me expectantly.

Michael cleared his throat, as he said, 'The only thing is, well, it's a bit delicate. It's the money.'

'The money?' I repeated.

'Yes,' said Michael. 'The thing is, all in, we're looking at about £100,000. I'm afraid Sylvia and I just don't have that sort of capital to invest anymore. So, we wondered if you and Simon would be able to put it up?'

'Me and Simon?' I was so stunned that all my mother's insistence that it was never 'me and X' but always 'X and me' was forgotten.

'We have the money, Ellen,' Simon said quietly. 'Our own mortgage is paid off, and your remaining app money is enough to do this.'

'But the app isn't making any money anymore!' I said, as I surreptitiously kicked my latest purse under the table out of sight.

'It is actually, darling. It's not making the pots of money it once did, but it's still bringing in a few thousand a month.'

'So you want me to give all MY app money to Louisa? So she can move to France and DRAW FUCKING PICTURES?' Oh my God, this is what an out-of-body experience feels like. I could hear my own voice shrieking and see myself hammering on the table like a mad woman, but I didn't seem able to stop myself.

Simon and Michael were saying something about how, no, it wouldn't be giving the money, we would own the house and land and Louisa would live there, but all I could really hear was the blood roaring in my ears as I fought the urge to throw myself on the floor and shriek and kick like a thwarted toddler as I yelled that I was going to scream and scream until I THREW UP! I couldn't help but feel that would be deeply satisfying and the main impulse stopping me was that I was wearing a fairly short skirt and if I did that, I would almost certainly flash my underwear at everyone and it was distinctly grey with dubious elastic, and my bikini line also left a lot to be desired.

Everyone continued to talk at me as I struggled to breathe, the single thought running through my head of 'MY MONEY, MY MONEY, MY MONEY!' as well as fury at Simon for springing this on me in front of everyone. He obviously knew this was coming, had discussed it with his parents and Louisa and yet didn't think that it might be a good idea to talk to me about it first. What the fuck did they think I would say?

'Oh yes, jolly good, excellent plan, I'm completely happy with that, absolutely, let's give Louisa (who hasn't actually done a stroke of work in the last ten years) all the money that I have made for *my* family's future so she can piss off abroad and live *my* dream in her adorable tumbledown villa, which will almost certainly have olive groves and probably an ancient retainer called Pascal, who lost his only true love, Marie Claire, in the war, and she will draw pictures for a living, which is practically the same as painting watercolours, and in the meantime, I will just carry on drudging away in a sodding office, trying to juggle the children and work and everything bloody else, and I won't even have a Pinterest-worthy cottage in Wells-next-the-Sea to keep my excess shoes in, or even a DREAM because LOUISA HAS STOLEN MY DREAM! Will I buy her a nice shady hat as well SO SHE DOESN'T GET SUNBURNT IN THE OLIVE GROVES WHILE SHE IS STEALING MY DREAM? Will I? Just so her stolen dream is complete? WILL YOU ALL BE HAPPY THEN?'

I hadn't actually realised I was shouting all this out loud until it dawned on me that everyone was looking at me in confusion and consternation, possibly not entirely sure who Pascal and Marie Claire were, so I stood up with what dignity I could muster and announced I was going out now and I may be some time, and stormed out of the house. I got as far as the end of the front path before I realised I had no money, phone or keys with me, so had to storm back in, collect my purse and re-storm out, which rather spoilt my dramatic exit, as a second storming is never as effective as the first, however hard you might slam the door.

Sunday, 7 August

Louisathedreamstealergate rumbles on. Simon has attempted appealing to my better nature, pointing out that, realistically, Louisa will never survive in the real world on her own and that it will be the children who will suffer. Apparently she needs to be somewhere that she will have the support of her family, to help her with the children, and since even with the app money (MY app money) buying or even renting a house for her round here would not be feasible, the best thing is for her to move near to Michael and Sylvia, where everything is so much cheaper. I hear the rational side of his argument but unfortunately it seems I don't have a better nature – I expect better natures are for people who have seaside cottages and haven't had their DREAMS STOLEN!

Eventually, sick to the back teeth of the bloody Russell family harassing me, and since Sam and Hannah were both on vacation, I rang Jessica to ask her out for lunch to attempt a little family solidarity of my own.

I poured out the story to her as we ate overpriced salad and Jessica decorously sipped a single glass of white wine and I downed glassfuls with abandon. Finally, I said, 'So you see? They are all being so unreasonable. It's just NOT FAIR! Why do they think they can ask me this?' and sat back to let Jessica's indignation soothe my battered soul.

'Actually, Ellen, I know it seems unfair, but I think you should let them have the money,' said Jessica.

'WHAT!' I sat bolt upright, having been slumped in my chair waiting to be told I was right. 'WHY should I give them the money?'

'Well, firstly, you're not *giving* them the money, are you? You're investing it in a property that Louisa will happen to live in.'

'DETAILS! That's just details. She is stealing my dream! She will be Pascal's confidante about Marie Claire, not me.'

'What? Who are Pascal and Marie Claire? You're not making any sense, Ellen,' she said as she moved the wine bottle out of my reach. 'The point is, the money will still be yours, just in another form. And it is the right thing to do.'

'No, it's not,' I mumbled sulkily.

'Yes, it is,' admonished Jessica sternly. 'She's Simon's sister. I'd give *you* the money if you needed it.'

'No, you wouldn't!'

'Yes, I would, because you are my sister.'

'You don't even like me!'

'That's not the point. And we're not talking about you and me.'

'You could at least pretend to like me. You are supposed to say, "Of course I like you, Ellen, I love you." Even if you don't like me. Which you don't.'

'Ellen, for someone who has spent the last forty-five minutes complaining to me that Louisa is a petulant child, you are behaving very like one yourself. If you don't help Louisa, what will happen to her? And more importantly, what will happen to her children?'

'Don't care.'

'Ellen! You are infuriating. Grow up.'

'Shan't.'

'Louisa will end up on welfare, probably miles from anyone she knows and minus any family support. Without help with the children, she probably won't be able to do this freelance work she's got, which will mean that once the baby is old enough, she will end up in some dead-end job, barely able to support her children. It will be a wretched life for all of them. And yes, Louisa is feckless and irresponsible and she should never have had so many children without any sort of plan about how she was going to support them, but the fact is, she *has* had them, and now that must be dealt with. And how do you think Simon will feel if you condemn his sister and nieces and nephews to a life like that?'

I felt a strong temptation to stick my fingers in my ears and sing 'Lalalalalala, I can't hear you!' Bloody Jessica, why does she have to be so morally upright about everything? She was supposed to be on my side. S'not fair. She wouldn't give the wine back either.

I continued to seethe and mutter indignantly to myself on the train home, which earned me some odd looks, but it did have the advantage of stopping anyone from trying to talk to me, because normally I seem to have one of those faces that says, 'Yes, please do sit next to me and tell me your life story/ask me impertinent questions about myself/invade my personal space'.

Friday, 12 August

Tomorrow Michael and Sylvia are returning to France with Louisa and the children, Gunnar having been scrapped and an old mini-van purchased instead to convey them there. I was still refusing to give up the money, and everyone hated me.

After another hideous row with Simon about it, I walked out again, unable to stand the resentful glares and loaded silences in the house. It was so unfair that everyone was blaming me when this whole mess was of Louisa's making due to her bad decisions. All I wanted was a Pinterest-worthy seaside cottage or some olive groves with ancient retainers. That wasn't so much to ask, was it?

Eventually, at a loose end, I got the bus to Hannah's house. Charlie answered the door and took one look at my tear-stained face and said, 'Oh my God, what's happened?'

Over several enormous glasses of wine, I sniffed and sobbed

out my sorry story, as Hannah patted my hand and made the sympathetic noises that I wanted to hear. That is why Hannah is my best friend. We long ago made a pact that no matter what we did, we would always be on each other's sides. Us against the world. I finished snottering out the tale and waited happily for the proper indignation that my wretched sister had been so unforthcoming with.

Charlie and Hannah looked at each other. Where was my indignation? Where? Charlie sighed.

'Ellen, this isn't you.'

'Yes, it is. It is absolutely me. It's MY money!'

'Yes, of course it is,' put in Hannah. 'But this mean-spiritedness isn't you, not at all.'

'Well, I'd give *you* the money, Hannah, in an instant. I just don't like Louisa.'

'That's not really the point though, is it?' said Charlie. 'The point is that she is Simon's sister, and this is the right thing to do.'

'It is, Ellen,' said Hannah. 'And you know it is.'

'You are meant to be on MY side!' I wailed at Hannah. 'What happened to us against the world?'

'I *am* on your side!' said Hannah. 'I am trying to stop you making a terrible mistake and destroying your marriage.'

'Look at it this way,' suggested Charlie. 'How are you going to feel, sitting in your beachfront cottage in Wells-next-the-Sea (why there, by the way, you seem obsessed with the place?), knowing Louisa and your children's cousins are sitting in some dismal hovel with peeling wallpaper?'

'I would feel fine. Possibly smug. And I googled it and it looked nice. Beaches and tea shops. And cheaper than Cornwall. And not so far.'

'No, you wouldn't,' said Charlie. 'You'd feel like shit, and deep down, you know you would. Do the right thing.'

Oh FFS.

I went home and marched in, giving the door a good slam (if they were going to make me do this, I was determined to extract every ounce of drama possible from it).

Simon was watching *Wheeler* Fucking *Dealers*. Louisa and the children had moved into Michael and Sylvia's hotel a few days before.

'FINE!' I shouted. 'They can have the money.'

Simon jumped up. 'Are you serious?'

'Yes,' I muttered grudgingly, still not quite believing I was actually saying this.

Simon was hugging and kissing me and telling me I was wonderful and marvellous and how much he loved me, which was all very nice, if not an adorable cottage. Then he rang Michael and they agreed that, yes, I was very marvellous and I started to think maybe this wasn't actually the stupidest decision I'd ever made.

Later, after some more wine, Simon showed me Louisa's new house on his computer. I had refused to look at it before, not wishing physical evidence of my stolen dream rubbed in my face. It was actually a rather ugly little modern bungalow, quite dark and dingy inside, and not nearly as nice as my own house. I am clearly a terrible person, because this made me feel a great deal better.

'Where are the olive groves?' I cried. 'Where will Pascal wander to mourn his lost love, Marie Claire?'

'I think you've had enough wine, darling,' said Simon, as he steadied me to bed.

Thursday, 25 August

We are in Cornwall, being properly middle class. The children have frolicked on beaches (kicked sand in each other's faces and screamed because someone stamped on their sandcastle), and splashed in rock pools (tried to drown each other).

We have picnicked to the max, and frankly if I never see another hard-boiled egg or chicken sandwich, it will be too soon. Peter and Jane have taken to throwing the eggs at each other, which then results in the dog wolfing them down. Eggy dog puke is so not part of the middle-class dream.

I still press my nose longingly against the windows of every real estate agency I pass, mourning my lost dream, but I know I did the right thing, however much I may have grudged it. Coventina sent me a letter shortly after they arrived in France, thanking me for her new home and life, which went some way towards mitigating my grudges. I remind myself of this whenever I spot the perfect 'Honeysuckle Cottage' and the bile abates somewhat.

Tonight, after Peter and Jane were in bed and I was futilely trying to shake sand out of wetsuits while keeping a close eye on the dog for any more signs of retching, muttering 'FML' to myself once more, Simon came up behind me and put his arms around me.

'I love you,' he said. 'And I don't tell you that enough.'

'No, you don't. Not nearly enough.'

'And I will try harder to make sure you know how much I appreciate you.'

'Good. I like the sound of that. You could appreciate me by giving me shiny things. I like shiny things.'

'I can do shiny things, my little magpie,' he said. 'I also thought you might like a little treat for your birthday next month?'

'I am trying not to think about that. I don't want to be forty. I will just pretend it isn't happening!'

'Oh. So you don't want to go to Paris then?'

'Of course I want to go to Paris! What about the children? They are not very Parisian?'

'All sorted!' he said smugly. 'Sam and Hannah are having one each for the weekend. And we are off to the City of Love for romance. And wine.'

'Will we go to jazz clubs?'

'You hate jazz. We can go to jazz clubs if you want, but all you will do when you get there is moan that you don't like the music.'

'Then can we sit in a bar in Montmartre and watch the world go by while you whisper sweet nothings in my ear?'

'Isn't Montmartre very busy? There will be people and –'

'SIMON!'

'Okay, we will sit in a bar in Montmartre and I will whisper sweet nothings in your ear, even though you probably won't be able to hear them because of *all the people*!'

'Good.' I said. 'I love you too.'

It seems that, all in all, turning forty won't be quite as awful as I thought it would be.

We are no longer broke, which is a wonderful thing to be able to say.

My mother-in-law can no longer make subtle digs at me (though I am almost certain she will continue to try) because I am the Saviour of The Family – and also because we bonded that one time over gin.

I no longer alternate between terror and hatred of the other mothers at the school gate but have in fact discovered they are all just human, though I am still strongly resisting joining Fiona Montague's book club, because apparently she makes everyone read terribly highbrow books and then she just downloads other people's critiques of them from the internet and passes them off as her own, to make herself look cleverer than everyone else.

I have made not one, not two, but three wonderful new friends in the form of Charlie, Katie and Sam, and I also get to feel slightly smug about being responsible for setting Hannah and Charlie up together, so if there is a wedding I will almost certainly be the guest of honour. Plus, there is the benefit of Katie being a kindred spirit just across the road to drink wine with.

And, best of all, I no longer want to sit in smoky jazz clubs with unsuitable men whispering sweet nothings in my ear – it turns out that just one very suitable man grumbling that there are *People* here and he is *too hot* will do for me.

I think being forty will be okay. It even gives me hope that one day I will manage to instil a modicum of civilisation into Peter and Jane, and they will stop trying to kill each other. Well, everyone needs a dream!

ACKNOWLEDGEMENTS

I used to look at the acknowledgements pages at the end of books and wonder how on earth it took so many people to help write a book – surely it was just the author, together with an editor and a proof-reader and maybe someone to do the typing for you if you couldn't type. And then I wrote a book and found out just how many people you actually need around you. So here are just a few of the many, many people who deserve such huge thanks for their help with this book!

First, thank you so much to all the fabulous people at HarperCollins and Harper 360 for giving me this amazing opportunity, but especially Grace Cheetham, Polly Osborn, Katie Moss and Jean Marie Kelly, who have been endlessly patient with my constant emails full of silly questions.

Massive thanks also to my fantastic agent Paul Baker of Headway Talent, who is another remarkably patient person.

Special thanks to my lovely friend Donna Pilcher for all her help and advice, and her generally calming presence. Thanks are also due to all the Dahlings (you know who you are), who supported me and encouraged me and gave me the belief that I might actually be able to do this.

To the FIAF crew – Tanya and Mairi and Eileen – thank you for keeping me sane.

Jim Peters deserves a massive thank you too for his patience, photography skills and anecdotes.

Helen and Martin – thank you for entrusting Judgy Dog to me; and Judgy Dog, thank you for keeping my feet warm while I was writing.

My amazing parents-in-law deserve enormous thanks, not only for all the emergency childcare and hot meals they provided throughout the writing of this book, but for always being there over the years to step in and rescue me from my various crises.

Thanks too, to my fabulous brother-in-law, for all his help with the nuances of the common language that divides us!

And most of all, of course, to my very own Gadget Twat and Precious Moppets – thank you for all the cups of tea and glasses of wine and for putting up with me.

And last but not least, thanks to Claire Scott for starting all this with a chance remark one day.

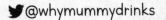 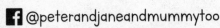